Aftermath

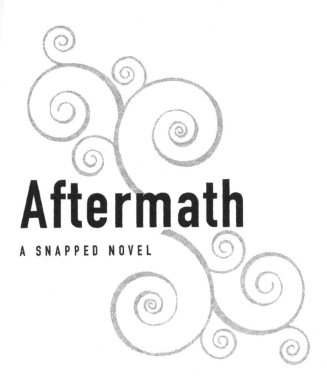

Aftermath

A SNAPPED NOVEL

Tracy Brown

St. Martin's Griffin

New York

This is a work of fiction. All of the characters, organizations, and events portrayed in this novel are either products of the author's imagination or are used fictitiously.

www.stmartins.com

Library of Congress Cataloging-in-Publication Data

Brown, Tracy, 1974-
   Aftermath : a snapped novel / Tracy Brown.—1st ed.
      p. cm.
   ISBN 978-0-312-55522-1
   1. African Americans—Fiction. 2. Inner cities—Fiction.
3. Revenge—Fiction. 4. New York (N.Y.)—Fiction. I. Title.
   PS3602.R723A69 2011
813'.6—dc22   2010038759

First Edition: February 2011

P1

For Daddy, in heaven.
I hope I continue to make you proud.

Acknowledgments

Monique, Matthew, Holly, Katie, Abbye, Talia, and all of the wonderful people at St. Martin's Press . . . thank you so very much.

Kareem Moody (Moodswing Entertainment), you are always helping me go the extra mile and I am eternally grateful.

To Arthur Smith, thanks for being my bestie. I value your friendship even though I may not always tell you so.

And to my baby, thank you for being so supportive, for giving me great ideas, and always looking out for me. I love the way you teach me something new each and every day. You are the best!

My readers across the globe, I appreciate your love and your positivity more than you can ever know. Every now and then, when I'm having a bad day, I'll get an e-mail from one of you telling me to keep going, that you're inspired by me and by what I do. Please know that I am just as inspired by each of you. XOXOXO

Aftermath

The Right to Remain Silent

January 5, 2008

Misa sat in the stillness of the house and closed her eyes, realizing that nothing would ever be the same. She heard someone come in through the front door and she held her breath. She waited to see who it was, but didn't move from where she sat, transfixed. This was it, the moment she'd been waiting for, she thought. Someone was home and would soon discover what she'd done. Her body trembled slightly as she heard footsteps moving through the house.

Camille walked into her home and immediately sensed that something was awry. First of all, Misa's car was parked outside, which was strange since Misa's son, Shane, had been with his father, Louis, for several days. Second, the house was dark and quiet. Most nights Camille's brother-in-law, Steven, came in from the guesthouse and drank up the beer in the fridge while watching TV in the living room until the wee hours of the morning. Instead, tonight the house seemed empty and eerily silent.

Then she walked into the kitchen and screamed.

Steven's cold, dead body was lying in the middle of the floor. Blood was splattered across the walls and had pooled on the floor. A gun lay on the floor near the body. Steven's eyes were wide open, and a broken beer bottle was near his right hand.

Immediately, Camille panicked and looked around the room in fear. Her husband was part of the Nobles crime syndicate, a crew that had come under attack in recent weeks. As retaliation for the murder of Dusty, an enemy of Baron Nobles, both Baron and his father, Doug Nobles, had been gunned down recently. Seeing her brother-in-law's dead body, Camille's heart raced. Had Steven been killed by someone trying to target her husband? Was the killer still in the house?

She saw a dim light coming from the dining room. She took a knife from the block on the counter and walked bravely, and slowly, toward it, following the glimmering light. She prayed that the gun lying on the floor, not far from Steven's body, was an indication that the perpetrator was now unarmed. Camille stepped into the room and came up short, stunned to see who was sitting at her dining room table. After a few beats, she slowly inched toward the woman.

Camille could see that Misa had blood on her hands and she was oddly calm despite the presence of the dead body just yards away. The only sign that anything was amiss were Misa's trembling hands.

"Jesus . . . oh my God, girl, what have you done?" Camille asked, breathlessly.

Misa didn't answer. She stared silently back at her sister, her hands continuing to quiver from the shock of all that had happened.

Camille's eyes searched the room, taking it all in. There

was blood splattered on the wall, and Misa had some blood on her clothes as well. Camille thought her sister looked so eerie sitting there, the candlelight illuminating her face and the sinister, blank expression it held. "Are you hurt?"

Misa shook her head no but said nothing.

Camille glanced toward the kitchen and Steven's body. She couldn't get her thoughts straight. What had she just walked into? Her husband's brother was dead, laid out across her kitchen floor. Her sister was sitting in the dining room, clad in a blood-splattered winter-white DKNY coat and staring absently into space. She looked again at the blood on the wall and on Misa's hands. The room was dark except for the candle flickering at the center of the table.

"Misa . . ." Camille had no idea where to start. She was shaking like a Parkinson's victim, and trying desperately not to panic. She didn't want to set Misa off. Seeing her sitting there so quiet and calm was making Camille even more of a nervous wreck. "What happened?"

Misa had been sitting there, entranced for so long, replaying the events of the evening again and again, that it was difficult for her mind to rewind all the way back to the beginning. It had all started when she returned home from visiting her love interest, Baron, in the hospital.

Camille tried to coax her to speak. "I want to help you. But you have to tell me what the fuck is going on."

"What was I supposed to do?" Misa asked softly, shaking her head from side to side. "I've put up with a lot of people's shit. First Louis, then Baron." She looked at Camille and her eyes welled up. "But not anymore. I fought the fuck back for once."

"I want to understand you," Camille said, her frowning

face expressing the desperation she felt. "But I'm confused. What are you talking about? You had to fight back . . . against Steven?"

"If I didn't kill him . . ." Misa's voice trailed off. "If I didn't kill him," she began again. "I had to kill him," she said at last.

"Why?" Camille pressed.

Misa looked at her and a few tears fell from her vacant-looking eyes. "I had to do it. He was . . ." She shook her head, her voice barely audible even in the silence that shrouded them. "I had to do it, Camille."

"*Why*, Misa?" Camille was losing patience. Frankie's brother, whom he loved and protected and looked out for, was lying in a sea of his own blood, riddled with bullets. And Misa seemed to be full of riddles herself. "You have to tell me what he did to you."

"He was molesting Shane," she said through clenched teeth. More tears came and Misa cried silently for her son.

"What?" Camille's knees buckled and she leaned on one of the dining room chairs as she listened intently to what her sister was saying. "S . . . Steven?" Camille stammered.

Misa spoke slowly and deliberately, her eyes expressionless as she addressed Camille.

"Tonight, I came home from visiting Baron at the hospital. I missed Shane." Misa's voice cracked and Camille watched her struggle to gain control of it once more. "I called to talk to Shane but Louis cursed me out. He said that I would never see my son again, that somebody has been molesting him."

"Oh my God," Camille breathed.

Misa continued. "I was shocked at first. I couldn't believe it was possible, but Louis said there was no doubt. And the more I thought about who spent time alone with Shane, I kept coming back to Steven. He's been babysitting him for the past few weeks . . . ever since Baron got shot."

Camille covered her mouth with her hands. While her sister had been at Baron's bedside, Shane had been left in Camille's care. But Camille had been sidetracked by her failed marriage and Steven had been all too happy to help out by babysitting Shane. She felt a surge of guilt at the idea that she had unwittingly handed her nephew over to a predator.

"I kept calling back, but Louis kept hanging up on me. Then he stopped answering the phone at all. I went over there to see my son, to talk to Louis . . . and he wouldn't let me in. He kept calling me a stupid bitch, a cheap tramp, a gold-digging slut. He spit at me."

"What?" Camille was outraged.

"He missed me," Misa said, as if that were some small triumph. "Nahla held him back, but he wanted to kill me. I could tell. Finally, I left and I sat and thought about it for hours." Misa had a sort of twisted smirk on her face that sent chills up Camille's spine. "I parked my car near the Verrazano Bridge and seriously considered jumping off. But I had to get that bastard first." The more Misa thought about the horrors Steven must have perpetrated against her son, the more she wanted to kill him all over again. "The only person who could have done that to my baby was Steven." Misa shook her head as if to shake away any doubt that she'd killed the right person. "It had to be someone that Shane trusted . . . someone who spends a lot of time with him."

Camille was in a daze as she listened. Could it be possible that her brother-in-law had sexually abused her nephew? He had certainly had the opportunity, and Camille had never particularly cared for Steven. To her, he was a listless and lazy user who took advantage of her and Frankie's kindness. But did that make him a monster?

Misa continued. "I came over here to confront Steven."

Camille leaned in closer. "And?"

"When I got here, the house was empty. I sat here for a while, just trying to think about everything and make sure that I wasn't making a mistake. But the more I thought about it, the more I was convinced that Steven did it. Then he came in from the guesthouse."

Misa's face took on a look that Camille had never seen before. Her beautiful sister with the cocoa-brown skin and the beautiful dimples now looked like a woman possessed as she sat there by candlelight, picturing Steven's face in her mind.

"I went into the kitchen and surprised him. He wasn't expecting to see me and he looked like I caught him off guard. So, I got right to the point. I told him what I knew."

"What did he say?" Camille felt like she was bursting at the seams. Her nerves were jittery and it occurred to her that Misa appeared calmer than she was.

"He laughed at me. He called Shane a liar." Misa looked at her sister and made a decision. "He lunged at me," she lied. "And I pulled out the gun Louis gave me years ago when he first moved out. I had brought it with me just for protection in case he got physical. He kept coming towards me like he wasn't afraid that I'd use the gun. And I . . . snapped. I shot him until he stopped moving." Misa shut her eyes tightly and shook her head.

Camille slumped down into one of the nearby chairs. She stared at her sister as she tried to calm herself. She was wondering if the neighbors had heard all the commotion. Homes in this neighborhood were pretty far apart, so it was possible that the gunshots had gone unheard by those living closest by. Still, Camille thought about the fact that the violence that had taken place in her home would eventually be played out publicly and her neighbors would soon know what happened. She cringed at the thought of being the only black family on the block and the first with a murder scene at their home.

Camille felt guilty for thinking of her own embarrassment at a time like this. Misa had *murdered* her brother-in-law. Surely, her sister would be arrested tonight. The thought occurred to Camille that perhaps they should try to dispose of the body, but she quickly came to her senses. She knew they would never get away with it. She had watched enough episodes of *Forensic Files* to know that the police would be able to locate even trace levels of DNA or blood no matter how thoroughly someone cleaned up the scene. Plus, how would she explain Steven's sudden absence to her husband? And where would they dispose of a body in the middle of the night? Camille couldn't believe that she was actually having these thoughts. She was the epitome of a housewife, and here she was sitting and trying to come up with a plan for getting rid of a dead body.

Camille wasn't sure what to say, think, or feel as she looked at her sister and then glanced in the direction of Steven's body. Next, she quickly tried to recall if she had anything illegal in her house. Surely her home would be thoroughly searched when the police got there. Camille took a deep breath and looked at Misa, truly at a loss as to how to proceed.

Misa seemed to sense her sister's hesitance. "Call the cops, Camille," she said, softly. "I'm ready to face what I did."

Just at that moment, the phone began to ring. Camille nearly jumped out of her skin, startled by the sudden noise. Misa, however, sat stoically and waited for Camille to answer it.

Glancing at her Cartier watch, Camille noted that it was 2:52 A.M. *Who the hell could this be?* On shaky legs, Camille walked over to the wall and flipped on the light switch. Next, she picked up the nearby phone.

"Hello?"

"Camille!" Frankie's voice sent chills up her spine. "I've been calling you for like an hour now."

Camille fought to catch her breath. "Frankie . . ." She looked over at Misa, who shrugged. It seemed that Camille's sister had resigned herself to her fate and didn't care what happened next. "What's wrong?"

Frankie was confused. "*What's wrong?*" he asked rhetorically. "You just came over here and dropped a bomb on me, and now you're asking *me* what's wrong?"

Camille was confused for a moment, before it all came back to her. She had completely forgotten about the events of her evening prior to coming home to a crime scene.

She had been following her husband and his best friend/ mistress, Gillian, for days. Their affair was now public and Camille had been humiliated by it. She'd been stalking them nonstop, pretty much consumed by her jealousy. She couldn't come to grips with the fact that her marriage was over and that Frankie seemed oblivious to what people were whispering about them.

"Camille," Frankie interrupted her thoughts, "are you really pregnant?"

Camille's heart was racing in her chest, and she tried to swallow the lump in her throat. "Yes," she answered weakly.

Frankie sighed heavily and held his head in his hand. "How is that possible?" To his knowledge, Camille had been on birth control for years, and he hadn't even been intimate with his wife in ages. Frankie had been very vocal about his desire to remain childless and it was evident even now. "How can you be pregnant?"

Camille could sense Frankie's disappointment, and it stung. She had already been humiliated by Frankie and Gillian's betrayal. For the past several weeks she had become obsessed with it and hadn't eaten or slept much. So when she fell ill and felt slightly weak, she had assumed it was due to her recent lack of attention to her health and poor nutrition. Camille had gone to her family physician expecting to be scolded for her poor eating habits and excessive drinking. To her surprise, she discovered that she was pregnant.

Camille had secretly stopped taking her birth control pills more than six months ago. It had bothered her that Frankie insisted on her using them because he was reluctant to be a father. And when he began spending most of his time with Gillian, Camille had decided to take matters into her own hands, and neglected her pills. It had seemed that her efforts had been in vain, since she had only been intimate with her husband once or twice since then. And then their lives had gone into a tailspin and they'd separated, leaving Camille distraught. While she had noticed that her monthly visit was lighter than usual, she had chalked it up to all the stress of the past few weeks. But it was official: She was pregnant, and tonight—while Misa had apparently been executing Steven— Camille had been over at Gillian's Upper East Side town house delivering the good news.

"I don't know, Frankie," Camille said. "It just happened."

Frankie laughed, although he found nothing funny. "How the hell could this shit just happen all of a sudden, Camille? I've been with you for years and nothing like this ever just happened before." He spoke through clenched teeth. "I feel like you're trying to trap me."

Camille shook her head and closed her eyes, trying to imagine the look on her husband's face at that moment. She wondered if it resembled his expression when she had appeared at Gillian's door earlier that night.

She had rung the doorbell and waited nervously. Gillian had answered and immediately asked Camille to wait in her car until Frankie came out to find out why she was there.

"Please don't bring drama to my door, Camille," Gillian had said. "Frankie will be out in a minute."

Camille wanted to snatch the bitch out and throw her down the stairs. Instead, thinking of the miracle growing in her womb, she calmly looked Gillian in the eye and shook her head. "I want to talk to *both* of you." Camille had boldly pushed past Gillian and entered her house. Camille had been prepared for a fight. Fuck it. If Gillian took it there, so be it. But, to her surprise, Gillian had simply sighed deeply and shut the front door. Camille looked around, musing that this was the place Frankie longed to be as opposed to the home he'd built with her. Just as she thought of him, her husband appeared from around a corner and walked toward her looking angry as hell. Camille didn't care.

"I'm not here for no bullshit, so I'll keep this short," she'd said, looking at each of them. She noticed that Frankie was shirtless, walking around in his socks—so comfortable in another woman's home. "I'm pregnant."

Frankie's face fell instantly. "Pregnant?" His body language showed that this news had caught him completely off guard. He put his hands in his pockets, then wiped his mouth. Finally, he folded his arms across his chest.

Gillian, on the other hand, didn't flinch. To Camille, she looked almost numb, as if the pain of losing her father had drained all the fight out of her.

"Nine weeks," Camille confirmed, staring at her rival. She turned her attention back to Frankie. "You may not want to be with *me* anymore, but now there's a child. When you're ready to talk, I'll be at home waiting."

Gillian had looked to Frankie for his reaction. He had stood there in obvious shock as Camille calmly sauntered out, confident that she'd ruined their fairy-tale plans.

Frankie had been calling the house ever since. Camille's cell phone battery was dead so his calls went straight to voice mail. Frustrated, Frankie had started calling Camille at home. There had been no answer, and the ringing phone had tormented Misa, who had just committed first-degree murder.

Camille glanced at her sister, who was sitting there looking so dazed. She gripped the phone tighter, wondering how the hell she could tell Frankie that his brother was dead—that Misa had killed him.

"We have to talk," Frankie said.

Camille shook her head. He had no idea how right he was. "Frankie, I can't right now . . . Misa's here . . ."

"Camille, come on. This can't really wait."

"I'll call you back." Camille hung up before Frankie could protest further, before he could ask if his brother was there. She looked helplessly at Misa. "We have to call the police."

Misa shrugged her shoulders again. She didn't care. The pain of knowing that Shane had been touched inappropriately by a perverted freak was more punishment than any the police could dish out. "Call 'em."

Camille took a deep breath and dialed 911. Two rings later, an operator answered.

"What is your emergency?"

"Somebody's been shot."

Truth and Consequences

Police swarmed Camille's beautiful home. They sealed off the kitchen—the crime scene—as well as the dining room where Steven's blood stained the wall, and were attempting to interrogate Misa in the living room. Misa, however, had so far refused to answer most of the officers' questions. She had acknowledged that she was the shooter. But aside from that, she was not cooperating much. To each of their questions, she answered simply, "I want to talk to my lawyer."

Camille had to laugh at that. Misa had no damn lawyer. Neither did Camille. In fact, Camille didn't have shit! *Everything* was Frankie's. And Misa had just murdered Frankie's brother. Camille trembled as the enormity of the situation became crystal clear. Her sister was going to jail, and Camille had no idea how they would manage to get her out. Now, the police were asking where her husband was—the brother of the dead man. Camille felt as if everything were moving in slow motion.

"I'll call him."

They watched as she slowly, deliberately dialed Frankie's cell phone number. Camille didn't miss the irony that he was eagerly answering her phone calls ever since she'd dropped the pregnancy bombshell on him. Recently, he'd been ignoring her repeated attempts to reach him, but not tonight. She took a deep breath as his deep voice filled her ear after only two rings. "Hello?"

"Frankie . . ." Camille's voice was barely above a whisper. She looked around at the police milling about her home, snapping pictures and searching through things that had nothing to do with the crime scene. She looked at her sister again and saw that Misa was trying to be tough. Still, Camille could tell that she was scared to death and that she wanted to cry but was fighting that urge. Her own voice was shaky as she spoke. "Steven is hurt. You need to come home right away."

Frankie immediately panicked. Had Jojo—the Nobles family's murderous enemy who'd had a thirst for revenge ever since his brother Dusty had disappeared—come gunning for Steven as a way to get at Frankie? He climbed out of bed and walked into the nearby bathroom, leaving Gillian lying awake in the dark. She sat up and tried to listen closely to his end of the conversation.

"What's going on, Camille?" he asked, the desperation in his voice so clear. "Are you all right? Is somebody there with you? Where's my brother?" Frankie whispered, too, now hoping not to alarm Gillian.

Camille began to cry. How could she tell him that Steven's body was at that very moment being toe-tagged and bagged up? Thankfully, the senior officer on the scene took the telephone from her and cut to the chase. He identified himself as Sergeant Denton and asked if Frankie was the homeowner. When Frankie confirmed that he was, Sergeant Denton explained briefly that the residence was being processed as a crime scene and they had a suspect in custody at the scene.

"Mr. Bingham, we have a deceased victim here, whom we'd like you to come home and identify, as your wife informs us that you are his next of kin."

Frankie heard the word "deceased" echoing in his head again and again. He closed his eyes and tried to digest all of it. "My brother? He's dead?"

"We believe so, sir," the officer answered honestly. "But we'd like for you to come down and—"

Frankie hung up and felt like he was living a nightmare. Steven was dead. First his father figure, Doug Nobles, had been murdered, and now his brother. Tears filled his eyes as he sat in the darkened bathroom, digesting what he'd just been told. He wondered if things could possibly get any worse.

Frankie went into defensive mode and called some of the goons to come over and secure the house until he came back. Assuming that whatever had happened to Steven was retaliation for Dusty's murder, Frankie surmised that the entire crew was now under attack. And as far as he was concerned, Gillian was the most important person among all of them. If a hair on her head was touched, he would never forgive himself. Hanging up with his boys, he went into the bedroom where Gillian was still lying in bed, and started getting dressed.

He replayed the conversation with Sergeant Denton in his mind. Steven was dead. A suspect was in custody. With a million thoughts racing through his head, Frankie spoke over his shoulder as he put on his clothes. "Danno and Biggs are coming over to keep an eye on things until I get back."

Gillian was confused.

"What's wrong? Why do they need to come over here? What did Camille want?"

Frankie looked at Gillian. Her long hair hung loosely

around her bare shoulders and the moonlight caught her face so delicately that she looked like a porcelain doll. It had already been a whirlwind evening since Camille had dropped her bombshell. Frankie had spent the past two hours reassuring Gillian that, kid or no kid, he was in love with her and not with Camille. Now, he was being called home to deal with the apparent death of his brother and the possibility that Camille was also in danger.

Gillian got out of bed and pulled on her long black silk bathrobe with concern etched on her face.

"I thought I heard you say that your brother is . . . dead?" She covered her mouth with her hands as she said it, her voice catching in her throat. She prayed that she hadn't heard him correctly.

Looking at Gigi, Frankie felt so sorry for her. Her father had just been murdered and her brother seriously wounded. Doug Nobles's funeral had just occurred only days prior and Gillian was still clearly fragile. Frankie didn't want to upset her further—at least not until he had all the facts.

"I don't know if it's him for sure. I'm gonna go and see. But I just want to make sure you're all right while I'm gone." Frankie quickly kissed Gillian on the forehead before dialing Tremaine's number.

"I need you to come with me to Staten Island," he said into the phone. "We got a problem."

Earlier that evening, Toya had come home from work, exhausted. Noticing that her screen door was unlocked, she had cursed herself for being careless and forgetting to lock it when she'd left for work that morning. But when she saw her front door was also unlocked, she knew immediately that something was wrong. Toya pulled her gun out of her purse and slowly opened the door, stepping quietly into her house.

She looked around for her dog. Her Pomeranian, Ginger, usually met her at the door, eager for a walk after being locked up all day with the wee-wee pads. But Ginger was nowhere to be found. She noticed the kitchen light on and knew that someone was in there. She slowly inched toward it, ready to fire at the slightest movement. Entering the kitchen, she cocked her gun and stopped, stunned.

Her father, Nate, stood against the kitchen counter holding her dog in his arms. He had picked her locks and waited for her to get home. Toya would have shot him on sight, but he had an advantage. Ginger was her weakness and there was no way she would ever put her dog in danger. Nate knew this, after having watched her from a distance for weeks, and was using it to his advantage.

"I just want to talk to you, Latoya. Now I've tried to call you, tried to come by here and you keep refusing. I didn't want to go this route, but you forced me."

She had wanted to spit in his face. "Talk, bitch! And it better be good or I swear to God, I'll kill your ass tonight."

Nate had known that his daughter wouldn't be happy to see him. After all, he'd been a brutal and often cruel parent and Toya had certainly suffered the worst of it. Knowing she wouldn't need much of an excuse to shoot him, he wasted no time getting right to the point.

"I'm about to die, Latoya," he had said solemnly. "And before I die, I wanted to come and tell you that I'm sorry."

Toya had slowly lowered the gun then. She wasn't sure why, since part of her wanted to pull the trigger and speed up his death. But there was something in his tone that made her pause. Toya could hear defeat in his voice, something she'd never sensed from him before. Nate had always been ready for a fight, but tonight he looked as if life had kicked his ass. Sizing him up, she noticed for the first time that he appeared to have lost a lot of weight. She had always recalled her father being a menacing presence in her life. Now, he looked frail, thin, and drawn.

Nate cleared his throat.

"I need a bone marrow transplant and so far they can't find a match for me."

Toya smirked and held her gun tighter. "Mmm-hmm. So you thought you could come here to convince me to be a donor?" She shook her head. "Let me save you the trouble. You can drop dead as far as I'm concerned."

Nate cringed a little. "Latoya, I'm not here to ask you for nothing."

"Good."

"I came here to talk to you. And all I want is a chance for you to hear me out. Hear what I have to say to you. Then you can cuss me out and kick me out if that's what you want."

"What could you possibly have to say to me?" she asked, shaking her head.

"I do want to tell you that I'm sorry, Latoya, but there's a lot of things you don't know, a lot that I need to explain to you before it's too late."

Toya thought about it. It seemed to her that this tyrant wanted to clear his conscience before he went to meet his maker. Again, she considered squeezing the trigger and ending it all. He didn't deserve a chance to be heard.

Sensing her hesitation, Nate said, "Please, baby girl. Just hear me out." He held Ginger close to his chest, and the dog squirmed and looked pleadingly at Toya.

Toya hesitantly put the gun's safety on and led the way to

her dining room. She sat at her dining room table across from her father, and he finally set Ginger free. The dog ran over and jumped into her lap.

"Hurry up and say what you gotta say," she demanded.

"I watched my daddy kill a man when I was twelve years old," Nate said, matter-of-factly. "And by the time I was seventeen I had killed a man myself while defending my mama. I came home from work one night and found Mama arguing with our landlord. The nigga called my mother a bitch and when she protested, he slapped her." Nate shook his head. "He ain't never slap nobody else after that." He sighed. "By the time I met your mother I had seen a lot of things. I had grown up long before I moved out of my mama's house. Seeing the shit that I saw made me tough. I guess it made me a bully sometimes. But when I met your mother . . . she brought out the best in me."

Toya sucked her teeth. "That ain't how I remember it."

Toya's mother had been a teacher. And although her salary had been paltry, she had a degree and a career—two things Nate had never had in all his life. Nate had quit school at the age of fourteen and worked at a steel mill, long hard hours for such little pay that it frustrated and angered him. That anger reared its head whenever he drank, which eventually became a daily occurrence. And Nate was a mean drunk.

"I have a thousand memories of you telling her that she was a dumb bitch, that she was lucky to have a nigga like you for a husband." Toya shook her head, recalling those painful words.

She had never understood why her mother—a woman who came from a family of college graduates, old money, and prestige—had fallen for and married a man as good for nothing as Nate. Hailing from Georgia, Toya's mother, Jeanie, had moved to New York City in search of some fun and excitement and found both in Nate. He lived in her Brooklyn neighborhood and was a fixture there. He worked at a steel mill in New Jersey but his main source of income was his gambling. Everyone in the neighborhood knew Nate. Jeanie was a lovely new face on the scene. The unlikely pair had an unmistakable chemistry in the beginning. Nate was proud to be the object of Jeanie's desire and had considered himself lucky to have found such a good woman. His lack of education didn't bother her. She was too impressed by his Brooklyn swagger, good looks, and sense of humor to care. Plus, Nate was making a decent wage at his job, and in the beginning things had been perfect. As their family grew, Nate worked longer hours to make ends meet. By the time Latoya, their fourth child, was born, the family was barely getting by. Nate's drinking had increased and Jeanie was dismayed when he was finally fired from his job. She had to shoulder the financial burden all by herself and it seemed that no matter what she did, it was never good enough.

"I was cruel to your mother," Nate admitted, his eyes downcast. "I used to cuss at her, call her names."

"You used to kick her ass." Latoya didn't want Nate to forget that little detail. "Brutally! You used to kick all our asses."

Nate looked at his only daughter and was ashamed. He nodded. "Yes, I did."

Latoya was relentless. "You felt like a man when you did that? Beating up on females and little boys made you feel powerful? Is that what it was?"

Nate didn't know how to answer that, so he sat in silence and looked at Toya.

"Wanna go down memory lane?" she asked facetiously. "Let's talk about the time I came home from school and found you fucking that bitch Miss Crystal right there in my mother's bed!" Toya shook her head as if her father should be absolutely ashamed of himself. "Your wife's best friend. You couldn't keep your dick out of anything!" She felt her blood boil, felt her hand instinctively inch toward her gun lying on the table. "Remember that night when you came in my room when my friend Stephanie had spent the night?"

"Now, Latoya, I told you—"

"She was only thirteen years old, you fuckin'—"

"I was high . . ."

"You tried to pull her pants down and fuck my friend . . . She was just a little girl, you sick bitch!"

"Latoya, I told you I was out of my mind that night." Nate lowered his eyes, ashamed of the ugly truth. He had spent years getting high and drunk as a way to forget the events of that night. He had come home and found that Jeanie wasn't there. For some reason—a reason he was never able to fully come to terms with—he stumbled into Toya's room and found her friend sleeping there in the spare bed. Nate had snapped out of a twisted trance only when Toya clawed at his face and Stephanie kicked him in his nuts.

"I didn't know what I was doing."

Toya's fingers brushed against the cold steel of her nine as she glared at her father, remembering the terror she felt that night when the father she already hated had the nerve to cross a very sick line. "I should have killed you then," she said. "I should have plunged a knife into your chest and watched you die."

Nate stared at her, knowing that she was contemplating it now.

Toya thought back on that hot summer evening when her sweaty and belligerent father had entered her room, clawing at her friend in ways they both knew weren't right. Toya had fought him off savagely, crying and kicking at her father until he retreated in pain when she hit her mark. She was embarrassed, ashamed of what had happened to her friend. Stephanie had been scared and so had Toya, and Nate only made them more afraid, as they watched him go from apologetic to menacing in minutes. Nate had apologized to Stephanie, begging her to keep her mouth shut about what happened and swearing that it was all a misunderstanding. Then he threatened to kill Toya if she ever told her mother. Toya had kept that dirty little secret among many others over the years, never wanting to bring more pain to her mother than what she was already enduring.

"I was never a good father or husband," he said.

Toya laughed as if this were the biggest understatement. Nate tried not to notice and continued.

"When you guys were little I used to drink a lot. And when I would get drunk, I would turn into somebody else."

Toya recalled how her father barked orders at her and her brothers, even when they were little. Whenever he came home, the drama erupted.

"I mean, you come in here and make it sound like you were just unkind. You were a muthafuckin' monster! You would go out there in the street and get so drunk and so high that you would pass out on the fuckin' porch and sleep out there all night in a heap on the doorstep. We would have to step over you on our way to school. All of our friends used to see you out there like that. And then when you woke up, you would terrorize everybody. You cheated on your wife *openly*. You used to beat the boys until they cried like girls. You would make my life hell and beat your beloved wife bloody all the time. Don't you think that's why God is snatching your miserable life away from you?"

Nate shrugged, unsure how to answer that. "It was the liquor, Latoya. I was—"

"You were a fuckin' embarrassment, out in the streets every day, stumbling around and falling down drunk. You would yell our names from down the block and we would *die* from embarrassment. I was so ashamed that people knew you were my father."

Nate hated to hear her say that. But he had to admit that he deserved it.

Toya got lost in thought for a moment, recalling the terror she'd suffered at her father's hands. As she'd gotten older and blossomed into an adolescent, Toya, like most girls her age, began to like boys. Toya recalled how her drunken father would see her on the block talking to a boy and bellow her name. When she went over to him, he'd ask her what the boy was saying to her. It never mattered. Before she could even answer him, he'd slap her in the face and tell her not to be a dumb bitch.

"Niggas only want one thing from you," he'd say. "You keep being a dumb bitch standing around here listening to these fools and you ain't gonna be shit. All you'll be is another dumb bitch with a whole bunch of kids. All these muthafuckas want is some pussy. Take your black ass home!"

Toya snapped out of her reverie and heard her father apologizing for the umpteenth time. She had hated Nate for as long as she could remember. Cutting him off midsentence, her words left him momentarily speechless. "And then, as if being a drunk bum in the street wasn't enough, you started using crack."

Nate closed his eyes and nodded. That had been the worst mistake of his life.

Toya knew she had hit him where it hurt. "You're a fuckin' crackhead."

Nate opened his eyes and looked at his daughter for several long, silent moments. "I *was* a crackhead."

"Once a crackhead, always a crackhead."

He put up his hands as if he didn't want to fight. "Okay," he allowed. "I got caught up with that shit and couldn't get off." As she listened to him talking about his alcoholism and how he got hooked on drugs, she kept flashing back to incidents in her childhood that were forever etched in her memory.

"I realized I had a problem. But I couldn't stop using crack," Nate was saying. "Whenever I wasn't high, I would think about all the shit I had did to y'all and I—"

"Remember when you would wake me up in the middle of the night, even when you knew that I had school the next day, so that I could walk with you to get drugs?" Toya interrupted. "Remember that shit? How you would take me with you to go get that shit because you were too twisted to walk and get it by yourself?"

Nate didn't respond. Of course he remembered it. He knew that she was trying to hurt him, and it was working.

"How about the time when I was sixteen and on my way out to a party and you tried to stop me from going—said I was going out to be a fuckin' tramp. When I tried to walk past you, you pushed me down the stairs and broke my arm. Remember that?"

"Latoya—"

"Or the time when you knocked my tooth out." Toya popped her false tooth out to reveal a hole where her front tooth had once been. Few people knew that she had a missing tooth, but for her it was a painful daily reminder of the abuse she'd suffered at her father's hands. "Punched me in my mouth like a fuckin' man 'cuz I had the nerve to try and defend my mother when you were putting a foot in her ass." She sighed. "You would beat her until she cried and curled up in a ball. Then you would take her money, her jewelry, *our* shit . . . whatever you could find. And you would go and get high. Didn't care how we survived, what we ate, or if the bills got paid. Didn't care that all the neighbors were calling *your* wife a dumb bitch, and that all the kids in school were laughing at us and the shame you brought on all of us. All you ever cared about was yourself. No wonder Derrick started selling drugs at sixteen. Somebody had to take care of the family. And your no-good ass was too fucked up to help."

"I'm so sorry, Latoya."

"Fuck you."

"I deserve that."

"You deserve to die, bitch!" Her voice reverberated off the dining room walls and she saw her father wince ever so slightly.

Nate sighed, then nodded slowly. "Maybe you're right."

They both sat in silence for a few moments. Toya thought back on the day when her mother had finally left her father. Nate had run their house like a dictatorship for years, using violence to keep his wife and kids under his control. Toya's three older brothers had moved out and as far away as possible as soon as they were old enough. Derrick, the youngest in the family, was incarcerated on a drug charge. And Toya had finally fled the confines of her brutal home and gone away to college to escape the clutches of her tyrannical father and her enabling mother. So it had come as quite a surprise to her when she got a phone call from her mother one rainy Sunday morning telling her that the family home had been foreclosed on and Jeanie was moving back to Atlanta to be closer to her sisters. She was finally leaving Nate, and for the first time in her life she didn't care how he made it without her. Decades of abuse and oppression had at long last taken their toll on her. Toya had been thrilled to hear that her mother had somehow gotten the strength to rid herself of her useless husband. Years passed with no word from Nate and Toya had been relieved that he was gone at last.

Now, here he was, sitting at her dining room table with his life hanging in the balance. Toya had to chuckle at the absurdity of it. She had told herself that her father was dead for so long that she'd begun to believe it. Seeing him now, seated across from her, felt somewhat surreal. Especially because he looked like a shell of his former self. She had been so afraid of him when she was a young girl. Her father was the very definition of the boogie man to her. But she wasn't afraid anymore. In fact, now she had the upper hand and she wanted nothing more than to bask in that.

"You know something, Latoya?" Nate said at last. "You probably don't know this, but I saw you on the street once."

Toya looked at her father, wondering what he was talking about.

"It was about two years after your mother and I split up. I was still out in them streets getting high and I was panhandling in front of a Popeyes chicken joint. A black Mercedes pulled up and a man got out wearing a Coogi sweater, iced-out chain, fancy watch."

Michael . . . Toya thought, recalling her ex-husband in all his finery. *God, he's talking about Michael.*

"He came around and opened the passenger door and you stepped out. You had on a fur jacket, diamonds, jeans, and high heels and I was shocked. I hadn't seen you in a long time, and you looked good. I waited to see if you recognized me, but you didn't. My clothes were dirty and I looked and smelled like shit. I had a coat on with a hood, a hat pulled low on my face. Anyway, you and the man came closer to where I was standing and I said, 'Can you spare some change?' I was still hoping you would look at me and recognize who I was. But you didn't. You looked right past me. Your friend stopped and was fishing around in his pocket for some change or something to give me. But you pulled him towards the restaurant and told him not to give me shit. You said, 'That nigga's a bum. Don't give him a damn thing. Let him get a fuckin' job or starve.' He listened to you and I watched you both walk away."

Toya felt no guilt. She only wished she had recognized her father so that she could have berated him even more.

"I was so proud of you that night," Nate said. He could tell that Toya was surprised to hear him say that. "I used to always tell you not to give nobody shit. Make 'em work for it. Don't let muthafuckas take advantage of you. And when you spoke that night, you sounded just like me."

"I'm nothing like you."

Nate smirked and nodded. "Yes you are. You're strong just like me."

Toya had no comeback. She hated to admit to herself that he was probably right. Toya's mother had always lacked strength. She was intelligent, articulate, and had done her best to be a good mother to her children. But she certainly wasn't strong. Even now. Nate knew where Toya lived, where she worked, and what her phone numbers were because Jeanie had provided him with the information, which meant

Toya's mom had been speaking to Nate, with her weak ass. Toya shook her head.

"You're not strong," she said. "You're a weak, heartless bastard, and you always have been."

Nate didn't respond right away. "I see that you've done well for yourself, Latoya," he said finally. "I'm proud of you. I'm sure that doesn't matter to you, but it's true. I'm very proud of you. Out of all my kids, you're the one I always admired the most."

"Please!"

"I'm serious. I was hard on you. I admit that. But even when I was getting high, I used to notice that you never took none of your brothers' shit. You fought them back. Shit, you fought *me* back. You threatened to kill me. Your mother never dared to do that."

Toya hated to hear him criticize her mother. All Jeanie had been guilty of was loving a no-good nigga too long. "She should've waited till your evil ass went to sleep and blew your fuckin' head off."

Nate chuckled a little. "She probably should have. Nobody would have blamed her."

The silence returned.

"I wanted to talk to you so I could explain that I was out of my mind in those days. I know I fucked up. And there's nothing I can do to take back all the shit I did. But I love you, Latoya. I love your brothers, and I've told them that. I just wanted to come and tell you, too. I'm sorry, baby girl. So sorry for all that I did wrong in your life."

Toya felt unwanted tears stinging at her eyes. She hated to think that this asshole was wearing her down. She was about to launch into a tirade to prevent herself from crying, but her phone rang and interrupted her. Toya looked at the time and saw that it was 3:30 A.M. She glanced at the caller ID and saw Camille's name and number. Frowning, since Camille never called at such a late hour, Toya answered.

"Camille? What's wrong?"

"Toya, I know it's late . . ."

"That's okay. What happened?"

Camille's words spilled out in a torrent. "Misa shot Frankie's brother, Steven. He's dead, Toya! And they're taking Misa to jail. Frankie is on his way over here now and I'm scared, girl. Can you come and meet me at my house? I'm afraid of what he's gonna do when he gets here."

Toya sat there speechless and listened to her friend. She could not believe her ears. "Misa killed your brother-in-law?" she finally asked.

"Yes," Camille said. "I know it sounds crazy. I'll explain everything when you get here. Please come as soon as you can, Toya."

"Okay," Toya agreed. "I'm on my way." She hung up the phone and looked at her father. "I gotta go. I hope you got all your shit off your chest."

Nate had heard his daughter's end of the conversation and was concerned. "What's going on? You running off to a crime scene in the middle of the night?"

Toya rose from her seat and frowned down at her father. "Where I run off to is none of your concern. You said what you had to say. Now I gotta go."

Toya grabbed her purse and led the way to the front door. Hesitantly, Nate followed.

Standing in her front yard, Nate watched as Toya locked up her home, taking extra care to ensure that all of her locks were secure. She didn't want any more unwelcome visitors. When she turned and faced him, Nate carefully reached for her hand. Toya drew back and frowned at her father. Putting both hands in the air as a sign of surrender, Nate backed off. "I just want you to know that I love you. I've always loved you. Even in the midst of my bullshit. And I always will."

Toya couldn't handle this. Too much was happening tonight and she couldn't process it all at once. She turned her head away from him, looking off into the night at nothing in particular, and Nate finally began to walk away.

"Good night, Latoya," he called over his shoulder.

Toya didn't bother to respond. Instead, as tears spilled down her cheeks in the darkness of the night, she climbed into her car, put the key in the ignition, and peeled out, heading to Staten Island.

Set It Off

Dominique sat in her car and looked at the dashboard clock in dismay. It was just past 3:45 in the morning and she had had no luck finding her fourteen-year-old daughter. Hours earlier, Octavia had run away, leaving behind a note that now sat crumpled and tearstained in the passenger seat. She had been driving around for hours looking for her child and had been unable to find her anywhere.

Dominique had been under the mistaken impression that everything was fine with Octavia. As far as she knew, ever since her father's sudden death, she and Octavia had grown closer and established a routine of sorts. Particularly since Dominique's sister Whitney had proven to be so undependable as the family grieved, Octavia had seemed to sense the importance of being good for her mother. Three days out of the week, Octavia had been attending dance class at the prestigious and expensive Bardwell Dance School not far from their luxury apartment on the Upper East Side. However, tonight when Dominique arrived home from a long night at work, she found Octavia gone and a voice mail from her dance teacher informing her that Octavia hadn't attended class in weeks.

Dominique had been completely confused. To her knowledge, her daughter had never missed a dance class. The message from the dance school made her more worried than ever about Octavia's whereabouts. She had gone into Octavia's room to look for clues as to where she may have gone. She hadn't had to look very far.

An envelope sat atop the pillows on Octavia's bed. On it, she had written "Mommy" in her fancy cursive handwriting. Dominique had torn open the envelope, read its contents, and gone running out to search for her child.

That was hours ago, and here she sat in front of the Port Authority Bus Terminal near Times Square praying that Octavia hadn't left town. She had scoured the terminal with pictures of Octavia and had enlisted the help of the Port Authority police to help in the search. They had no way of knowing whether or not she had jumped on a bus before Dominique got there. But they promised to be on the lookout for her throughout the night. They told Dominique that it was too soon to file a missing person's report since her daughter was a teenager and had admittedly run away. They advised her to go back home and wait for Octavia to come back and to hope for the best.

But Dominique couldn't just go home and give up. She could tell from the tone of the note that Octavia wasn't coming home that night. She seemed to be hiding something, running from something. Dominique picked up the note for the umpteenth time and reread it.

Ma,

I got myself in some trouble. I'm not really who you think I am and I don't want to let you down anymore. It's time for me to grow up sooner than I thought I

*would and to take responsibility. I love you and I'll be
in touch soon. Don't worry about me. I'm okay. You
just have to accept that I'm not your baby girl anymore.
In time you'll understand.*

Octavia

Dominique was confused. She felt like she was reading
some kind of puzzle that she was supposed to decipher. She
had racked her brain for hours in an attempt to figure out
what kind of trouble Dominique was in. Her grades in school
were good. Dominique always kept on top of that. It had to
be something deeper, something personal, and Dominique
felt like a terrible mother for not having noticed that something was clearly wrong with her child.

Her cell phone rang and for a brief, fleeting moment, she
got excited thinking that it was Octavia calling. But one glance
at the caller ID dashed those hopes. Toya's name and number
flashed across the screen and Dominique let out a disappointed sigh.

"Hello?" she answered.

"I expected you to be asleep," Toya said, speaking into her
earpiece as she drove along the BQE.

"No such luck," Dominique answered, closing her eyes
as the beginnings of a headache crept up on her. "Octavia is
missing and—"

"Missing?" Toya swerved the car a little. "What the fuck
is going on tonight?"

"I came home and she was gone. She left a note behind
and I've been looking for her ever since." A thought occurred
to Dominique. "Have you heard from her? It just dawned on
me that she might go to your house since you two hit it off so
well the night of my father's accident."

Toya hated to disappoint her. "No, girl. She hasn't called me and she didn't come by." Toya shuddered as she recalled the hours-long conversation she'd had with her father that evening. "I can't believe this crazy fuckin' night!"

Dominique frowned. She had been so caught up in her worries for Octavia that she hadn't asked what prompted Toya's late-night call. "What else happened?" she asked, wondering what her friend was alluding to.

"Camille just called me. I'm heading to her house right now. She said Misa shot Frankie's brother."

"What?" Dominique couldn't believe her ears. "Shot him?"

"That's exactly what I said. She told me she'll explain when I get there. Frankie's supposedly on his way over there and Camille is scared. Misa was being questioned by the cops when I spoke to her."

Dominique started her car and put it in drive. "Oh my God. I'll meet you there."

"Are you sure?" Toya asked. "You got a lot going on right now with your daughter."

Dominique shrugged. "I feel helpless just driving around. Trying to find a teenager in the middle of the night in New York City is like trying to find a needle in a haystack." She sighed again. "The cops told me to go home and wait for her. I can't sleep anyway, so let's go find out what's going on."

Toya agreed. "Okay. See you at Camille's. Get there as soon as you can."

"I'm on my way."

The phone rang in Baron's hospital room in the middle of the night, startling him awake. He glanced at the bedside clock and pushed the button to raise the top of his hospital bed. When he was in an upright position, he reached over and answered the phone. It was Tremaine.

"Aye, Baron. I know you were sleeping, but I had to get in touch with you ASAP. Frankie got me meeting him at his house on Staten Island right now. He said somebody shot his brother, Steven. Killed him. The police are over there right now. He got Biggs and Danno over at Gillian's house to keep her safe. I just wanted you to be alert, my nigga. Shit is real right now."

Baron's face froze. He felt so vulnerable lying there in his hospital bed hooked up to what felt like a thousand machines. On the night that he was shot and his father had been murdered, Baron had sustained gunshot wounds to his chest, stomach, and both legs and had been grazed in the head by a bullet, as well. Luckily for him, none of the injuries had cost him his life. However, they had rendered him practically immobile. His head was wrapped in a bandage, as were both of his legs. He had a heart monitor, an IV, and even a colostomy bag attached to him. He was defenseless and he couldn't help taking note of the fact that Frankie had secured Gillian safely, but had left him open to attack.

Tremaine could hear the fear in Baron's voice as he spoke. "I can be as alert as I want to, Trey. But if somebody comes up here, what can I do?" Baron buzzed for the nurse. He wanted to see how long it would take for someone to get to his room if he needed help at this hour of night. For weeks he'd been stuck in the hospital—mostly lying dormant in a coma while he fought for his life. In the days since he'd regained consciousness, his mother, Celia, and Misa had taken turns sitting at his bedside each day, doing their best to keep him comfortable and helping him come to terms with what had happened. But it was the middle of the night, and both Celia and Misa had gone home hours ago.

"I hear you, son," Tremaine said. "But I'm already on Staten Island to meet up with Frankie. All I can do is tell you to keep your eyes open."

The nurse came in and asked if Baron was all right. Ironically, she offered him something to help him sleep, but he refused. Sleep was the last thing he needed right now. He asked for some water and she left to retrieve it.

"Yo, Trey, good looking out. But tell Frankie not to leave me fucked up like this. He can send somebody up here the same way he sent goons to my sister's house."

Tremaine was pulling up in front of Frankie's house at that moment and saw the chaos that surrounded the sprawling home. He put his car in park, turned off the ignition, and wiped his hand across his face in amazement. "I'll let him know, Baron," he said. "I'll call you back in a little while."

Tremaine hung up the phone and sat in the dark of his car, the flashing lights from the police and emergency vehicles illuminating his face. He started to dial Frankie's number, not wanting to go into the house without his friend. But then he spotted Frankie running toward the driveway and Tremaine climbed out of his car and followed.

Frankie saw all the emergency vehicles outside of his house. As he ran toward it, he heard someone call his name. Turning, he saw Tremaine headed his way. He didn't greet his friend, but Frankie's eyes said it all. He was definitely scared of what awaited him on the inside of his house. Together, they walked up the stairs and right into Sergeant Denton who was waiting in the doorway.

"Mr. Bingham?"

Frankie nodded. "Where's my brother?"

The sergeant led them into the foyer of the home and paused, holding his hand up in front of Frankie. "Mr. Bingham, let me bring you up to speed on what we know so far."

It felt odd to Frankie, having this cop stop him from moving freely about his own home. But he was anxious to find out what was going on. Frankie was all ears and Tremaine, too, hung on the officer's every word.

"We were called here tonight by your wife . . ." The sergeant looked at his notepad and found the name he was searching for. ". . . Camille. She informed us that she arrived home to find that your brother had been shot in the kitchen. According to her, he was dead when she arrived."

Frankie felt the blood drain from his face.

"The murder weapon was found lying beside the deceased. Camille picked up a knife nearby and then proceeded to the dining room where she found her sister seated at the table."

"Misa?" Frankie couldn't believe what he was hearing.

Sergeant Denton referred to his notes again. "Yes, sir. Misa Atkinson. Your wife found her seated in the dining room with blood spattered on her hands and on her clothes. There were also some bloody handprints found on the wall in the dining room. When we arrived, Ms. Atkinson was still seated in the dining room, in somewhat of a . . ." The sergeant seemed to search for the right words. ". . . a state of shock. We've since moved her to another room where detectives are talking to her. She has so far refused to answer our questions but she has acknowledged that she is the person who committed this crime. We're attempting now to establish a motive for what happened here tonight. And we're hoping that you or your wife may be able to shed some light on anything that may have transpired recently between your siblings."

Frankie leaned against the wall, feeling like he might pass out at any moment. "You're telling me that Misa killed my brother?" A million thoughts raced through his head. What possible reason could she have to hurt his brother? The two rarely even spoke to each other as far as Frankie knew.

Sergeant Denton nodded. "That's what we believe based on what we've been told and also based on the fact that there were no signs of forced entry into the home. Nothing has been stolen, according to your wife, and your sister-in-law admits that she shot the victim until the gun was empty."

"Shit!" Tremaine muttered under his breath.

"We'd like to have you come with us into the kitchen where we've collected your brother's remains for transport to the medical examiner's office. If you can confirm his identity, we can process the case much faster since he's now listed in our report as John Doe. We'll need to perform an autopsy and will need your permission to do that."

Frankie stood there in silence for a moment or two.

"*. . . your brother's remains . . .*"

He felt his heart pounding in his chest, and felt his palms sweating despite the freezing January cold. On shaky legs, Frankie followed the officer into the kitchen and Tremaine trailed behind, taking in the whole scene. With each step through his home, Frankie felt as if he were walking through a nightmare. He looked around for signs of a struggle, but saw no clues as to what could have made Misa kill Steven. It felt surreal, and as they entered the kitchen it became downright horrific. A large pool of blood was in the middle of the floor. Broken glass crunched under Frankie's feet as he entered. A few officers were snapping pictures of the blood all over the room for use as evidence. Steven lay on a gurney, his cold and lifeless body shrouded in a black body bag. The bag was zipped up to his chin, revealing only his face, which was frozen in a ghastly expression, eyes wide open.

Blinking back tears, Frankie nodded. "That's him."

Sergeant Denton nodded toward one of the junior officers and they zipped Steven's body all the way up and wheeled him out past Frankie and Tremaine who stood in stunned silence. Frankie looked around the kitchen. He watched one cop walk past with a .38 Special zipped up in a plastic bag. Gathering that this was the murder weapon, Frankie turned his attention back to Sergeant Denton.

"Where is she?"

"Your wife?"

Frankie shook his head. "Misa."

The sergeant seemed to hesitate, as if unsure whether or not it would be wise to let this man, who was clearly upset, be in the same room as the suspect. He decided to go for it. After all, it might be interesting to see how Misa reacted to seeing her brother-in-law. Figuring that the worst that could happen would be that some questions might get answered, Sergeant Denton led the way to the living room where Misa sat surrounded by detectives.

Camille stood with her back to him, flanked by Toya and Dominique, both of whom had just arrived. When Frankie entered the room, Misa's face resonated with fear. Turning around to see what had caused Misa's reaction, Camille came face-to-face with her husband.

"Frankie," she said, not knowing what else to say.

He ignored his wife, instead staring straight at Misa. The officers on the scene stood guardedly, waiting to see what would happen. But they said nothing as Frankie stared at his sister-in-law and walked slowly toward her.

"You did this?" he asked, his gaze fixed on her.

Misa's jaw clenched. Her body seemed to tense and she stared right back at Frankie as he drew nearer. She nodded, and in one swift motion, Frankie lunged at her, snatching her by the neck as officers hurriedly pulled him off her. Camille ran to him, trying to plead her sister's case. But Frankie shoved her off him.

"Get the fuck off me!" he bellowed as Tremaine and Sergeant Denton restrained him.

"Calm down," Tremaine urged. "You don't want to go to jail tonight, Frankie."

"Listen to your friend, Mr. Bingham," a detective warned.

Frankie's chest heaved as he glared at Misa, who was holding her neck as if he'd managed to hurt her in the few seconds he'd tried to squeeze the life out of her. "Why'd you do that to my brother, Misa?" he asked, tears streaming down his face. Steven was Frankie's Achilles' heel—his weakness. By hurting Steven—who Frankie had always tried to protect from any kind of harm—Misa had crushed him in a way she couldn't possibly imagine.

Misa shook her head as tears fell from her eyes, too. She hadn't thought this far ahead. It hadn't occurred to her that she would hurt *Frankie*, that his marriage to her sister might never survive this. Frankie had always been generous to her. But she still had no regrets about what she'd done to Steven. The bastard deserved what she'd done and more! She said nothing as her brother-in-law looked at her with hate in his eyes.

"I asked you a fuckin' question!" he yelled. "Why'd you shoot my brother?"

Toya and Dominique held Camille back as she still struggled to get free and get close to her husband. Toya had to fight the urge to slap her friend. Instead, she hissed at her, "Don't go near him right now, bitch! He's *pissed*! Be easy."

Finally, Misa spoke up, her voice low and calculated. "He was fucking with my son, Frankie," she said through clenched teeth. "He was molesting Shane!"

Frankie's expression conveyed utter disbelief. He looked at Camille, then back to Misa. "You're crazy!"

Misa was enraged now. "No, your muthafuckin' brother was crazy!"

"Easy," one of the detectives warned her, as Tremaine got a tighter grip on Frankie.

Frankie looked at his friend and took a deep breath. He looked Tremaine in the eye and said, "Let me go. It's all right. I'm not gonna touch her."

Slowly, and hesitantly, Tremaine released his grip on Frankie. Frankie took two steps back, closed his eyes, and cupped his hands in front of his face as if in prayer. Looking at Misa, he frowned. "You think my brother was touching Shane?"

Misa didn't answer. As far as she was concerned, the subject was not up for debate. She didn't *think* Steven had done it. She knew he had.

"You got this idea in your head and you came over here . . . to my house. And you killed him?"

Again, Camille stepped gingerly toward her husband. "Frankie . . ."

He held one hand up to her as if to stop her from coming any closer. "Nah," he said calmly. "Stay away from me."

He was unmoved by Camille's tears as Dominique hugged her. Frankie shook his head. Camille was carrying on like she was the victim. Meanwhile, his poor brother had been pumped full of lead and accused of a heinous act against a child. He turned his attention back to Misa, who was again refusing to answer the detective questioning her.

"Misa, you just said that your son was being molested. Can you elaborate on that?"

She shook her head. "I want a lawyer."

The detective nodded. She had already told him that a thousand times in the past hour and a half. "You understand that we have no choice but to place you under arrest and take you down to the station?"

She nodded. She couldn't wait to get the fuck out of here. She felt like she was in a fishbowl, with all eyes on her. Frankie, more than anyone, was making her want to get out of this house as soon as possible.

The detective rose and guided Misa to her feet. Handcuffing her behind her back, he noticed that she was shaking despite her icy demeanor. He could tell that she was scared to death as he read her rights.

"You have the right to remain silent," he said. "Anything you say can and will be used against you in a court of law. You have the right to an attorney . . ."

As Misa acknowledged that she understood what she was being told, Camille looked at her husband. Frankie had an expression on his face unlike any she'd ever seen before. Clearly, he was devastated by his brother's murder. But the pain of what Misa had accused Steven of was evident on his face as well, as he stared at her being led out of the house and into a police car. Sergeant Denton was explaining to Camille that a bail hearing would not be held for Misa for hours, that she'd be spending the rest of the night down at the precinct and would be brought to court to appear before a judge sometime after noon that day. As he finished giving her this information, Sergeant Denton suggested that Camille find somewhere else to spend the night. The home was still being processed as a crime scene, plus the last thing he wanted was to leave the Binghams alone together after what he'd just witnessed.

"You can come back to my house, Camille. You can stay for as long as you want," Dominique said.

Camille was still staring at Frankie. Their eyes met and for a few silent moments, she pleaded with her eyes for him to talk to her. Instead, he stared at her blankly before he turned away, tapped Tremaine on the arm, and strode right past Camille and out the front door. She called after him, but he ignored her and kept on walking.

"Let him go, Camille," Toya said. Her tone of voice conveyed that she was sick of her friend calling after Frankie. "He just found out that his brother was killed. It's a lot to digest in one night."

Camille took a deep breath. She knew that Frankie needed time to sort out everything that was happening. Shit, she hadn't processed it all herself. But, as she packed a suitcase to take to Dominique's house, she admitted to herself that it was deeper than just tonight. She knew that things in her family would never be the same again. Frankie had left her for Gillian. Camille was pregnant with his child. Steven was dead. Misa was in jail. And poor Shane had been victimized. In a daze, Camille left her million-dollar home amid the flashing lights of news cameras and the curious stares of her neighbors. As she climbed into Dominique's MKX, shielding her face from the news photographers, she cried for all of them. This was worse than anything she could have ever imagined.

Reckoning

The sun had come up, and Gillian had brewed a fresh pot of coffee by the time Frankie returned to her Manhattan home. By then her imagination had gotten the best of her. Last she'd heard, Frankie was running off to the home he shared with his estranged wife—who, incidentally, had just announced that she was pregnant. Gillian had lain awake all night while Danno and Biggs patrolled her home like pit bulls. She wondered what had happened to Steven, wondered why Frankie hadn't bothered to call. Gillian was worried sick.

When Frankie came through the door at just after seven-thirty in the morning, Gillian was standing near her floor-to-ceiling kitchen windows gripping a coffee mug. Seeing him enter, she set the mug down on the nearby marble countertop and looked at him expectantly. Her eyes seemed sad, and Frankie almost dissolved in a puddle of tears at her feet. He hated having to burden her with more horrible news. But what had happened to his brother was not something he could keep from her.

He walked over to her and pulled her close to him. His strong arms overwhelmed her as he inhaled her scent. With his nose nestled in her hair and her face buried in the crook of his arm, Frankie openly cried. Gillian's hair became damp with his tears and she clung to him, aware that his underlings were still present and that Frankie had never been one to cry in public before. Despite the grimmest of circumstances, he kept a stiff upper lip. But now he openly wept, seeming not to care who saw him fall apart. Finally, he loosened the grip he had on her and she reached up and touched his face, wet with tears. Glancing around she noticed that Danno, Biggs, and Tremaine had had sense enough to withdraw to her study.

She looked at Frankie, his eyes squeezed shut as if to stop the torrent that was pouring forth. "What happened?" she whispered softly. "Come here." Gillian kissed Frankie's exquisite lips and wiped his face. "Tell me, Frankie. What happened?"

Frankie shook his head back and let out a deep and seemingly calming breath. When he looked at Gillian again, his eyes were red and puffy. She led him by the hand to her living room and got him situated on the couch. Sitting beside him, she squeezed his hand as he began.

"My brother is dead." Frankie's voice was monotone, his eyes distant. "Misa shot him. She . . ." His voice caught in his throat then. Clearing it out, he clenched his jaw, folded and unfolded his hands, and then went on. "She went to the house while no one was home last night. She had keys." His voice got louder. "You know what I'm saying? We trusted that bitch with keys to the house 'cuz her son was over there all the time. She let herself in. And she waited for him. And when he came in, she shot him." Gillian couldn't believe what she was hearing, but she kept quiet as he continued. "Pulled the trigger six times and then sat there. Camille found her in the dining room."

Gillian couldn't be silent any longer. She almost didn't believe what he was telling her, but then how could he possibly make up such madness? "Frankie, what are you telling me? Misa shot Steven . . . for what? Why would she just go over there and kill him?"

Frankie stared at the floor. His mind was reeling. After leaving his home, he had ridden in Tremaine's car to the morgue and signed the forms necessary to perform the autopsy. It all felt like a bad dream to him. Like he was trapped in his worst nightmare but couldn't wake up no matter how hard he tried. Steven, the little brother he had nurtured, attempted to mentor, and protected, was dead. Frankie knew that their mother, whom he hadn't spoken to in at least two years, would be devastated. This might be the thing it took to finally kill her.

Gillian stroked Frankie's head and spoke softly. "Why did she do it?" Gillian had to know.

He looked at her, silent for a while.

"She thinks he was molesting her son."

Gillian's expression changed and she stopped stroking Frankie's head. She frowned slightly and touched her diamond necklace absentmindedly. Frankie took note. He expected that everyone would respond that way, questioning the possibility that Steven was a pedophile. Frankie had seen the local newspaper reporters assembling at his home in the wee hours as word spread of a bloody crime scene in his upper-crust neighborhood. He had heard what Misa said, seen her conviction. He knew that his dead brother would be judged publicly without ever having the chance to defend himself.

"Oh my God," Gillian managed.

Frankie cleared his throat again. "She sat there and looked me in my face . . ." He didn't complete the thought, but it was obvious that Frankie was struggling with what had happened.

Gillian had one eyebrow raised. Gently, and in her most angelic voice, she prodded. "Steven couldn't be capable of something like that . . . could he?"

Frankie didn't move. He didn't respond. He simply stared off into space as if he were mesmerized by some long-ago thought.

Gillian didn't nudge any further out of respect for the fact that he had just lost his brother. But she began thinking about Steven—about all the times she had interacted with him over the years, trying to assess if she had missed any warning signs that he could be a pervert.

"Nah . . ." Frankie said at last. "I mean . . ."

Silence lingered between them for so long that Gillian got up and poured herself some of the coffee she'd made earlier. She made some tea for Frankie, since she'd been around him long enough to know that he hated coffee. When she returned to the living room, Frankie was holding his head in his hands. Meanwhile, Tremaine and the goons came in and told Frankie that they were going to leave. Gillian noticed that Tremaine's demeanor seemed just as downtrodden as Frankie's. After all, Tremaine had witnessed the carnage up close and personal. He had seen Steven's bullet-riddled body, watched his friend come to terms with the loss of his brother and what he was accused of. The two friends shared a strong handshake embrace and when they were all gone, Frankie sank back down on the couch, and again the silence came.

"Drink your tea," Gillian said, wondering how things could get any worse. First her father had been slain, her brother maimed, and now Steven was dead, Camille was pregnant, Misa was in jail. And Frankie sat mute before her.

"I'm so sorry, baby," she said, watching him ignore the steaming mug in front of him. She knew that he probably wanted something much stronger than peppermint tea. "I know you looked out for Steven all his life." She thought back to a conversation she and Frankie had only weeks earlier, on the night when they made love for the first time. He had shared with her some painful details of his childhood. They were things that Frankie had never shared with anyone; how his father suffered from some type of mental illness that had gone undiagnosed for so long the family seemed to have just found a way to cope with it.

Frankie looked at Gillian. "I told you that my father was crazy," Frankie said, as if reading her mind. "He was the type to go off—just snap at any minute."

"Yeah," Gillian said, nodding. "You told me that he would sit down for dinner and smile, he'd tell your mom that it was delicious, and then he'd bug out and ask why she was looking at him like that. He accused her of poisoning his food."

Frankie nodded. "That wasn't the half of it." He stared ahead before looking at Gillian again. "He was like a psychopath."

Gillian felt like a psychologist. "You said that he used to bully everybody, and beat you."

Frankie looked at her in a way that made her stop speaking. "We were all scared of him." He frowned. "But my brother was the most afraid because he was the little one, you know? He was a little kid, bony and frail, and my father used to tease him, call him Gimpy and shit like that."

Frankie had told Gillian that his father committed suicide one night as his brother and mother lay asleep. By then, Frankie had fled the home and was working for Gillian's father, Doug Nobles. Frankie admitted to Gillian that he had

felt no sorrow when his father died. He had only been relieved that he hadn't taken the rest of the family with him.

"After I left home, I would sneak in and see Steven all the
time. He told me that Dad wasn't beating them like he used
to. I never knew if that was true or not, 'cuz I wasn't seeing
my mother. She was like a slave to my father, you feel me?"

Gillian nodded, but truly had no idea what that kind of
upbringing must have been like. Her father had doted on her
from the moment she entered the world and her mother had
been smothering, as opposed to distant and nonparticipatory.
Her parents' marriage had been a happy one and she had rarely
heard her father raise his voice at her mother.

Frankie continued. "I never knew what happened after I
left. I got out and got away, but he probably bore the burden
of it."

"You feel guilty about that?" she asked.

Frankie nodded. "Yeah, I do. I left. And Steven and my
mother were left behind to deal with my father."

"Don't blame yourself, Frankie."

He shrugged. "Nah," he said, as if trying to shake off the
feeling of guilt that so obviously haunted him. "It ain't that. I
did what I could to protect him. And I thought I did a good
job." He looked in her eyes. "Camille never understood why I
took care of him; why I let him hang around in our kitchen
and eat up our food, run up our bills." He chuckled awkwardly. "I just wanted my little brother to feel like he had a
place he could be . . ." Frankie seemed to lose the words he
needed to convey the sense of comfort and safety he had
wanted Steven to enjoy after years of being belittled and demeaned at the hands of their tyrannical father.

"I understand," Gillian said. "I know how you felt about
Steven." She couldn't believe that Misa had killed him.

"Frankie, I'm so sorry." She shook her head, feeling helpless to ease his pain. "Where is she now—Camille's sister?"

"She'll be in court this afternoon," Frankie said, moving forward in his seat as if he needed to say something. He paused and looked at Gillian. "I can't let her get away with this."

Gillian wondered for a moment if Frankie was going to hurt his sister-in-law. She searched his eyes for the answer.

Frankie was staring at the floor as if in a trance. "I have to break this to my mother somehow." He pictured his mother's face—Mary Jane Bingham. She was once a beautiful woman, tall and brown, statuesque and ladylike. She was always quiet, had always been shy and soft-spoken. But it had gotten worse over the years, and Mary had remained a scared and beaten-down wife long after her husband was dead.

"Why didn't you feel the need to take care of your mother the same way you did for Steven after your father died?"

Frankie stared at Gillian, having asked himself the same question over and over. "Because my brother had no choice but to stay there and deal with it. He was a kid, you know what I'm saying. But my mother? She could have left whenever she was ready. She could have got us out of there. She was always so fragile, and . . . maybe I shouldn't fault her for it."

Gillian shook her head. "No, I think I would feel the same way." She wondered how the news of Steven's death would affect poor Mary Bingham. "When are you going to tell her? I want to be there with you."

He laughed a little. "How do I tell her this shit? It's gonna destroy her."

"I don't know how we'll tell her. But we'll figure it out, Frankie."

She made it sound so easy, but Frankie knew that it

wouldn't be. He breathed a heavy sigh and sat back against the pillows on the couch. He couldn't block out the recollection of Steven's face in his head. He saw his brother lying in the body bag, his eyes frozen in horror as he lay dead. There was no question in his mind that somebody—Camille, Misa— somebody was going to pay for what had been done to Steven.

Gillian looked at him as if she could read his mind. Frankie realized then how much he loved her. She was all that was good in his life at the moment. In his mind, Camille had held him hostage in a marriage he no longer wanted to be in. He had felt obligated to Camille for all the years of loyalty and love she had given him, but truth be told he hadn't been happy in years. And now, just as he found the courage to leave her and to live his life doing what made him truly happy, she was pregnant with his child. Camille's sister had killed his brother and accused him of an atrocity, dredging up years of Frankie's own childhood nightmares, which he had managed somehow to suppress in order to survive. Now he'd have to face his mother with more bad news in a life that had been riddled with nothing but. His "brother" Baron was laid up in the hospital, responsible for the death of his father figure, Doug Nobles. But as he looked at Gillian sitting there, Frankie felt reassured. She was beautiful, she understood him, she had his back and he was grateful.

"I love you, Frankie. And no matter what, nothing's gonna change that. We're gonna get through this together."

Frankie kissed her, pulled her close to him. She lay against his chest and he held her, hoping that their bond could indeed stand the trials that loomed ahead of them.

Fingerprints

It was tight in the back of the squad car as Misa was driven to the police station that night. With her hands cuffed firmly behind her back—the female officer who put the handcuffs on had expressed concern that Misa might slip out of them with her small wrists—she sat uncomfortably as she listened to the two officers in the front seat joke about each other's mamas.

Misa thought about the look on Frankie's face. She tried to block it out as she gazed out the window at the passing motorists. She thought instead about Shane, her sweet boy with his big innocent eyes and his beautiful smile. Misa missed him more than she ever had before. She felt tears stinging at the corners of her eyes as she acknowledged her role in what had happened to her son. Misa hadn't been there to protect Shane. In fact, she'd been so busy trying to be everything Baron Nobles had ever dreamed of that she hadn't even noticed her own child's misery.

She had been a terrible mother, she decided. It didn't matter that her heart had been in the right place; that she had only been out trying to secure a place in Baron's life so that she and Shane could have a better existence. None of that mattered now. Shane had been victimized and Misa felt that it was all her fault.

They arrived at the precinct and Misa was ushered inside, the cold winter wind howling in her ears, whistling through the trees and nudging them all forward toward the big doors leading into the police station, to her fate. Once inside, one of her captors ordered her to sit on a bench as he approached the desk sergeant and was handed a logbook.

Misa sat on the bench and shivered slightly as her body warmed up from the cold January air outside. She watched the officers gather around and talk about her in hushed tones. *"Murdered the guy . . . said he was molesting her kid . . . her brother-in-law, can you imagine?"*

She felt like an exhibit at the zoo. After several agonizing minutes, she was led up an old, paint-chipped staircase that reminded her of the one in her former high school. The handcuffs still tore at her wrists and she hoped, as they reached the landing, that someone would take them off her soon. They stepped into a room and a heavy iron door shut behind them. She looked around and saw four officers and a few holding cells. She was mercifully uncuffed and ordered to step out of her shoes. Misa was searched again and made to pass through a metal detector. Once they were satisfied that she had no weapons of mass destruction, they gave her back her shoes — without the laces. Next, she was led into a cell that was smaller than her tiny bathroom at home, and she sat on the bench inside as the officer shut and locked the cell door behind her. She massaged her sore wrists as she peered through the bars at the officers filling out paperwork and milling about.

Misa looked around. This place was filthy. Previous poor, unfortunate souls had carved their names into the bench on which she sat, onto the walls surrounding her. Misa couldn't imagine what would possess a person to want to leave their mark *here* of all places. She had certainly never imagined that she would find herself in this situation. No one could have predicted that things would've turned out the way they had.

Her thoughts were interrupted by a female officer who came and unlocked Misa's cell. She informed her that she was about to be fingerprinted and photographed. Misa let out a soft moan as she was led to the photographing station. She was familiar enough with the justice system to know that her mug shot would inevitably appear in the newspaper the next day. She stepped into the white-painted square on the floor as the officer instructed her and looked into the camera as she was told.

"How's my hair?" Misa half jokingly asked the woman wielding the camera.

The brunette seemed caught off guard by the question, but nodded, offered Misa a weak smile. "Good."

It was true. Compared to most of the people who slid through the precinct late at night, she did look all right. Misa had a fresh new weave, which was less than a week old and still looked great.

She glared into the camera, her expression defiant. The officer told her to turn to her left and another picture was taken. Then she was led over to a high-tech fingerprinting station and processed. When she was done, the officer who had brought her in appeared again and handcuffed her, looser this time, before leading her up another flight of stairs. This time, Misa was led down a maze of hallways and brought into an office where an older white woman with glasses and plainclothes sat behind a large oak desk.

The cop ushered her into a nearby room and ordered her

to sit on a folding chair. He left her in there and went back outside the room to speak with the woman at the desk. Misa stared at the wall in the room she had been left in. Photos lined the wall like poorly applied wallpaper—pictures of crime victims. Misa read their names, read the details of their murders.

Trina Samuels, shot numerous times in the head . . . Darin "Dusty" Fernandez, missing since August 2007 . . . Martin "Murk" Payton last seen leaving Top Cuts Barbershop . . . found with a bullet to the back of the head in the basement of 555 Steuben Street . . . a witness stabbed to death in his home . . . another bludgeoned to death in the parking lot of Staten Island Savings Bank.

Misa looked at all the faces and all the stories and immediately felt like something was wrong. First of all, Frankie owned Top Cuts Barbershop. It was one of the many legitimate businesses he used as fronts for his illicit drug empire. She had also heard Baron mention Dusty's name on at least one occasion—particularly in hushed tones during late-night phone calls with Frankie during a trip he had taken with Misa to Miami.

Misa recalled the Miami trip now as she stared at Dusty's name and face on the poster. She remembered hearing Baron admit to having killed Dusty, recalled how she had judged him for taking the life of another human being. And now she had done the same thing. She had never been the most religious person, but she did believe in God. She knew that murder was a sin, no matter how you cut it. Misa's faith taught her that God himself would exact revenge against Steven for what he had done to Shane. But Misa's maternal instincts hadn't allowed her to wait patiently for justice. She had had to get some kind of immediate closure, and she had done that. Even as she sat there, knowing that she was facing a horrible immediate future in prison, she felt better knowing that Steven was dead—that she had killed him.

She turned her attention back to the wall and read some more of the posters, although no other names, faces, or details jumped out at her. The white woman who had been seated at the desk came into the room, but the other officer stayed outside. She sat across from Misa and offered her a halfhearted hello.

"So, what happened tonight?" she asked.

Misa ignored the question. She had asked for an attorney so many times she was sick of saying it. Plus, she was certain that the rookie outside had filled this lady in on all the details.

The woman smirked at Misa. "You're probably smart not to say too much. Is there anything you need? Any phone calls you need to get out of the way?"

Misa shook her head. "No."

"Well, it's late and I'm sure you'd like to get settled in for the night and lay down for a spell. Why don't you take a look behind you and tell me if you recognize anybody?"

Misa spun around in her seat and looked at the wall behind her. Unlike the wall she'd been facing, this one was papered with photos of wanted criminals and descriptions of the crimes they were accused of. Her eyes danced across it and settled on a photo of Daniel "Danno" Henriquez, an associate of both Frankie and Baron Nobles.

Misa's stomach flip-flopped.

. . . *wanted in connection with the rape and torture of Trina Samuels . . . DNA evidence found at the scene . . .*

Misa didn't want to overreact, but she was stunned.

"If you recognize someone on that wall, I'm sure it would look good for you in court."

Misa wondered if they already knew that she was familiar with Baron, had vacationed with him, spent nights in his bed. She wondered if they knew that she had seen Danno plenty of times before. Her connection to Frankie was unmistakable, but she wasn't sure if they knew how close she had gotten to the criminal side of it all, the things she'd heard over the past few months. Misa decided that now more than ever, she needed to keep her lips sealed. She had permanently burned her bridges with Frankie Bingham. The Nobles family was powerful and Misa couldn't afford to make any more mistakes.

She looked at the woman who hadn't bothered to identify herself and shook her head. No matter how grim her future seemed at the moment, she couldn't see snitching as a means of bettering her chances at trial. "I want to talk to my lawyer," she said.

The woman looked disappointed. "You sure?" she asked. "Take another look."

Misa didn't bother. She had seen enough the first time.

The woman nodded. Her glasses were ugly, Misa decided. Far too big for her face. She scribbled something in yet another logbook and called the rookie to come and get Misa. The officer came back in and ushered Misa all the way down the two flights of stairs they'd originally climbed and then farther down another stairwell, into what seemed like the dungeon of the precinct. It turned out to be the holding cells for the female prisoners. A blond female cop took over at that point and the rookie disappeared for good. Misa was led by the blonde to what would be her cell for the night.

Upon seeing it, Misa paused. The tiny cell was filthy, covered in graffiti that had been carved into the walls, into the hard metal bench and even the floor. A disgusting stainless steel toilet with a sink on top of it sat in the middle of the cell and the smell of urine was overpowering. Yellowed tissue clung to the seat of the toilet and Misa had to fight the urge to gag.

"I can't sleep in here," Misa said, shaking her head and backing away.

Blondie took Misa by the arm and urged her forward. "I know," she said, sounding as if she felt genuine sympathy for the pretty young lady in her charge. "It's not easy, but you have to go in there. Just try to get some sleep and before you know it, it'll be morning and you'll be on your way to court."

Misa looked again at the cell she was being forced to spend the night in and shut her eyes as if to block it out. She pictured her own bed at home, Baron's big beautiful bed in his big beautiful house. Looking at the metal bench she was being made to sleep on tonight, she shook her head as Blondie uncuffed her and nudged her forward into her evening accommodations. Misa slunk down onto the bench and leaned her fresh weave against the dank and dirty walls as Blondie locked her cell. She heard another door slam as Blondie retreated, heard still another door shut loudly outside of that one, and knew there was no escaping this fate. She was doomed to live like an animal for the time being. Misa could hear other voices in neighboring cells and listened to the conversations being shouted out from one woman to another. But she refrained from joining in. Instead, she laid her small body on top of the hard metal bench and shut her eyes. Sleep never came for Misa, but she still dreamed of seeing her son smiling

at her, free of his predator, no longer scared of the big bad
wolf.

Camille had showered, changed, and was lying across the chaise in
Dominique's living room. Toya, too, had freshened up and
was sipping a cup of coffee while seated on the sofa, looking
at the sunlight spilling through the huge windows of Dominique's apartment. Dominique was walking back and forth,
frantically dialing the numbers of some of Octavia's friends
in hopes that they had heard from her during the night. So
far, she'd had no luck. Both Toya and Camille had been dis-
heartened to learn about Octavia running away. Toya had
assured Dominique that her daughter was a smart young lady
and that she was okay and would come home soon. Dominique
wanted to believe that, but her maternal instincts tugged at
her still. None of the women had slept a wink in close to
twenty-four hours. And what an unbelievable twenty-four
hours it had been.

After leaving Staten Island, the three friends had arrived
at Dominique's Upper East Side apartment and Camille had
immediately called her mother to tell her about Misa's arrest.
Her mother, Lily, had been understandably distraught, and
when she called Misa's ex-husband, Louis, it had been even
more difficult. Louis had at first been dead silent, leaving
Camille wondering if he was still on the line. When he finally
spoke again, his words were cold.

"I don't feel sorry for her," he said. "None of this would've
happened if she was doing her job as a mother." He had paused
again. "But I would like to be in court tomorrow to answer
any questions about Shane." Louis was secretly relieved that
someone had paid the ultimate price for what had been done

to his son. But he still held Misa one hundred percent accountable. Camille didn't argue with him. Instead, she gave him the information for Misa's bail hearing. She advised both her mother and Louis to watch what they said to the media and to their friends about the situation in the days to come.

Even as she helped Camille calm down after a long and tragic evening and watched as Dominique paced the floor waiting for word from her daughter, Toya couldn't get her father out of her mind. She lay across the sofa and exhaled loudly.

Looking over at Toya, Dominique noticed that her friend looked exhausted. She knew that she personally wouldn't be able to sleep no matter how she tried, and assumed that the same was true for Camille. But Dominique saw no reason why Toya shouldn't get some rest.

"Toya, are you sure you don't want to go lay down in Octavia's room? Misa won't be in court for hours." They had agreed that Toya would accompany Camille to Misa's court appearance that afternoon while Dominique stayed home and waited for word from Octavia.

Toya shook her head. "Can't sleep," she said. "Got too much on my mind. Y'all ain't the only ones dealing with some bullshit."

Camille looked at her, frowning slightly. "What's on your mind?"

Toya looked at her troubled friends and felt less embarrassed to share the drama she was dealing with. She sighed. "My piece of shit father came back from the dead tonight."

Dominique stopped pacing then, and sat down in the recliner and crossed her legs. Camille seemed rapt as well, since neither of them had ever heard Toya speak much about her family.

"You thought your father was dead?" Camille asked, confused.

Toya shook her head. "No. I just wished he was."

Dominique's eyes widened.

"Damn," Camille said.

Dominique shook her head. "You're gonna have to elaborate."

Toya filled her friends in on the events of her childhood
and noticed that they seemed amazed by what she'd been
through. She knew it came as a surprise for them to learn that
someone as tough as Toya had endured such abuse. She regaled her friends with story after story of her father's verbal
and physical torment. When she showed them her missing
tooth, their facial expressions were priceless. She got emotional
at one point as she described the way her father had talked to
her, how he had belittled her mother. His words had often
been more painful than his blows, although his blows had
often been crippling. Toya's eyes grew sad.

"I used to hear my mother crying in her room at night
sometimes when she thought I was asleep. He would fuck her
up, but she would fight him back. Don't get it twisted, she
was not the kind of bitch to sit there and be his punching bag.
They used to go *at it*!" She laughed a little at that, though she
didn't really find it funny. Toya became lost in thought momentarily as she thought about how weak her mother still
seemed to her despite the fact that she had fought back. She
may have struck back, but she also kept returning to the monster she had married. Her mother, Jeanie—whom Nate had
nicknamed "Sweets" in the early days of their relationship—
had been gullible enough to be lulled back with empty prom-
ises and what Toya imagined must have been some really
good sex, since Sweets had stayed so long and had so many of

Nate's children. Toya hated the weakness she perceived in her mother, even on the nights when she battled Nate blow for blow.

"But he was a man and she couldn't win," Toya said at last. "I jumped in once and he knocked me out cold. So I learned to stay in my room, stay out of sight. Because as much as I loved and felt sorry for my mother, I couldn't understand why she kept taking him back." Toya shook her head as if still at a loss for an answer to that question. "But she wouldn't cry, she wouldn't break down at all until he left the house. She would shut her bedroom door and cry into her pillow and I don't know if she ever knew I could hear her." Toya stared off momentarily before clearing her throat and continuing. "I have a lot of respect for my mother," she said. "Even though to everybody in our neighborhood, she probably looked like a dumb bitch for putting up with Nate, to us she was a hero. She fed us, kept us going to school, kept clothes on our backs. It was more than my bitch-ass father was ever good for."

Finally, Toya described the times he had awakened her in the middle of the night and forced her to go with him to some of the seediest parts of Brooklyn and witness things she wasn't old enough to understand.

"He was a pig, you know what I'm saying?" Toya wiped her eyes. "Had me out there with him in the middle of the night watching him throw his life away." She shook her head. "Plus he cheated on my mother. Right in front of me, he would grab asses—nasty, fat, ugly, broke, nobody bitches. Tongue 'em down, joke around with them. And then he would dare me to tell my mother. Bitch-ass nigga." She sniffled and took the tissue Dominique passed her. "Anyway, his ass is dying. He needs a bone marrow transplant or something."

Dominique shook her head, her facial expression one of pure compassion for her friend. She had no idea that Toya had been through so much in her childhood.

"Will you be tested to see if you can be a donor?" Camille asked.

Toya seemed surprised and appalled by the question. "Hell no! I told him to crawl back under the rock he climbed out from."

Dominique knew that Toya was a tough woman, but that sounded harsh. "You're just gonna let him die?"

Toya didn't expect Dominique to understand. After all, her father, Bill Storms, had been the model parent. She looked at her friend like she didn't get it.

"Dominique, your father was perfect. He loved you, supported you, took care of you. My father didn't do any of those things. All he ever did was hurt my mother and all of us. I feel no pity for him. And if he really wanted my forgiveness, he would've asked for it before his time started running out."

Neither Dominique nor Camille could argue with that logic.

Eager to change the subject since she was uncomfortable being pitied, Toya looked at Camille. "Do you believe that Steven really molested your nephew?" she asked.

The look on Camille's face suggested that she'd been asking herself that question for the past few hours. She shook her head and looked at the ceiling before shrugging her shoulders. "I'm not sure, Toya," she said at last. Camille looked at both of her friends. "Steven was a weird guy, you know? For as long as I've known him he's been that way. Quiet, no friends, no luck with women, unmotivated . . . he was all those things. But to think that he could be capable of touching a three-year-old boy?" She shook her head again. "I just don't know, girl."

Dominique frowned. "I remember seeing him at that barbecue you had last year. He was hanging around the pool where all the kids were and I recall being concerned about that. Octavia had been there with that tiny bikini she had on that day and I was worried that the grown men were checking her out. Steven was one of the few adults hanging around over by the pool and I was worried that he was trying to get close to Octavia. But now I'm wondering if it was because all the little kids were playing over there."

Camille nodded. She remembered that as well. In fact, Steven always wanted to be around her nephew. Whenever Shane spent the night with Camille—a constant occurrence since Misa was always out partying or running behind some man—Steven would play with Shane, watch TV with him, and babysit him while Camille slept. "I feel a little guilty about leaving Shane alone with Steven," she admitted.

Both Toya and Dominique frowned. "Don't start blaming yourself, Camille," Toya said. "If that muthafucka was a pedophile, you had no way of knowing it. And besides, you took care of Shane as often as you did out of the kindness of your heart. Misa was the one who chose to spend so much time away from her child." Toya hated to sound as if she were blaming Misa for abandoning Shane, but the truth was the truth.

Camille shrugged. "I know you're right. But I still feel . . . responsible in a way." She sighed. "Ever since Frankie moved out, I've been drinking like crazy." Camille knew her drinking had gotten out of control long before Frankie left her, but she wasn't ready to admit that to her friends just yet. "I was sitting up all night downing drink after drink. In the mornings, I would be so hungover that I couldn't get out of bed some days. Shane was always with me and always so full of energy, and Steven would volunteer to take care of him while I slept."

Camille closed her eyes, wondering if her brother-in-law had been using those opportunities to get close to Shane so that he could prey on him. "I never thought that he was capable of doing something so sick. Shane is just a baby . . ."

"Nobody could have imagined something like that, Camille," Dominique said. "Whether you were drinking or not, Steven was Shane's uncle through marriage. It was inevitable that they would interact on some level. Yes, Misa left Shane behind a lot. And, okay, you may have been drunk a time or two while Shane was with you, but no one gave Steven a reason or a right to touch that child. And if he really did that to Shane, I say good for Misa. I'm glad she killed the freak."

Toya nodded. That was the smartest thing Dominique had said in a long time. "Amen."

Camille managed a weak smile. She was happy to have the two of them as friends at a time like this. She would have felt so alone had it not been for them. "I have to tell you both something."

Toya sucked her teeth and threw her head back in anguish. "Come on now, bitch. It's been too much bullshit tonight already. Don't tell me you got some terminal illness or something! No more bad news, 'cuz I can't take it."

Camille had to laugh and it felt good to do so after all they'd been through lately. Dominique, too, chuckled and waited to hear Camille's announcement.

"Well, it's not necessarily bad news," she said. "I'm pregnant."

Dominique's pretty face spread into a broad smile and she sat forward in her chair. "Camille! Really?"

Camille nodded and smiled back at her friend. She glanced at Toya to see her reaction. Toya wasn't smiling. She looked at Camille and the severity of the situation in her family became painfully clear to Toya. Not only had Camille's husband left her for his beautiful best friend, but Camille was now pregnant with his child—a child that Frankie never wanted. To make matters worse, Camille's sister had murdered Frankie's brother in retaliation for molesting her son. Toya wanted to put on a smile and be happy for her friend. She wanted to say something lighthearted and sweet the way Dominique had. But all that came to her was, "Wow."

Camille smiled weakly. "Yup. Nine weeks. I told Frankie tonight when I went to Gillian's town house to confront them." Camille explained the events leading up to her coming home and discovering a murder scene in her home; how she'd announced to Frankie and his mistress that she was expecting a child.

Toya couldn't keep her game face on for too long. "So Frankie knows that you're pregnant and he still walked out like that tonight?" She thought back to how coldly Frankie had acted, not just tonight, but on every occasion on which she'd seen them together in the past few weeks. The once-doting husband seemed to have no love left in his heart for Camille. Toya knew then that things between him and Camille would only be worse now that she was having a baby.

Camille nodded. "I mean . . ." Camille's voice trailed off. She seemed to be searching for words, and she swallowed hard before continuing. "I can understand him being upset. His brother is dead and my sister is responsible." A tear fell from her eye and Toya shut her mouth.

"Am I crazy to want to still make it work with him?" Camille asked, looking from one friend to the other, her eyes flooded.

"No, Camille," Dominique said, hoping to soothe her before Toya said something negative. "You're *not* crazy. You

love him. He's your husband and having a baby is a blessing."
She smiled at her friend, hoping to reassure her at what was
obviously a terribly painful and confusing time. "You're
gonna be a great mom, Camille. And with or without Frankie,
you're gonna be all right. And so is your baby. Frankie is
hurting right now. You have to let him have space to deal with
what happened. The Gillian situation aside, you and your
husband need to take a time-out for a little while and sort a lot
of things out."

Toya agreed. "Exactly. Right now you have to focus on
yourself and on Misa. She's all alone and I can't imagine how
she must be feeling locked up in there right now."

They all thought about that and Camille seemed to tremble
at the thought.

Toya thought about the fork in the road each of them was
facing at that moment in time. She had often likened them to
a black version of *Sex and the City*. But those fictional characters had no problems compared to the ones their foursome
was now dealing with.

"Ladies, let's promise to stop keeping shit to ourselves."

Camille and Dominique looked confused, so Toya happily elaborated.

"All of us had a problem tonight and none of us reached
out to each other until blood was spilled. Camille, when were
you gonna tell us that you're pregnant?"

"I was—"

Toya cut her off. "As a matter of fact, until tonight you
never admitted out loud that Frankie left you." Toya looked
at Camille as if to dare her to correct her.

Camille closed her mouth. It was true. Camille had been
so ashamed to admit that her marriage—the picture-perfect

million-dollar marriage—was over. She had clung to Frankie for dear life in an attempt to save face.

Toya continued. "We all knew the deal. We could tell that you two were having problems. But you kept it all to yourself." Toya saw Camille nodding and knew that she had made her point. "Dominique, you came home and found your daughter missing and you ran out into the night all by yourself like you were Wonder Woman."

Dominique had to smirk at her friend's sarcasm. "You're right," she admitted.

Camille had to turn the tables on Toya. "Well, you just got around to telling us about your father and what you went through as a kid," she said. "All this time, we've all been spilling our guts out about our problems and you never once shared your own pain."

Toya nodded. "Exactly. That's what I'm saying. We all have to stop keeping shit to ourselves." She shook her head. "Yesterday Misa found out some terrible information. And instead of picking up the phone to call one of us, she spazzed out. Now she's in serious trouble. We can't let this happen again."

Camille and Dominique agreed. "No more secrets." Camille yawned and soon Toya and Dominique were doing the same.

"Let's try to get some rest," Dominique said.

Camille stretched and nodded in agreement. "Misa's going to need to see our faces in that courtroom when she walks in."

Dominique helped Camille and Toya get comfortable—Camille in Dominique's bed and Toya in Octavia's—and then lay down on her sofa with a chenille throw wrapped around her. She closed her eyes and tried to block out the horrible scenarios playing out in her mind. She imagined Octavia being victimized in countless ways, and the worry that tugged at her heart and mind kept her from getting one wink of sleep. More than ever, Dominique wished that her man Jamel was there with her instead of incarcerated in a correctional facility upstate. She would have given anything to be wrapped in his arms and reassured that everything was going to be all right. Instead, she snuggled into the cold leather couch and shut her eyes, praying for the safe return of her only child.

Not Guilty?

The courtroom was packed. Camille, her mother, Lily, and Toya sat just behind the defense attorneys and watched as the prosecutor presented case after case against a myriad of defendants. They had arrived early in order to get the best seats, hoping to place themselves in a position to be the first faces Misa saw when she was escorted into the courtroom. They had already been waiting for hours. It seemed that the court was determined to call every case besides Misa's, and it was hard not to get antsy. As each poor, unfortunate soul was dragged out into open court, the women had watched to see what kind of judge Misa was about to face. So far, he had put bail on every single defendant who had come before him. So they resigned themselves to the fact that it was highly unlikely that Misa would be released on her own recognizance.

Camille fidgeted slightly in her seat. She wore a red wool crepe Michael Kors dress that used to fit her quite well. Today it felt snugger than usual, but that wasn't the only reason she shifted uneasily. She was waiting for Frankie to come through the door at any moment. Despite all that he had put her through, Camille still loved her husband and was eager to see his face.

She had told her mother about her pregnancy on their way to court that afternoon. Lily had been so overcome with emotion that the usually stoic woman had burst into tears. Camille had been unable to tell whether they were happy tears or not. The reality was that Lily *was* happy for her daughter, but so worried for her, as well. Both of her daughters were in for the fight of their lives, and it would either make or break them. Misa being jailed and Shane being torn from them was enough to send Lily's blood pressure soaring. Now, Camille would be facing extreme emotional turmoil in the months to come. So much was happening that the timing of Camille's pregnancy seemed ill-advised. Still, Lily was happy that her eldest daughter was about to become a mother for the first time. It had been a long time coming. Lily hugged Camille, congratulated her and assured her that whether her husband came to his senses or not, she and her baby were going to be just fine.

Toya sat beside Camille and soaked it all in. She crossed her legs and noticed that her Pour La Victoire T-strap platform pumps were smudged. She felt a mess today anyway. She had borrowed an outfit from Dominique and it didn't feel right. Dominique wore fine clothing, just as Toya did, but their styles were entirely different. Toya loved to accentuate her figure and wore body-baring silhouettes every day. Dominique's style was more modest. Toya had searched through Dominique's wardrobe for something she could tolerate and settled on a gray sheath dress with black piping that wasn't tight but was, at least, short. She couldn't help thinking about her dog, Ginger, whom she hoped was safely accounted for at Dominique's place. Dominique had reluctantly agreed to dog-sit once Toya argued that she needed company, something to occupy her while everyone else was in court and Octavia was still missing. Toya wondered if it was selfish that she was praying Dominique was treating her "baby" well.

As another defendant was led in, Camille anxiously waited to see if it was her sister. To her disappointment, it was not. Turning around to gaze at the spectators seated behind her, she spotted Louis walking in with his girlfriend, Nahla, on his arm. She was a Bajan beauty with a nice body, but the permanent scowl on her face took away from her appeal. Every single time Camille had seen this woman, she was frowning for some reason. It seemed that she was in a perpetual bad mood and Camille had often wondered how Louis put up with such a bitch. Louis made eye contact with Camille and nodded in her direction. He sat, however, on the opposite side of the courtroom, behind the prosecution, and faced forward.

Lily frowned, looking at Camille. "Who is taking care of Shane?" she asked.

"Good question," Toya chimed in.

Lily shook her head in amazement. "That bastard couldn't leave his pit bull home today? She had to come here, too? And *where* is my grandson?"

Before either of them could respond, Lily was out of her seat and headed in Louis's direction. Toya and Camille watched as Lily rushed to the empty seat beside Louis's girlfriend and spoke in hushed tones to her former son-in-law. Nahla's facial expression showed her discomfort as Lily leaned over her in order to speak to Louis. It seemed as if something Lily was saying made Nahla uncomfortable. She looked amazed by the older woman's brazenness. Finally, after Louis seemed to explain himself, gesturing with his hands and nodding

vigorously, Lily returned to her seat and filled Toya and Camille in on what she'd learned.

"Louis's mother is taking care of Shane while they're here
today." Lily shook her head. "Shane don't hardly even know
that woman!" She looked at Camille incredulously. "I asked
him why he brought the pit bull in a skirt with him and he
said she wanted to be here to support him." Lily rolled her
eyes. "Hmm! If you ask me, she came to be fucking nosy!"

Toya had to resist the urge to giggle. She liked Lily. She
was a plucky old lady who seemed to possess the balls that
Camille didn't have. Toya made a mental note to ask Camille
how she turned out to be such a punk with a mother as
straightforward as Lily.

"Anyway, I told him I'm coming over there *today* to see
my grandson. Just me by myself and I don't want no shit
when I get there."

"What did he say?" Toya asked.

"What could he say?" Lily asked as if the question was
idiotic. "He nodded his peasy head and that was that."

A commotion seemed to stir up just outside of the courtroom, as raised voices could be heard through the closed
doors. When the doors swung open, Frankie and Gillian entered like a black Brad and Angelina, flanked by court officers
who were trying to keep reporters in the lobby at bay. Since
Camille, Toya, and Lily had arrived early, they had missed the
crush of reporters who had assembled outside. Frankie and
Gillian, however, had walked right into it.

Camille looked at her husband and swooned. He looked
so handsome, his mustache and goatee groomed to precision.
He wore a Banana Republic blazer, Thomas Pink shirt, and
black Kenneth Cole pants and shoes. He walked in beside
Gillian, who wore a long-sleeved blue dress with Louis Vuit-

ton boots and bag. Spotting Camille and her mother sitting in the front row, Gillian squeezed his hand tighter. Frankie returned the gesture and ushered her into the row of seats behind Louis and Nahla. Camille couldn't help noticing the irony. Louis and Frankie had both positioned themselves on the opposite side of the courtroom from the defense, showing Camille that the lines had most certainly been drawn. It was she and Misa versus Frankie and Louis. How drastically things had changed! Camille shook her head and struggled to keep her tears in check. Seeing her daughter battling with her emotions, Lily took her hand and winked at her. Camille smiled and together they faced forward.

At last, Misa was finally brought into the courtroom, her wrists cuffed behind her back. She looked defeated, her posture slightly slumped as she shuffled in. It had been a long night for her. Misa had lain atop that hard, cold metal bench, tossing and turning all night. She felt stiff and eager for a shower, for some real food. For a brief moment, her eyes seemed to brighten slightly as she scanned the courtroom and she saw her mother, sister, and Toya seated nearby. Then her gaze settled on the opposite side of the room where Louis sat with his girlfriend and her expression turned melancholy once more. Behind them were Frankie and Gillian and the icy stare Frankie sent Misa's way made her turn and face the judge quickly.

Camille had retained an attorney that morning. Teresa Rourke was a criminal lawyer with an impeccable reputation. Dominique had suggested that Camille hire her after watching Teresa win an unlikely acquittal in the case of one of the rap industry's biggest stars. Infinite Knowledge was a rapper from Bed Stuy who had opened fire in a crowded nightclub in Manhattan in 2004 after an altercation with a

hater. No one was hit by the gunfire, but the ensuing stam-
pede for the exit caused a young lady to be trampled to
death. Infinite had been charged with manslaughter, but in a
stunning victory, Teresa Rourke had won an acquittal on
the unlikely grounds of police misconduct. That high-profile
case had earned her a reputation as a female Johnnie Cochran.
She didn't come cheap and Camille was praying that she
would be worth every penny. Misa just couldn't spend the
rest of her life in jail.

Teresa sauntered over to Misa's side decked out in a fabulous custom-fitted black D&G pantsuit. Her Stuart Weitzman
pumps made her five-foot-nine frame seem even longer. She
wore her hair in neat microbraids and, standing beside Misa,
the contrast was evident. To her loved ones, Misa looked broken and haggard.

The case got under way with the court officer announcing, "*The People vs. Misa Atkinson*, case number 688973. The
charges are New York State Penal Codes 265.04, criminal
possession of a firearm in the first degree; 265.09, criminal use
of a firearm in the first degree; and 125.27, premeditated murder in the first degree."

"How do you plead?" the judge barked without so much
as glancing at Misa.

"Not guilty," Misa said, her voice cracking a little at the
end.

A slight stir could be heard from somewhere behind her,
but Misa didn't dare turn around. The prosecution wasted no
time laying out its case. Misa's lawyer touched her arm comfortingly and offered her a reassuring smile. It did little to
soothe her as they listened to the district attorney speak.

"Your honor, the defendant shot Mr. Steven Dennis Bingham a total of six times at point-blank range with an unli-

censed revolver. She has expressed no remorse for her actions and has been uncooperative with our investigation. The charges she is facing carry a possible life sentence, and she is the sister-in-law of Mr. Frank Bingham, who owns and operates two successful local businesses. Mr. Bingham also came into sole ownership recently of the popular Manhattan restaurant Conga."

Frankie noticed Gillian glance at him questioningly then. He avoided her gaze and kept looking forward, listening to the prosecution use his wealth against his wife and sister-in-law. Gillian didn't ask him about it then, but he knew that her curiosity had been piqued. Gillian had no idea how Frankie had come to own her mother's restaurant.

The prosecution finished stating its case. "By virtue of her access to cash, we assert that Ms. Atkinson is a flight risk and ask that she be held without bail."

Misa looked over at the DA and shook her head. He wore a blue pinstriped suit and shoes so shiny she could see the light shining off them. He was a pale, snarling, gray-haired, bespectacled old man who looked like he'd been an asshole his entire life.

Teresa Rourke wasted no time with her rebuttal. "Your honor, my client poses no flight risk. The deceased, whom my client shot in self-defense, was the brother of Frankie Bingham. Therefore, it isn't likely that Mr. Bingham would be willing to be of any assistance to her—monetary or otherwise—in this . . . imagined effort to escape prosecution." Teresa shook her head as if the idea was absurd. "Mr. Bingham's assets and apparent wealth should have no bearing whatsoever on whether bail is set for Ms. Atkinson."

"Your honor—" The prosecutor tried to interject, but Teresa wasn't having it.

"She is the mother of a three-year-old son who has been traumatized." Teresa paused to let that sink in. "That child is now in the custody of his father and Ms. Atkinson is anxious to reconcile with her son. Going on the lam is not an option for her. And I assure the court that she *is* eager to cooperate with the investigation. Despite repeated requests for an attorney on the night in question, my client was forced to remain at the scene of the crime under grueling questioning by police for more than an hour with the deceased's body lying just feet away. She was in shock and was denied her rights to an attorney."

"That's not true, your honor." The prosecutor was raising his voice now.

"Again, my client is eager to answer these charges against her and has no intention of fleeing prosecution."

The judge made some notes and flipped through Misa's file. For seconds that felt to Misa like hours, the judge read silently and then peered over his glasses at Misa. She held his gaze, hoping to convey that she was harmless, that she wouldn't try to run. Her lawyer had briefed her in the holding cell on what to expect today. She said that Judge Mitchell Williams was a stern bulldog with a permanent frown. He was no-nonsense and no-holds-barred and brought down his decisions with a finality that often left jaws ajar. But despite all that, Judge Williams was pretty fair. Misa was counting on that today. Her eyes locked with his and she spoke silently, willing him to see that she was not the heartless bitch the prosecution had made her out to be. The judge looked again at the papers before him, and then spoke up at last.

"Bail is set at five hundred thousand dollars." He banged his gavel, and the hearing was over just like that.

"I'm going back to jail?" Misa asked, innocence resonating in her tone.

Teresa looked at her watch and sighed. It was already after two-thirty in the afternoon. "It's pretty late, but there's a chance we can get you out tonight. If you have collateral or if your sister has assets she can use as collateral, she can bail you out before the bus leaves for Rikers at five o'clock."

Misa's heart sank and she looked at the floor. The court officer came to bring Misa back to the holding pen. Teresa told her she would come and talk to her about what her options were in a few minutes. Misa turned to look at her mother and sister and mouthed the words, "Get me out." As she was hustled back to the holding pen, she avoided looking in Frankie and Louis's direction and for a fleeting moment she wondered if she'd be better off staying in jail.

Frankie and Gillian were the first ones out the door. He had always been careful to avoid publicity, eager to remain in the shadows instead, where he was safe from the scrutiny of anyone who might connect him to the shady ways he truly made his money. All these photographers and reporters were the last thing he needed.

Camille marveled at how swiftly the two of them had slithered out of the packed courtroom and into the lights and cameras flashing in the lobby. Louis tried to pull the same maneuver, but Lily was on him before he could reach the door.

"I'm going to be there to visit with Shane in about an hour. Let him know that Grandma is coming to see him."

Louis nodded and slunk out with his screw-faced girlfriend in tow.

Misa's attorney came over to Camille and explained Misa's bail situation. "Basically, you would need to put up cash totaling five hundred thousand dollars in order to bail her out tonight. Or, you can present collateral in the amount of twenty percent of her bail. In this case, that would mean assets totaling one hundred thousand dollars."

Camille was at a loss for words at first. Teresa made it sound so easy, with her designer suits and expensive bags. Camille figured the prominent attorney probably had that kind of money to burn. Camille did not.

"Oh my God . . ."

Toya stood there and wondered if her friend was one of those dumb bitches her father had warned her about growing up: a dumb bitch who didn't know her worth, who never saved for a rainy day, who never asked a nigga for shit or planned for the day when he wasn't there. She felt a headache coming on as she watched her friend—the wife of Frankie B, head of the Nobles crime syndicate—struggle to come to terms with what had just happened.

"I don't have that kind of money," Camille said.

"You can put your house up, Camille," Toya pointed out.

Teresa nodded in agreement. "Yes, the court will accept the deed to your house as collateral."

Camille shook her head. "The house is in Frankie's name. Everything is in Frankie's name."

Toya almost wanted to choke Camille to death. "Everything?"

Camille felt like the dumbest bitch on the planet. "Yeah." She nodded sadly. "Everything." The severity of the situation made her weak in the knees and she sat down on the courtroom bench before she collapsed.

Teresa seemed dismayed, as well. "Well, then . . ." She began to pack her belongings into her briefcase, assuming that if these ladies couldn't afford bail, they couldn't afford her.

On her way out the door, she handed Camille a business card. "Call me when you're able to work things out with your husband."

They watched Teresa Rourke, Misa's ticket to freedom, saunter out the door one dollar sign at a time.

"You have . . . sixty seconds remaining on this phone call." The voice recording let Dominique and her incarcerated boyfriend Jamel know that time was winding down on their collect conversation.

Dominique had spent the past half hour telling Jamel all the events of the past twenty-four hours. Toya had accompanied Camille to Misa's court appearance and Dominique had stayed behind in order to wait for word from her daughter. Hearing from Jamel had been a welcome distraction from the nonstop worrying she'd been doing since Octavia's disappearance. She felt so alone. Octavia's father was not an active part of her life, never had been. Stationed overseas as an army sergeant, he supported his only child with monthly checks, but never visited or sent for Octavia. Dominique sent him a school picture of their daughter each year as a courtesy, but she suspected that he couldn't care less about them. She hadn't even bothered to contact him to inform him that Octavia had been missing for the past few days. He wouldn't be of any help to her. The person she wanted to cling to the most—her father Bill Storms—had died only a couple of months ago. Bill would have known what to do, where to look for Octavia. Without him, she felt so alone even with her friends' support.

"Baby, I'm gonna hang up and call right back so we can talk about this," Jamel said, his tone at once calming and reassuring.

Dominique didn't feel reassured, though. Still she managed to say, "Okay."

She hung up and hated that this was the closest she could get to being comforted at a time like this. So many thoughts had gone through her head all night. Octavia was only fourteen years old. What if she had trusted some stranger and was in peril? Dominique hadn't slept a wink all night and now she wanted nothing more than to fall into some strong arms and be held. She wanted to be hugged and kissed and told that everything was going to be all right. But with Jamel still in prison, she had to settle for the ringing phone and his words of comfort through the receiver.

"I have a collect call from . . . Jamel . . . an inmate at . . ."

Instinctively, she pressed 3 to skip the monotonous recording.

"Baby?"

"Yeah." Dominique lay across Octavia's bed, feeling drained and anxious at the same time. She ran her fingers across the soft brown fur of Octavia's favorite teddy bear and sighed, tears pouring forth involuntarily. She imagined poor little Octavia being raped, beaten, and left for dead somewhere and a sob escaped her lips.

Jamel leaned against the wall as he spoke into the receiver, picturing Dominique's pretty face in his mind. He could imagine how she must look right now, so scared and worried about her only child. He wished, more than ever, that he could somehow escape the confines of the prison walls that held him.

"I can't imagine how you must feel right now," he said honestly. "But I bet you're probably thinking the worst."

She was. Dominique squeezed her eyes shut to block out the horrible thoughts going through her mind.

"You can't think like that," Jamel said. "Octavia's a smart girl. She's probably staying with a friend of hers until she can get up the nerve to call you. She's gonna come back home soon, ma. You gotta believe that."

Looking around Octavia's room, Dominique did believe that. She'd called the police that morning after Camille and Toya had left, and filed a missing persons report. The officers who had come out to her home and taken her statement had collected pictures of Octavia and searched her room for clues as to what may have caused her to run away. They'd indicated it was likely that a child who had grown up as sheltered and as privileged as Octavia would come back to the luxuries she'd miss on the streets. That is, one officer suggested, unless she was on drugs. Either way, they'd said, she hadn't packed much of her clothes and shoes. She would be more likely to come back for those things (if nothing else) in the coming days.

Dominique had never had any indication that her daughter might be using drugs. She hadn't noticed any drop in her grades or any overly rebellious behavior. There was no drug paraphernalia in her room and Dominique hated to think that was the case. But the truth was, she hadn't been spending much time with her daughter. And she had really no idea what might be troubling her so much that she would run away.

"Jamel, I haven't been a good mother to Octavia," Dominique said, as she smoothed Octavia's pillows.

"Now you're playing yourself," Jamel said. He hated how women always had to try and find a reason to blame themselves for everything. "You're a great mother, and you know it."

She shrugged. "We have a nice home, she wears nice clothes and goes to a good school. But I don't spend any time with my kid, Jamel. I'm always traveling, and always working late. When I'm not working late, I'm going upstate to see you!"

Dominique hadn't meant for it to sound that way, hadn't wanted to make Jamel feel as if she was blaming him. Nevertheless, that was exactly how he took it.

His face fell. Here he was trying to soothe her in her time of need, and she was shifting the blame for all this to him. "Okay," he said. "So I'm sorry if coming to see me makes you a bad mother."

Dominique wanted to toss the fucking phone across the room. She was in no mood for Jamel's pity party. "I'm not even saying that! What I'm saying is that the police came over here today and asked me if I've noticed any change in my daughter's weight, in her sleep patterns, her moods . . . and I struggled to think of the last time I even noticed, Jamel! Octavia is so independent and I've been so used to this non-stop pace that my life moves at that I've been . . . I've been neglecting my daughter." She shook her head as she said it. "And that's the bottom line."

Jamel was about to respond when a CO rudely interrupted them. "Hang up the phone," the officer barked. "It's count time!"

Jamel seethed, but had no choice but to comply. The count was a mandatory lineup during which prison officials tallied the inmates to ensure that everyone was accounted for. "I gotta go, ma," Jamel said, hating to have to leave their conversation at a time like this. "I'll try to call back in a little while."

Dominique shook her head, frustrated and sick of the way her life was playing out. She hung up the phone without even saying good-bye. She got on her knees and prayed that the next time the phone rang, it wouldn't be Jamel calling, but Octavia instead.

Frankie seemed too big for his mother's house, looming large on her tiny sofa. Gillian looked around Mary's humble home and tried to imagine Frankie as a child, the way he looked in the countless pictures of him dotting his mother's living room. Framed photos of him riding his bike, playing basketball, dressed up in his Easter suit—in all of them, he was staring back at the camera with the same serious and stoic expression on his face, never smiling. Steven was present in some of the pictures, too. Always peering from behind his older brother or from behind a tree, always half hidden or shielded by his own hands as if he never wanted to be immortalized in a photograph. It was kind of eerie to Gillian seeing the two brothers playing the same roles in childhood as they did in their adult lives. Frankie out in front, all serious and no-nonsense; Steven playing in Frankie's shadow, seemingly more comfortable there than anywhere else.

Frankie watched his mother rushing around her kitchen nervously, trying to find her best glass to pour something for Gillian to drink. Frankie knew she was making the task harder than it had to be and when he saw her reach way in the back of her cabinet, he grimaced. She was still so scarred from years of abuse by her husband, so accustomed to being alone and without company that she was going out of her way to do everything right.

"Ma," he called out to her. He noticed that the sound of his deep voice caused her to jump a little. "You don't have to go through all of that. Gillian will drink from any glass you got."

Gillian felt bad now for taking Mary up on her offer of something to drink. All she wanted was a glass of water, and

Frankie's mother was acting like she had to go to the well to get it.

Finally, Mary came back into the living room and set a glass of water with a perfect slice of lemon inside of it on a coaster on the table in front of Gillian. Gillian smiled and thanked her for it, noticing that Frankie's mother seldom made eye contact with anyone.

She had been wondering why Frankie was so hesitant to break the news of Steven's death to his mother. He had been so wound up that he hadn't slept at all. That morning, he had locked himself in the bathroom for what seemed to Gillian like a never-ending shower. Then he had emerged, only to busy himself with calls to his lawyer and accountants. And when she suggested breaking the news to his mother before Misa's hearing, Frankie had ignored her. Gillian had pressed him, emphasizing how devastating it would be for Mary to hear about her son's death on TV or to see it splashed across the front page of the newspaper. Still, Frankie hadn't budged. Seeing the docile and nervous woman now, Gillian understood his reluctance a little bit more.

Mary was wondering why Gillian was with her son today instead of his wife. The last time she'd had the pleasure of a visit from Frankie, Camille had been by his side and Mary had fallen in love with her daughter-in-law. Camille was lovely, sweet, and so attentive to Frankie. Mary had never met Gillian before, but judging by the chemistry between them it was apparent that she was now the woman in Frankie's life.

Mary sat across from her son on the rocking chair she'd had since she was a little girl. Her father had given it to her for Christmas when she was six years old and it was one of her most treasured possessions. That chair was one of the few pieces of her life prior to marrying Frankie's father, John, that he hadn't destroyed in one of his many tirades over the years.

"I'm so surprised to see you, Frankie." Mary's voice was soft and sweet.

Gillian was heartbroken, knowing that they had come to deliver terrible news to the fragile woman who sat before her.

Frankie offered a weak smile and stared at his mother for a few moments. He took in her facial features, her body language. She was thinner than he'd ever seen her before, but still just as pretty as he remembered. It had been two long years since the last time he had come by to visit her. He called her every now and then, sent money to her each month. But he had found it difficult to be around her, to see her still so meek and so powerless even though her oppressor was dead.

Her long thick hair was pulled back into a neat bun, her beautiful brown skin seemingly aglow. Her long dark eyelashes fluttered each time she dared to look up at him and her long dainty fingers toyed with the napkin she held in her hand.

Finally, Frankie spoke as his mother looked at him expectantly. He felt a surge of guilt as she smiled at him, unaware that he had nothing positive to say.

"Ma," he said. "I came by here today to talk to you about Steven."

Mary's facial expression changed then. She always felt a mixture of emotions at the thought of her youngest child. Steven was so much like her. He was weaker than his brother, less outgoing, not as resilient. He wasn't a fighter the way that Frankie was and Mary had noticed this early on. For that reason, she had always worried about Steven far more than she worried over Frankie. Ever since they were kids it had been that way. She felt a strange feeling in the pit of her stomach hearing Frankie mention his brother now. Something wasn't right. She could sense it.

Her hands were shaking involuntarily and both Frankie and Gillian noticed. They exchanged glances and Gillian nodded at him, encouraging him to keep going. There was no way around it. Mary had to know what happened.

"How is he?" she asked, softly, her eyes focused on the napkin in her hands instead of looking at Frankie.

He took a deep breath.

"You know he's been staying with me out on Staten Island."

Mary nodded, looked at him expectantly.

"He's been staying in the guesthouse and I look out for him. He keeps to himself most of the time, but sometimes he comes over to the house and watches TV. Camille's nephew has been staying with us a lot lately . . ." Frankie's voice trailed off and he looked at Gillian for help. There was no easy way to tell his mother this story. The look on Gillian's face was reassuring and he continued.

"Anyway, me and Camille have been having problems lately. We're gonna be getting a divorce soon. Well, for the past few weeks, both of us have been away from home a lot and so Steven babysat for Camille's nephew a few times. Misa—that's Camille's sister—was never around so someone had to look out for her kid."

Mary was frowning a little and twisting the napkin in her hand absentmindedly. "*Steven* was babysitting for her?"

Frankie nodded, gulped as he went on to the hard part. "She picked him up a few days ago and took him home. And then she came back last night and . . ." Frankie saw that his mother was staring right at him, waiting for him to finish. But he had a hard time continuing.

Gillian watched him struggling and her heart went out to him. She sipped her water, since her mouth was suddenly dry, and watched Mary's reaction as Frankie spoke.

"Misa came back and accused Steven of touching her son. And she shot him."

Mary gasped and dropped the napkin on the floor. Her hands covering her mouth, her eyes began to fill with tears. "Steven?"

Frankie nodded, while Gillian moved closer to where Mary sat in case she needed comforting. Right now, the woman sat frozen in shock, her hands cupped over her mouth. She began rocking back and forth in her seat. Tears streamed down her face and her voice cracked as she responded.

"Where is he? Can I see him?"

Frankie wanted to disappear. He wanted to be anywhere else but here delivering this blow to his mother.

He shook his head. "He died, Ma." He sat forward in his seat as if he expected her to fall and would need to catch her. "He's gone."

Tears poured from Mary's eyes and down her cheeks as she sobbed. Gillian rushed to her side with tissues in hand and stroked the older woman's back lovingly as she cried.

Frankie watched his mother cry and his own heart broke all over again—not just for Steven, but for Mary, as well. She had endured years of abuse at the hands of her husband, had been the one to discover his lifeless body when he killed himself. And now she was going to have to bury her youngest child. She didn't speak another word that afternoon. Instead, her cries were the only sounds she made as Frankie and Gillian tried in vain to comfort her.

Lost and Turned Out

Lying on her cot, Misa stared directly into the bright light above her, hoping to make herself go blind. The light remained on twenty-four hours a day in her solitary confinement cell on New York's notorious Rikers Island where she'd been held for the past two days. She was on suicide watch, requiring that her tiny private quarters be lit around the clock and that guards monitor her every movement to ensure that she didn't take the easy way out. During the psychological evaluation portion of her intake interview, Misa had expressed how badly she wanted to die. She told the psychologist she had seriously considered killing herself before going to confront Steven on the night she killed him. She also told them she was still contemplating it. Death might bring her some relief from the guilt she was now drowning in. They had her on surveillance cameras as well as under the watchful eye of guards on foot patrol pacing outside the iron door. Staring into the severe light, she figured blindness would be a decent start in her determination to punish herself for what had happened to Shane. Blindness was the least of what she deserved.

Her mind drifted to Baron, wondering how he was, what

he'd been told about her. An almost sinister laugh escaped
her then. At that moment, Baron was probably not even thinking about Misa, and here she was wasting time thinking about
him. She pushed him to the back of her mind then, tried to
focus on her own issues, focus on Shane. And then it dawned
on her.

That was her problem. She always had to push some nigga
to the back of her mind in order to concentrate on her child.
It was as if the men in her life—first Louis, then some nigga
named Cyrus, and now Baron—were all at the top of her list
of priorities, ahead of Shane and even ahead of herself. Misa
sat up and closed her eyes, which stung from the glare of the
light. She pictured Shane's face in her mind and smiled to
herself when she recalled his laughter. He was such a beautiful
little boy and she loved to see him smile. For so many years
she had searched for a man who would complete their lives.
And it had only now dawned on her how perfectly complete
their lives could have been without any man.

Her heart had been in the right place. She had always
wanted Shane to have the father that Louis had failed to be.
She wanted to have a man to snuggle up to at night, someone
to toss a ball around with her son and protect them both. And
she had tried to force it, again and again with man after man.
After a few sexual encounters, Misa would begin to envision
the fairy-tale ending with the man she'd set her sights on and
the rest played out the same way over and over. Inevitably,
Misa and Shane wound up right back where they started
out—just the two of them.

She wished she could end it all. After court, she'd been
told that her case was being elevated to the State Supreme
Court and she'd be facing a whole new judge the next time
she went to court. Since Camille hadn't gotten her out, Misa

assumed that her sister was fucked up financially. Everyone knew that the money was Frankie's, after all. Misa knew she could be sitting in this hell for months while she awaited trial. More than ever she wanted to take one last breath and let go of all the anguish in her heart over what had been done to Shane. She wanted to die and escape the prying eyes of the media and the questions from her family. Over and over she recalled the look of utter disgust Louis had given her as she walked into the courtroom. She hadn't missed the sneer on that bitch Nahla's face, either. Still, Misa had absolutely no regrets about what she had done. Steven had deserved to die.

But she did long for Shane. She did regret having abandoned him while she searched for a fairy tale that never existed to begin with. She remembered him yelling that he hated her, thought about what he must have endured, how scared he must have been. And she was consumed with guilt.

Throughout the night, the guards heard Misa crying herself to sleep, chanting "Shane" again and again, each gut-wrenching wail slicing the air around her like a sword.

Camille sat perched in the window seat in her upstairs bedroom, gazing out at the softly falling snow. She loved snowy days, loved the silent calm that accompanied the icy flakes as they drifted from the sky. There was a need for that kind of peace in her life these days. Everything in her world had gone horribly wrong.

Camille had been unable to come up with the money to bail her sister out, and she felt helpless. Everything of intrinsic value—the house, the cars, the artwork, their stock portfolio—was all in Frankie's name. Camille owned nothing but the clothes on her back and those items hanging in her massive closet. Even the jewelry she thought she owned had been insured in Frankie's name. Once again, her husband wasn't taking her calls, and what little money remained in their joint accounts was barely enough to cover the bills. Frankie had withdrawn the bulk of the funds the morning of Misa's arrest.

In the three days since then, the public scrutiny had been nonstop. Neighbors drove by Camille's home at all hours of the day and night. News crews returned nightly to the scene of Staten Island's most scandalous crime in years, leaving Camille a virtual prisoner in her opulent home. Still too spooked to venture into her kitchen, she had been ordering food from local eateries and relying on Toya to swing by each night and bring in her mail and drop off incidentals. Camille had been holed up in her huge bedroom day after day, trying to come up with a mere hundred thousand dollars in assets to get her sister out on bail.

After Misa's court appearance, their mother Lily had visited with Shane and found him to be withdrawn, but still happy to see his "Gamma." She had noticed that he was sucking his thumb now and seemed less energetic than usual. But he was being well taken care of, and for that Lily was grateful. Louis had shared with her the physician's report he'd been given after having Shane examined. The doctor had confirmed that Shane had been sodomized, and the department of social services had been called. Lily had been dismayed to learn that Misa had been too preoccupied with Baron in the days that Shane was left in Steven's care to notice something was amiss. Reading the doctor's report, it had broken Lily's heart to imagine Shane being abused. The precious three-year-old fell asleep on her lap toward the end of her visit and she laid him down in his bed before going home for the night. Lily had thanked Louis for stepping up and taking good care of his son when Shane needed him most, and asked him to try to understand that Misa wasn't the only one at fault for what had taken place. Surely, she had never expected anything like this would ever happen to her child.

Camille hated thinking of her sister left to languish on Rikers Island. Even harder to accept was the fact that the only thing standing between Misa and her freedom was money. Five hundred thousand dollars in cash or one hundred thousand in assets—Camille couldn't believe that she was having such a hard time coming up with that. The trouble was, she'd been blind enough to think that Frankie would never abandon her this way. All but one of her credit cards had been suspended. Their joint accounts had been wiped nearly clean, leaving her with a little over seven thousand dollars in liquidity.

She was embarrassed. During the course of their marriage, Camille and Frankie had blown a hundred grand like it was nothing on countless occasions over the years. Frankie loved to gamble and Camille loved to shop. So, she knew that it wasn't about the money. Frankie was holding out on her on purpose. Camille understood Frankie's stance. Part of her didn't blame her husband for what he was doing. She was only angry with herself for never listening to Toya or to her own intuition telling her to put away money for a rainy day. She had never anticipated this, though. Never in her wildest dreams.

Her telephone rang and she didn't even bother to glance in its direction. She knew that it was some reporter wanting an exclusive. She cracked the window open and caught a few snowflakes in the palm of her hand, watching them disappear into her skin, and wishing she could disappear just that easily.

Toya stared at the computer screen absentmindedly. She had been working harder than usual lately. But working in real estate during what was beginning to look like a recession was proving to be a challenge for her financially. In an attempt to turn a greater profit, she was putting in longer hours and doing her best to bring in new clients. Her long hours were also a thinly veiled attempt to avoid talking to either one of her parents.

Toya's father had apparently made amends with all the members of her family except for her. Over the course of the past several weeks, Nate had reached out to her siblings one by one and apologized sincerely for the pain he'd caused them. It had been her mother, Jeanie, who had given Toya's contact information to her father. That was an unforgivable offense in Toya's opinion, and she hadn't spoken to her mother in days. Her brothers had called and admitted to Toya that they'd been reluctant to reconcile with Nate, as well. He had, after all, been a terrible father to all of them.

"But, he's dying, Toya," her favorite brother Derrick had said. "It don't make no sense being mad at a ghost."

"I shouldn't have to let him off the hook for all the shit he did just because he's on his deathbed. You reap what you sow. Whatever happened to that?"

Derrick had sighed then. "Toya, I know he was a fucked-up father," he said. "But he wasn't always that way. He wasn't always a bully. Don't just think about the bad things. You have to remember the good stuff, too. He used to take us to

Coney Island every summer . . . before he got strung out. We would ride the Cyclone, eat cotton candy, play games. Remember that? He used to play with us, laugh with us and he was fun. We used to love him once upon a time. Don't forget that."

Toya was thinking about that now as she stared blankly at her computer. She blinked finally, then ran her hand lightly across her face. She picked up her purse and opened up her wallet. There, she found the piece of paper on which Derrick had scribbled her father's cell phone number when he met her for breakfast a few days earlier. She snickered at the notion that Nate's bitch ass had a cell phone. He had come a long way.

She dialed the number, and took a deep breath as she listened to the ringing. She heard Nate answer, "Hello?" His raspy voice made her skin crawl, and she hung up, tossing her phone aside as if it were contaminated.

"Fuck that nigga," she said aloud to herself. She wasn't scared of ghosts anyway.

Baron was having his bed linens changed when Gillian arrived to visit him. The nurses had assembled at his bedside and drawn the curtain closed around them as they bathed him and changed his dressings and bedsheets. As Gillian peered into the room, his mother, Celia Parker-Nobles, approached and greeted Gillian with a smile.

"Gillian," she said. "Good to see you again." Celia had noticed in the weeks since Baron's shooting that Gillian rarely visited her half brother. Gesturing toward the drawn curtain, she rolled her eyes. "His favorite part of the day," she quipped. "Sponge bath."

Gillian chuckled. She had always enjoyed Celia. Despite the fact that Baron's mother and Gillian's mother were archrivals, Celia had always exuded an air of class and sophistication that was hard not to admire.

"All done!" the perky, big-breasted brunette nurse announced with a smile, pulling the curtains back.

As the nurses filed out, Celia approached her son's bedside and rubbed his arm lovingly. "Gillian's here to see you."

Baron turned toward the door as much as he was able to and saw his lovely baby sister entering the room with a lone GET WELL balloon in her hand.

"Hello, big brother," she said with a smile that, to Baron, seemed forced.

"Hi," he said, smiling back. "I thought you forgot about me in here."

Gillian added the balloon to the others lining the far wall of his room. She stood at the foot of her brother's bed and shook her head. "I could never forget about you, Baron," she said.

Gillian also couldn't forget he was the reason her beloved father was dead. She looked at Baron all bandaged up and broken and wasn't fully satisfied. She knew that he was hurt, that he had suffered terribly as a result of the shooting, and that he, too, had lost his father on that fateful night. But, she wanted him to feel the loss the way that she felt it; even *more*—to suffer the way that their father had as he lay dying from bullets meant for his son.

"Thank you for the balloon," Baron said, snapping her out of her reverie.

She shrugged. It had been a halfhearted gesture. "You're welcome." She noticed that Celia was flipping through television channels to find something Baron might like to watch.

"I'm sure you heard about what happened to Frankie's brother."

Baron nodded. "I heard about it, but I don't understand why I had to hear it from Tremaine," he said. "You're my sister. You could have come and told me yourself."

Gillian wanted to rip out his fucking catheter. The nerve of him! "Baron, it's not like you could do anything about it. Why would I rush to tell you? You can't even walk, so it's not like you can help investigate," she spat. She saw the wounded expression on her brother's face and saw Celia's body tense up. Gillian sighed. "I'm dealing with a lot, you know? I'm still not over Daddy being gone, for one thing."

Celia didn't turn from the television, but she was damn sure all ears. She heard the venom in Gillian's voice and it confirmed what she'd suspected ever since Baron had woken up from his coma. Gillian blamed Baron somehow for their father's death. Celia had to find a way to get her son to tell her the truth about the circumstances of Doug Nobles's death.

Gillian continued. "And now your little girlfriend or plaything or whatever she is . . . she killed Frankie's brother. I'm sure you can understand if I have more things on my mind these days than just you."

"I'm just saying," Baron replied, looking her in the eye. "I'm still your brother, Gillian." Baron's tone had an underlying message and Gillian looked at the floor, convicted.

Celia spoke up. "Gillian, can you tell me exactly what happened at Frankie's house that night?" Celia's face showed genuine concern. "I've met Steven many times over the years. And I've gotten to know Misa, as well, since Baron's been hospitalized. I can't imagine how the two of them came to this."

Gillian pulled up a chair and told them what she knew: that Misa had accused Steven of the unthinkable and then killed him and surrendered to the police willingly. Both Baron and his mother hung on her every word while pondering whether or not Steven had the makings of a pedophile. Finally, Baron asked, "Do you believe Steven did it?"

Gillian stared at her brother silently before answering. "We'll never know now, will we? Thanks to Misa."

She clenched her jaw at the realization that Baron and his little bitch had wreaked havoc on Frankie and Gillian's lives in the past few weeks. She wondered whether it was irony or destiny. Gillian hadn't bothered to mention that Camille was apparently pregnant with Frankie's child. She was still trying to wrap her mind around that fact and was secretly hoping that Camille was lying in a desperate attempt to hold on to her husband.

"Misa's bail is five hundred thousand cash or a hundred grand bond." Gillian smirked. "She's been locked up at Rikers for days because Camille doesn't have any money of her own to bail her sister out."

Celia didn't appreciate the smug expression on Gillian's face as she spoke of Camille's personal business. Celia knew how it felt to be left alone by a man who got bored of his marriage, since her own husband Doug Nobles had done the same when he left her for Gillian's mother. Unlike Camille, Celia had been smart financially, but she sympathized with both Camille and Misa just the same. "Please extend my condolences to Frankie," Celia said. "And let me know when the funeral services are being held. I'd like to attend since I've always loved Frankie."

Gillian nodded. "I will." She rose to leave and looked at Baron. "I have to go. But I'll be back to see you before the end of the week." She squeezed her brother's hand and waved farewell to Celia before slipping out of the room, her heels clicking down the hall as she walked.

Celia sat beside her son's bed and held his hand in hers. She shook her head. "This is all so much to take in at once," she said, referring to both recent shootings. "Misa never seemed like the type to kill someone in cold blood that way. I wonder if Gillian has all the facts straight."

Baron was thinking about it. Misa had a feisty side to her, one he'd seen when their rough sex got rougher than usual on more than one occasion. But she had never given him any indication that she was capable of murder. Thinking back on the brutal way he'd treated her in the past, he thanked God that she hadn't unleashed her murderous wrath on him instead. He'd certainly given her reasons to do so. He felt sorry for her then, sorry for what he'd done to her, and wondered if his poor treatment of her had somehow contributed to her coming undone.

"If Misa killed him for the reason Gillian said she did," Baron stated, shaking his head slowly, "then he deserved it. And if it was my son, I would've done the same thing."

Celia nodded in agreement. "To molest a little baby . . ."

They both thought about it and shuddered.

Baron's conscience continued to tug at him. His mother had told him how day after day Misa had held vigil at his bedside while he lay comatose. He wondered why she had done that, since he hadn't always been so nice to her. But he was grateful that he hadn't been alone while he fought for his life. It comforted him somehow to know that someone had held his hand while his future hung in the balance. When Baron had finally awakened, it was Misa's face he'd seen first and her tears that he'd felt fall on his face as she realized that he was going to make it. He felt a sense of gratitude as well as a sense of guilt for how he'd treated her in the past. Lately, with him lying vulnerable in the hospital while his shooter was still on the loose, Baron had been thinking about death more than ever. He'd been trying to come to grips with the inevitable and wondering if he was doomed to burn in hell. It occurred to him that he was in a position to help Misa and perhaps nudge himself toward the pearly gates when his time came.

"I want to bail her out," he told his mother.

Celia looked at Baron to see if he was serious. She could see that he was and she was surprised. "Really? That's a lot of money, Baron."

He nodded. "I know, but I want to do it. We can't leave her in there—in Rikers! She's not built for that."

Celia agreed. Misa was a little thing and certainly wasn't tough enough to hold her own amid New York's City's worst female criminals. "I'll call Camille."

Camille and Lily stood and waited as Misa was finally brought through the heavy door followed by a large corrections officer. Camille had to resist the urge to gasp as she looked at her sister. It had only been five days and already Misa's body looked frail, her face sunken. She had been stripped of her beautiful weave and her hair appeared barely brushed, pulled back into a messy bun. Misa's facial expression was blank, bearing no smile or hint thereof. Still, Lily looked at her daughter and managed to still see her natural beauty. She noticed that Misa's head hung low and her eyes were downcast as she approached them. Lily walked toward her daughter, meeting her halfway, and pulled her into her arms. She placed her hand on the bottom of Misa's chin and inched it upward, forcing her to look into her mother's eyes. Lily smiled at Misa.

"I love you," she said. "And everything is gonna be all

right." She pulled Misa close and hugged her tightly. Misa dissolved into sobs and Camille came and joined in a group hug. Together, the women wept, overjoyed that Misa was finally coming home where she belonged.

Finally, they pulled apart and Lily glanced around. "Let's get the hell out of here before these idiots change their minds about letting you out." She took both of her daughters by the hand and led them out the prison doors.

Once they got to Camille's Range Rover and climbed inside, Misa finally exhaled. She couldn't believe she was out of jail—for the time being at least—and she couldn't wait to get the chance to see her son again. Teresa Rourke was suddenly representing her again, and had come that day to ensure that bail was posted and that Misa was immediately released. Teresa had explained that Misa wouldn't be able to see Shane until a hearing was held in family court regarding visitation. Misa couldn't wait to have her day in court so that she could see her baby again. She prayed that Louis wouldn't make it too hard for her.

She looked at her sister. "How did you find the money to bail me out?" she asked. "And who is paying that high-priced lawyer, Camille? I know Frankie isn't giving you any money." Misa hated being a burden financially or otherwise to her sister, especially under the circumstances. Misa knew that Camille and Frankie's marriage had been on the rocks for some time. But she still felt guilty for having driven what was sure to be the final nail in that coffin by killing Steven.

Camille sighed and gave her mother a sidelong glance. Lily had been questioning her as well, wondering the same thing. But Baron had sworn Camille to secrecy, demanding that she not reveal that he'd given her the means to bail Misa out. The last thing he wanted was for Frankie and Gillian to completely

cut him off when he was most vulnerable. So Celia had arranged to have the big house in which Baron lived put up as
collateral. The house was still in Celia's name and was worth
close to two million dollars. It was enough to get Misa out
and secure Teresa Rourke as her attorney. Celia brought the
deed to Camille's home under cover of night, and Teresa had
gone to bail Misa out, while Camille and her mother waited
in the vestibule. No one knew the true source of the bail
money except Camille, Celia, and Baron himself.

"I got the money from an old account I had set up years
ago and forgotten about," Camille lied, regurgitating the
story Celia had told her to give people.

Misa knew it was a lie, but didn't bother to push it. After
all, she was just happy to be going home. The specifics didn't
matter much. She stared out the window at the snow on the
ground and realized that she hadn't even known that snow
had fallen during the past few days. It had seemed as if time
had stopped, as if her whole world had stopped spinning the
moment Louis had told her that Shane had been abused.

"Mama, tell me again how Shane was when you saw him,"
she said softly.

Lily smiled and detailed her visit with her grandson days
prior. As the three women drove toward Long Island, where
Misa had agreed to stay with her mother in an effort to avoid
all the media on Staten Island, they all wondered what the
future held. For now, they tried to make Misa's first day home
as pleasant as possible.

U-Turns

Frankie climbed out of his car and shut the door, pressing the lock button on his key ring. He pulled the hood of his black jacket closer to his face as the January wind whipped around him. Gillian joined him and together they walked over to a long black limousine. Frankie opened the door and helped his mother, Mary, out. Side by side the trio neared Steven's casket, which was perched above the hole in the ground where his body would rest for eternity.

The small gathering of funeral-goers included Tremaine, Baron's mother Celia, and a young lady named Angelle who did big, illicit prescription drug business with the Nobles syndicate. Only a handful of Frankie's goons made up the rest of the crowd that gathered together around the hole in the ground as the wind whistled eerily through the naked trees. Conspicuously—and understandably—absent were Camille and her family. The press arrived and stood at a respectful distance, snapping pictures of the mourners as they gathered around and listened to the preacher saying things about Steven that weren't even true. He *hadn't* actually been a loving and devoted son, since neither Frankie nor Steven had interacted much with their mother since becoming adults.

Mary Bingham had been so broken down, so destroyed by the abuse her husband had dished out that she was a shell of her former self. It had been hard to watch her shrinking into herself whenever they visited her, so her sons had stayed away. Even now, as Frankie looked at her—all frail and bony underneath the full-length mink coat he'd given her years ago—he shook his head.

Gillian squeezed his hand, her Isotoner gloves warming his hand as she did so. He caught her eye and winked at her to let her know that he was okay.

When the minister was finally done bullshitting, Frankie took his mother by the arm and led her over to Steven's casket. Her legs shook from a combination of the biting wind and the fact that she was approaching her baby's gravesite. Her knees buckled and Frankie reached and caught her before she hit the ground.

Gillian gasped and rushed over to help Mrs. Bingham get her bearings. A heart-wrenching wail escaped the old woman's lips and Gillian looked to Frankie to see how he would react. She could tell that he was trying to be strong as his mother collapsed into his arms, her tears staining his coat. He held her as she sobbed into his chest.

"I'm so sorry . . . Steven! Oh God! I'm so sorry . . . Steeeeven!" Mrs. Bingham was distraught.

Frankie frowned hearing his mother's words and tried his best to quiet her. He was aware that the photographers were clamoring closer in an effort to get the money shot and he shielded his weeping mother from them as best he could.

"Ma . . . come on. It's not your fault." He held her close to

him, realizing then how skinny she was, how weak. He recalled the blows his father dealt her and realized the damage
that had been done to her. He fought the urge to cry as he
spoke to his mother.

"He's at peace, now, Ma." Frankie's voice cracked, but he
didn't let a tear fall.

His mother's sobs began to lessen.

"He's at peace now." Frankie rubbed her back, held her
up. He led her over to the casket and together they stood
there looking down at Steven's coffin.

Mary held on to Frankie, leaned on him. She thought of her
youngest son lying dead in the box before her; pictured him as
a baby running around in his footy pajamas with a pacifier in
his mouth. A sad smile appeared on her face as she thought of
Steven that way—young, innocent, pure. She thought of the
way he had looked in his coffin earlier that day, before they'd
closed it at his funeral service. His body was bigger, his face
had matured and hardened, his facial hair had grown in. But
he was still her baby, had always been her baby. Now her baby
was dead. Mary Bingham squeezed her eyes closed, the cold
winter wind flogging her body like a cat-o'-nine-tails.

Slowly, painfully it seemed, she reached forward and set a
single white rose on top of her child's casket. Her fingers lingered there for several moments, all was silent except for the
clicking of the photographers' cameras. Frankie didn't say a
word as he watched her fingers dance across the surface of
Steven's casket, her eyes brimming with tears. Seconds felt
like hours as she stood there this way. In a voice as gentle as a
whisper, she spoke at last.

"It should have been me."

She seemed to take in a deep breath, then let it out. Finally, she took her hand away and held it close to her heart as she turned and walked back to the car, nestled in Frankie's arms.

Gillian followed them, her hands tucked into the pockets of her lynx coat. She watched as Frankie assisted his mother into the limousine alongside Celia. When they climbed back into Frankie's black Escalade, Gillian looked at him. Emotionless, he started the car and put it in drive.

"Frankie—"

Slamming on the brake, he held his hand up. "I don't want to talk right now," he said, sternly, not even looking in her direction.

Gillian shut her mouth and silently they drove back to his mother's apartment in Flatbush.

Just then, her cell phone vibrated and she saw Saadiq's number flash across the screen. She turned her phone off and looked at Frankie, dazed and driving with his eyes focused intently on the road ahead. She wondered how long they could truly last if he continued to shut himself off this way. She wanted to talk about what was going on, while Frankie seemed intent on avoiding that at all costs. When they pulled up to Mary's apartment, Frankie started to get out of the truck, but Gillian reached over and stopped him, holding him by the arm.

"Frankie," she said again.

This time he looked at her with a pained expression on his face.

"I just wanted to tell you that I love you." She smiled faintly. "And everything is gonna be all right."

Frankie sighed and shook his head. He wished he was as sure as she was.

Toya jumped for some strange reason when she heard her doorbell ring. She clutched her chest as she felt her heartbeat quicken. Her father's reappearance in her life had her on edge more than she cared to admit. Camille was out on Long Island with her mother and sister while Dominique was becoming a ghetto version of Nancy Drew in search of her missing child. Toya had been enjoying a rare night at home without any interruptions.

As she neared her front door, she breathed somewhat easier as she realized that it was only Russell, her pesky, terribly ugly neighbor from across the street. This was the first time she was actually relieved to see him. Even a visit from this monster was better than another visit from her father.

She opened the door and greeted Russell. "Yes?"

He smiled, his face not looking any better despite his sunny disposition. "I understand that you're a real estate agent," he said, getting right to the point. Toya had slammed her door in his face on more than one occasion, so he knew he had to talk fast if he expected to get anywhere with her. "I'm tired of renting the house across the street. I'm looking to buy a house of my own in this area. I was hoping you could take me around and show me what's available."

Toya frowned and shifted her weight as she looked at him. "Wait a minute. You *rent* the house across the street? You don't own it?"

Russell nodded, not understanding her change in demeanor. "I rent right now, ma'am. But I'm interested in buying a house."

She smirked and folded her arms across her chest. This amateur was *renting* while she had been a homeowner for years, and he'd had the nerve to continuously harass her for a date. Just as she had suspected all along—based solely on his hideous facial features—he was beneath her.

"I'm very expensive," she said, hoping to dissuade him. "And don't call me 'ma'am.'"

He fought the urge to smile. He was trying to get his mack on and Toya was a tough nut to crack.

"Okay, well . . . I'm sure I can afford you," he said. The look on her face told him that she was about to go for his jugular vein, so he immediately corrected himself. "Your fee as a real estate agent, I mean. I'm a fireman, great salary, no kids." He hoped she was happy to hear that. "I make good money, and I have a nice amount saved. I just wanted to know if you're interested in doing business with me."

She raised an eyebrow. He was talking money now, speaking her language.

"Okay. Come into my office when you have a chance and we'll see what you're working with."

Russell loved the sound of that. She reached over to her purse lying nearby and handed him her business card. He read it aloud: "Toya Blake, Independent Real Estate Agent."

"Very good," she said sarcastically. "You can read. Have a nice day."

She shut the door in his face and still Russell's smile didn't fade one bit. He had made progress this time. At last, he had her attention.

It was Octavia's seventh night away from home and by now Dominique was a big bundle of nerves. Her child hadn't been to school, hadn't contacted any of her friends (or so they claimed), and hadn't so much as texted Dominique to say that she was alive. Dominique had taken time off from work, determined to stay close to home in case Octavia came back.

She had been hitting the bar in her expansive living room pretty hard on this Friday night, having nearly downed an entire bottle of Grey Goose as she sat alone listening to WBLS FM. Her doorbell chimed and she set her glass down on the coffee table. Her feet snug in a pair of fuzzy socks, she shuffled across her hardwood floors toward her front door clad in a lavender pair of Juicy sweats.

She glanced at her high-tech security system and saw that it was Archie, the guy she got her high-grade marijuana from. He stood just over six feet tall with a slim build and a rugged sex appeal. His brown skin and pearly white teeth gleamed on the screen and she unlocked the door and ushered him inside. Usually, she met Archie in the lobby of her Upper East Side condominium. But tonight she was too afraid to be away from the phone, too paranoid that she might miss Octavia's one attempt to call home. So, for the first time, she invited her Dominican friend to come upstairs to sell her some hydro.

As he stepped into her huge apartment, his eyes widened. "Daaaaaamn," he muttered. He looked around at the sheer size of her home and was amazed. An apartment this large in Manhattan was a true rarity—and carried a huge price tag. He looked at Dominique, his eyes wide with surprise.

She smiled at him, aware that her home was a treasure. Archie glanced around at all the furnishings, the art on the walls, the elegant décor, and he was impressed. Dominique had been his customer for years, even though he lived in burgeoning Harlem and she lived in this upper-crust part of town. She didn't spend much money when she called him, but she had a beautiful face and an awe-inspiring ass, so it was worth the trip each time he came to service her. As he stood in her living room now, he couldn't disguise his amazement upon seeing her home for the first time.

His accent was thick as he addressed her. "You have a beautiful home. I knew this was a nice building, but I had no idea it was *this* nice."

She thanked him and tried to maintain a smile. Her mind wasn't on prime real estate, though. She was worried sick about Octavia. "Let me get the money." She walked over to the sofa where her purse lay.

Archie strolled over to her entertainment center, and saw pictures of Dominique and a little girl who looked like a younger version of her. "This is your beautiful daughter, I presume."

Dominique looked up and nodded. "Yeah. She's the reason I couldn't meet you downstairs this time. I'm waiting to hear from her." Dominique sifted through her purse for her wallet.

Archie smirked. "What, she's out past her curfew or something?"

She shook her head. "No. She ran away."

Archie was surprised. "What?"

Dominique's face was dismayed as she nodded slowly. "*Days* ago, and I'm gonna have a heart attack from worrying about her." She finally fished her wallet out of her purse and flipped through it for a hundred-dollar bill.

Archie held his hand up to stop her. "Wait a minute. How old is she?"

Dominique's arms fell to her side. "Fourteen." She slumped down on the recliner, the Grey Goose finally starting to feel like it was taking effect.

Archie walked toward her, genuine concern marking his face. "*My God!*"

She held her head in her hands and blew her breath out in exasperation. "I have no idea where she is."

Archie didn't know what to say. He was a man of few words anyway. But when it came to kids in danger—especially precious daughters—the rage he felt was hard for him to express.

She made eye contact with him. "Do you have any kids?"

He nodded. "I do. But not here. Back at home." His brow furrowed. "I'm so sorry to hear about your daughter." He handed her the weed and she handed him the cash. He put the money in his pocket and looked at her. Still he didn't move. He frowned. "If you don't mind . . . why she run away from all this?"

He looked around at the lavish surroundings. Archie had known Dominique for years, ever since she'd started getting her hair done at his aunt's hair salon uptown. Each weekend, he and his family hustled their various products out of that shop and Dominique had caught his eye whenever she came in to get a relaxer or a wash and set. From his aunt, he'd learned that she worked in the music business, though she wasn't boastful about it. She always kept to herself and never gave any play to the men who vied for her attention—at least not from what Archie had witnessed. He had assumed that she had a man, but looking around he saw no sign of one.

Dominique shrugged. "Your guess is as good as mine," she answered. "I came home the other night and found a note. Haven't heard from her since."

He shook his head, hoping that the young girl was okay. "Wow."

She noticed that Archie was still standing there despite the fact that she had already paid him. Politely, she gestured toward the sofa. "You can have a seat if you want, Archie. Have a drink if you want."

He looked around warily. "I don't want your man to come home and get the wrong idea."

She laughed at that. "My man isn't coming home for two more months," she said.

Archie seemed surprised yet again. "He's locked up?" Dominique didn't seem like the type to deal with a street nigga.

"Yup." Dominique nodded. "Finishing up the last few weeks of a three-year bid." Dominique looked him in the eye. "He was selling coke."

"Okay," he said. He sat down on the sofa, thinking that her man was a damn fool for going to jail for that long with a woman like this at home. Archie himself had numerous run-ins with the law in his past. But those days were long behind him. These days, he hustled smart and flew below the radar. He and his family had been in the game for years and learned to play it well. Marijuana, after all, was a far lesser evil than whatever he assumed Dominique's man had been peddling.

She walked over to the bar and got him a glass. She dished some ice cubes from the bucket into his glass and then looked at him. "What'll it be?" she asked, gesturing at the bar.

Archie could tell she was feeling whatever she was sipping on, only because she was being far more outgoing tonight than she had ever been before. "How about some Absolut?"

"Okay." Dominique brought him the entire bottle along with the glass. She reached into the mini-fridge behind the bar and handed him two small bottles of cranberry and orange juice.

Archie smiled. "Thank you."

Dominique settled back into her seat on the recliner and sipped her drink. She noticed that he chose the cranberry juice. "So, your children . . . do you have boys or girls?" she asked.

"Oh, I have just one. A daughter. She's seven." Archie smiled as he thought of her. "I just traveled back to visit her this past summer."

Dominique nodded. She thought that was nice—a father who cared for his daughter so much that it lit up his face. She had been blessed to have that. Unfortunately, Octavia hadn't and Dominique couldn't help wondering if that was what she was rebelling against.

"I go there to see her. But then it's hard to come back here. I miss home. But the money is here, ya know?"

Dominique nodded.

Archie sipped his drink. Then he reached into his pocket and pulled out a spare bag of weed and held it up. "You wanna smoke now?"

She nodded, and handed him a Dutch Masters cigar from the drawer of the end table. Archie proceeded to roll up a perfectly packed blunt as Dominique watched.

"What's it like where you're from?" she asked, eager to take her mind off her troubles. Imagining a place like the Dominican Republic was a very welcome distraction.

Archie smiled, showing all his pearly whites, and regaled her with stories of his island culture. He was animated as he spoke, clearly in love with the place he still called home despite the fact that he'd been in America for more than ten years.

They smoked the blunt until it was gone as they talked. Soon, they'd shared many laughs, various stories and several drinks. Without noticing it, so much time had passed with them talking this way that it was after midnight.

Archie rose to leave and Dominique wasn't sure why she was sad to see him go. This was the most they'd ever talked before, since their conversations thus far had been limited to idle chatter whenever they saw one another. He seemed smart and compassionate. And she had been so focused on being faithful to Jamel that she had barely noticed how cute Archie was. The full, thick head of hair, the accent, his eyes, and sexy lips all came together in perfect synchronicity and resulted in a one beautiful man. Dominique stood next to him and he towered over her, his hair hanging past his collarbone. She was staring at him without realizing it, completely unaware that she was practically undressing him with her eyes as she imagined what he looked like underneath his winter clothes.

He smiled at her and moved in closer. "Why're you looking at me that way?" he asked, his accent casting a spell over her.

She blushed a little and looked away, but Archie stepped toward her and turned her face back toward him. Leaning down, he kissed her lips and was pleased that she kissed him back. Their tongues danced together and he pulled her body roughly toward his. Dominique was aware that this was crossing the line. And for one brief, fleeting moment, she thought of Jamel and considered pulling away. But Archie's kiss had her stuck. He held her face firmly within his hands—firmly and yet so gently that she felt secure. She clung to him, his T-shirt fisted in her grasp. She had never been kissed like this and she wanted Archie more than ever.

The music coming from the speakers did little to quell the fire that burned between them. Aaliyah's "Rock the Boat" seemed to only intensify their passion. Her inhibitions completely gone, Dominique led Archie to her bedroom.

"Stroke it for me . . . stroke it for me," Aaliyah sang and

Dominique had never wanted anything more in her life. Boldly, she climbed up onto her bed and Archie eagerly climbed on top of her, roaming her body with his hands while kissing her in a way that made her feverish. He made her feel alive, the way he touched her, his hands so unyielding and so tender at the same time. Archie undressed her and she eagerly stripped him out of his clothes. Through clenched teeth, she sucked in her breath as he put on a condom and entered her dripping wetness.

Dominique felt like she'd gone to paradise. His long, thick penis slid in and out of her, his hair shrouding her face as he ground into her.

"Oh . . ." she moaned. "Shit!"

"Yes," he panted in her ear. He kissed her and she faded out of this reality and into a whole new space and time. Dominique was aroused in ways she'd never imagined by his hunger for her. Archie touched a part of her that had gone undiscovered until then. For more than an hour he made love to her, stroked her, bit her, sucked her, licked her, kissed her, and entered and exited her, driving her to the point of no return. His rhythm was something magical that swept Dominique up into a frenzy of ecstasy she had never known. Her legs began to tremble from the sheer magic she was feeling. Her moans intensified and he knew that she was nearing her climax.

"Come," he whispered to her, his face mere centimeters from hers. "Come on."

"Ohhhhhhhh," she breathed as she came so viciously that her pussy pushed him out of her.

He held her close to him and resisted the urge to reenter her. Instead, he hugged her body tightly next to his as she panted breathlessly. When her breathing steadied, he looked at her. They stared into each other's eyes, silent except for the music playing during this lull in the nonstop sex they'd been having.

"Weak" by SWV played and Dominique had to smile. She indeed felt weak from their lovemaking. They just lay there in silence, nestled together, their limbs intertwined, and stared at each other. They looked into each other's souls and saw the possibilities that lay there. They kissed, giggled, touched, and held each other and soon came back together once more. Tossing and turning, they alternated in their hunger for each other. Dominique rode him and watched his face contort in rapture. Archie made her purr, feasted on her, fucked her until she came again. He felt empowered then, she could tell. His facial expressions matched hers and his intensity increased. He could feel her constricting around him, every part of her tensing and releasing in a way that squeezed his dick into a volcanic eruption. He came and it felt wonderful.

Lying beside her, Archie propped a pillow up on his arm and pulled Dominique closer to him. He snuggled her so close that she could feel his heartbeat and he could feel her breath falling steadily on his body. It felt like they were one, and evening faded into morning.

All Rise!

The telephone rang at four-thirty in the morning and stirred Dominique awake. Her home phone seldom rang, since most people called her cell. So the shrill sound shook her from her blissful slumber with a jolt. Her abrupt reaction roused Archie, as well, as Dominique scrambled for the telephone.

"Hello?" she stammered, realizing she was still naked. She pulled the sheet closer to her body.

"Ma?"

Dominique wanted to cry with joy. "Oh my God!" she exclaimed. "Octavia, where are you?"

It sounded like Octavia was crying. "Brooklyn."

"Are you okay?" Dominique was already out of bed and halfway dressed. Archie watched her, surmising that her daughter had finally gotten tired of running. He climbed out of bed himself and gathered his clothes.

"Um . . . yeah." Octavia sounded so unsure. "I'm at my friend Holly's house . . . Holly, from school. Her mom wanted me to call and tell you that I'm here. And I'm okay."

Dominique was so confused. Holly's *mother* wanted Octavia to call. "You've been there all this time?"

"No . . ."

Before Dominique exploded and demanded to know what the fuck was going on, someone took the phone away from Octavia.

"Mrs. Storms, this is Holly's mom, Rebecca. Octavia came by our house tonight and spoke with my husband and me about her situation. We've persuaded her to call you so that you can come over and talk with her. I'm sure you've been worried sick."

Dominique sat down on the bed and Archie sat, too, searching her face for clues. "She just came there tonight?" Octavia had been away from home for seven days.

"Yes," Rebecca said. "I think that once you come over here and talk with Octavia, everything will make sense." The woman paused. "I think she's sort of scared. I assured her that you would be happy to hear from her, but she's still very nervous."

Dominique didn't want to curse or yell or do anything to scare Octavia or the white woman on the other end of the phone. She calmly asked for Holly's address and wrote it down with her hands trembling the entire time. Dominique hung up and was aware of Archie's hand stroking her back. She turned to him, shaking.

"I have to go."

"Where is she?" he asked.

"Brooklyn. Williamsburg. I have to get there now." Dominique snatched her sneakers out of the closet.

"You cannot drive like this," he said. "I'll come with you."

She shook her head. Was he crazy? "No. I have to go and

see about my daughter. I like you, Archie. But I don't need you coming with me at a time like this."

Archie tried to explain. "I understand—"

"Thank God she's okay!" Dominique threw her hands up in praise. She looked toward the ceiling as if truly grateful to the Almighty. Looking at Archie again she shook her head. "But why hasn't she called me in seven muthafuckin' days? I'm gonna kill her!"

He had to resist the urge to laugh as he listened to her rant. He understood her being this upset, but he found it amusing that she was happy her child was alive and eager to kill her at the same time.

"Calm down," he said firmly. "Listen, I will drive you there in your car and take the train back to the city. I'm not going to stay there with you. You can handle your business with your daughter and bring her home. Call me whenever you get the time." He kissed her trembling hand and rubbed it gently. "But you can't drive like this."

She nodded. He could have told her that he was going to drive her to Jupiter and she would have gone along with him as long as he kept touching her the way he did.

Together they got dressed and Dominique grabbed her car keys off the dresser. She turned around and faced Archie once more. She wondered how she'd gotten herself into this situation with him, yet she was grateful he was there with her at a time like this. It felt so good not to be alone for once.

He pulled her close to him, holding her tightly at the small of her back. His pillowy lips pushed into hers and he lingered within a breath of her. "Ready?"

She nodded and he took her by the hand, leading her out the door.

Toya had known that peace wouldn't last for long.

"What are you saying?" she asked Dominique as she sat up in bed cradling her BlackBerry in her palm.

"Octavia is in Brooklyn, Toya!" Dominique was nearly breathless. "Can you go there and make sure she doesn't try to run away again before I get there?"

"Where?" Toya switched her bedside lamp on. "Give me the address and I can meet you there." She glanced at the clock. It was just after 5:00 A.M. She loved her friends, but they were definitely some early-in-the-morning and middle-of-the-night bitches these days! She took down the address and warned Dominique to drive carefully.

Dominique glanced over at Archie in the driver's seat of her MKX and decided that Toya didn't need to know about this. "I will," she said, before ending the call and holding on for dear life as they sped to Brooklyn.

Along the way, Dominique looked at Archie in a new light. He had ravaged her and made her feel things she'd never felt before. She wondered if it was his passion for her or if it was the fact that she'd gone so long being faithful to Jamel during his incarceration. She had been without sex for close to three years as she waited patiently for the man she loved to come back to her.

And now she had been intimate with Archie—intimate in a way that she had never been with any man before him. She knew that she should feel guilty. But as he looked at her and smiled, laugh lines creasing his handsome face, she felt nothing short of joy.

They arrived at Holly's house at precisely the same time

as Toya. She made Archie turn the engine and headlights off, and Dominique watched as Toya climbed out of her Benz, hurried toward the front door, and then as she was ushered into the house. She was thankful that Toya hadn't noticed her car.

Dominique turned to Archie. "Thank you," she said.

He nodded. "You're welcome, Dominique." Her name rolled off his lips like music.

For a few silent seconds, he looked at her. "You're so pretty," he said, gazing at her with a smile spread across his face.

She was wondering whether or not she should promise to call him. She wasn't sure that she ever would. She didn't want to lie. As she battled within herself, he leaned in and brushed his lips against hers one more time. Then he handed her the keys to her car and climbed out. Dominique got out, too, and watched as he crossed the street and walked toward the subway station two blocks away.

"Don't kill the poor girl, ya heard?" Archie called over his shoulder.

She laughed, blew him a kiss even though his back was turned, and walked up the walkway to greet her prodigal child.

Octavia sat on the sofa, tapping her foot nervously on the marble floor in Holly's living room. She may as well have been facing the guillotine, her fear of her mother's wrath was that great. Her heart beat so rapidly in her chest that she wondered if it was possible to have a heart attack at her age. Holly and her family had been tiptoeing around her for quite a while now, everyone anticipating the moment the doorbell rang and the festivities began.

Octavia kinda wanted to kick Holly's ass. She had gone to her classmate in confidence, since the two of them had gotten to know each other while working together on a science project. Holly had always talked about what pushovers her parents were; how they never went in her room and let her friends stay the night without question. Octavia had remembered that and had hoped they would be lenient enough to let her stay there until she could figure out what to do next. But Octavia—Holly's only black friend—would've been hard to conceal. So, Holly had gone to her mother in confidence and asked her if Octavia could stay there for a few days. Holly had persuaded Octavia to tell her parents the truth about why she was there. Instead of understanding, her mom had filled her husband in on everything and together they had forced Octavia to call her mother. Octavia's entire plan had crumbled before her eyes and now her back was up against the wall.

When the eerie, doomsday-sounding doorbell finally did ring out, it sent chills up Octavia's spine.

She heard voices at the door and knew instantly that it wasn't her mother. The person at the door sounded downright pleasant, and as the voices came nearer Octavia didn't hear her mother. When Holly and her mom Rebecca came into view, followed by Toya, Octavia breathed a huge sigh of relief. Until then she'd been lamenting that the only person capable of preventing her mother from killing her that day was her late grandfather. Toya suddenly seemed like a good stand-in.

"Well! *Hello*, Octavia," Toya said, locking eyes with the teenager. Her voice said so much more than just "hello." It said, *Where the fuck have you been, Octavia?*

"Hi, Miss Toya."

Holly's mother, Rebecca, offered Toya a seat near Octavia, which she happily accepted. "May I get you something to drink?" Rebecca asked.

"Yes, please." Toya nodded. "Do you have any wine?"

Rebecca smiled and breathed a sigh of relief. "Absolutely! I was just about to have some myself." She needed to take the edge off after talking to Octavia. "Red or white?"

"Red, please."

Rebecca scurried off to pour the wine and Toya turned her attention to Octavia. The only other person in the room with them was Octavia's friend Holly. Apparently, Holly's dad had fled the scene since Octavia's surprise visit.

"Where've you been all this time?" Toya asked her. She kept her voice low, so as not to alert any of the adults in the house. She spoke loudly enough for only the teenagers to hear. She glared at Octavia.

Octavia and Holly looked at each other. Toya saw that they were having a silent conversation and she mushed Octavia, shoving her roughly in the forehead with her hand. It caught both Octavia and her friend off guard, and Toya's smile faded into a sinister snarl.

"You better start talking, Miss Thang. 'Cuz when your mother gets here, she is going *off*! You'll want to have me on your side then, pleading your case. So what the fuck is going on, Octavia? And where have you been?"

Holly didn't look at Octavia, but prayed silently that she told the truth. This Miss Toya seemed like she meant business.

Thankfully, Octavia needed an ally so she started talking. "I've been staying uptown . . . in Harlem at my boyfriend's place."

"Your *boyfriend*?" Toya asked. "What boyfriend?"

Octavia shrugged. "I'm not supposed to have one so I was keeping it a secret." She shook her head, feeling like a complete fool. She looked at Toya, hoping for some sympathy as she spoke about her plight. "Then . . . I got pregnant and now I'm not sure what to do."

Toya had been praying all along that this wasn't Octavia's big secret. She was all too familiar with this story, having seen it happen again and again to friends of hers back in high school. She sighed. "Octavia . . ."

The doorbell rang again. Surely, this time, it was Dominique. Rebecca rushed in, Toya's wine in hand, and gave it to her before rushing back out to answer the door. This time, the voices that mingled in the foyer were far more subdued and Octavia looked to Toya for consolation. She found none.

Toya shook her head at her and said, "This is the last thing your mother needs."

Dominique walked into the room and the oxygen seemed to escape all at once. The air was thick with tension and Octavia glanced sheepishly in her mother's direction. Rebecca went and stood behind Holly and together they watched something better than reality TV.

"Octavia." Dominique's tone was flat and held no emotion. She was happy to see her daughter but scared to death of what she was about to reveal. In light of Shane's recent revelation, Misa's first-degree murder charge, and Toya's newly uncovered past, it seemed that anything was possible. Numbly, Dominique walked toward her daughter and hugged her, happy to see that she was in one piece.

Pulling away, she looked at her closely, scanning Octavia from head to toe. "Have you been hurt?" she asked. "Why haven't you called?"

"I . . . w-was . . ." Octavia began to stutter.

"Dominique, why don't you sit down?" Toya suggested. Dominique was small in frame but was somehow looming large over her daughter at the moment. Toya gestured to the empty seat across from her. "Come sit down."

Reluctantly, Dominique did as Toya urged. She took a seat and stared at her daughter, eager to get to the bottom of this.

"I can't keep tap-dancing around this," Dominique said. She was perched, literally, on the edge of her seat. She looked at Octavia. "Tell me where you've been, why you haven't called, and why we're all *here* instead of at home where you belong."

All eyes were on Octavia.

"I have a boyfriend."

Toya looked at Dominique to see her reaction. Dominique didn't budge, her facial expression shifted only slightly. Toya looked back at Octavia. "Continue," Toya urged the youngster on.

Octavia swallowed hard. "I was meeting him after school instead of going to dance class. We would go to his house . . . he lives in Harlem . . . and we would talk and get to know each other."

Toya noticed that Dominique's breathing was getting heavier. She touched her reassuringly and smiled. "Just listen, Dominique."

Octavia was so glad that Miss Toya was there. She looked at Holly and her mom and saw their rapt expressions. She had never been more embarrassed and ashamed in her life.

"We started having sex."

Dominique didn't bother to hide her disappointment. She looked at Octavia, with her baby face and braces, her innocent eyes brimming with tears. This baby girl was having sex already. Dominique shook her head in disappointment.

"And now I'm pregnant."

Dominique was silent then. She didn't move, didn't even seem to breathe. Everything in the room seemed to freeze and she wondered if she'd heard her daughter correctly.

Octavia had begun to cry. "I don't know what to do . . . because I told Dashawn about it."

"Dashawn?" Dominique was frowning.

Octavia nodded. "That's my boyfriend."

Toya looked at Dominique and noticed her right eye was twitching.

"He's a good person, Ma." Octavia was speaking more confidently now. "And he said that he would take care of me if anything like this ever happened."

That was when Dominique lost it. She lunged at her daughter, and Toya caught her in midair, toppling her onto the ottoman. Octavia had sense enough to get out of the way then. She ran toward the front door and Holly's mother blocked her exit.

"Don't do this here, Dominique!" Toya hissed at her friend. "I know you want to kill her. I do, too."

That didn't make Octavia feel any better. She moved toward the door again, but Rebecca blocked her once more.

Toya continued to restrain Dominique. "But that's not gonna solve anything. Think about Misa."

Holly, Rebecca, and Octavia all frowned, not knowing what Toya was referring to. But Dominique understood. She didn't want to end up in jail like her friend had. She stopped trying to wriggle free and closed her eyes in dismay.

"I don't mean to butt into your business," Rebecca said. She looked at young, pretty, naive Octavia. "But I can't let you keep running. Your mother is here. She loves you, and that's why she's angry. This boy is not your boyfriend, Octavia."

Rebecca sighed and looked at Dominique. "Mrs. Storms, he told her that he loved her," Rebecca explained. She turned her attention back to Octavia. "But that is not love at all, sweetheart. You told me that when you gave him the news of your pregnancy, he let you stay with him for a few days until his mother found out. And then they kicked you out. Just threw you out in the street with no place to go. That's not love, Octavia."

Dominique hated another person having to school her child on what was so obvious. Toya wasn't feeling the vibe in the room, either. She looked at Rebecca. "Is there some place where Dominique and I can talk alone?" Toya glanced at Octavia.

Rebecca quickly sprung into action. "This way," she said, gesturing toward her kitchen. Toya took Dominique by the hand and led her in there. Once they were inside and Toya felt certain that no one could hear their private conversation, she spoke to her friend in a hushed tone.

"You can't attack her right now, even though I know you want to," she said. "Shit, I want to kick her ass myself. But for one thing, she says she's pregnant."

Dominique squeezed her eyes shut hearing her friend say that. She opened them again and looked at Toya with tears in her eyes.

Toya felt so sorry for her friend who had already endured so much. Octavia's pregnancy was only the latest misfortune in Dominique's life. "For another thing, this ain't Big Mama's house from back in the days. You can't kick her ass in here without going to jail. Pull yourself together and help me convince Octavia to come home. She only called you to meet her here in order to protect herself. So make her feel safe, bitch. Then when you get her home, you give her the third degree."

Dominique fought back tears. "How could she be so stupid, Toya? Did you hear her in there? Did you hear how pathetic she sounded?"

"That was you once, Dominique."

Toya hadn't meant to hurt her friend's feelings, but the expression on Dominique's face said she had done just that.

"I'm not trying to put you down, but you have to see things clearly. She doesn't need you to beat up on her right now. She needs a hug, and some motherly talk, and a reality check. Right now you have a lot on your mind. You've been worried sick about her for a whole week, and you're still dealing with losing your father." She took Dominique by the hand. "Let's just be happy that she's okay."

Dominique managed a faint smile, nodded, and took Toya's advice. She put her game face on and went back out into the living room. She hugged Octavia, told her that she loved her and that she was going to help her figure out the right thing to do. She reminded her that she, too, had been a teen parent and assured her that she wouldn't bug out. Holly and Rebecca were happy, feeling that they'd done the right thing. The only person who remained unconvinced by Dominique's Oscar-worthy performance was Octavia.

Octavia looked at her mother and knew that this was far from over. She knew that when they went home, a million questions would be asked and what happened here at Holly's house was only the tip of the iceberg.

Still, Octavia had to hand it to her mother. She seemed awfully calm and far less tightly wound than usual. There was almost a smile behind her eyes as she assured Octavia that everything was going to be all right.

Dominique was actually devastated. She hadn't wanted her daughter to repeat the mistakes she'd made. She also blamed herself for Octavia's pregnancy, in part because of her preoccupation with Jamel and with her career and even with her father's death over the past few months. She had the weight of the world on her shoulders. But the way that Archie had soothed her just a few short hours ago helped her keep her sanity. It wasn't just the sex, it was the intimacy she had experienced for the first time in years. Archie had awakened her senses. As Holly and Rebecca smiled and reminded them that they were available to talk if Octavia ever needed them, Dominique flashed back to the scissor position Archie had twisted her into and had to suppress a smile. Toya noticed, but figured Dominique was just slowly losing her mind.

They left Holly's house and Dominique led the way to her car in silence. Toya took the opportunity to pull Octavia to the side.

"Whatever you do, don't *ever* run away again." Toya's face was serious as she spoke and she gripped Octavia's hand tightly. "Your mother was worried sick about you and so was everybody else. She just buried her father—your grandfather. And she's doing the best she can to be a good mother to you, Octavia. Don't send her over the edge by running away again. You wanted to act grown and have a boyfriend when you weren't supposed to and have sex before you were ready." Toya shook her head as if those were the dumbest things in the world. "So now you have to face the consequences like a grown-up and stop running away from your problems. Sit with your mother. Talk to her. And I'll come over in a few hours to make sure she hasn't killed you."

They got to Dominique's car and Toya ushered the little girl inside. She turned to Dominique and sighed.

Dominique shrugged. "I'll probably never be able to repay you for everything you've done for me, Toya. Thank you so much."

Toya waved her hand as if to stop her friend from gushing about it. She wasn't comfortable with emotional outpourings. "Girl, please! That's what friends are for." She hugged Dominique and patted her reassuringly on the back. Looking her friend in the eye, she summed up her case. "Don't hit her, no matter how much you may want to. She's scared to death, and what she did was dumb. But she's safe. And she wasn't out there being hurt or God knows what. Just listen to her, talk to her. And I'll come over later and we'll all figure out what to do about her situation."

Dominique smiled. "Okay."

Toya frowned slightly as she watched her friend climb into her car and buckle her seat belt. If she didn't know any better, she'd think Dominique seemed more relaxed than usual. Toya chalked it up to her relief over having finally found her daughter. She yawned, eager to get back to her bed, and walked off toward her car as Dominique honked and pulled away from the curb. Octavia looked out the window as her mother drove her back to their Manhattan apartment in silence.

Regrets

"What are you doing here?" Gillian stood with her front door cracked, her body blocking her uninvited guest from gaining entry to her home.

"I just want to talk to you," Saadiq explained. He had been dating Gillian for more than a year. But after her father's death she had cut him off, ignoring his repeated phone calls, text messages, and e-mails. It was clear that their relationship was over as far as she was concerned, but he just wanted an explanation.

"Talk about what?" Gillian looked aloof, standing there with her arms folded across her chest and a scowl on her face.

"What happened with us?" Saadiq asked. "I mean the last time I saw you was at your parents' anniversary party. I left that night and I knew you were upset, but I didn't think it was that serious. I picked up the paper the next day and read about what happened to your father and your brother. So, I called you, I came by here, and I couldn't find you anywhere. Then I saw that his funeral had taken place and I've been trying to get in touch with you ever since."

Gillian shrugged. "It's over," she said matter-of-factly. "Everything is different now."

"Different how?" Saadiq asked, frowning.

"I'm with Frankie now," Gillian explained.

Saadiq stared at her, his temper flaring by the second. "Frankie?"

Gillian nodded and watched the wheels turning in Saadiq's head.

"So all that time you were swearing that you two were just friends . . ."

"We were," she said. "But losing my father brought us closer."

"And now you're with him?" Saadiq's voice dripped with hurt and anger.

Gillian nodded again. "I love him."

"You don't love him."

"I don't love *you*." Gillian didn't blink as she said it. "And I would appreciate it if you could leave me alone and let me be happy."

Saadiq wanted to knock her lights out. "You're a cold bitch, you know that?"

Gillian smirked. She didn't care what he thought of her. She had bigger concerns right now. Saadiq could kiss her ass. She stepped back inside her house and shut the door in his face, then watched as he pathetically retreated down her stairs with his tail between his legs.

Turning on her heel, she walked back into the living room and sat down once more on the sofa across from her guest.

Biggs sat stone-faced before Gillian, but he was actually feeling quite anxious. Gillian was asking him to do a very serious thing.

"So," she said, picking up where she left off. "Can you handle that for me?"

"You want me to kill Jojo?" Biggs confirmed.

She nodded, crossed her legs, and looked him dead in the eyes.

Biggs cleared his throat. "Does Frankie know about this?"

Gillian frowned slightly, annoyed that Biggs seemed to be questioning her authority. "No. He's got other things on his mind these days," she said. It was true that Frankie had been understandably sidetracked by the tragedy in his family. But Gillian was still thirsty for the taste of Jojo's blood. She wanted desperately to avenge her father's murder so that she could find some peace at last.

Biggs watched Gillian's facial expression vacillate between irritation and control. "And, for the record, I'm in charge of this family now," she said, her perfectly glossed lips tightly pursed.

Biggs stared back at her, listening to her assert her power. For a moment, he thought about calling Frankie and clearing it with him, just to be on the safe side. After all, Gillian was new to the powerful position she now occupied. He understood her bloodlust, but he wondered if she was being a little hasty. Looking at her now, he could see that she was serious.

"You thought this out all the way?" he asked.

She nodded once again. "All the way."

Biggs nodded finally and licked his lips. Leaning forward in his seat, he clasped his hands together. "I'll make it happen."

Jojo stumbled out of the bar and toward his car. The crowd at Lucky Lefty's bar in the Bronx had been a smattering of familiar faces from his days growing up in the Boogie Down borough. It was his birthday weekend, and he had been celebrating hard all night. In fact, his birthday hadn't been the only thing he'd been celebrating. His beef with the Nobles family was over. The war had been won, Jojo believed, once he and his goons had killed Doug Nobles and critically wounded Baron. With news of Frankie's brother's recent death at the hands of his own sister-in-law, Jojo was celebrating what he deemed to be the demise of his rival crew.

He climbed behind the wheel of his Benz, although he knew that he had no business driving as drunk as he was. He waved at his boy Day-Day as he pulled out of the lot, and then headed toward the FDR. He stayed to the right, opting for the slowest lane of traffic in his inebriated state. So he was a little befuddled when he saw flashing lights in his rearview mirror and realized that he was being pulled over.

Reluctantly, Jojo pulled over to the shoulder and stopped his car. The unmarked vehicle with the flashing lights pulled up behind him and Jojo dug in his pocket for his wallet. He looked in the mirror to see if his eyes were red as he retrieved his license. He watched the tall officer clad in all black approaching his car and popped a mint in his mouth to cover up the smell of tequila. Next, he reached into glove compartment for his registration. Sitting upright with his paperwork in hand, he lowered the power window on the driver's side just as the individual who had pulled him over approached. Glancing up, Jojo came eye-to-eye with Biggs.

He recognized Frankie's henchman immediately. Instinctively, he tried to reach under his seat for his gun, but it was too late. Biggs shot Jojo three times in the face, the silencer on his .45 caliber avoiding the detection of the passing motorists. Calmly, he walked back to his truck with the smoking gun concealed at his side. He climbed inside, tucked away the phony police siren, and drove off.

Her eyes were downcast as she spoke, her voice low and her hands intertwined.

"I met him on the six train. He struck up a conversation with me and I thought he was cute."

Octavia had showered and was feeling cozy, so glad to be back at home in her pajamas. She had twisted her shoulder-length hair into a single braid and was perched on the living room chaise, her knees pulled close to her chest. She looked more like a child than ever, Dominique thought. Seated in the recliner across from her daughter, she listened silently as Octavia told her the story of how her misfortune began.

Octavia was relieved that her mother was calmly listening to her. It made it easier to be honest as she told the story of the torment she'd been dealing with alone for so long. She wondered what Toya had said to her mother to calm her down enough that she could listen so raptly. Whatever it was, she was glad as she continued.

"We exchanged cell phone numbers and he would call me. Granddad was going to dialysis three days a week and I was supposed to be in dance class those days. At first, I just missed one day, then the next week I missed two. If the dance teacher called, I would delete the messages. He wanted to take me out to the movies and I knew you would never go for it. So I snuck and did it anyway." Her tone was flat and she finally made eye contact with her mother.

"That's interesting," Dominique said, her gaze locked on her daughter. "Obviously, you knew better than I did."

Octavia didn't know how to respond to that. She proceeded with her story instead. "Yeah, so I was skipping dance class and meeting him. We would go to get pizza or just sit in the park, a couple times we went to an arcade or to a movie. But then he invited me to his house instead."

"His house . . . where exactly is his house and who does he live with?"

"He lives in Harlem River Houses."

Dominique closed her eyes, shook her head. Here she was busting her ass to afford a luxury condo, a private school for her child, and all the perks of good living. And all the while, Octavia had been up in a project apartment getting fucked by some hoodlum named Dashawn.

"His mother just got custody of him again."

Dominique rubbed her temples.

"She was on drugs, but she's clean now." Octavia thought back to how Dashawn's mother had treated her during her week on the run. She hadn't held any punches when she told Octavia what ordeals awaited her if she chose to keep her unborn child. "She's kind of like . . . tough all the time. Not mean, but just tough. Anyway, when she wasn't home I would go over there with him and we would . . ."

"Have sex," Dominique filled in the blank. "Continue."

"Yeah." Octavia shifted a little in her seat. She hadn't had many conversations with her mother about sex. Having one now, as she sat pregnant before her at the age of fourteen, felt awkward. "We used condoms most of the time. But sometimes we didn't. I would tell him to use one, but he would say he didn't need to, that I could trust him." She wiped a tear that fell from her eye.

Dominique felt like kicking this bastard's ass. "Did he force you, Octavia?" she asked, through clenched teeth. "Did he make you do it?"

Octavia shook her head. "No. He didn't force me. But I told him that I was scared to get pregnant and he swore that I wouldn't. And he said that if I did, he would take care of me. So I didn't think about it."

"How often were you having sex with him?" Dominique looked at her daughter and knew that she didn't really want to know the answer to that question. She prayed that Octavia hadn't contracted any diseases having unprotected sex with this idiot.

"I don't know." Octavia shrugged. "A few times."

Dominique swallowed hard, clenched her fists involuntarily.

"And then right around the time when Granddad got sick, I realized that I wasn't getting my period. I got scared and I didn't know how to tell you." Octavia glanced sheepishly at her mother. "There was so much going on, and you were already upset about Granddad."

Dominique knew that things had been crazy around that time. She looked at her daughter and her eyes narrowed. "Did you tell Dashawn?"

Octavia nodded.

"And what did he say?"

"He was stressed, just like me, worried about what his mother would say. But he said he would handle it. He said I could stay with him if you kicked me out."

Dominique frowned. "But you didn't even give me a chance to kick you out, Octavia. You just left."

Octavia didn't know what to say. Her mother was right. Fear of disappointing and angering Dominique had been only part of the reason Octavia had run away to her boyfriend's house. Truthfully, she had wanted to feel grown-up, to live with Dashawn, wake up beside him, and have the freedom her mother wouldn't give her.

Dominique leaned forward in her chair. "And, for the record, I wouldn't have kicked you out. You're my daughter. I love you, no matter what you do or what mistakes you make. And you should know that by now."

"I know." Octavia did know that her mother loved her. It was just that Dominique was busy all the time and so much more strict than her friends' parents.

"And you already know that I had you when I was a teenager myself. How could I dare to throw you out when I've walked a mile in those shoes already?"

Holly's mom had asked the same question. Octavia still came up blank for an answer.

"So you ran away, why?" Dominique pressed.

Octavia took a deep breath and thought about the question posed to her. She looked at her mother and came clean.

"I wanted to be with him. I was hoping that he would let me stay there with him like he said he would, and that we could have our baby." Octavia began to cry. She shook her head in shame as Dominique watched her. Octavia looked to see if she saw disgust in her mother's eyes. She knew now that the idea of finding her Prince Charming at the age of fourteen and living happily ever after was nothing more than a little-girl fairy-tale fantasy.

"But after a couple of days, his mother started wondering why I wasn't going home."

"After a couple of days? What kind of mother wouldn't question you spending even *one* night in her home when she hadn't even spoken to your parents?"

Octavia shrugged again. She didn't really care too much

about what type of mother Dashawn had. She only wanted to be with the boy she had fallen in love with.

Dominique was sick of seeing her daughter shrug her little fucking shoulders. "What is this woman's name? What is this nigga's last name?"

"Her name is Dee Dee. Jackson is their last name."

"And what did she say when she finally found the time to question you?"

"She sat me down in the living room and asked me what was up."

Dominique pictured the scene in her head. She hated the thought of her daughter being at someone else's mercy.

"I told her that I was pregnant and she told me to get rid of it." Octavia was crying, still. She reached and took the box of Puffs that sat on the end table. She took out a tissue and wiped her face as she glanced at her mother.

Dominique did not respond, instead she watched Octavia compose herself.

"She told me that she got pregnant when she was young. She had Dashawn and regretted it from day one." Octavia thought back to how badly she felt hearing Dashawn's mother admit that in front of him. It was bad enough that she hadn't raised him, but to state her regret over his birth so blatantly seemed foul. "She talked about how she worked as a stripper to support him and then started using drugs; how she lost custody of him and he grew up in foster care. Now he's sixteen and he's just getting to know his own mother."

Dominique had heard enough about the woes of the fucker who had gotten her precious child pregnant. She wanted to know where he stood now on that issue. "So what was he saying while his mother was telling you to have an abortion?"

Octavia's face fell. She toyed with her hands and sadness

swept across her. "He told me he agrees with his mother, that we're too young to have a kid." She shrugged. "Then they told me to go back home and talk to you."

Dominique sat back in her chair and looked at her child. She thought about what Octavia was saying.

"So they sent you home, and instead of coming home you went to Holly's house."

Octavia nodded.

"Why?" Dominique asked. "What could be so horrible about me that you decided to keep running instead of coming home to talk to me like everyone was telling you to?"

Octavia looked at her mother and her mouth suddenly felt dry. "I didn't want you to be disappointed in me."

Dominique felt a tug at her heartstrings. She could tell that Octavia was happy to be home and relieved to have gotten the burden of the truth off her shoulders. She sighed. "So, what do you think you should do now?"

Octavia's eyes watered again. "I'm scared, Ma. I don't know what to do. I just . . . want to get some sleep in my own bed again." She sighed. "I want to just enjoy being back home."

Dominique smiled. She wanted that, too. She was relieved that her daughter was back and she reiterated Toya's assertion that running away was not something Octavia should ever do again. She watched Octavia yawn and she stood up and reached out her hand to her child.

Octavia looked up at her mother and felt so grateful that she wasn't yelling and screaming. She took Dominique's hand and stood up. As they stood eye-to-eye, Octavia knew that her mother was indeed disappointed in her. But as Dominique pulled her into a loving and firm embrace, she also knew that her mother still loved her. She held on tight and vowed to herself that she would never take that for granted again.

Gillian lay awake wondering where Frankie was and praying that he was all right. She had a strange feeling in the pit of her stomach and she couldn't figure out why. That feeling had been there for days. Ever since Steven's death, Frankie had been quiet and withdrawn. Gillian understood since she, too, was still coping with the loss of her father. It felt as if there were a dark cloud hovering over them, and Frankie seemed to be immersing himself in work as a way to deal with all that had happened.

She flipped on the lamp at her bedside and pulled open the drawer to her nightstand. She reached in and moved a few things around before pulling out a small framed picture of her seated in her father's lap on the night of her senior prom. In the photo, she wore a poofy pink taffeta dress and sat nestled in her daddy's embrace, her arms wrapped around him as if he were the world's biggest teddy bear. As clear as it was from the photo that she was a young lady—tall, buxom, and all made-up—it was equally clear that she was still her father's baby girl. That had never changed, and now that he was gone she found herself longing for the comfort of his arms more than ever.

She sighed and stared down at the picture, then smiled as she remembered his insistence that she attend the prom with Baron that night. It had been a joy for all her girlfriends who thought her green-eyed brother, who was nearly ten years older, was the finest thing since Al B. Sure! But to Gillian, it wasn't so thrilling. She had fun with her brother and made the most of the night, but she had envied her friends who came with real dates. Truth be told, Gillian hadn't really wanted to go with any of the boys from her exclusive prep school. Frankie was the only one she could have imagined herself with. But he was eight years older than her and married. Her father would have had a heart attack at the mere suggestion.

She put the picture back in its original spot on her nightstand instead of returning it to the drawer. It wasn't so painful to look at it anymore. At first, in the days and weeks after he passed away, she'd found it difficult to look at pictures of him, to hear his favorite songs or smell his cologne. But now, those things gave her comfort and a sense of calm in the midst of all that was going on around her.

Gillian climbed out of bed and walked over to her bedroom window, looked out at the streetlights, the taxis zipping up her block. She thought about Frankie again, wondered what was keeping him out all night, and she chuckled a little at herself then. Here she was—Gillian Lourdes Nobles—sitting up waiting for a man to come home to her. She felt somewhat pathetic at the thought of that. It felt as if she had switched places with Camille, whom she all but despised.

Frankie came in at 5:55 A.M., and found Gillian standing in the silence of her bedroom facing her large window, the curtains drawn back as if she'd been gazing outside. She looked over her shoulder at him as he came into the room.

"Hey," he said, wishing she'd been asleep so that he could lay awake in the dark and think. He stood off to the far side of the room and began to disrobe.

Gillian watched him. They had so much to talk about, but she didn't want to bombard him the moment he walked in the door. The last thing she wanted to turn into was the nagging wifey. Camille had that role sewn up all by herself.

"I couldn't sleep," she said, sitting on the bench at the foot of her bed. "I was worried about you."

He walked over to her and kissed her softly. "I'm all right."

He wasn't, though. His entire world was still turned on its ear and he was convinced that the only good thing in his life was the beauty who sat before him. He looked at her sitting there, so patient, so soft, and yet so strong despite everything happening around her.

Gillian watched Frankie walk into the bathroom and shut the door. She heard him turn on the shower and felt better knowing that he was there, that he was safe. She crawled back into bed and waited for him to emerge. When he did, she watched him climb into bed beside her and wrap her in his arms, whispering that he loved her.

Gillian searched his eyes for more. She knew there were things he wasn't telling her, but she'd been raised to know better than to ask questions. She was, after all, a Nobles.

She knew that Misa had been mysteriously bailed out by her sister. The DA had called to tell Frankie personally, and Gillian had been with him when the call came in. She knew that Frankie had been wondering how Camille had managed to get her hands on that amount of money. Gillian was convinced that Camille wasn't such an idiot after all. Obviously, she'd stockpiled money that Frankie didn't know about. This only added to Frankie's disdain for his wife, and he wanted her out of his life more than ever before.

Camille and her mystery cash were the least of Frankie's worries. Misa had murdered his brother. Worse, she'd accused him of an atrocity toward a three-year-old kid, and Frankie hadn't been able to stop thinking about it ever since. He had been tormented by his brother's face in his dreams, his mother's cries in his ears; her cryptic words: *"It should have been me."*

Frankie hadn't been able to sleep much as a result. He had

found comfort in the arms of Nobles's beloved daughter. He knew that the old man would approve, but still felt tormented by the sudden loss of someone who had been so pivotal in sculpting him into the man he had become. And now Steven was gone, too.

Then there was the fact that Baron was in the hospital recovering from his wounds, responsible, in Frankie's eyes at least, for what had happened to Nobles. Frankie hadn't been able to visit Baron. He wasn't ready to make peace with him yet. He was starting to wonder if he ever would.

Gillian took a deep breath, looked him in his weary eyes. "Frankie, I need to ask you something."

He nodded, hoping it wasn't some bullshit.

"In court the other day, they mentioned that you owned Mommy's restaurant. When did that happen? Daddy's will hasn't even been read yet."

Frankie leaned back against the pillows and sighed. This was where he had to hold out on Gillian a little bit. He couldn't tell her everything. Not yet, anyway. There was more he needed to know before he divulged too much about the conversation he had had with Nobles about Conga.

"Your father and I had a conversation the night before he died. He thought something wasn't right. He was pressing me to get Baron to step aside and telling me that he wanted me to take over. Pretty much the same thing we talked about when all of us were together. Only this time, I think he . . . kinda suspected that he had to start hiding his assets. I think he was maybe a little paranoid . . . Anyway, he signed your mother's share of Conga over to me that night. He asked me to keep it quiet. He didn't want anybody to know."

Gillian raised an eyebrow. This was certainly news to her. Her father hadn't mentioned any desire to hide his assets when she was around. And if what Frankie said was true, why had her dad been determined to keep it a secret, even from her?

"Really?" Her voice was at once inquisitive and skeptical.

Frankie knew she had a million questions. "He didn't say why he wanted to hide things and who he was hiding it from," Frankie lied. Doug Nobles had, indeed, shared his suspicions with his heir apparent, but Frankie wasn't ready to divulge all the details of that conversation just yet. "He just made it clear that he knew what he was doing and that he wanted me to keep my mouth shut about it. So I did." He looked at Gillian, saw the pained expression on her face. "I planned to tell you about it after he passed away, but . . ." He gestured with his hands helplessly. "Everything just started going crazy."

She nodded. "I understand." She looked at him seriously. "Does my mother even know about this?" Mayra certainly hadn't mentioned that her husband had stripped her of owning her beloved eatery.

Frankie shook his head.

"Did he know about Baron coming to me for a loan against the restaurant?" She wondered if Frankie had told her father her little secret; that she'd given her brother fifty-five thousand dollars to repay a debt to Jojo—a debt he hadn't bothered to pay back.

Frankie told the truth this time. "No. I never told him about it. You know we put that money back and that was the end of it."

Frankie had discreetly given Gillian the money to pay back Baron's debt and balance out the books at Conga. Then he had set about getting Gillian acclimated with the ins and outs of business with the various sectors of the Nobles family business so that she would be ready to take over. It had become clear to him, and to Doug Nobles, as well, that Baron was a loose cannon who was compromising the family's future.

At first, Frankie had assumed that it was Baron, therefore, who had aroused his father's suspicion and caused him to begin to sign away his assets. But, in fact, it was Mayra—Gillian's mother—whom Doug Nobles had been worried about.

Nobles had sat down with Frankie and told him that he was fearful that Mayra was having an affair, he was beginning to have doubts that she stayed with him out of love alone as his health failed. He had sworn Frankie to secrecy, making him vow on his life that he wouldn't tell another soul for the time being. He asked Frankie to keep an eye on Mayra, especially those days when he'd been confined to a wheelchair most of the time, and sluggish.

Frankie didn't want to tell Gillian these things; didn't want to taint her relationship with her mother until he knew whether or not Nobles was right.

Gillian could tell that there was something Frankie wasn't saying. She knew him better than he thought. She didn't press further, though. She knew that he loved her, that he had loved her father. And she trusted that whatever he wasn't telling her was for her own protection. But her antennas were up.

"Get some sleep. You look like you need it." She smiled at him ever so slightly and it warmed Frankie's heart.

He pulled her close to him and laid his head back against the mound of pillows, shut his eyes. He held her so close that she could smell the scent of the soap on his skin. She kissed him lightly on his stubbly face and watched him fall asleep holding her tightly against his strong body as if he'd never let go.

She missed her father more than ever then. She wished he was still alive, telling her his secrets and his fears the way he'd told them to Frankie.

Emancipation

Misa sat in her mother's living room on Long Island feeling apprehensive. Today would be her first supervised visit with her son, and she felt a thousand emotions at once—joy, excitement, fear, sadness, pain, all mixed up in one overwrought cocktail. Shane was being brought to his grandmother's house by a social worker and Misa was wondering what condition her son would be in today. She hadn't seen him in close to two weeks—one week prior to her arrest and one week since—and she missed him terribly. All she'd had to get by on for the past few days were updates from the social workers assigned to Shane's case. Misa wanted to see him for herself so that she could judge how well her baby was coping with what had happened to him.

She bounced her foot as she sat with her legs crossed, scared to death.

Lily stood across the room near the baby grand piano Camille had given her for Mother's Day. She watched her baby daughter and would have given anything to ease the burden she so obviously bore. Misa had been eerily quiet and contemplative. She'd been spending most of her time sitting in her room, writing in her journal, and speaking on the phone with her attorney about her defense. She wasn't eating much, hadn't talked much. In fact, Misa wasn't doing much of anything except worrying about the meeting that was now about to happen.

The doorbell sounded and Lily noticed Misa jump just a little. Lily walked quickly to the door and said a silent prayer along the way. She came to the door and opened it to find Shane in the arms of a Latina social worker, sucking his thumb and looking meekly at his Gamma. A smile spread across Shane's face when he saw Lily and she returned the gesture.

"Hello," Lily said, as she ushered them inside quickly with the winter wind howling behind them. She noticed that Shane was bundled up and was grateful that her grandson was being well cared for.

Shane allowed her to unzip his snowsuit while the social worker continued to hold him. Misa watched from her seat on the sofa, frozen there. She had seen his familiar smile spread across his face at the sight of his grandmother and it made Misa smile, too. Shane hadn't noticed her yet, and she watched as if captivated by the sight of him. Misa could tell that the social worker, who introduced herself as Ms. Thomas, was trying to slowly reintroduce Shane into the familiar setting. They had chosen Lily's home for today's visit because it was the one location that Shane was familiar with where it was certain that no abuse had taken place. It was important that he feel comfortable and safe.

When he was out of his winter gear and standing hand-in-hand with Lily, she led him toward his mother. Shane froze when he saw Misa sitting on the sofa. She stood to greet him and he turned as if to run back toward the social worker. Lily caught Shane by the hand. She scooped him up in her arms as she saw the frightened expression on his face. None of them could know the horrors the poor child had suffered at the hands of the animal who'd abused him. It was clear that whatever had happened to Shane was something so dreadful that he was tormented by it whenever he looked at his mother.

Misa was only beginning to comprehend the fullness of the damage that had been done to her only child. She felt so unworthy of him. He was better than her, even at his young age. He was pure, undamaged—or at least he had been. She had robbed him of that; it had been her selfishness that had cost her son his innocence. So when Shane clung to his grandmother and didn't face his mother anymore, Misa was fine with that. She felt she deserved it.

The social worker watched, took note that Misa made no move toward her child as he ran from her. She watched as Misa looked at the floor as if too ashamed to look anyone in the eye.

Lily comforted Shane.

"It's okay, baby," she cooed in his ear, soothing him enough to stop his squirming at least. "Shane, say hi to Mommy." Lily didn't dare put him down as he clung to her, his little arms wrapped around her neck like a vise grip.

Misa glanced at them, then at Ms. Thomas. The social worker cleared her throat and spoke to the seemingly fragile young woman before her.

"Try talking to him, Ms. Atkinson," she addressed Misa. "It may take several visits before he begins to feel comfortable around you again."

Misa's facial expression changed drastically. She looked pissed and her brow was furrowed. "I know how to make my son feel comfortable."

Ms. Thomas bit her tongue. She wanted to point out that the opposite was evident, but she kept her mouth shut. Instead, she looked at Shane and nodded.

"Okay, then. Perhaps you can try to talk to him, coax him to interact with you."

Misa sat silent and let the words marinate in her mind.

". . . *coax him to interact with you.*"

She knew it was her fault that her only child, her sweet three-year-old son, needed to be coaxed into interacting with her. She thought of all the times she'd abandoned him, leaving him with Camille or her mother—at times even leaving him with her girlfriends for a few hours—all in an effort to party or to chase after some man. She looked at her son and was ashamed of herself, of her selfishness, and knew that she had been a terrible mother thus far. And the person who'd paid the biggest price for that neglect had been Shane. She was so mad at herself now for having been such a poor mother.

Misa stood slowly and forced herself to walk toward her son. He was still clinging to his grandmother and had his face buried in her neck. Misa stepped in close and rubbed his tiny back soothingly. She felt him tense slightly at her touch, but he didn't cry, didn't turn to face her, either. She spoke to him softly.

"Hey, papa." She looked at her mother and saw the encouraging smile on her face. Lily was willing her daughter to keep trying even though Shane wasn't responding. "Mommy is so glad to see you. I missed you, Shane."

He didn't budge. Instead, he nestled his face in closer to Lily's neck, so close, in fact, that Lily could feel his warm breath rising and falling on her skin.

Ms. Thomas watched like a hawk. "Let's come into the living room," she suggested. Lily nodded and led the way, still cradling her grandson in her arms. Once they got to the large, carpeted living room, Ms. Thomas held up Shane's Backyardigans backpack. "We have some of Shane's favorite toys," she said. "Maybe it will help him relax and unwind if he's able to play freely without pressure." She looked at Misa. "I suggest that your mother and I sit nearby while you and Shane play on the floor with his toys. Hopefully, he will open up with time."

Misa nodded. She hoped that he would come around before their one-hour visit was over that afternoon. She took Shane's backpack from Ms. Thomas and sat down Indian-style on the floor. She unzipped the pack and began pulling out the contents one by one, beginning with his favorite toy car.

Misa pushed it around on the floor and made a *vroom* sound with her mouth as she did so. Shane peeked at her and decided she was having too much of a good time with his toy. He struggled to get down out of his grandmother's arms and Lily placed him gently on the floor. He marched over to his mother and snatched his car out of her hand. Turning away from her, he walked a few feet away. He knelt down and pushed the car around himself.

Misa looked in the direction of Ms. Thomas and her mother. The two women seemed to read each other's minds as they simultaneously headed toward the adjacent dining room.

"Would you like some coffee?" Lily asked.

"Sure," Ms. Thomas agreed. She sat down at the dining room table, watching Misa and Shane as Lily walked off toward the kitchen.

Misa watched her baby playing with the car, glancing every few seconds in her direction to ensure she wasn't coming any closer to him. Misa smiled at him, but Shane didn't smile back. She watched him this way for close to twenty minutes, tried futilely to make conversation.

"I remember the day we bought that car, Shane."

Silence.

"It was the day that I took you to Toys 'R' Us for your birthday and told you that you could get whatever you wanted. And that was the only thing you wanted that day. Do you remember that day, Shane?"

He didn't respond.

Misa reached into the bag and pulled out another toy—this time an action figure. "I remember this toy, too," she said. "Your teacher, Mrs. Falco, gave it to you for Christmas last year."

Again, Shane stomped over and snatched the toy out of his mother's hand before retreating to what he'd established as his turf on the other side of the carpeted room. Misa fought the urge to smile. He was so cute when he was being mean.

She repeated the game they were now playing with each other for several more minutes, pulling a new toy out and telling a memory connected with it. Each time, Shane came over and confiscated his toy. And each time, Misa looked forward to Shane coming close to her and the feeling of his hand brushing against hers as he snatched his toy away.

Ms. Thomas watched and took notes. She saw that Misa was being patient with her son and allowing him to retreat to his own space without pushing him. She noted this and watched as Misa pulled the final toy from the bag. It was a small bag of plastic army men. Misa hadn't bought this for him, and she assumed that it was something Louis had gotten during the past few weeks. She decided to try a different approach this time.

She opened up the plastic bag and emptied the army men out onto the carpet. Lining them up one behind the other, she began to make believe.

In a raspy voice, she said, "Okay, listen up! This is Captain Mommy and I demand that all you soldiers pay attention!"

She maneuvered one army piece so that it faced the others. Shane watched out of the corner of his eye while keeping a firm grip on the toys he'd already repossessed.

Misa saw that she had his attention as she continued. "I have a big job for you today! Today, we're going to be protecting someone very important. And that person . . ." Misa paused for added effect, "is Shane!"

Shane seemed to be trying hard not to look interested. Ms. Thomas had to suppress a smile as she watched the adorable little boy giving his mother a sidelong glance.

Misa dragged the plastic piece she'd christened Captain Mommy back and forth across the carpet in front of the other pieces, creating the illusion that the captain was pacing in front of his troops. "Lieutenant Grandma, step forward!"

Misa pulled one of the other pieces forward to face Captain Mommy and changed her voice to a higher pitch. "Yes, Captain?"

In her Captain Mommy voice, she addressed Lieutenant Grandma. "I need you to make sure that Shane has all of the hugs and kisses he needs."

The Grandma piece agreed and then fell back into formation.

Next Captain Mommy summoned Corporal Aunt Camille forward, and instructed her to give Shane all the yummy snacks he could ask for. Finally, Deputy Daddy was told to make sure that he tucked Shane in at night, to make sure that the boogie man didn't come anywhere near Shane.

Misa peeked at Shane and saw that he was staring directly at her now. He was swept up in the story so completely that for a moment he stopped seeing her as the person who delivered him up to the boogie man, and saw Mommy—Captain Mommy to be exact.

She looked at Shane and finished her story. "And Captain Mommy's job is to love Shane and to tell Shane that she's so sorry for ever leaving him behind." Her voice cracked and she felt emotional.

His eyes locked with hers and she got teary. "Come here, papa."

Shane hesitated, and in that second Misa held her breath. Then he stood, his superhero action figure clutched tightly in one hand, and went to his mother. Misa pulled him into a tight embrace and sniffed in his scent, baby lotion and powder. Her tears finally fell and she hugged him, rocking him gently in her arms as she knelt on the floor. Lily watched from the dining room, her gaze alternating between the heartrending scene and the social worker diligently taking notes.

Ms. Thomas glanced at her watch and cleared her throat again. Lily was beginning to realize that clearing her throat was a signal that she was about to speak up.

"I'm afraid our time is up today," Ms. Thomas said softly. "But it appears that we've made fast progress."

Misa seemed not to have heard her. Her eyes blissfully closed, she was hugging Shane close to her and rocking him in her arms. He clung to his mother, sensing her joy. Misa kissed his face and held it gently in her hands, his cheeks pushed together in the most adorable way. She smiled at Shane and, to her utter amazement, he smiled back.

"Ms. Atkinson, we're going to need to get going now."

Misa ignored the social worker's prodding and Lily softly

beseeched Ms. Thomas for just five more minutes. Begrudg-
ingly, she acquiesced.

Misa was speaking quietly to her son. "Mommy loves
you, Shane. Remember that. I love you, and I'm coming back
for you very soon. Ms. Thomas is going to take you back to
Daddy and he's going to make sure that you're okay, just like
I told you." She kissed him again, hugged him. "And I'll see
you soon."

"Bye, Mommy," Shane said softly.

Misa smiled, her heart breaking just a little, and watched
as Ms. Thomas led her son away. By the time Shane had his
winter gear on and was being carried off to the car, Misa's
smile had given way to tears. But they were happy, hopeful
tears this time. And she knew, as she fell into her mother's
arms and was comforted, that she had done the right thing
after all. She'd kill Steven all over again if she could. Now,
more than ever, Misa was determined to fight tooth and nail
for her freedom so that she could get down to the business of
rebuilding her relationship with her son.

Toya sat in the booth at Junior's and waited, tapping her finger-
nails on the table impatiently. It was two-forty in the afternoon, which made her twenty minutes early for her meeting
with her father. With every second that elapsed, she second-
guessed herself.

"What the fuck am I doing here?" she wondered aloud,
ignoring the questioning glance from a passing waiter. She
sighed, closed her eyes, and told herself to calm down. This
would be the first time she was seeing her father since the night
he'd broken into her house. Since then, a combination of her
own conscience and the prodding of her brothers and her

friends had given her the push she needed to call Nate. It had been an awkward telephone conversation, and Toya had paced the floor nervously as she spoke, finally ending the call by setting up a lunch meeting with him for the next day. And now here she was, dressed in all black as if Nate's funeral were about to commence, and second-guessing herself.

He arrived fifteen minutes early, only to find that Toya was already there. An involuntary smile crept across his aging face as he walked toward her table. Toya couldn't help noticing that his walk was still the same, that old gangster diddy-bop she remembered watching as a child. He came to the booth and stood there for a moment, towering over her, smiling. She looked up at him expectantly and his smile broadened.

"Hey, baby girl. Good to see you."

Toya nodded, shuddered a bit, and gestured at the seat across from her. Nate slid into the booth and clasped his hands together on top of the table. Silence fell between them as Nate took in the features of his only daughter's face—her eyes that looked just like his own, her nose and mouth that were identical to her mother's, and her cocoa skin. Toya cleared her throat and was happy for the distraction when the waiter came to take their orders.

Once he did so, the waiter left and Nate leaned forward in the direction of his daughter. "I know it wasn't easy for you to make that call to me, Latoya." Nate was staring at her in a way that told her he was sincere. "I want to thank you for agreeing to meet with me today."

Toya detected a hint of sadness in his eyes. Gone was the mean, menacing, boisterous drunk who had bullied her family for years. In his place sat a frail old man with fear in his eyes—fear of his own impending death.

Toya looked at her father unflinchingly. "I want you to

say everything that you need to say today. This is the last time
I plan to meet you, the last time I plan to even talk to you. So
this is your chance to let it all out." She sipped her water, set
the glass back down and stared at him. "We got interrupted
last time. So now I'm listening."

Nate looked at her, disappointed. He had hoped that
when she called it was a signal that she was ready to forgive
him. Apparently, that wasn't the case.

"I know I already said it, but I want you to know how
sorry I am for the way I was . . . I realize how bad it was
growing up with me as your father."

Toya nodded. It had been terrible.

"I don't know if this means anything to you, but I'm real
proud of you. I remember when you were in high school and
all the boys were checking you out." Nate smiled, as if at some
long-ago memory. "I used to tell you that all they wanted from
you was sex, and I probably went about it all wrong." He shook
his head. "But my intentions were good. I didn't want you being just another dumb broad out there in them streets, giving it
up so easy when you're worth more than that. I didn't want
you to end up with a whole bunch of kids by some no-good
nigga, or sitting around waiting for a welfare check. So I said
some mean things and from time to time I may have even embarrassed you." Nate saw her eyes water a little. "But I just
wanted you to be better than all them other girls out there;
wanted you to be smarter, stronger than them." He looked at
his daughter and smiled. "And you are."

The waiter brought their food and Nate watched as Toya
discreetly dabbed at her eyes with her napkin before spread-
ing it across her lap. She wasn't sure why she was crying. A
combination of emotions were barraging her—anger, frustra-

tion, and surprisingly, sadness. When the waiter was gone, Toya dug in to her salad while Nate sliced his T-bone steak and watched her.

"Look at you," he said, smiling proudly. "You got your own real estate business, that big ol' brownstone in Brooklyn. You got a beautiful car parked outside, diamonds on your fingers . . . you seem like you're doing all right."

Toya nodded. She had done well for herself, and she knew it. "Thanks," she managed.

Nate chewed on his steak. "I can't help noticing that you're single. No kids. What's up with that?" Nate asked. He wondered if he was to blame for that. He had instilled so much toughness in Toya that he hoped he hadn't poisoned her mind about love in general. His warnings about men and their ulterior motives may have caused her to run from love and from commitment.

Toya frowned. She didn't really appreciate him questioning her. After all, what gave him the right? But she found herself answering him anyway. "Ain't nothing up with that. I don't want any kids. Don't want to disappoint them." She shoved a forkful of salad in her mouth and watched her father chew on what she'd just said.

Nate didn't miss her barb. He nodded. "I bet you'd be a great mother, and a great wife, too."

Toya rolled her eyes. She didn't want to talk about this, not here and definitely not now.

"What ever happened to that guy you married?" he asked.

Toya nearly spit her Pellegrino all over the table. Nate noticed her reaction and knew that he'd hit a nerve.

"I mean I know he got sent to—"

"I don't want to talk about him," she said flatly. "Move on."

He nodded. "Okay, then." He took a sip of his drink. "Just tell me how you managed to land on your feet after all of that."

Toya glared at her father across the table and bit her lip. She wanted to say that she had survived it all on her own, with no assistance from the bitch nigga that sat across from her now. But she didn't say that. Instead, she looked away, took a deep breath and met her father's gaze again. "I just did. I'm a tough bitch."

Nate smiled, slowly nodded his head. "Yes, Latoya. Yes, you are."

She went back to her salad and Nate watched her, still smiling, before he resumed his meal, as well. After eating in silence for a while, Toya looked at her father questioningly.

"So what do you want from me?"

Nate seemed caught off guard. He stopped mid-chew and looked at his daughter.

"What do you mean?"

"You swoop back into my life after all these years, say all the things you needed to get off your chest and . . . now what?" Toya asked, gesturing with her fork. "What is it that you want from me now? A bone marrow transplant? Some money? What?"

Nate wiped his mouth with his napkin, set it on the table and sat back in his seat. He looked at Toya and shook his head. "I don't want none of that. All I want from you—from your brothers and your mother, too—is your forgiveness." His eyes narrowed slightly. "If you can find it in your heart to forgive me for all the shit I did—all the things I know you saw growing up—I could die a happy man." He shrugged then, looked down at his hands. "Maybe you feel like I deserve to die as miserable as I made y'all all those years," he said. "And I can't blame you if you feel like that."

Toya felt hot tears flood her eyes and she looked away, but not before a couple rolled down her cheek. Nate noticed and leaned forward and wiped her eyes, relieved that she didn't recoil. At that moment, some icy part of Toya's cold heart melted. She looked at her father and the hate that had been so evident in her eyes had gone away. Now, as he looked at Toya, Nate saw her for who she once was—a little girl longing for her father's strong hand to wipe away her tears. He smiled at her, hoping that it wasn't too late after all.

Something about seeing her father smiling at her made Toya's insides churn. Instantly, she tensed up and the serene expression on her face morphed into a grimace as she recoiled. He didn't deserve to smile, didn't deserve even a shred of happiness after the years of hurt he'd caused her. She pulled away and sat as far back in her seat as possible. Nate's hand still hung in the air where it had graced her cheek only moments ago, and he felt spurned. His smile faded as he suspected that his glimpse of Toya's soft side had been short-lived.

"You shouldn't die a happy man," she said coldly. "What happiness have you brought to my life? Huh? Did you ever wipe my tears when I was a little girl falling off my bike? Or were you too fuckin' drunk and high to notice? Did you ever tell me that you were proud of me when I was growing up and I needed to hear that shit? Did you ever do anything to build me up? Or were you so busy beating me down that you didn't have time?"

Several patrons were staring at them, whispering among themselves, and Nate was embarrassed. Still, he kept his cool knowing that everything Toya said was right.

She wasn't done yet. "You know what?" she asked rhetorically. "You might be right. You might be the reason I'm so tough. Shit, I've been fighting you since I was about twelve years old so I should be tough. Defending myself when your drunken, abusive ass would come home starting shit. You can take credit for that. But take credit for the rest of the shit, too. You're the reason your youngest son went to jail. You're the reason the other three can't get through one day without a fuckin' drink. It's your fault that we lost the house we grew up in. And you're the only one to blame for the fact that you're dying alone and miserable."

"Is everything all right?" the waiter asked. Neither Toya nor her father had noticed him approaching the table during her tirade.

"Everything is fine," Nate fibbed, forcing a smile at the young man. Satisfied that the yelling was over, the waiter retreated.

"Latoya," Nate said, his tone low and steady. "You're right about everything you said. I can't argue with the truth."

Toya sucked her teeth. In her opinion, this new improved Nathaniel Blake was a phony. This was all part of some new con that he had cooked up to get sympathy from his family, she thought. She snatched her napkin off her lap and tossed it on the tabletop. She had lost her appetite.

"I have a meeting to get to," she lied. "Are you done?"

Nate leaned toward her anxiously. He didn't want this to be the last conversation he would have with her. "Latoya, I love you," he said.

Her jaw clenched involuntarily. "Is that it?"

"I would like it if you would keep in touch with me. I don't expect things to be perfect overnight. But you can call me from time to time. Maybe we can try to fix our relationship. Start over."

Toya reached for her purse and cursed herself for feeling a twinge of sympathy. "Good luck finding a donor," she said halfheartedly. She stood up and walked out, leaving Nate staring after her.

As she climbed into her car and drove back home, she knew that even if she never saw her father again, she had gotten closure. She felt relieved and perhaps a little drained as she pulled up in front of her brownstone.

As soon as her heels hit the pavement, she saw Russell coming across the street in her direction and sighed. This ogre sure didn't let up.

He strolled up to her with that same hideous smile on his face and said, "Hey, I'm sure you're gonna say no, but I wanted to come and ask you to come out and have a drink with me tonight. Nothing serious, no strings attached, just—"

"Fine!" she interrupted him, too broken down after the emotionally draining day she'd had to put up a fight. "Let's go."

Russell was clearly caught off guard, but recovered quickly as he happily led Toya off toward his car. The smile on his face spread wider and he silently thanked the Lord that this was clearly his lucky day.

In a restaurant across town, Dominique sat with Octavia and waited as the waitress refilled their water glasses. She'd taken a leave of absence from her job in order to tend to Octavia's situation and had signed Octavia out of school, having her assignments forwarded each day from her teachers. Everyone was relieved that Octavia had come home and in the three days since then, a lot had changed. Dominique had taken Octavia to a gynecologist, who confirmed their worst fears—Octavia was six weeks pregnant. Once they knew for sure, Dominique had contacted Dashawn's mother, Dee Dee. Almost as soon as the conversation between the two women began, Dominique could tell what kind of person Dee Dee was. Her voice, her ebonics-laden language, and her incessant gum chewing all screamed HOOD RAT! It had come as no surprise when Dee Dee reiterated her assertion that the best thing Octavia could do was to "get rid of it."

Since then, Dominique had been spending all her time talking to her daughter about the situation at hand. Today was no different.

The waitress walked away and Octavia looked at her mother. "I think I've made up my mind," she said.

Dominique stirred some sugar into her coffee and met her daughter's gaze. "About the baby?" she asked, realizing immediately that it was a stupid question. Of course it was about the baby. Everything was about the baby at this point.

Octavia nodded. She toyed with the salt shaker absentmindedly. "I'm going to have an abortion."

Dominique took a deep breath, blew it out, and looked at her child. "What made you come to that decision?"

Octavia shrugged, stared at the table. "For one thing, I'm mad young."

Dominique smiled slightly at her daughter's use of slang. That sentence alone illustrated Octavia's point exactly. She nodded and Octavia continued.

"I'm only in the ninth grade and I have my whole life ahead of me. Plus Dashawn doesn't want a kid right now." Dominique noticed the dejected expression on Octavia's face as she said that. "This is just not the right time to bring a kid into the world."

Dominique was relieved. After the pregnancy was confirmed, she had said all the things to Octavia that she knew she needed to say. She had told her daughter that she loved her, that she would stand by her side no matter what decision she made. She told Octavia that if she kept the baby, they would make it work, that life wasn't over just because she'd made a mistake. And she'd also told her that if she chose to have an abortion or to put the child up for adoption, she would stand right by her side from start to finish. But the truth was, Dominique was not ready to be a grandmother. And although she had been a teen parent herself, she did not want the same for her daughter. She let out a silent sigh and squeezed Octavia's hand across the table.

"I think you're making the right decision," she said honestly. "But I want you to be sure. Once you do it, there's no turning back and I don't want you having any regrets when everything is said and done."

Octavia nodded. "I'm sure about this," she said. "It's all I've been thinking about." She looked at Dominique. "Ma, I want to tell you that I'm sorry about everything."

Dominique waved her hand as if to dismiss her apology, but Octavia kept going.

"I knew better than to sneak around behind your back . . . I was just in such a rush to be grown. I wanted to be able to go on dates and to have a boyfriend and I just wouldn't take no for an answer. I always thought that I would come and talk to you before I started having sex, but for some reason . . . I just couldn't. I didn't think I would get pregnant and I was dumb enough to believe Dashawn when he said that he would take care of me." A tear fell from Octavia's eye but she quickly wiped it away and kept talking. "I was dumb. And I got myself into all this trouble, had you worried about me for so many days. I'm sorry, Ma. From now on, I swear I'll talk to you about everything." Octavia felt like an idiot. She was ashamed of herself and embarrassed that the boy she'd given her heart to had played her. It was over between her and Dashawn. He didn't want her, didn't want their baby. Octavia just wanted the whole nightmare to be over.

Dominique smiled, patted her daughter's hand, and felt her heart fill with pride. True, her daughter had made a huge mistake. But she had learned from it and Dominique believed that this would be the start of a new beginning for them.

"Well," she said. "I think I owe you an apology, too."

Octavia frowned slightly.

"I've been so preoccupied with work, with Jamel, and with mourning Daddy's loss that I've neglected you. I'm hardly ever at home. And even when I am, there's always a letter to write to Jamel, a phone call to accept, or a visit to go on." Dominique shook her head, ashamed of herself. She was relieved that Jamel was coming home in a matter of days and prayed that his return to civilization would mean a return to some normalcy in her life for once. "Def Jam is working me harder than ever and I've been so busy with all of those things, that you've been practically raising yourself. So, I'm sorry, too."

It was Octavia's turn to smile. They finished their meal and ordered dessert, switching topics to lighten the mood. The next morning, Dominique scheduled an appointment for Octavia to have an abortion. She only bristled slightly when the receptionist scheduled the procedure for Monday, January 21. It was the same day that Jamel was being released from prison. Dominique shook it off and proceeded to schedule the appointment for ten o'clock that morning. Jamel would have to understand that, for once, she was putting her daughter first.

She hadn't spoken to Archie since Octavia had come home. She really wasn't sure what to say. True, he had made love to her in a way that no other man ever had. But, her heart still belonged to Jamel. She loved Jamel, wanted a future with him. And now that he was coming home, she had to decide whether or not to tell him about her indiscretion. She was battling within herself every time Jamel called, and she knew that seeing him face-to-face once he came home would only make it harder. Maybe it wasn't such a bad thing that Dominique wouldn't get to see him on his first day home.

On the morning of Octavia's procedure, she was awake long before her mother. She had barely been able to sleep because of her nervousness. She wasn't sure what to expect, and wondered if the abortion would hurt, if it would leave a scar, if she would feel any different afterward. By the time she and her mother had gotten dressed and piled into the car, Octavia was a bundle of nerves.

Dominique looked over at her daughter shaking in the passenger seat and gently pinched her cheek. "There's nothing to be afraid of," she said, as if reading Octavia's mind. "Everything's gonna be just fine."

Octavia wasn't sure why, but hearing her mother say those words and having her look at her so reassuringly was all that it took to put her at ease. They drove off toward the hospital, hand in hand.

Jamel stepped out of the prison without a guard escorting him and without the burden of any restraints and felt free at last. For three long years he had been treated like an animal and now that was all behind him. As he boarded the bus bound for New York City, he thought about Dominique. He couldn't help feeling disappointed that she was unable to be there to greet him on his first day as a free man. He understood that she had to accompany her daughter to her procedure, but it still felt bittersweet to be going home to no fanfare. He took a seat near a window and settled in for the long ride back to the city from the mountainous upstate region where the prison was located. He told himself not to dwell on Dominique's absence. He would see her soon enough, and in the meantime, he was free. Nothing felt better than that.

Suicidal Thoughts

Camille stood precariously on the edge of the roof and looked down. The ground seemed so far away, the tops of the trees swaying beneath her. She hated that this was the only option, but she had no choice. There was no way she could live like this anymore. Her mind was reeling. A driving rain was falling, and she lost her footing and slipped off the edge of the roof on which she stood. In that instant, she knew that she was making a mistake. She wasn't ready to die. It didn't matter, though. The damage had been done and she was falling, falling fast toward the earth and the ground was getting closer and closer by the second. A bloodcurdling scream escaped her lips as she braced for impact.

With a gasp, Camille woke up from her nightmare and felt her heart thundering in her chest. She breathlessly looked around the room at her belongings, feeling sweat forming on her forehead. She was alive, and it had all been a bad dream.

Well, not all of it. She was still pregnant with a child her husband had never wanted, still living in a palatial estate that doubled as a murder scene, still alone, broke, and afraid. She shut her eyes and took a deep breath, and rubbed her pregnant belly comfortingly. She smiled a little then, realizing that this was something she'd started doing lately—stroking her stomach this way, aware that there was a life growing within the safety of her womb. Whether Frankie was happy about it or not, they were going to be parents.

She felt her anger bubbling at the surface whenever she thought of her husband lately. The hurt she'd initially felt had given way to rage, which Camille had never known before. Frankie still hadn't been in touch with her, and was still depositing only enough into their joint bank account to keep the mortgage paid. There was not a penny left over for her to put gas in her expensive cars or to buy food, for that matter. Camille had resorted to borrowing money from her mother—an odd situation since it was Camille who usually paid all her mother's living expenses prior to Misa's arrest. It had been that way since the beginning of their marriage. Frankie and Camille both agreed that their mothers' bills would be taken care of out of the household expenditures each month, and so it had gone for years.

Thankfully, Lily had stored up her own money over the years and was able to maintain her quality of life now that Camille and Frankie were on the outs. But that didn't matter to Camille. She was pissed. The nightmare she'd just awakened from was the final straw. She had a right to live comfortably. She was Frankie Bingham's wife, and it seemed he needed a reminder. So, she climbed out of bed, threw on some jeans and a sweater and headed out the door at just after 2:00 A.M. to remind her husband just who the fuck she was.

Gillian was asleep, wrapped securely in Frankie's arms, when the doorbell started ringing incessantly. She was startled by the noise and so was Frankie apparently, as he jerked awake. Both of them scrambled out of bed and started off in the direction of the front door. Gillian peeked out the front window, half expecting to see the police or one of the family goons. When she saw who it was, her body stiffened. She looked at Frankie and he could see an instant change in her demeanor, from fear and anxiety to pure annoyance.

"It's Camille."

Frankie's heart sank. He knew it was inevitable that this would happen. He hadn't spoken to Camille since the night his brother was killed and he had been avoiding her at all costs. At the advice of his lawyer, he was still providing for her household expenses—and that was *all* he was doing. He had deposited the bare minimum into their joint account. Then he had withdrawn all the money in all the other accounts Camille knew about, and closed them for good measure. He knew he'd been playing hardball. But what the hell did she expect when her own sister was to blame for Steven's death?

Frankie took a deep breath as Camille continued to press the doorbell. He looked at Gillian and rolled his eyes, then reluctantly opened the door.

Camille stood there in the cold of the night with her mink bomber jacket zipped up to her neck. As she spoke, the cold air was visible as it escaped her mouth.

"Frankie, enough is enough. I've been calling you for days. No answer. I have no money and nowhere else to turn." Camille shook her head in frustration. "So, something's gotta give."

Frankie looked at his wife standing before him and felt a slight twinge of guilt. After all, Camille hadn't done anything wrong. It was her sister, Misa, who had murdered Steven. Camille was pregnant and it was freezing outside. He didn't object as she stepped into the house, seeking refuge from the bitter cold. He wasn't heartless, after all.

Gillian, however, was outraged. "Camille, I understand that you want to talk to Frankie," she said, as she watched Camille stroll into her home as if she belonged there. "But this is the second time you've come to my house uninvited, and I'm not comfortable with that."

Camille laughed slightly. "*You're* not comfortable, Gillian?" Camille shook her head. "Well, I'm so sorry to hear that. How 'bout I'm not comfortable with you over here fucking my husband?"

"Listen, Camille—" Frankie began.

"Your *husband*," Gillian interrupted with a hint of a smirk on her pretty face, "can call you later to talk to you. For now, why don't you go home and call it a night?"

Camille picked up a nearby vase and tossed it at Gillian's head with all her might. Narrowly missing its target, the Mikasa crystal piece hit the wall behind Gillian and shattered into a thousand pieces. Gillian cried out and ducked.

"Camille!" Frankie yelled her name this time, and rushed toward her before she could pick up anything else.

"I didn't come here to talk to *you*, bitch!" Camille unzipped her jacket and stepped closer to Gillian. Gone was the demure seen-and-not-heard Camille Bingham. She was a woman scorned and hell hath no fury . . . "Go sit the fuck down and be quiet!"

"Bitch?" Gillian frowned, looking from Camille to the glass at her feet and back again. It was clear that Gillian was piecing together the fact that Camille had officially lost her mind. "Do you know who the fuck I am?"

"Yeah," Camille said, her index finger pointed directly in the face of her husband's mistress. "*Bitch!*" Frankie was

holding her back and preventing her from getting close
enough to hit Gillian.

Gillian seemed as if she couldn't believe what was happening. "Don't make me fuck you up, Camille!"

Frankie looked like he had absolutely no control over the
situation at hand. Both women were furious. Calmly and in a
low voice, he spoke firmly to his wife.

"Camille, you can't come in here like this. Go home. I'll
call you in a little while."

But Camille wasn't trying to hear that. "Yeah, right.
Frankie, I'm here *now*. Talk to me now."

"I'm gonna ask you one more time to get out of my house
before I call the cops, Camille," Gillian said, her chest heaving with rage.

"Fuck you!" Camille was furious and Gillian's threat fell
on deaf ears.

Frankie blamed himself for this. He had seen the dozens
of missed calls from Camille over the past few weeks. He had
known that he was only prolonging the inevitable by ignoring her. But he had never expected Camille to come out of her
character the way she was now. He wanted to protest as Gillian made a beeline for the telephone. In their business, the
last thing they normally did was involve the police. But he
knew that if he protested, Gillian would think he was defending Camille.

Camille ignored the fact that Gillian had stomped into the
bedroom to get her phone and was apparently dialing 911.
She turned her attention to Frankie again. "I need money,"
she said. "The bills are paid, but I have nothing left to eat
with, no money for gas or for—"

"Here, Camille!" With the phone cradled between her ear
and her shoulder, Gillian emerged from her bedroom,

snatched her purse off the coffee table and pulled out a wad of cash. She tossed the bills in the direction of Frankie's unwanted wife. "Take it. And go home and wait for Frankie to call you tomorrow."

Camille couldn't believe her eyes. Was this bitch treating her like a charity case? She charged toward Gillian prepared to kill the whore with her bare hands. But Frankie stopped her, restraining her as she struggled to break free. "Don't throw money at me like I'm some fuckin' bum on the street. I'm not asking *you* for shit! I'm not even fuckin' talking to you. Mind your business!"

"This *is* my business, sweetie. It's my house."

"And this is my husband," Camille reminded her.

"Yes, I do have an emergency," Gillian spoke into the telephone. "The address is—"

"Go ahead and call 'em," Camille said. " 'Cuz I ain't going nowhere."

Frankie looked torn. There was no way for him to put an end to this amicably. The face-off he had been hoping to avoid was now upon him.

Gillian continued her conversation with the 911 operator. But she couldn't help thinking that Frankie was acting like a real pussy right now. She didn't understand why he hadn't kicked Camille the fuck out already. The bitch had barged into Gillian's house, cursed at her, and aimed a very heavy object at her head. Gillian paced the floor, thinking Frankie was lucky she hadn't murdered his little Stepford wife yet. She watched him struggling with himself about what to do next, how to defuse the situation. And Gillian couldn't help losing the slightest bit of respect for Frankie.

Camille's voice rose. "I can't believe you, Frankie," Camille said, shaking her head in amazement. "What kind of man are you? If someone had told me a year ago that we would be standing here . . . I wouldn't have believed that you would be so coldhearted and cruel as you've been lately. I know you don't love me anymore. I'm coming to terms with that. But I'm still your wife. I'm carrying your child in my womb. There's years of history between us . . . yet you can sit back and watch me suffer? You can sleep at night knowing that you cut me off from all the money, knowing that I'm pregnant and that my whole life has been turned upside down?"

"Well," he said softly, "you're not the only one whose life was turned upside down."

She nodded. "I know. But it's not *my* fault, Frankie. I feel like you're blaming me for what Misa did. I don't know if Steven did what she thinks he did. What I do know is that *somebody* was molesting Shane. So whether she was wrong or right about Steven, Misa is devastated by what was done to her son."

Frankie's jaw clenched. "That didn't give her a right to kill my brother."

Camille shook her head. "Maybe not. But that has nothing to do with me and you."

"Don't it?" Frankie asked incredulously. "I mean she is your sister."

"So what? You think that by hurting me, neglecting and ignoring me, that you're somehow punishing Misa? She's already going through hell with what happened to her son. Her only priority right now is Shane."

"Well, it seems kinda funny that you're coming to me for money, but you somehow found the money to bail her out."

Camille had wondered when he would bring that up. She knew that Frankie would wonder where she'd gotten that money from.

"You found hundreds of thousands of dollars for bail and

for that high-priced lawyer she got, but you can't gas up your Range?" Frankie had a confused expression on his face and Camille noticed Gillian smirking. She wanted to scratch that bitch's eyes out.

"Mama is paying for Misa's attorney."

"Yeah right!" Frankie scoffed. He knew all too well that Lily couldn't possibly have the money it took to bail Misa out, let alone to pay Teresa Rourke's exorbitant hourly fee.

"And we bailed Misa out with every penny we managed to scrape together. It wasn't easy, but we managed to do it. So don't go thinking I've been hoarding cash all these years because I wasn't. Obviously I should have been!" She held her arms out helplessly. "But I wasn't. I trusted that you would never leave me with nothing. Whether you want to be with me or not, I'm still the woman you married. And what about the baby? You haven't even mentioned the fact that you're gonna be a father!"

He shook his head. "How am I supposed to feel, Camille?" he asked seriously. Gillian had hung up the phone, having been assured that the police were on their way, and was standing nearby with her arms folded across her chest, hanging on his every word. "Am I supposed to be happy about a baby when I told you over and over again that I wasn't ready to be a father? Our marriage is basically over and you expect me to be overjoyed that you're pregnant? I'm not!"

Camille winced a little hearing him say that, especially in front of Gillian. "Well, whether you're overjoyed or not, there's still a baby. And not talking about it isn't going to make it go away."

"I know that," Frankie acknowledged. "So, let me talk to my lawyer and find out how much I should be giving you every month until—"

"Fuck that, Frankie!" Camille was outraged. "We don't need lawyers to tell us how to deal with each other. I'm your *wife*! You give me what you know I deserve and let's settle this like adults. You're treating me like a fuckin' stranger."

"It's not that simple anymore." Frankie looked at the floor.

"Why not?"

He looked at his wife as if she were blind to what was going on all around them. "Because, Camille . . . my brother is dead. Your sister killed him." Frankie shook his head. "Even before that, I told you I wanted out. I told you that it was over."

Camille cocked her head to the side. "Ohhhhh, I see," she said, nodding slowly. "So you think that because you want out of our marriage, and because of what Misa did, you're no longer responsible for me or for the baby I'm carrying? Does that even make sense to you?" Camille laughed, but she was far from amused. She was so hurt that her heart felt like it would burst inside her chest. "You let this bitch brainwash you into cutting me off because it makes her feel good. It makes her happy watching you ignore me and avoid me and you're such a fucking coward that you're letting her manipulate you."

"Ain't nobody manipulating me, Camille." Frankie shook his head. "And I already told you that I'll call you tomorrow so we can talk about the money. What you need to do now is—"

"Wait, let me guess. Go home and wait for your imaginary phone call?" Camille gave him a look that told him this wasn't a possibility.

The doorbell rang and Gillian stormed over to it and happily ushered two uniformed police officers inside.

Camille stood silently as Gillian explained the situation at hand.

"I've asked this woman to leave my house more than once. She came over here uninvited—"

"I came to talk to my husband, not to cause any trouble, sir," Camille addressed the younger black officer directly. She noticed that his Puerto Rican partner was busy ogling Gillian.

The black cop looked at Frankie. "Is this your wife?"

Frankie nodded and watched as both officers assessed the situation. Clearly, Gillian and Frankie had been in bed together as evidenced by their pajamas and the late hour. If Camille was this man's wife, it was obvious why they'd been called.

Gillian could see that they were beginning to take pity on Camille by the change in the police's facial expressions. "She barged in here and threw a fucking vase at my head after I asked her to leave."

The Puerto Rican cop walked over and observed the shattered glass on the floor. He looked at Camille and shook his head. "Did you do this?"

Camille looked at Frankie to see if he would intervene. Thankfully, he did.

"She was upset," Frankie explained. "I don't think she was trying to hit anybody with it."

Camille had to suppress a smile as she saw Gillian shoot a treacherous glance in Frankie's direction. Clearly, she was not happy hearing him defend his wife.

Frankie cleared his throat. "But I told her that I'm gonna call her tomorrow to talk to her and she should go home." He looked at Camille. He still wanted her gone, but he sure didn't want to see her hauled off to jail.

She shook her head. She knew that Frankie wouldn't be calling to talk about anything tomorrow. Tears gathered in her eyes and threatened to pour forth, so she squeezed her eyes shut and turned away from Frankie and his concubine. She didn't want to give them the pleasure of seeing her cry yet again.

While his partner spoke with Gillian and Frankie in hushed tones about the events of the evening, the black officer approached Camille and touched her softly on her shoulder.

"Ma'am, I can see what's going on here and I know you must be upset," he said. "But this is this woman's house and you can't just refuse to leave. She can have you arrested for trespassing and I know you don't want to give her that satisfaction."

It was as if he was reading her mind and Camille wiped her eyes and looked at him. Glancing at his uniform, she saw that his last name was King. She appreciated the fact that he was being so kind to her. Especially since his partner seemed so enamored with her nemesis.

"I just wanted my husband to talk to me, that's all. It's been weeks and I've been calling him for money, calling him to talk about what's going on . . ." Camille looked at the floor and shook her head. It was pointless. She let out a deep sigh. Making eye contact with Officer King once more, she shrugged. "But I guess I can't force him to be a real man." She zipped up her jacket and smoothed her hair down. "I'll leave."

Officer King felt sorry for the pretty lady with the cute fur jacket who stood before him. She looked so hurt and so disappointed by what was going on and he noticed that her so-called husband seemed especially cold toward her. Frankie stood across the room with Gillian looking like all he wanted was for Camille to be gone.

Camille stole one last glance at her husband as she headed for the door. Frankie met her gaze and felt a tug on his conscience. But then he thought of his brother, thought of Misa and what she had done, and remembered that Camille was on her side. He looked away as Officer King followed Camille out of Gillian's house and into the bitter night cold.

While Gillian thanked his partner, Officer King watched as Camille dejectedly descended the stairs and climbed behind the wheel of her truck. As she pulled away from the curb, he watched her wipe her eyes, the tears no longer kept at bay.

Painful Truths

Dominique put the last of the dinner dishes away and poured herself a glass of wine. The past twenty-four hours had been very trying. She had accompanied her teenaged daughter to have an abortion and then sat up with her for most of the night talking like schoolgirls. Truthfully, Octavia had been having trouble sleeping, believing that nightmares would plague her as a punishment for what she'd done. She didn't regret having the abortion, since she knew she wasn't ready to be a mother. But she still felt guilty for having gotten pregnant in the first place and now felt as if she had a permanent stain on her, for which she would someday have to answer to God. Her conscience troubled her, so it had come as a welcome distraction when her mother had crawled into bed with her and chatted for hours about everything and nothing at the same time.

Dominique had been equally as anxious for conversation that night. It was Jamel's first day home as a free man, and Dominique had not seen him at all. When she and Octavia had returned home from the procedure, Dominique had been happy to hear Jamel's voice on the answering machine announcing that he had landed in the concrete jungle safely.

"Hey, baby! I'm home! I just wanted to call you and let you know that I made it and that I love you. Feels good to be a free man. I hope everything goes well for you and your princess today. I'll call you tonight to hear that sexy voice of yours. Mwah!"

Jamel had sealed his voice mail with a kiss and it had made Dominique smile. That smile had faded now, as more than twenty-four hours had passed since that message and she hadn't heard a peep from Jamel since.

She was worried about him, wondering if he was hurt or if he was in trouble. She had expected to hear from him by now and was doing her best not to suspect the worst.

Octavia was in her room listening to sad love songs, while Dominique took comfort in the bottom of a wineglass. The doorbell ringing brought both ladies scampering toward the front door at the same time, eager for a distraction from their thoughts.

"Surprise!" Toya sang, as Dominique swung the door open. By now, Rafael the doorman was familiar with Toya from her previous visits and she had explained that this was a surprise girls' night in for her friend. Toya had slipped him a twenty and he looked the other way as they headed upstairs unannounced. She strolled into Dominique's apartment now as if she owned the place. Camille and Misa filed in after Toya and Dominique couldn't stop smiling. This was the first time that all four of them had been together since Misa's arrest.

Toya took one look at the wine in Dominique's hand and shook her head. Taking the glass from her hand, she replaced it with a pint of Rémy. "We're going *in* tonight! All of us need it. Hell, even Octavia might need a little sip, you feel me?"

Dominique started to protest, but noticed that Toya was laughing. She watched as her friends poured into her home and began unloading food and drinks for their planned slumber party.

Camille explained: "I needed to get away from Staten Island for a little while, and Misa can't take another minute of Mama." The girls laughed, all knowing that spending any length of time with one's mother could drive a person insane. "So, Toya suggested that we all crash over here tonight."

"I knew that if we invited you to my house, you would have said no. You wouldn't want to leave Octavia at home all alone. So here we are." Toya kicked off her shoes and went to the kitchen to get some ice.

Dominique couldn't have been happier. "I'm glad you guys are here." She watched Camille assisting Misa with the salsa, chips, and cheese and smiled. For the first time all day, she stopped wondering where Jamel was and what he was doing. Right now all she wanted was to chill with her girls and reconnect after several tumultuous weeks. She started laying out the shrimp ring.

While they set up shop in the living room, Octavia slipped into the kitchen where Toya was filling up an ice bucket. Toya smiled when she saw her and Octavia closed in for a hug. It caught Toya off guard, but she hugged her back.

"Thank you, Miss Toya," Octavia said, her face nestled against Toya's shoulder. "You made me appreciate my mother more."

Octavia pulled back and looked her mother's friend in the eye. "She acts so strong sometimes and so tough. But I know she misses Granddad. She works hard, takes care of me all by herself, and she never gets any thanks for it. I was playing myself before. But I'm gonna stay on the right track this time. I'm gonna make her proud. And I'll make you proud, too."

Toya was touched. "I'm already proud of you, sweetie.

You did something that wasn't easy. And you're not the only one who's done something like that, so don't go beating yourself up about it." Toya raised her hand as if acknowledging that she, too, had terminated an unwanted pregnancy before. Octavia seemed surprised. "Yeah," Toya said. "Everyone makes mistakes. It's how you handle the mistake that matters. Is it a lesson learned or will you keep repeating it? I think you've learned your lesson, and I'm proud of you. So is your mother. Just remember to never run away from your problems. They always follow you."

Octavia nodded and Toya pinched her cheek playfully. "You can always call me if you need to talk," Toya said. "I give good advice."

Together, they reentered the living room where Misa had set up shop on the floor with some nail polish and nail files. Seeing the look on Octavia's face, she smirked. "Yeah, um . . . I raided your room for some nail polish. Your mother's colors are boring, and the last thing I need is boring pale nails."

Octavia laughed. "It's all right," she said. "I think I'll do my nails, too." She joined Misa on the floor, while Camille, Toya, and Dominique took seats on the sofa and chaise, digging into the shrimp and hors d'oeuvres. Toya, Misa, and Dominique each poured a glass of Rémy and Octavia wished she was old enough to indulge as well. The playlist Dominique chose was perfect, a mix of old-school and newer music. Her job at Def Jam gave her access to an enviable music library and they enjoyed it as they made small talk. Finally, Toya got down to the nitty-gritty.

"Misa, are you okay? I mean, that's a dumb question 'cuz I know you're not okay. But . . ."

Misa nodded. "I understand. Yeah," she said. "I'm okay. I got the chance to see Shane and he hugged me. He still loves me." Misa smiled, and it seemed as if she had won the lotto. "That's all I need to keep me going." She looked at Octavia, unsure if she knew what was going on. Dominique cleared up any doubt.

"She knows what happened. We've been talking so much over the past few days that—"

"It's all right. She was bound to find out," Camille said, shaking her head. "It's all over the news and in every paper in town."

Misa glanced at her sister, aware that negative press was Camille's worst nightmare. She lived her life desperate for the approval and even envy of others.

"Who cares?" Misa said. "Seriously, what difference does it make? Those reporters don't know me. They don't know Shane."

"Exactly," Toya chimed in. "What matters is that you know in your heart that you did the right thing. All of us agreed that we would have done the same thing if we were in your shoes."

Misa looked at her sister again. Camille didn't seem so certain. The look on her face told Misa that Camille would give her right arm to go back to that night and prevent Steven's murder.

"How is Teresa going to handle your defense?" Dominique asked. She and Teresa were good friends and Dominique had always admired her hustle.

"She said that it was good that I didn't say too much when they picked me up. Now all I can do is tell my story when it goes to trial and pray that the jury sees it as a case of self-defense."

Dominique hated to pry, but she couldn't resist. "Can you talk about what happened that night?"

Octavia was so eager for the raw and uncut details of the

night her mother's friend had killed a nigga that she was damn near breathless with anticipation. She prayed that Misa would take a sip of that brown juice and spill her guts.

Instead, Misa did what Teresa had advised her. "I'd rather not even think about it, to tell you the truth. It's gonna be hard enough to relive that night when I get up on that witness stand."

"I understand," Dominique said quickly.

"But, I'll tell you this," Misa said, opting for a shade of polish the same color as Shane's favorite red Matchbox car. "I don't feel bad about it. Nobody's gonna make me feel bad about it." Misa smiled. "Shane is getting more comfortable around me now. At first he was kinda scared. He would cry if I came too close. But now, he comes and he runs to me, gives me a hug. He still gets a little mad at me sometimes. I can tell that he still has some trauma over what he went through." Misa thought about how it broke her heart whenever she heard about Shane's repeated nightmares and his refusal to let anyone near his rear end, even at bath time. She knew that the effects of what had been done to Shane would be with him for a long time. But she was confident that soon they could begin the work it would take to repair his damaged psyche. "But nobody's ever gonna hurt my baby again," Misa said. "Never again."

Toya couldn't let it go. "I just want to know. When you pulled the trigger, were you scared?"

Misa looked at Toya and nodded. "I was scared to death. But I wasn't gonna let him get near me. He kept coming towards me and I fired until he stopped." She trusted everyone who was present, so she told the truth. "I wished I'd had more bullets so that I could shoot him some more. I would have shot him all night if I had the ammunition."

No one knew what to say after that. Octavia cleared her throat and said softly, "Can you pass the top coat?"

Misa handed the polish to her and looked around the room at her friends who were all suddenly silent.

Camille stared back at her sister. "Misa, let's not talk about the case," she said. Camille wished she could have a drink. Her pregnancy prevented that, so instead she shoved a tortilla chip in her mouth.

Sensing some tension, Toya changed the subject. "I had lunch with my father the other day."

Dominique and Camille both looked surprised and Misa looked around in confusion. "What happened with your father?" she asked.

Toya had forgotten that Misa was absent for her explanation of her mystery dad. "I hadn't spoken to him in years because he was a dope fiend, crackhead, alcoholic bastard."

Octavia couldn't mask her amazement at Miss Toya's vocabulary. Her mouth hung open in shock. She recovered quickly, though, and listened closely. Of all Dominique's friends, Toya was definitely Octavia's favorite.

"Anyway, he crawled back from the dead the night that Misa—"

Not knowing how to finish the sentence, Toya searched everyone's faces and saw that they all understood what she meant.

"Anyway, he wanted to tell me that he's dying, and to ask me if I would talk to him, hear him out."

"Dying?" Misa asked, her face contorted in a frown.

Toya nodded. "Cancer." She seemed to try to shrug it off. "Yeah, so he's very persistent. He kept calling and finally I gave in. I had lunch with his ass."

Octavia and Misa seemed astounded.

"What did he say?" Camille tried to picture what Toya's father must look like.

"He wants me to forgive him. That's all he says he wants. No money, just forgiveness."

"So," Misa said. "Do you forgive him?"

Toya looked around the room and knew that they all expected her to say no. She had a reputation as a hard rock, but truth be told she had a soft core that she guarded fiercely. She shrugged. "I want to. But I can't."

No one responded and the music filled the void.

Misa finished her pedicure and sat back, admiring her work. She looked at Toya finally and said, "He must have been a real fuckup for you to have held a grudge for so many years."

"He was," Toya said. "And I *want* to keep hating him. I'm used to that. He deserves that." She shrugged. "But, truthfully, hating him is hurting me. And it's a new year, a clean slate. I want to start fresh."

She held her glass up as if to toast. Octavia quickly poured herself a glass of Sprite so that she could join in. Camille had been yearning for apple juice desperately and had claimed the bottle of Motts Toya brought all for herself. She held the bottle up as part of the toast. Misa, Toya, and Dominique clinked glasses with the rest of them and downed shots of Rémy in one gulp.

Sitting back afterward, they all listened to Michael Jackson singing about "Human Nature." Octavia thought of Dashawn and wondered if he was thinking of her. She hadn't told him about the abortion yet. She looked around the room at all the seasoned older women surrounding her and knew that none of them was perfect. Toya, although tons of fun, was often brutally blunt and a borderline bitch. Camille was estranged from her husband, the notoriously sexy and paid Frankie B, and Misa was under indictment for murder. Octavia's own mother was pining over a recently released convict. Still, she cleared her throat and asked for some advice.

"What do I say when I speak to Dashawn?"

Each of the women, particularly Dominique, seemed stunned by the question. Dominique cleared her throat and poured herself another drink as she answered. "Tell him what you decided to do. Let him know how you feel about it, how you feel about him and the way he handled everything."

"How *do* you feel about that?" Toya asked. "The way he handled everything."

Octavia rolled her eyes. "He played me." She shook her head and thought about how it felt to hear him tell her that he didn't want to be a father yet. He had promised to stand by her side and had quickly proven himself to be a liar. "I don't want to talk to him anymore or ever see his punk a—" She remembered her audience and caught herself. "Again," she finished.

"Tell him that!" Toya yelled. "Don't say nothing else but that! When he calls you, you pick up that phone and let him talk all that shit he thinks you want to hear. How he's sorry, how he was overwhelmed, et cetera. And when he stops talking, you tell his bitch ass, '*fuck you!*'"

"Toya!" Camille objected.

"Okay, okay, don't say that. But say, 'I don't have *nothing* to say to you and I don't want to see you ever again.'" Toya had to remember to tone it down for Octavia. Even though her hot ass had gotten knocked up already, in reality she was still a baby. "Women have to stop beating around the bush and trying to be nice. Tell that son of a bitch to eat a—"

"*Toya . . .*" Camille warned.

"Tell him to get the hell out of your face." Toya took another swig of the brown juice and sighed.

Misa had to laugh, and it felt good to do so. She hadn't had much amusement in the past few weeks.

Octavia laughed, too. But she heeded the advice she'd been given. She decided that when and if Dashawn got in touch with her again, she would cut right to the chase. For now, there was no use crying over him since he surely wasn't wasting his tears on her.

"Thanks," she said, smiling at her mother and standing up carefully so as not to smudge her polish. "I'm going to chill in my room now so you old ladies can really talk and get your drink on."

"I got your old ladies!" Misa said, tossing a cotton ball at Octavia.

"Good night," Octavia called over her shoulder as she left for her sanctuary.

Camille turned to Dominique. "She's a good girl; I'm so glad that she's back here at home with you and that she's okay." At least somebody's story had a happy ending. Camille knew that her own wouldn't wind up as nicely.

Dominique nodded. She was glad, too. She had prayed so hard for her daughter's safe return and was thrilled about it.

"I love her so much," she said of Octavia. "I just want her to know that she's not defined by any man. She has to stop worrying about guys and focus on building up her self."

"Well," Toya said, as nicely as she could. "She's watching you. Have you learned that same lesson yet?"

Dominique looked confused.

"What I mean is she's seeing you go upstate in the middle of the night to see a convict. Packaging up goodies for him like he's in Iraq fighting the war on terror instead of stuck up

in the mountains somewhere doing hard time. I'm not putting you down," Toya clarified. "But I'm just showing you
how it must seem to her. She sees you busting your ass at your
prestigious job, meeting celebrities and making wonderful
connections. And she sees that you still allow yourself to get
involved with a man who has no future, no potential whatsoever. Not even a pot to piss in. That has to be one of the reasons she saw no problem with being the girlfriend of a nobody.
Thank God you have a second chance to get it right, but you
gotta get it right this time."

Normally, Dominique would have argued that Jamel was
different. She would have cited the fact that he wasn't just
your average hustler on the corner who got caught; that he
was intelligent, well read, and articulate. But this time, Dominique let Toya's words sink in and realized that she was absolutely right. She sipped her drink.

"We all have to stop doing that," Toya said. "Women in
general. We dumb ourselves down for the men we choose to
be with. My mother did it, I did it, we've all been guilty of
spending precious time with men who don't deserve it."

Dominique gripped her glass and groaned in agreement.
"Jamel came home from jail yesterday. I was at the doctor
with Octavia while she was having her procedure. When I
came home, I had a voice message from Jamel. He's out and
he's safe and he said he was gonna call me later on. I waited
all night for that phone to ring. And all day, too."

"You still haven't heard from him?" Misa guessed. She
was familiar with that kind of story.

Dominique shook her head. "Not a peep." She shrugged.
"I don't know if he's hurt or if he's locked up again."

"Who cares?" Toya said, waving her hand. "He's probably
a faggot!"

"Toya!" This time it was Misa who said it.

"What?" Toya asked, her face frowned up. "He's been in jail for years! Now he's home and in no rush to get to some ass . . . what does that sound like to you?"

Misa laughed again. "Every man that does time in jail isn't gay, Toya."

Toya shrugged. "Men nowadays are *gay* until proven *straight* in my opinion."

Dominique smirked. Toya was a trip. "Well, regardless, I just want to know that he's okay. After all this time, I think I deserve at least a phone call!" She swirled the ice around in her glass and shook her head. "I realize now that I made a mistake with Jamel."

Toya gasped dramatically, clutching her imaginary pearls. "What did you just say?"

"I look back on it now and I can see that I wasted time traveling, writing, talking on the phone. All that time I should have been focused on Octavia. I should have seen that something was going on with her but I was too busy being thirsty for the wrong man."

"Well, when did you get this new epiphany that he's the wrong man?" Toya asked, intrigued. This was a complete about-face for Dominique.

Dominique shrugged. Toya's eyes narrowed in suspicion.

"You still celibate?"

Dominique tried not to smile, and her friends began to giggle.

"I slept with—"

Before she could even finish her sentence the room erupted in shouts of joy. Dominique laughed as her friends celebrated as if she had hit the lottery.

"Who?" Toya asked eagerly, once they had composed themselves.

"Just some guy I do business with," Dominique allowed, careful not to reveal the kind of business she was doing with Archie. "It's nothing serious, but . . . I like him."

Camille smirked. "It was good, wasn't it?"

Dominique closed her eyes dreamily and nodded. Opening them, she looked at her friends. "But I felt a little guilty about it, to tell you the truth." She shrugged. "Not anymore, though. Jamel obviously doesn't even think I'm worth a phone call."

"Who was better?" Toya asked, being nosy.

Dominique pretended not to understand.

"Jamel or the business associate? Who fucks you better?"

Camille and Misa leaned forward and waited. Dominique knew she shouldn't entertain the question, but the liquor had her feeling buzzed. Whispering so that Octavia wouldn't overhear, she said, "I've never been handled the way this man handled me. Jamel ain't got shit on him."

Cheers and applause came then and Dominique found herself wondering why she was so concerned about whether Jamel called or not. Still, she couldn't help hoping that he was safe.

"I know how that feels," Camille chimed in, her apple juice balanced on her lap.

"How what feels?" Misa asked.

"Not hearing a word from him. Wondering where your man is or if he's okay."

Dominique felt so sorry for Camille. Here she was complaining about Jamel—a man who added nothing to her life other than a financial drain—while Camille was struggling to get used to life without her wealthy husband. "Camille, I promise you that Frankie is gonna be sorry for how he's treated you. Eventually, he's gonna see that he's dead wrong."

"I went over there last night to raise hell. That bitch Gillian called the cops on me."

"What?" Dominique was dumbfounded.

Toya frowned and set her glass down since this was the first she was hearing about this. Misa shook her head, so sorry for having brought more problems to her sister's already troubled marriage. Misa had warned Camille about Gillian, though. Long ago, she had pulled Camille's coat about her husband's so-called best friend, only to be ignored and assured that everything was fine. Things were damn sure not fine now.

"It was late and I couldn't sleep. I was up thinking about my marriage and how Frankie has been carrying on. I got mad and went over there to talk to him. Gillian and I had some words, I threw a vase at the bitch's head and missed. I was so mad that I missed!"

Toya tried to stifle a laugh, but failed. Dominique and Misa joined in and they laughed hard at the thought of Camille going all Tom Brady on Gillian. Even Camille had to join the laughter.

When they recovered, Dominique looked at Camille in amazement. "Frankie stood by and let Gillian call the cops on you?"

Camille nodded. "Sure did. When they got there he told them that I wasn't really trying to hit anybody. But he did ask them to make me leave."

"So what did you do?" Dominique asked.

"I left," Camille said as if it was obvious. "No point in me going to jail, too."

Dominique and Toya winced a little, but Misa seemed to ignore her sister's remark.

"What are you gonna do about all of this, Camille? I mean you can't keep going on like this without any money. Frankie can't expect you to sit by and just let this all happen." Dominique couldn't believe that Camille's once doting husband was behaving so coldly.

"You need to—" Toya began.

Camille cut her off. "I don't really want to hear it, Toya," she said firmly. "I'm not in the mood for that shit tonight."

Toya sat forward, her face expressing her shock. "What shit?"

Camille was tired of being lectured by her friend. "*Your* shit, Toya. Every time one of us has a problem, you're the first one to tell us what we should do, how we should handle it, when you've never been through the shit yourself. You can't tell Dominique not to love Jamel just because he made a mistake that put him in jail. Have you ever loved a man doing time? You can't tell me or Misa how to deal with our shit, either. You've never been married, never been facing jail time. So save it!"

Everyone was caught off guard. They all assumed that the pressure of everything going on in her family coupled with her pregnancy hormones had made Camille hostile. That outburst was so out of her character. But, Misa and Dominique both silently cosigned. After all, Toya *hadn't* walked a mile in their shoes.

Toya calmly stared at Camille before pouring herself another glass of cognac and sitting back, crossing her legs.

"Actually," she said. "I've been through *all* of that."

All three of her friends looked confused, and Toya decided that it was time she solved the mystery.

"Unlike you girls," she said. "I don't open up easily about the things I've been through in my past or what I've survived. So there's a lot you don't know about me." She guzzled the contents of her glass and felt the warm liquor coat her chest. "On the night that Misa shot Steven, I told you girls that we should stop keeping things to ourselves. So let me practice what I preach." She sighed and told them a story.

"You already know about my father, how he got drunk and high all the time and made a fool out of my family. But what you don't know is that eventually things got really hard for my mother. She was working her fingers to the bone and that muthafuckin' father of mine would spend the money faster than she could make it. Times were hard and to make matters worse, he would put his foot in her ass every now and then for good measure." Toya rolled her eyes in disgust. "Anyway, it was the eighties and crack was making average Joes into millionaires. And I met this guy named Michael. He was from Antigua, but had an unmistakable thoroughness, a swagger that could only come from the streets. I was about to graduate from high school and I couldn't wait to get the fuck out of my parents' house. My father was a fuckup and my mother was an enabler and I was sick of watching it. Three of my brothers were older than me and had already moved out. But I was still there and so was my little brother Derrick. He was sixteen, I was almost eighteen and we both used to talk about how eager we were to get grown and move out.

"So I met Michael and he pursued me something terrible. He was the same age as me—actually he was a year older— but had dropped out of school already. I would see him when I was on my way to school and he would follow my ass all the way there. At first, I ignored him. My father had drilled into

my head that men only wanted me for sex. I had the body of
a video chick—big boobs, phat ass, small waist—and my father made me feel like that was all I had to offer a man, like
no guy would ever want me as anything but a sex object. So I
was leery of Michael at first. But he was so *fine*! I liked him, I
just wouldn't give in and let him take me out or anything.

"Well, I graduated high school and I spent that summer
getting ready to go away to college. I would see Michael from
time to time and we would chat. I told him that I was going
away to school and do you know that he offered to take me
shopping for my dorm room?" Toya paused her story, smiled
at the memory of the beautiful Antiguan man who had swept
her off her feet. "I didn't accept it, but eventually, he wore me
down. I started seeing him secretly behind my parents' back.
By the end of that summer, I was in love with him. But my
father had done a number on me. I still wouldn't let myself
believe that he wanted anything from me but sex. So I went
away to school on a scholarship and didn't look back. Then I
came home for Thanksgiving and I wound up never going
back to Atlanta."

Camille was hanging on Toya's every word. She had gone
to high school with Toya at Brooklyn Tech, but hadn't known
about her father's tyranny. Since Camille traveled to school
from Staten Island, she had been oblivious to what had gone
on in her friend's family life. The Toya she had known was a
pretty, around-the-way girl who all the other girls in school
wanted to be friends with. After graduation, the two had
kept in touch, but only via occasional letters and postcards,
until one day they just stopped. "Why not?"

Toya looked at her, smirked. "I came home and found out
that my father was worse than ever before. He was getting
high more than ever, still kicking my mother's ass, but my

brother had started fighting him back. One night, while I was away at school, my father had punched my brother in the face and Derrick lost it. He kicked my father's ass!" Toya chuckled, wishing she had been there to witness that. "My father kicked Derrick out, even though he was only sixteen years old, and my mother let him do it. Nobody told me about all of this while I was away at school, so I didn't find this all out until I came home. I was pissed! I went out in our neighborhood looking for my brother and eventually I found him with Michael. He was working for Michael."

Dominique shook her head. She had never known that Toya had dated a drug dealer, let alone one who had put her little brother to work. "What did you do?" she asked.

"I went *off*! I called Michael every name in the book and Derrick dragged me away, pulled me into some apartment building lobby and tried to calm me down. He told me that he had been kicked out with nothing but the shit he could fit in a duffel bag, that my parents had left him with nothing. He knew he could come back around when my father wasn't there and my moms would have given him money or made him something to eat. But my brother was too proud to do that. He felt like since they kicked him out, fuck them. He was gonna make it on his own. He went to Michael, because he had seen him around the way, knew what he was doing, and saw that he was getting money. He asked Michael to put him on and at first he refused because of me. Michael knew that I wouldn't approve. But Derrick was persistent and eventually Michael gave in. My brother was a drug dealer."

Toya took a break from her story and poured another drink. Her friends waited with bated breath for her to continue.

She sipped her drink and finally went on. "Well, at that

point I was mad as hell—not just at my father, but my mother as well. This was her baby boy she allowed to be tossed out in the street like that. So I kept to myself. I stayed in my room most of the time and ignored both of them. When I did go outside, I spent most of my time with Derrick and Michael and their crew, watching them do their thing and keeping an eye out for cops. Derrick had found a room in a rooming house on Saratoga and he was renting it by the week. It was small, but it was warm and clean and that's all he cared about. Michael was living nice! He had a big old apartment on the top floor of a building with a doorman and everything. I was impressed, but I tried not to show it. I would chill with them, help them bag up their shit and then I'd go home and lock myself in my room until the next day. Then one night, I came home and my father was waiting for me at the front door. He told me that he needed money. I said I didn't have none, but he knew that I was lying and I wouldn't give it to him. He slapped me so hard that my ears were ringing and I swear I saw stars. So I packed my shit, went back out there in the cold and told my brother and Michael what happened. Michael told me that I could stay with him. I didn't even think twice about it. I knew I wasn't going back home, otherwise I would have wound up murdering my father. From that night on, Michael and I were official.

"I eventually dropped out of college and spent most of my time with Michael and Derrick. I was part of their team, and even got to know some of the other hustlers' wives in their circle." Toya looked at Camille. "So this was when I got married."

Camille looked amazed. "You married Michael?"

Toya nodded. "Yup. I was so fucked up at first by all the shit my father had drilled in my head over the years—a man won't marry you if you give up the ass too soon; the only thing a man wants from most of the women he meets is some pussy; once a nigga gets the pussy he's looking for the exit—and I believed that. So I started expecting Michael to push me away, to do all the things my father said men do. But he didn't push me away. In fact, he tried to undo all the damage that had been done to my self-esteem throughout my upbringing. He loved me." She nodded matter-of-factly. "No doubt about that."

"Did you have a big wedding?" Misa asked.

Toya shook her head. "Nah. We went right down to City Hall and did it. And that was the happiest I've ever been in my life. Michael had it all—a nice home, fancy car, clothes, cash, so much fucking cash!" She shook her head at the memory of it. "We used to travel all over the place—Mexico, Aruba, Barbados, all around the United States!"

Camille smiled. "That's when you were sending me postcards from all those places," she recalled. "I thought you were traveling while you were on break from school."

Toya smiled, too, remembering. "That's what I wanted you to think," she said. "But I was Mrs. Michael Nash, and I was on top of the world. I had furs, diamonds, expensive furniture, but most of all I had respect. People respected me in the streets 'cuz they knew I was Michael's wife. I even went back home and told my mother that I got married. She was happy for me, but my father said it wouldn't last. I didn't give a fuck what he said. I was happy and I was finally out of their house for good."

Toya looked at her friends seriously. She took a long swig of her drink and stared at the floor. "We were happier than anybody else in the world," she said. "I was so in love with him! I'm sure he cheated on me, but I never knew about it. When we were together, it was all about me and everybody knew us as a team. I felt powerful, and I was more in love with him because *he* was so powerful. He made a lot of money. They all did. My brother was driving fly cars, getting all the prettiest girls. My mother was mad because she didn't approve of us being involved in the drug game. Meanwhile, she was still with my drug-addicted father." Toya shook her head at the absurdity of that. "Years went by and we were untouchable."

She looked at Misa. "Then my brother got arrested. I thought it was my fault—definitely that it was Michael's fault. We never should have let him sell drugs in the first place. I think at that point that I started looking at the whole thing differently. Michael became the bad guy in my mind, because if it wasn't for him, Derrick wouldn't be in jail. At least that's how I looked at it. Derrick wouldn't rat, so they sent him to jail for five years. He was only twenty-one." She sighed. "That was hard to handle. My parents turned their backs on him. My mother was embarrassed that a child of hers—a teacher who worked hard to make ends meet—would resort to selling drugs. My father was disappointed for God knows what reason! It seemed like neither of them saw that my brother's hand had been forced, that my father's bullshit contributed to it. Anyway, I held Derrick down. I sent him money orders, food, cigarettes, sneakers, letters. I accepted collect phone calls and went on visits . . . I did *all* of that!" She looked at Dominique pointedly. "And I watched women go up there week after week, dragging small kids with them and getting treated like shit by the prison guards. Then the same unappreciative bastard they were traveling hours to see would have some next bitch sitting up there at the next visit. I listened to the stories Derrick told me about guys in there dealing with faggots on the low and then kissing their wives when they came to see them; heard story after story about chicks paying thousands of dollars in phone bills because their punk-ass man couldn't do his time without touching base every night. And I even watched women get arrested and their kids taken away because they tried to smuggle drugs into the prison hidden inside their baby's diaper. So all the things I warned you about, all the things I said to you about Jamel . . . I was speaking from experience. From day one, I could tell that he ain't shit! I was just trying to save you the trouble of finding out the hard way."

Dominique smiled. "All I know is the hard way," she said, though she wished now that she had heeded Toya's advice.

"So, okay," Misa said. "Did Michael ever get caught?"

Toya smiled and nodded. "Unfortunately, he did. We both did."

Camille shifted in her seat, tucked her legs underneath her and rested her chin on her hand as she listened intently. She couldn't believe what she was hearing.

"We were home one night and the police raided our apartment. One of his boys snitched on him and they found everything. Drugs, guns, everything! I got arrested right along with him and spent a few weeks in jail because my mother wouldn't accept my calls. It was bad enough that her son got arrested for drugs, but her daughter?" Toya shook her head in dismay. "That was the last straw."

"So how did you get out?" Dominique asked anxiously.

"Eventually, one of his cronies posted my bail. Michael was denied bail because he took the fall for everything. He told them that it was his shit, that I had no idea all that stuff was in our home, that I was blind to the fact that he was hustling. The police didn't believe him, but they had to let me go. They had no evidence against me, I had no priors and he was admitting being the one who did it. So I got out, while he got sentenced to fifteen years."

Dominique's chin dropped. She had been struggling with Jamel being locked up for three years. Fifteen sounded like an eternity!

"So now, you had to visit him *and* your brother in jail," Misa assumed.

Toya frowned, shook her head. "I guess you haven't been listening," she said. "I had seen all that I needed to see by then to convince me that men in jail don't give a fuck about anyone but themselves. I wasn't going to be traveling for hours to visit him, spending my last money on packages for him, when he was bound to play me just like the rest of them incarcerated niggas do to the women in their lives."

Camille frowned, sat up. "What are you saying? You left him while he was locked up?"

"I sure did," Toya said, with no hint of regret or remorse. "It was one thing to do all that for my brother. But I wasn't about to do it for just some ordinary man. Husband or no husband, Michael knew I wouldn't be willing to put my life on hold for that long. He loved me, but he knew that I wasn't built for that life. I could never be some prisoner's wife, running upstate every weekend for a nigga who would ultimately give me his ass to kiss."

Silence filled the room until Mary J's "Take Me As I Am" filled the speakers.

"So what ever happened to him?" Dominique asked.

"He did his time and as soon as he got out, they deported him." Toya crossed her legs and looked at her friends. "I took the money the police hadn't seized and put a down payment on my brownstone. Been living there ever since."

Everyone was floored. Dominique stared at Toya wide-eyed. "So all this time you've been talking shit about what we *need* to do," she said teasingly. "You were speaking from experience. You've been married to a drug dealer like Camille, been locked up like Misa and—"

"And I was *still* smart enough to know not to waste my time on a convict like you did."

Dominique threw an olive at Toya playfully. Their giggles lightened the mood somewhat.

Camille felt that Toya had been a little heartless, though. "Do you ever feel bad for turning your back on your husband? Ever wonder where he is now or how he's doing?"

Toya sighed. The truth was that she often wondered that. She thought about Michael all the time, about the patient love he had given her, allowing her to feel protected and adored after all that she had been through. And in the end, she had walked away from him without thinking twice about it. She realized, as she thought about it now, that she had been able to shut her emotions on and off so easily because she had never allowed herself to believe it was all real in the first place. Even now, part of her believed her father—men could never be trusted with her heart. "I don't feel bad," she lied. "But I do think about him sometimes. Then I think about something else." She refilled her glass and Dominique and Misa held theirs out for refills, too. "Oh, and I divorced him while he was in prison. So he's not my husband anymore."

Camille's head was spinning after all she'd just heard. "Wow," she said. All along, Camille had thought Toya hadn't been through the kinds of the things that the rest of them had endured. Now she realized that Toya had been through all of what they were dealing with and more.

"Let me tell y'all the new drama in my life," Toya said,

eager to change the subject. Thinking about Michael always made her heartsick.

"There's more?" Misa asked. Hearing about Toya's past had been enough of a shock.

"Yeah," Toya said and sighed. "Lately, this guy named Russell has been bothering me, begging me to go out with him. He comes to my house and brings me flowers, gives me compliments every time he sees me. But he's as ugly as sin." Toya shuddered for emphasis. "Anyway, the other night, after I had dinner with my father, I ran into this son of a bitch and he asked me out for the hundredth time."

"Did you go?" Camille sat up slightly.

Toya nodded. "I did. He took me to a nice restaurant and we had dinner. I ordered the most expensive shit on the menu hoping to turn him off and make him mad. But he paid for it with no problem. In fact, every time I ordered something expensive, he ordered something even more expensive than that."

Dominique raised an eyebrow, intrigued. "Nice!" she said. "So, what was the conversation like over dinner?"

"It was interesting," Toya admitted, somewhat reluctantly. "He's a fireman, no kids, no wife, no baby-mama drama. He lives on his own—rents an apartment across the street from my house. He says he likes to travel, that he likes a challenge, and he noticed me as soon as he moved into the neighborhood."

"Okay," Camille said. "So far, he sounds good."

"But she said he's ugly," Misa reminded.

"Beastly!" Toya clarified. "This muthafucka is . . . ugh!"

They all burst into hysterics again. When they got it together, they listened as Toya described the rest of the night. Russell had paid the bill and left an exorbitant tip in order to sufficiently impress her. Then he and Toya had gone to a local bar and had a couple more drinks.

"Long story short, I got twisted and went home with him."

"Did you go because you were having fun with him or because you were tipsy?" Misa asked.

Toya thought about it. "I think it was the liquor. I was vulnerable after seeing my father and I was distracted by the fact that he managed to hold my interest during the date . . ."

"He hit it, Toya?" Camille asked incredulously. She couldn't believe it.

"And it was *fabulous*!" Toya bellowed. "I mean I was seeing stars, bitches!"

Laughter and hollering erupted all around and the ladies talked all over each other with a million questions about Toya's beauty-and-the-beast love story.

Despite the turmoil unfolding in each of their lives, the women found solace in laughter and in Toya's shenanigans for the rest of the night. And once again, together they faced a new day.

Motives

Frankie came bursting through the door of Sugarcane like a gust of wind. Gillian sat at a corner table near the back and watched as he stormed through the small but popular Brooklyn restaurant. He reached her table and sat down across from her, leaning in close so that she could hear him over the loud music and chatter from other diners.

"What the fuck!" he hissed. "You put a hit out on Jojo without telling me?"

Gillian sipped her rum punch and stared back at Frankie over the rim of her glass. "It needed to be done, Frankie." Her voice was soft and light. "I knew that you were preoccupied with what's going on. So I just took care of it, that's all."

He watched her with his jaw clenched in anger. The waiter approached their table and Gillian cleared her throat. "I took the liberty of ordering for you," she explained. "I know how much you like their jerk chicken."

Speechless, Frankie sat back as the waiter set the steaming plate of food before him. When Gillian's red snapper was placed before her, she said a quick and silent prayer before digging in. Frankie was becoming increasingly aware that

Gillian was taking her new position of power and running with it. As if ordering the hit on Jojo without his knowledge wasn't bad enough, now here she was ordering his food for him. When the waiter was gone at last, Frankie leaned in closer to her.

"You're acting like this is no big deal, Gillian. But since when do you not talk to me about shit like this?"

Gillian chewed her fish and looked at Frankie. Swallowing at last, she said, "Well, you haven't been talking to me much either, lately." She wiped her mouth with her napkin and took a long sip of her drink before continuing. "You come in the house late at night, hoping that I'm asleep. You think I don't realize that's what you're doing, but I'm not stupid. You go about your day-to-day business and you act like you're handling everything just fine. But you're not. You don't talk to me. Instead, you spend your whole day talking to Tremaine about business, or talking to the DA about the case against Misa. When I try to talk about what's going on, you make excuses for why you don't want to discuss it. You're shutting me out."

"So you pay me back by doing something like this behind my back?"

Gillian shook her head. "I didn't do anything behind your back."

"So why didn't you tell me about it? Why did I have to read about that shit in the newspaper? And why won't any of the goons own up to it? Who did you put on it?" Frankie was pissed. He felt that his control of the crew was nonexistent if no one would tell him who had actually done the hit.

Gillian was pleased that Biggs had kept his mouth shut. She knew now that she could trust him. "Maybe I did it myself, Frankie." She smirked at him, hoping to make him laugh. He didn't find anything funny. Gillian sighed. "Listen, I took care of it. If things weren't so crazy, you would have done the same thing. We're a team, aren't we? Bonnie and Clyde? We're supposed to be in this together."

"So why did you give the order by yourself?" Frankie was just as mad at himself as he was at her. He felt that it made him look weak in the eyes of the crew. *He* should have been the one to take care of Jojo, not Gillian. By her giving the order, she had made him appear to be too preoccupied by his grief to lead the crew effectively.

Gillian watched Frankie sulking, his pride wounded since she had gotten to her father's killer before he did. "I should have told you," she allowed. "I just didn't want to stress you out any more than you already are." She reached for his hand and stroked it. "I love you," she said. "And I'm worried about you. I just want to do my part to keep things moving forward for all of us. Maybe then you'll stop shutting down on me."

"I'm not shutting down on you," he said defensively.

She nodded. "Sure you are. You're doing the same thing to me that you were doing to Camille not so long ago. You're keeping busy so that you don't have to talk to me. You're throwing yourself into your work in order to keep yourself from thinking about what's really on your mind. I don't even think you realize that you're doing it," she said. "But I'm not Camille. And I'm not gonna keep pretending like I don't see what's happening until it's too late."

Frankie looked at the woman he loved and wished he could be more open with her. "I'm sorry," he said. "I just got a lot on my mind." He sighed.

Gillian nodded. She smiled at him, reassuringly. "I understand. But you can't deal with what's on your mind by pulling away from me. It's not healthy for our relationship."

He knew she was right. "I know," he acknowledged. "It's just the way I've always been. But I'll try to change that."

She smiled again, nudged his plate closer to him. "Eat," she said. "It's delicious."

Frankie put his napkin in his lap, picked up his fork, and picked at his chicken. He glanced at Gillian once again. "No more ordering hits without talking to me."

Gillian nodded. "Deal."

Frankie shoved some chicken into his mouth and winked at her. Gillian winked back. She knew that he could never stay mad at her for long.

Dominique sat in her freshly detailed Lincoln and waited for Jamel to come out from his mama's house. It was the place he'd been paroled to at the ripe old age of thirty-one. She reflected on that as she waited. She had gotten to know Jamel's family during his time away and had a lot of love for his mother. Still, she saw the situation clearly for once and noticed the contrast between her world and his.

She glanced at her fox jacket tossed across the backseat, looked down at her wrist and saw the tennis bracelet she'd gotten for herself last Christmas. Looking up, she saw him coming. He approached her car with the same sexy walk she'd always swooned over. This time, though, it seemed more childish than attractive; more pathetic than it had seemed before.

As he neared her car, she took him all in. He wore the sneakers she had bought for him, a pair of baggy jeans that were at least four sizes too big for him, a white tee and black hoodie that were equally as large. His black winter hat sealed the look and it seemed to Dominique as if Jamel had come

home and stepped right back into his uniform as a soldier in
the same mean streets that kept swallowing him.

"This nigga . . ." she mumbled. She was most bothered
by the fact that today he was accompanying her to a community outreach program that was supposed to encourage inner
city kids to embrace the arts rather than criminal alterna-
tives. Here Jamel was looking like a recruiter for the wrong
army.

"Hey, stranger!" he opened the passenger side door and
greeted her, smiling from ear to ear.

Dominique smiled back, gave him a kiss when he leaned
in for one and decided to keep her mouth shut about his outfit. After all, what had she expected? Surely, he wouldn't be
caught dead in anything that fit him right. They set out for
the venue in Far Rockaway and the tension was palpable as
they crossed the Verrazano. Jamel turned up the radio and
Dominique said nothing, wondering why he was being so
distant all of a sudden. Finally, he spoke up.

"I didn't want to call and bother you while you were dealing with Octavia's situation," he explained. She glanced at him
briefly and kept driving. "I know that must have been hard
for both of you to deal with, you feel me?"

Dominique didn't answer, she simply nodded.

"And I came home that first night, kicked off my shoes
and sat on my mother's couch and it was lights out. I woke up
and ate, and fell back asleep. I woke up and Shonda was there
with J.J."

Dominique almost skidded to a halt on the Belt Parkway.
She looked at him in surprise. Shonda, his son's mother, had
seen him first.

He continued quickly—just a little too quickly. "That's
how I felt. I was like, wow! So anyway he was so happy to see

me, 'cuz you know it's been months since the last time she brought him up north. He got so big."

Dominique plastered on the fakest smile.

"So, you know my moms had cooked, everybody ate, and it got late. Shonda went to take J.J. home and he lost it! He didn't want to leave me. So I went back to the house with them."

"You went to Shonda's house?" Dominique asked without taking her eyes off the road. The speedometer crept to the right.

Jamel knew this wouldn't be easy. "Yeah. But just to play with J.J. Anyway, so J.J. falls asleep and I go to leave. That's when she started with her bullshit. She tried to stop me from leaving, telling me how she's sorry for not being there for me while I was gone."

Jamel noticed that she swerved a little. He cleared his throat. "You okay?"

"Mm-hmm. Continue."

He knew what that meant. "So I tried to leave, she blocked me."

"She blocked your big ass from leaving, Jamel?" He was six two, nearly three hundred pounds.

"She was running her mouth. I told you how Shonda is. So before I knew it, my curfew had passed. Now she's holding it over my head that if I try to leave, she's gonna call and tell the cops to pick me up on my way to my mother's house 'cuz I'm out past my curfew."

Dominique had to laugh. She had to hand it to him. He had worked out the perfect scenario in his mind.

Jamel thought Dominique was laughing *with* him at Shonda's tactics. "Word!" he chuckled. "So I stayed there on the couch. I didn't really sleep, though, 'cuz all she did was run her mouth all night." He looked at Dominique sincerely. "I didn't touch her. I swear on my son."

Dominique listened in silence as he filled her in on the rest of the events that had occupied the past two days since he had been released from prison. He had reported to his parole officer within twenty-four hours as required, gone looking for a job but nobody was hiring. He had spent the morning "babysitting" his son while Shonda went to work.

Dominique noticed that despite his grim circumstances, Jamel had a cell phone. She stared at it and rolled her eyes, let out a sigh.

"Jamel, you know you don't have to lie about—"

"See? I knew you would think I was lying!"

As Jamel pleaded his case, insisting that he was through with Shonda, that his mama had given him the phone, that he didn't even know the number to it, that's how little it mattered, Dominique said nothing.

She was too close to the venue to turn back now. If she went home, she would have disappointed the kids who had put together an entire musical repertoire to impress the "Def Jam exec" coming to see them. She tuned Jamel out as he babbled, listened instead to the CD playing. It was Amy Winehouse.

"Kept his dick wet, with his same old safe bet."

She turned it up. Jamel stopped talking midsentence and looked at her. He knew then that she wasn't trying to hear him.

They arrived at the Queens high school and were met by airport-level security. Metal detectors and handheld scanners were necessary to gain entry. Dominique looked at Jamel questioningly, praying that this fool hadn't brought anything illegal with him. She had already made up her mind that he had fucked Shonda. She wondered now if he was back to all of his old habits or just one.

Thankfully, the search went without incident and they proceeded to the next level of security at the poorly performing school.

"May I see ID, please?" a security guard asked.

Dominique fished in her purse and pulled out her driver's license, explained that she was there as a guest for the assembly. The security guard nodded and looked to Jamel. He looked like he had swallowed a lemon.

The only ID he had was his prison ID card. Reluctantly, he pulled it out of his pocket and handed it to the security guard.

The guard's eyes flew open and she looked at Jamel suspiciously. She handed him back his card and waved them on, but the damage was done. Dominique's world and his had collided embarrassingly.

The assembly was wonderful and Dominique did her best to motivate the young people present to know that they could do everything they had ever dreamed of. The whole time, she was glancing at Jamel, sitting in the corner looking like one of the students—and a bored one at that. She knew then that it was over.

When the long day was over and the two of them climbed back into the car, Dominique stuck the key in the ignition and started the car, letting it warm up.

She looked over to the man she had wanted so badly to be the one. She had convinced herself that he would be ready to grow up this time, that he was done with the lifestyle of a hustler. She had convinced herself to accept him even though he had no job, no ambition, and no experience being anything but a drug dealer. And he couldn't even believe in *himself* for a full three days. She shook her head.

"I'm so mad at you," she said. "You let me persuade myself and everybody else that you were different and the whole time you knew you weren't."

"Can I speak?'

"No," she said. "I heard what you had to say. I thought you would at least try, Jamel. You talked all that shit while you were locked up about being in it to win it this time. You fuckin' loser!"

He looked like she had sucker-punched him.

"Yo, I hate you." She put the car in drive and argued with Jamel for most of the ride back to Staten Island.

By the time they pulled up in front of his mother's house, he had finally come to grips with the fact that his scam was over. Dominique had cried, yelled, cried some more, and rambled on and on about how much she had trusted him, loved him, believed in him. He knew that she was right. He was a loser. He had lost his desire to be anything more than what he already was, and lost the willingness to try something new. All he had ever been was Shonda's baby's father, Betty's son, Jay from around the way. And Dominique wanted him to be a whole lot more.

"I'm sorry," he said. "I really wanted to do what we talked about. I wouldn't have wasted your time if I didn't want to change. And you're acting like I did something I didn't do and I respect it," he said, lying till the end. He shrugged. "But I want you to know that I really do love you."

Dominique wanted to spit in his face and tell him that his dick was smaller than she would have liked, that she had cum all over Archie's while he was away. Instead, she hauled off and slapped the shit out of Jamel, leaving him looking like he wanted to hit her back. Instead, he climbed out of her car and watched as she sped out of his life for good.

"He's dead?"

"Word, son. I can't believe nobody told you. They found that nigga's body slumped over in the driver's side of his S-Class with three shots to the face."

Baron was sitting in a wheelchair in his hospital room waiting for his mother to finish handling some paperwork at the nurse's station. He was being released from the hospital today and had been talking to Tremaine on the telephone about his plans to settle the score with Jojo as soon as he was back on his feet.

"What's Frankie saying about that?" Baron asked. He was careful about what he said on the telephone these days, but Tremaine still understood the question. He was asking whether Frankie was the one who handled it.

"He ain't sad about it," Tremaine said. "But your sister's the one who really does most of the talking these days."

Baron couldn't believe his ears. *Gillian?* "Word?"

"Yeah," Tremaine confirmed. "Gillian's been holding her own lately. Frankie has his hands full with everything going on in his family. But your sister still has her eyes on the prize. Seems like she has everything under control."

Baron sat and chewed on that for a moment. Gillian had ordered the hit. Now that Jojo was dead, and Nobles's death had been avenged, Frankie and Gillian had no loyalty to Baron anymore. Baron knew that both his sister and Frankie blamed him for what Jojo had done. Truth be told, Baron blamed himself. His father had warned him that shit had gotten out of hand. But hothead Baron was never one to back down from a fight. He had gone too far in his war with Jojo and it had cost him his father's life, had nearly cost him his own, and had apparently cost him his status as the head of his family. While he sat crippled in a wheelchair, Gillian had rushed in and saved the day and was riding off into the sunset with Frankie and the Nobles family's loyalty. Baron seethed.

"What about Camille?" Baron asked. "Frankie just deaded her?"

Tremaine sighed. Even he thought that what Frankie was doing to Camille was grimy. "Yeah," he said. "He cut her off altogether. No money, no nothing. She's out there in Shaolin by herself in that house and Frankie just said fuck her. He's with Gillian now."

"Damn," Baron said. It sounded like losing Nobles had turned Frankie's heart to stone. He was cutting everybody off who he felt had crossed him. Baron wondered how Camille was handling that. She always seemed so meek, such a doting wife. He wondered how she was dealing with the fact that Frankie had left her for Gillian. If what Tremaine said was true, then Camille was broke and had nothing. Baron thought about Misa then, wondered how she was getting by since he'd paid to spring her from jail.

"You still there?" Tremaine asked since the line was dead silent.

"Yeah," Baron said. "Aiight, then. I'm gonna hit you back when I get home."

Tremaine knew that Baron had gotten the message. His reign at the top was over.

Camille and Misa sat in the back of the church and listened as the reverend spoke on the subject of tithing. Camille closed her eyes, remembering a time when she had something to donate ten percent of. She remembered the lyrics to a song that her mother used to play years ago. *"Ten percent of something beats one hundred percent of nothing at all."* How true.

She felt a tap on her shoulder and turned around to see that Celia Parker-Nobles was seated behind her.

"Hi." Camille smiled brightly and clasped hands with Celia. Misa turned around and smiled at Baron's mom.

"What are you ladies doing after service?" Celia whispered.

The sisters exchanged looks and then shook their heads. "Nothing," Camille whispered back.

Celia nodded. "Come with me."

Camille and Misa agreed and turned back around to give their attention to the reverend. Camille had never seen Celia at this church before all the way out in Long Island near Lily's house. That meant that Celia had come there specifically to see them, and she wondered why.

Misa thought about what Celia had already done for her. Camille had finally told her out of their mother's earshot that Celia had basically bailed her out. Misa had been wondering ever since then whether it had been Celia doing it as a favor to Camille or a message from Baron that he cared about her. She hoped that after service she would get some answers.

Celia sat there with her big red hat putting all the other parishoners' Sunday finery to shame. She watched Misa and Camille as they participated in the service. She had a special place in her heart for both of them. Camille reminded Celia of her younger self. Like Camille, Celia had been the first

wife of a very handsome and powerful man. She, too, had
been abandoned in favor of a woman she had known, someone who had been in her home. As Celia watched Camille
come unraveled by Frankie's behavior, she had warned her to
keep her dignity. Celia herself had never compromised her
dignity for anybody. Not even the late, great, notorious Doug
Nobles. She had acquiesced and divorced him, watched as he
married Mayra Leon and had Gillian, and she had laughed
all the way to the bank. Today, Celia was going to teach Camille how to do the same thing.

Service ended and the congregants spilled out into the
parking lot, all of them hurrying toward luxury cars in this
affluent community.

As they walked along, Celia linked arms with Camille.
"It's good to see you again," she said. "I want to take you out
to lunch, have a talk just me and you."

Camille smiled. "I'd like that." She glanced at Misa. Celia
winked as if she had a plan.

"Misa," Celia said, smiling and taking the young lady by
the hand. "I've been praying for you and for your son. Everything is going to be just fine. Keep the faith."

Misa nodded and allowed Celia to lead her over to a black
Town Car. A balding, round black man opened the car door
for her as they approached and Misa turned to Celia, confused. Camille was but a few steps behind.

"My son was released from the hospital the other day and
he's been asking about you. I told him how you held vigil at his
side for so many days while he was comatose. He appreciates
that because he's feeling deserted by a lot of other people."

Misa nodded. She completely understood.

Celia gestured toward the car and driver. "He asked me to
send the driver for you so that you can go and see him. He's

at my house in Montauk, and I think it might be good for you to get away for a little while. Security is tight and all that. No reporters or anybody else will bother you while you're there. You can rest assured."

Misa wanted to jump up and down, but instead she hugged Celia and said, "Thank you so much." She hugged her sister, too, before she turned and greeted her driver.

Camille and Celia watched as Misa climbed into the car and was whisked away. Then they walked back toward where Camille had parked her Range Rover. Climbing inside, Camille asked, "Where will we go for lunch?"

Celia smiled. "IHOP."

Camille burst out laughing. Celia seemed too classy for the International House of Pancakes. "You're kidding."

Celia took off her extravagant hat, shook her head, and frowned. "I'm not playing! I want some of that butter pecan syrup on mine, now let's go."

Camille knew there was one about a mile down the road, so she drove off in that direction. She hoped Celia knew she was broke, that she couldn't even pay for her own meal at IHOP. As if she read her mind, Celia turned to her.

"I know times are hard, Camille. I just want to treat you to lunch, give you some advice, some girl talk. You know?"

Camille did know. She wanted badly to get some good advice from someone who had actually walked a mile in her shoes.

They arrived at the restaurant, got seated, and ordered their meals before Camille shared her good news.

"So, I'm having a baby."

Celia couldn't hide her surprise. "A baby? What?" She sat back in her chair and took a good look at Camille. "I knew I saw something different in your face."

Camille smiled. "Yeah. Frankie and I haven't really had a chance to talk about it, so it feels . . . kind of unreal."

Celia thought Frankie was a true ass for treating his wife this way while she was pregnant with his child. On the drive over, Camille had shared her sad story—how Frankie had cut her off financially, how Gillian had called the cops on her. Celia was astounded now to find out that there was also an unborn child involved in all of it.

"Camille, what are you going to do?" she asked.

Camille held her hands up helplessly. "I have no idea."

Their food arrived and Celia said a quick yet poignant prayer before dousing her pancakes in syrup. Camille nibbled on her turkey sausage and looked at Celia.

"What would you do?"

Celia smirked as she chewed on her pancakes. "You really want to know?" She was thrilled that Camille had asked. Unsolicited advice was often unwelcome. But now that she'd asked . . .

Camille nodded.

"Sell that house out there on Staten Island. The market ain't great right now, but it's something."

"None of it is in my name."

"So what? You're his wife."

"The barbershop and most of his other big assets are in his mother's name. At least that's what Teresa told me. Frankie doesn't own much on paper besides Conga, and he just came into owning that recently. It's the other money that matters most, and legally I can't touch that."

Celia stared at Camille. "Legally," she repeated.

Camille chewed on her eggs and on what Celia was alluding to.

Celia stirred her tea. "Frankie is giving you no choice but

to play hardball. So, you have to do just that." She sipped from the steaming mug. "I've spoken to Teresa, too."

Camille nodded. After all, Celia had every right to. She was the one who was financing Misa's defense.

"She tells me that you're still hoping to reconcile with Frankie."

Camille shrugged, embarrassed. She had, in fact, told Misa's attorney that she didn't want to go too far in her efforts to get money from her husband out of fear that he would divorce her. "I was," she admitted, wiping her mouth with her napkin and sitting back in her seat. "But after he stood there and watched the police escort me out of that bitch's house . . . after how he looked at me and told me that he wasn't happy about this baby . . ." Camille was so clearly hurt by that episode that Celia could tell it had been a turning point for her. "I'm done. I'm ready to file for divorce."

Celia nodded. "Good," she said. "I know it's hard because you still love him. I've been there. But you can't make a man love you back, even when you know he's making a huge mistake." Celia shook her head. "I spent the whole weekend in my mother's house crying when Douglas married Mayra. She was clearly only with him for his money, and I really, truly loved that man."

Camille saw the sincerity in Celia's eyes and it made her smile. That was exactly how she felt about Frankie. She wasn't sure why Gillian wanted Frankie, of all the men she could have. But what Camille knew for sure was that Gillian couldn't possibly love him more than she did.

Celia sighed. "But I had to let him go. He wasn't in love with me anymore. Thankfully, Doug had sense enough to provide for me willingly. He put the New Jersey house in my name, the Hamptons house, and one in Coral Gables, Florida. He set up a trust for Baron and made me cotrustee over it. And he sent money over every month, no questions asked. He didn't make it hard for me. But if he had, I was fully prepared to get what was mine."

"How?" Camille asked. "What do I do to get what Frankie owes to me and to my baby?"

"First step is, you have your girlfriend Toya prepare that house for sale. Have it appraised and have her list it. When Frankie raises hell about it, you lay your case down. You don't want the public scrutiny of his finances, and neither does he. But, if need be, you're willing to provide proof of the lifestyle you've become accustomed to. You tell him that you can't live in that house under a microscope any longer. And since he won't give you the money you need to find a safe place for you and for your child, selling the house and having the courts decide how to split the profit is your only option." Celia looked Camille in the eye. "You remind Frankie of how loyal you've been to him over the years. Faithful and trustworthy. How silent." She sipped her tea, holding Camille's gaze over the rim of the cup. "Make him see how beneficial it would be for you to keep being silent that way."

Camille nodded.

"If you play your cards right, Camille, he can't deny you. You've been married for eight years, you gave up a modeling career to be a dutiful wife, and now you're carrying his child. He's abandoned you with no money, no means of supporting yourself or the baby. He has to pay. Period." Celia shook her head and the expression on her face told Camille that this was the worst part. "Unfortunately, you can't make Frankie be a good father to his child. Douglas never was a good father to Baron. Especially once Gillian was born."

Camille was surprised to hear Celia say this. She had always had the impression that Doug Nobles had loved both his children equally.

"I watched him lead Baron into the business even though I begged him not to. What mother would want her son to be groomed for the drug business from the age of thirteen?" Celia had a pained expression on her face. "You're about to be a mother, so soon you'll understand. You *know* your child; know what they're capable of, what's outside of their reach, what can make them or break them. And Baron has always been seeking his father's approval. He wanted to be just as notorious, just as flashy. But he kept falling short, while Gillian managed to remain the apple of her father's eye." She leaned forward and rested her chin in her hand. "Baron has been broken because of it. Nothing he ever did was good enough, and now he seems so depressed, so empty inside that I'm worried about him."

Camille sighed. "It's funny because Frankie always envied Baron for being Nobles's real son. Frankie always wished that you and your husband had been his parents instead of the two that he was given." Camille had often heard Frankie express his admiration for Celia and she could see why. The woman was as real as it gets.

Celia smiled. "I loved Frankie like a son, as well. And Baron loves him like a brother. I think it's hard for him to understand being ignored by Frankie and Gillian like this."

"Frankie hasn't contacted Baron at all?"

Celia shook her head, sat back. "Baron has tried calling both of them and gets no response. If it weren't for Tremaine, my son would be completely in the dark about everything." She looked at Camille. "I don't pretend that Baron is a saint. There are some things he's not telling me. I'm not blind to

that fact. He feels responsible for his father's death in a major
way. He won't talk about it. But sometimes—when the pain-
killers get him feeling fuzzy—"

Both ladies chuckled at that.

"He tells me that he feels like the bad guy. Like in the
movies . . . he says he's been bad to everybody including himself, and that he deserves everything that's happened to him.
He told me that he's in exactly the same position his father
was—stuck in a wheelchair while life goes on around him."

They sat in silence for a moment and thought about that.
It was true.

"I think he's finally had a chance to stop and think back
on everything he's done and it's a tough pill to swallow.
Baron isn't the bad guy." Celia realized that she sounded like
she was trying to convince herself. "At least he doesn't mean
to be."

Camille nodded her understanding and smiled. "You've
been a good mother to Baron," she said, hoping that Celia
wasn't blaming herself for his shortcomings.

"I know!" Celia chuckled. "If it wasn't for me, that boy
would be broke. So much of the money Doug gave me over
the years is still there. I didn't need much to survive or to
raise Baron. Hell, once he got in the drug game he was living
with his father and his newfound family more than he was
with me."

Celia had seen her son on weekend visits and holidays
while he was being groomed as his father's successor. She had
often wondered how Baron would have turned out had she
had a stronger hand in his upbringing.

"I had the properties Doug gave me and the money he
gave me each month to pay for it all. And I got my hustle
on—legally."

"What did you do?" Camille was intrigued.

"I invested. I bought some art, some stocks and bonds, some T-bills. I invested in some real estate, long before the recent surge in home buying. I made a lot of money that way. I didn't tell anyone about it until now. All these years, everyone assumed that I was just sitting around living lavishly off of my ex-husband's money." She shrugged. "I guess it was partly true, but I doubled and tripled it by myself without having to look over my shoulder the way that he did."

Camille was amazed. As the two women enjoyed their meal and talked strategy, Camille felt hopeful for the first time that she could actually come out on top. Finally, she had accepted that Frankie wouldn't be playing the role of model husband and father in her happily-ever-after. But Camille was still about to have the child she'd always longed for, and she was willing to do whatever it took to ensure that he or she got the best life had to offer.

"I'm not saying that you're wrong," Baron was saying. He sat in his wheelchair, still unable to walk, though he was much more comfortable in his mother's Hamptons estate than in the cold and sterile hospital. "But how do you know for a fact that it was Steven who did it?"

Misa looked at Baron, her expression steely. "It was him. I just know it."

Baron didn't press her. Her conviction had him sold on it, as well. It must have been Steven. What else could have made this petite and typically mild-mannered young woman commit murder?

They'd been sitting together for close to two hours talking about the events of January 5, 2008. Misa had been reluctant to open up about it at first. But when Baron assured her that he was no longer in cahoots with Frankie, that in fact Frankie had abandoned him the same way he had abandoned Misa's sister, she told him everything that led up to the shooting that night. She had gone into detail about her determination to remain at Baron's bedside while he lingered in a coma; about the time she found Shane curled up inside Camille's bathtub, hiding from Steven; how Steven had told her that Shane loved to play hide-and-seek, and how it haunted her now to think of the terror her child must have felt every time he tried to find a hiding place secure enough to keep a pedophile from hurting him.

Baron sat there in silence for a while and watched as Misa got comfortable on the sofa. She seemed so calm and matter-of-fact now as she talked about it. But he could also see the torment in her eyes, the pain that lay just beneath the surface of her pretty brown eyes.

He thought about what his mother had told him in the hospital, what Misa had confirmed for him tonight. She had sat by his side day in and day out for weeks, despite their checkered history. Knowing that he hadn't always treated her well, Baron looked at her questioningly.

"Why did you do it?" She looked at him as if she didn't understand the question. "Why did you care about me so much that you sat with me all those days?"

She had been asking herself that question over and over again. The answer wasn't an easy one. She had done it because she hoped to show Baron that she was worthy of being his one and only. She had hoped to secure a spot in his life so that she could live better, so that Shane could have it all. But admitting that to Baron now as he sat in a wheelchair stripped of his seat at the helm of his family seemed cruel. Misa shrugged.

Baron stared at the floor. He had been thinking a lot lately—about everything. And he had finally begun to ask himself some hard questions. One of the things he pondered was why he had been so violent toward the women in his life— particularly his ex-girlfriend Angie and then Misa. And Trina Samuels.

"I wasn't always nice to you," he admitted. "I beat you so bad that time before I took you to Miami." He seemed to cringe at the thought of it.

Misa saw him struggle with the memory. She, too, recalled that trip with mixed emotions. On the one hand she had been overjoyed about being by Baron's side, in his life and in his bed. But he had beaten her so mercilessly that she still felt sore at the thought of it. Misa decided to be honest in the hopes that he would see he wasn't the only one in the wrong.

"I wanted you to be that someone special in my life no matter what. So when you got physical I overlooked it because I wanted you to be Mr. Right. I wanted to be with you and I wanted you to be Shane's father figure. I had it all pictured perfectly in my mind." She shook her head at the absurdity of it now. "When you got shot, I guess I felt like you needed me." Misa sighed, realizing now that it was her son who had needed her the most then. "I wanted to be there when you woke up so you would see that you hadn't been alone."

He smiled slightly. "And your face was the first one I saw when I opened my eyes. You looked shocked as hell!"

Misa smiled, too, remembering how happy she had been when she saw Baron's beautiful green eyes focusing in on her.

"I was so happy. It was Christmas morning, and I knew that your mother would be so ecstatic when she saw that you were awake."

Baron knew that it wasn't his fault what had happened to

Shane. But he felt obligated to let Misa know how much he appreciated the fact that she—the unlikeliest of all the people he had been close to in the months before his shooting—had been the one to stand by his side when the chips were down.

"I've been doing a lot of thinking about the shit I've done, you know?"

Misa could see that he was serious. He appeared to be struggling with his emotions as he spoke to her.

"Same here," she said. "They got me talking to a psychiatrist once a week, so I'm forced to think about it even when I don't want to."

He smiled. "Sometimes I think I need a psychiatrist."

Misa didn't know what to say.

Baron stared at her for a few minutes and remembered her as merely the sex toy he used to take out and play with at will. The months preceding his accident had been an endless cycle of weed, alcohol, sex, women, and cash—lots of cash he had flushed down the drain. In the midst of all that had come Misa, and he had taken it all out on her—his frustration with Gillian and his father, with Frankie, his financial misfortunes. Poor Misa had borne the weight of Baron's fury simply because she was there and she kept coming back.

"I know that I have a problem with my temper. I take shit out on people like I did to you, like I did to Angie." He looked at his hands as if they were foreign objects. "I go too far with shit sometimes. And I don't know why." He got quiet again and then looked at Misa, locked eyes with her. "I'm sorry," he said. "For what I did to you and for what I did to everybody else." He looked so serious.

Misa nodded, but couldn't help thinking that it sounded as if she was the representative—in Baron's mind at least—of all the people he had ever done dirty.

She decided not to sugarcoat what she was thinking. Misa cleared her throat and spoke her mind.

"You should be sorry," she said, her eyes penetrating his. "You're not the only one who's been doing a lot of thinking. I have, too. And I know I never should have tried to make you love me. I should never have chased after you the way I did, because it caused me to neglect my son." Her voice cracked and she took a deep breath. "But instead of appreciating the time I was spending with you, all you did was treat me like shit. And I was dumb enough to think that you could learn to love me. I thought that if I was patient with you, if I kept being there for you when you needed me, and showing you that I was on your side, that you would change." Misa shook her head in disgust. "I thought that your money, your power, and your status were all the things I needed to make a perfect life for me and Shane. It seemed like all you were missing was a woman in your life to complete you, and I wanted to be that woman. I wanted the money, the status, and the prestige of being Baron Nobles's wifey. And when you got shot, I thought that if I sat by your side every second you would wake up and realize how much I loved you. And then you would love me, too. I was so stupid." She looked at Baron again. "I'm so mad at myself for taking time away from my son when he needed me the most. But I'm mad at you, too, Baron. I didn't deserve what you did to me."

Baron felt himself getting choked up. He hadn't expected Misa to be so hard on him. He was already sorry for his poor treatment of her, but hearing her spell it all out for him made him feel even worse.

"You're right," he said. "I can't go back and undo what I did to you. But, Misa, I am sorry. I really am. And I didn't deserve for you to treat me as well as you did. Covering up the things I did to you so that Frankie wouldn't find out, sitting by my side at the hospital . . . I kept you away from your son. I treated you bad. And I probably don't deserve your forgiveness now. But I'm still asking for it."

Misa stared back at him. "Is that why you bailed me out? 'Cuz you feel guilty?"

He started to deny it, but decided against it. "That was part of it," he admitted. "But I also knew that you could use a friend. I owed you that. I couldn't sit back and watch Frankie keeping you locked up on Rikers Island when I don't feel like you deserve that."

Misa held his gaze. "Thank you," she said.

Baron shrugged his shoulders and gave her a half smile. "You coming here today and giving me a chance to try and get you to forgive me is all the thanks I need."

Misa felt awkward. She wasn't sure what to say to fill the void.

Finally, Baron spoke again.

"I know I fucked up. I made some wrong moves. But to be left out in the wind like this . . ."

Baron stared off into space momentarily. "Everybody except for you and my mother abandoned me." He seemed to chuckle slightly at the thought of that. "Half the niggas working for Frankie right now are my so-called friends. Gillian is my *sister*. My own flesh and blood hasn't called me or come to see me since I got out of the hospital."

Misa frowned, having always been under the impression that Baron and Gillian were as close as two siblings could get. "Maybe she's too busy stealing Frankie from my pregnant sister to call you."

"Camille is pregnant?" Baron couldn't believe his ears.

Misa nodded, smirking a little. "So she didn't mention

that when she came and told you how broke my sister is, huh?"

Baron had explained to Misa that it had been Gillian's visit with him in the hospital that had prompted him to send Celia to bail her out of jail. Hearing how alone Camille and Misa were in the world was something Baron was all too familiar with. But Gillian hadn't mentioned that Camille was pregnant with Frankie's child.

"Wow. That's crazy." He shook his head. "He left her when she needs him the most. I know exactly how Camille feels."

Misa crossed her legs, decided to do a little prying. "If Gillian and Frankie cut you off altogether, then how do you have the money to stay out here, the money to bail me out and pay a fancy lawyer like Teresa Rourke?"

He smiled then. "My mother," he said. "She's the most wonderful mother anybody could ever ask for." Baron shared with Misa how he had awakened from the coma distraught not only that his father was dead, that he may never walk again, and that he had been shunned by his family, but by the fact that he was now flat broke and without a penny to his name. Every one of his resources had dried up while he lay stricken by Jojo's bullets.

"I poured my heart out to her when no one was around. I told her how much money I had left—next to nothing. And I thought she was gonna be stressed out over how we were gonna pay the hospital bills and where I was gonna live without money coming in. None of that happened."

"What did she say?"

"That she had known for years that I wasn't ready for what my father gave me to handle." Baron shrugged, still not in complete agreement with Celia on that point. "So she always planned for 'what if.' She told me she hoped that it would be more like 'what if Baron stops being a criminal and wants to go to college?' But it turned out to be 'what if Baron gets shot, gets his father killed, and blows damn near all the money?'"

"Don't say it like that. It sounds so—"

"True?" he laughed. "Fuck it. It is what it is."

Misa had never heard Baron sound so defeated.

"Anyway, she had some money put away, some property nobody knew she had. It's funny 'cuz I doubt that Mayra or Gillian know all of what my father actually gave to my mother when they broke up. It almost seems like he was hiding some of his shit from Mayra by giving it to my moms."

Misa smiled. "Men can be so deceitful toward their wives," she said, willing to bet that neither Camille nor Mayra knew the half of what their husbands did behind their backs.

"Well, in my mother's case, that was a good thing. Thanks to the fact that she was smart with what my father gave her, I'm not worried about nothing." He looked at Misa sincerely. "And you don't have to worry about nothing, either."

She seemed a little surprised.

"You can stay here if you want. You can stay for as long as you want. Nobody has to know," Baron continued. "My moms got a nurse coming in here around the clock to help me out. But she don't let them do their job. My mama's always gonna be the one who takes care of her baby."

Misa laughed. She knew the feeling. Lily had been hovering over her like an umbrella for weeks.

"So you don't have to worry about being stuck taking care of me or no shit like that if you decide to stay."

Misa felt sorry for Baron then. "I wouldn't feel 'stuck,' Baron," she said. "Don't say it like that." She recalled a time when she would have jumped at an invitation to move into

Baron's home, into his life. But now, everything was different. Too much had changed for Misa to even consider his offer. "I'm comfortable staying at my mother's house," she said. "But I appreciate the offer. I'm grateful for everything you've been doing for me, Baron."

He shrugged, humbled by his disability. He had always been a loudmouth, a hothead. Not being able to walk and having to be at the mercy of nurses and his mama had taken his ego down several notches. "Well, the bottom line is that I know how you must feel. Everybody's looking at you like everything is your fault." He pointed toward himself. "You're not the only one."

Misa understood what he meant. She knew that everyone blamed him for Nobles's murder. Baron was just as much an outcast in his family as she was in hers. She was still quite surprised by how despondent Baron seemed overall. He sounded like he had reached the end of the line.

"I know I'm the one that made Jojo do what he did," Baron admitted, his voice low and monotone. "I knew that he could come back at me at any minute. But I never thought he would hurt my father." Baron got emotional and then gathered himself. "He didn't have nothing to do with it. And I feel just as bad as everybody thinks I should." He wiped his eyes quickly. "But I feel like Frankie and Gillian forgot the good shit I did for this family. It's like they forgot who brought us this far over all these years. It was me." Baron thought back on all the moves he'd made, the connections and money he'd made. "And I know I fucked up this time. But, damn. They just left me out here like an outcast."

Misa understood how Baron must feel.

"And I want you to know something else," he said. "I admire you for what you did."

Misa seemed surprised to hear that.

"I think it took guts to go and face the muthafucka who did that to your kid. A lot of people would have called the cops and let the justice system handle it. But it took a lot of heart for you to go over there and face him by yourself. I think that says a lot about your character."

"Thank you," Misa said, genuinely touched.

"You got a lot of heart, Misa. Your son is a lucky little boy to have you for a mother."

Misa's eyes watered then. She wasn't sure that she agreed with Baron's assessment, but she was praying to have another chance to get it right. She smiled through her tears. "He's a lot more comfortable with me now. We put together puzzles and color together during our visits." She seemed to glow just from the thought of it. "And when he has to leave, he gets sad. Each time, I promise him that he'll see me again soon and he calms down." She looked at Baron. "I'm so grateful that he still wants to see me."

He smiled at her.

"I'm gonna give you some money," he said, very matter-of-factly. Then his face contorted into a frown. "Frankie is playing himself. Camille is pregnant, and he's so far up Gillian's ass that he's not thinking." He looked at Misa and his expression softened. "I want you and Camille to have whatever you need. You have enough on your mind to not have to worry about money. I'm gonna give you something to hold you over for a little while. And when you need more, I want you to come back to me without hesitation."

"Wow," Misa said. "Thank you, Baron."

Misa felt conflicted. She agreed that Frankie was wrong, but she felt bad accepting legal help, bail money, and now financial assistance for her destitute sister from Baron. She hated feeling like a charity case and was sure that Baron was doing all of this in an effort to ease his guilt over a bevy of other things. She wished there was a way for her to show her appreciation. She thought of something that she had been meaning to tell him about ever since it happened.

"Oh, yeah," she said. "The night I was arrested, they brought me into this room where they had all these pictures of fugitives and victims of crimes and all kinds of shit. Anyway, your friend Danno was in one of those pictures."

Baron froze. "Danno?"

Misa nodded. "Yeah. The poster said something about he was wanted for the rape, torture, and murder of somebody named Trina . . . um . . . Trina Samuels."

Baron kept his game face on, but his ears were ringing, his head began to throb.

"It said that they found his DNA at the scene and—"

"You're sure it was Danno?"

"Yeah." Misa nodded. "They had his picture. Hers, too. She was a pretty girl." She saw Baron shift uncomfortably in his seat. "Have you seen him?"

Baron looked at her. "No," he said. "Did you tell them that you knew who he was?"

"Hell no!" Misa snapped. "I'm not crazy. I told them that I didn't recognize anybody on that wall."

"Did they believe you?" Baron was wondering how close he was to having the walls close in around him.

"I think so. They didn't press me about it. They just sent me to my cell and that was the end of that."

He nodded. "Thanks for letting me know," he said. He began thinking of how he would handle this now. Danno was on the police's radar in connection with a murder Baron had committed. Sure, Danno and his two nephews had been the ones to rape and torture Trina. But Baron had pulled the trigger and killed the girl. Now he had to decide how to handle the situation in order to save his own ass.

Just outside the room, Celia listened to their conversation. Having just returned from her lunch with Camille, she had come home and heard the two of them talking in the living room. She had heard Baron admit to having hit Misa, had heard him acknowledge that he hadn't been good to Misa. Celia had often wondered whether her son had laid his hands on his ex, Angie, and hearing Misa confirm her worst fears, Celia let out a sigh. Baron also seemed pretty interested in the murder of this Trina girl.

Celia walked upstairs to her bedroom, making a mental note to have a long talk with her son the next chance she got.

Red-Handed

Gillian stood at her father's gravesite, fighting back tears. She missed him with all of her heart. She had always been the apple of her father's eye. No matter what she did, whether it was making some toast for breakfast or winning a golf tournament, Doug thought it was the most amazing accomplishment and would always tell her how proud he was of her.

The winter air was breezy and the cloudy sky only made her dark mood worse. She felt so alone. Frankie was preoccupied with the drama unfolding in his family. And she was still too angry with Baron to forgive him for their father's death. Her mother wasn't grieving the way that she was. In fact, Gillian was beginning to wonder if Mayra had ever loved her father at all.

She had hoped that settling the score with Jojo would make her feel better. She had been waiting for some sense of closure to come over her. But it never came.

Gillian's tears fell slowly and she bent down to touch her

father's tombstone. "I miss you," she said softly. "I feel so alone."

She closed her eyes and felt the wind wrap itself around her body and imagined that it was her father hugging her tightly, reassuring her that everything was going to be all right and that he was still there with her. The thought made her smile and she opened her eyes and peered up at the cloudy sky.

"Thanks, Daddy," she said. "I needed that."

Camille had only returned to her Staten Island home to retrieve her mail and to gather some more of her belongings. She had finally accepted that this house she loved so much was no longer the haven it had once been for her. Reporters were fewer now, but still present. Her neighbors still stared at her and offered to lend a listening ear if she needed to talk just so that they could get into her business. She had put her beloved house on the market. She would miss the luxurious estate, but was eager to move on to a new chapter in the lives of her and her unborn child. These days she was staying with her mother out on Long Island. It allowed her to achieve some sense of normalcy in her otherwise chaotic life.

In her bedroom, she packed some of her underwear and sweaters, her important papers and her pictures. She zipped the duffel bag and was descending the stairs to the living room when the doorbell rang. Camille sighed, assuming that it was one of her "concerned" neighbors. She glanced through the peephole and was surprised to see the cop who had escorted her out of Gillian's house a few weeks ago. He wasn't in uniform, but she recognized him nonetheless.

Camille opened the door and he smiled at her, said hello.

"Hi," she said. "Officer King, right?"

He nodded, flattered that she remembered his name.

"What did I do now?"

He laughed, shook his head. "No, you didn't do any-thing." He looked around as if he had something painful to admit. "I looked up your license plate number and got your address. I'm not supposed to do that, so I hope you're not planning to rat me out."

Camille frowned. "Why?" Her paranoia made her won-der if he was a stalker, or if perhaps he was part of a larger investigation into her husband's illegal operations.

"I thought about you after that night at your husband's . . . at his um . . ."

"Girlfriend's house." Camille saw no point in beating around the bush.

"Yeah," Officer King said, laughing uneasily. "Anyway, you're a beautiful woman."

Camille smiled involuntarily.

"And I just couldn't help noticing that. I think your hus-band is a fool."

Camille found herself reluctantly flattered by the lengths this man had gone to in order to tell her this.

"Wow," she said, otherwise speechless. She realized that she hadn't been complimented by a man—her husband more specifically—in months. It hadn't occurred to her until now how much she had missed that.

"So . . ." He seemed like he hadn't thought his plan out this far ahead. "I'm sure you're not looking to get involved with somebody new right now, but I just wanted you to know that I'm available for friendship."

Camille giggled a little.

He smiled again. "I have great credentials for friendship. I

make a good listener, I won't borrow money." He stopped
joking around and got serious. "If you want to go and get
something to eat or something, I would be honored to—"

"Officer King," she interrupted.

"Elijah. You can call me Eli."

She smiled despite herself. He was cute. "Eli, I'm broke,
so there's no going Dutch. Is this your treat?"

His smile broadened. He assumed, based on the opulence
of her million-dollar home, that Camille was joking about
being broke. "Absolutely."

She nodded, grabbed her keys and her bag. "Let's go."

Misa sat with her legs crossed, her hands folded in her lap as ca-
sually as possible. Her shoulders were relaxed, her gaze was
steady and she didn't fidget, not even once. Her voice was firm,
and the chignon in her hair gave her the illusion of being an
innocent young mother. Her attorney Teresa Rourke was impressed. She decided then that Misa would make an excellent
witness. The two of them had spent the past two hours going
over grueling testimony, practice cross-examinations, and
things to avoid doing in front of the jury. Misa had gone over
her story step by step by step and it all added up. Everything
could have happened exactly the way Misa said it did.

The only problem was that Steven wasn't alive to tell his
side of the story.

"I think you're ready," Teresa said. "But when we step into
that courtroom next week, you have to know that every eye in
that room is going to be on you. They're going to attack your
character, your parenting, and even your family's reputation.
So, you have to be blind and deaf to all of that and stick to the
facts at hand. You believed he was molesting your son."

"He *was* molesting my son." Misa wasn't going to allow anyone—not even her own attorney—to question what she knew in her gut to be true.

Teresa nodded. "Okay. And you confronted him, armed to defend yourself in case he got violent. He lunged at you and you shot him in self-defense. To your credit, you didn't run or try to elude the police in any way. You have a good case, Misa."

Misa was glad to hear that. Still, she felt a "but" coming on.

"But I want you to know that they're going to question whether or not Steven was truly guilty of what you say he did. He didn't admit it, according to your story. In fact, he denied it."

"I don't give a fuck what he said!" Misa was vexed and her voice loomed larger than she was. "*He* did that to my son! And anybody sick enough to do that shit deserves to die."

"See?" Teresa shook her head, her long hair bouncing as she did so. "You can't do that on the witness stand. *That* right there will make a jury turn against you."

"Why? Because it's true?" Misa was sick of all this judicial bullshit.

Teresa sighed. "No. Because it sounds as if you made yourself judge and jury that night. You didn't call the police, Misa. You went over there and killed him. Self-defense is the only way this is a winnable case."

Misa understood that. But it was hard not to erupt in anger whenever anyone suggested that Steven was somehow a victim in all of this.

"If you give off the impression that you planned this, they will convict you. We want them to see you as a scared young mother who only wanted to protect her baby, to protect her-self."

"Okay," Misa said, and she knew her attorney was giving her good advice. But in her mind, she wondered if she could really sit silently and watch them paint that devil as a saint in court. She nodded, apologized to Teresa for her outburst, and prayed for a miracle.

It was Grammy night, and Dominique felt like such a grown-up. Tonight, she could party guilt free until the wee hours of the morning for once. She had been spending every spare moment of her time with her daughter in order to make up for lost time. She enjoyed her child's company, but she was eager for a night to let her hair down and be a grown-up! Octavia was safely accounted for at Toya's house for the night while Dominique had been at L.A. Reid's Grammy party to celebrate the success of some of the label's biggest acts. But all the dancing had taken its toll on her. The loud music and louder outfits worn by the entertainers and their entourages was enough to make Dominique feel like an old lady. She wanted to be anywhere else but here.

The party was jumping. R&B sensation Kiara was performing and Dominique was seated at a table with three of the five nominees for best new artist. Sangria and conversation flowed nonstop. Dominique sucked on a piece of fruit from the bottom of her glass and glanced at her phone to see what time it was. It was 1:54 A.M. She took a chance and text messaged Archie.

Are you still up?

After a few minutes, a reply flashed across the screen. *Yeah.*

She smiled, encouraged by the alcohol in her system and typed a reply.

Can I come over?

She thought about Jamel and his constant phone calls lately. He was full of apologies and excuses for why he'd gone back to selling drugs, back to his baby mama, back to everything he swore he was finished with. He had even resorted to passing messages to her through his mother, hopeful that hearing how sorry he was might soften Dominique's determination to hate him forever. She didn't want to hear anything he had to say. To her, he was a scared little bitch, deceitful and full of shit. There were two things she hated more than anything—liars and cowards. Jamel fell into both categories.

Minutes more passed, with Dominique second-guessing herself. If Archie didn't respond or if he said no, she'd be humiliated. Then she felt her phone vibrate in her bag and looked at the screen.

Of course.

Dominique was overjoyed. She spent another few minutes at the party before hurrying out and hitting the FDR. Traffic was surprisingly light and it wasn't long before she parked her car outside of Archie's apartment building and refreshed her lip gloss. She climbed the stairs to his apartment and knocked. Archie quickly opened the door.

Ushering her inside, he noticed that Dominique was teetering slightly on her four-inch Louboutin boots.

"Are you all right?" he asked.

She stepped into the living room, stripped out of her black leather jacket, and grinned. "Nope."

Archie smirked, caught off guard. "You are *not* all right?" His accent was so thick and so sexy to her.

Dominique shook her head. "I'm a little tipsy," she admitted before slumping onto his love seat and crossing her legs.

Archie smiled and joined her there. "So you shouldn't be driving."

She knew he was right. "I know. I just didn't have the patience to sit at the party till I sobered all the way up."

He nodded. "I guess you had fun tonight?"

She smiled. "Yes. I was drinking sangria . . . Delicious!"

She kicked off her boots and regaled him with some details of her evening rubbing elbows with the music industry's elite. Together, they watched an old Eddie Murphy movie on cable and before long, Dominique had sobered up somewhat. Archie didn't want her to be too tipsy tonight. He didn't want her to forget what he was going to do to her.

Laughing at one of Eddie's jokes, Archie leaned close to her. With little room between them, and their faces merely inches apart, their kiss happened easily. Archie pulled her onto his lap and she straddled him as they tongued one another passionately. Firmly, and ever so carefully, Archie palmed her ass and stood up, lifting her easily in his arms as he carried her slowly toward his bedroom. Their kiss uninterrupted as he walked down the long corridor, Dominique wrapped her arms around his neck and her legs around his waist. She felt herself melting into his arms, feeling so safe there and so wanted. Finally, they entered his bedroom. Gently, he placed her on his bed and shut the bedroom door behind them.

Archie stripped her out of her clothes and she helped him, eagerly pulling her Rachel Roy dress over her head. Climbing out of his pajamas, he mounted her, stroking her face and sucking ever so softly on each of her breasts with an erotic mixture of pleasure and pain. Their lovemaking spanned hours and sounded nearly animalistic as she came over and over again. He palmed her ample ass in his big hands, kneading it as he grinded into her and felt her wetness engulf him in a creamy tidal wave. Finally, after nearly two hours of alternating positions and unparalleled pleasure, Archie came.

Sweaty and out of breath, he collapsed on top of her, his long dick still lodged limply within her sugar walls, and fell asleep, cradling her in his arms. Dominique smiled, feeling more content than she had in all her years of fucking with bitch-ass Jamel, and drifted into a peaceful and euphoric sleep.

It was four o'clock in the morning when she awoke to Archie spooning her. Her hair was a mess, the sheets were wet from a mixture of sweat and secretions and morning breath had crept up on them both. Still, Archie pulled her close to him from behind, her ass resting against his hard dick. Slipping on a condom, he entered her sideways, stroking her to paradise once more.

She didn't recall falling asleep again, but apparently she had. It was now after ten o'clock in the morning and Dominique hadn't even bothered to check in at the office. True, it was Friday and it was unlikely that any real work would get done the day after the Grammys. But it was so uncharacteristic of her to play hooky so boldly from the job she cherished.

She pondered going into work, and it seemed as if Archie read her mind. As he stirred awake, he noticed her sitting up in bed and pulled her back down beside him. Wrapping her in his strong embrace he kissed her neck.

"Don't leave yet," he said. "I don't have anywhere to be today."

Dominique was tempted. His voice seemed to pull her toward him, but she resisted. "I have some things I need to do."

He frowned. "What you have to do?"

She thought about it. There was really nothing that warranted her immediate attention. Still, it seemed odd for her to remain there with him in the daylight hours. She shrugged. "I don't know. But I don't do this," she said, gesturing at the bed in which they lay.

He pulled away slightly and smiled at her. "You don't do what? Relax?"

Dominique was caught off guard by that.

"You *don't* really relax, do you?" he pressed. "Every time I see you or talk to you, you are going somewhere or doing something."

She thought about it. It was true. She felt as if her life was in a constant state of self-imposed "fast-forward." "You're right."

"So stay. Relax."

Dominique took a deep breath and thought it over. *Fuck it!* She settled into the crook of his arm and draped one of her legs across his. Archie grabbed the remote to the large-screen TV perched on his bedroom's far wall and turned on a Showtime series on demand. He explained the premise to her and before she knew it they'd watched five consecutive episodes. With their bodies intertwined, they napped off and on throughout the day. They'd wake up and have long conversations, their faces merely inches apart.

One such discussion involved her relationship with Jamel.

"So, your man is home now, no?" Archie asked.

Dominique rolled her eyes. She shook her head. "Not for long." She looked at him with an expression that showed her disdain. "He came home a month ago, got right back on the block and right back in his baby mama's bed."

Archie scoffed at that. "With a good woman like you behind him?"

Dominique nodded. She knew she was a good woman and that Jamel was too dumb to realize it.

"Well, he's a fool, then. If he couldn't see that he had a good thing, it's his loss."

Dominique agreed. "I just feel kinda dumb, you feel me?

I should have known better," she said. "He ain't shit, and everybody realized that but me. It's just a matter of time before he winds up right back in jail."

Archie listened as she blamed herself for her ex's shortcomings and rubbed her feet as they lay in bed. "Well, you learn lessons as you go along. Don't beat yourself up about it."

Dominique grinned. "I think the lesson is to lock my heart away inside a fortress."

Archie smiled. "I don't think that's it."

"What is it then?" Dominique propped herself up on one elbow and looked at him for the answer.

"You have to peep the warning signs sooner next time. You can still love. Just make sure you're gettin' the same love and respect in return. And just because one man doesn't appreciate you don't mean that no other man ever will."

Dominique thought about it as she massaged his chiseled chest. Archie gave her some purple kush to puff on while she relaxed. It felt blissful and the entire day passed with them lying there that way. The sun had risen and gone down again without either of them bothering to stray too far from the comfort they found in Archie's big bed.

From time to time, they checked their cell phones and noticed missed calls relating to each of their businesses. They responded to the quick fixes and ignored anything that would separate them for an extended period of time. For the first time in far too long, Dominique felt like a man not only appreciated her presence but cherished it. He made her feel so good that she wanted to make sure she did all she could to make him feel the same way.

At last, at nearly 7:00 P.M., Dominique gathered her things, kissed Archie for endless moments as she bid him a reluctant good-bye, and headed home to get her heart in check.

"So you're pregnant?"

Eli didn't hide his disappointment, and then felt badly for that. "I don't mean it like that. I mean I'm happy for you, but . . . damn."

Camille had to admit that this was pretty tough luck—that she would meet a handsome, single man who liked her right after she'd discovered she was pregnant by her philandering husband. "I think I'm in this by myself, though," she said, sadly. "My marriage is over, so I gotta move on. New year, new start, you know?"

Eli knew she was trying to sound optimistic, and he felt sorry for her. It had to be hard watching her marriage fall apart before her eyes. "I hear you," he said. She ate her grilled chicken sandwich and Eli watched her as she chewed. He thought she was adorable.

"Yeah, I know exactly what you mean." He took a bite of his quarter pounder and thought about the other things she had told him. "So you said you're staying in Long Island now?"

She nodded. "Yeah, with my mom. I needed to get away from it all." Camille didn't elaborate.

"I live in Queens. That's not so far away. Since you're pregnant, you'll probably be hungry a lot over the next few months. I can meet you at your neighborhood Mickey D's. Cheer you up every now and then." He took another bite.

Camille stared at him for several seconds and then frowned. "Why?" she asked. "I mean why to *all* of this? You live in Queens. So on your day off you drive all the way out here to Staten Island to ring my bell and ask me out . . . all because you thought I was cute when you kicked me out of—"

"I didn't kick you out," Eli corrected, his mouth half full. "I was very nice."

"Whatever." Camille was confused. "You came all the way out here for what?"

"To ask you out," he said. "It *is* my day off, but I had to go to court downtown this morning to testify in a case. Afterwards, I thought about you. Like I told you, I had your address and I decided to stop by and take my chances."

"You came all that way to find me because you thought I was cute?"

He nodded and Camille twisted her face into a doubtful expression.

"You must think I'm younger or dumber than I really am."

Eli shrugged. "I was curious," he admitted. "Your husband is laid up with his mistress in a multimillion-dollar Upper East Side town house. You got on a coat worth more than what I make in a month, driving the brand-new Range. And despite all that obvious wealth, I thought you seemed . . . *sad,* really sad and kinda fragile. So I was intrigued. I kept thinking about you and I wanted to find out more, to see if you were willing to give a guy like me a chance with a woman like you."

Camille wasn't buying it. "A woman like me. You don't even know me."

"I'm trying to get to know you."

"And now I tell you that I'm pregnant by my husband and you still want to hang out with me. Why?"

Eli finished chewing and wiped his mouth with his napkin. He looked at Camille and figured he had nothing to lose by leveling with her.

"I've only been a cop for two years, but I see women like you all the time," he said. "Battered women with beautiful faces and expensive homes."

"I'm not a battered woman," Camille corrected, slightly offended. This nigga thought he had her all figured out.

"Not physically maybe. But emotionally, verbally probably, he batters you."

Camille listened, hearing the truth in what Eli was saying to her.

"And he has you living lavishly and wearing big fur coats and bigger diamonds. So you deal with it." He sipped his Fanta. "I think—and correct me if I'm wrong—that after a while, when you deal with shit like that for so long, it lowers your self-esteem. You start to forget that there's more to you than a pretty face and pretty clothes."

Camille thought maybe Eli was on to something after all.

"So, when I saw you that night standing there looking so beautiful and so upset at the same time, my heart went out to you, first of all." He popped a French fry in his mouth. "You were *mad*! And even though you were pissed off, I thought you looked so much better than his side chick."

Camille laughed, which made Eli smile. "Seriously," he said. He opened up a packet of ketchup. "I couldn't help noticing how pretty you were even though you were obviously hurt. Your husband seemed like an asshole for letting his side chick call the cops on you. So I'll admit that I drove out here to ask you out, hoping that we would hit it off and I could make you forget that lame husband, maybe give you a shoulder to cry on."

Camille didn't respond.

"So now . . . I see that you got a situation." He ate another fry and looked at her. "But I still think you're beautiful. And I still think you need to forget about him. Just 'cuz you got a bun in the oven doesn't mean we can't hang out. It's not like you got the cooties or something." He grinned, revealing dimples.

Camille sipped her milkshake. "You really think I'm cuter than she is?"

He nodded. "Definitely." He passed her an apple pie, which she readily accepted. "I'm a good guy. You should get to know me."

Camille finished her lunch and did just that.

Mayra Nobles sat on the edge of her bed and lit a cigarette. Her lover ran his fingers through her long thick hair and she smiled. Guy was so affectionate with her, so attentive. She closed her eyes as he glided his fingertips down the small of her back, kissed the nape of her neck.

"Stay with me," she purred. "Spend the night."

Guy was tempted. He wanted her so badly that he would have gladly sacrificed everything in order to have Mayra all to himself. She was a lovely and voluptuous woman with sexiness dripping from her every crevice. But money was important to her, and until Doug Nobles's will was executed, Mayra was playing the role of grieving widow to the hilt. If her affair with Guy was uncovered, she knew that Celia, Baron, or even Gillian might try to shut her out. As long as that was the case, Mayra would do anything she could to preserve that inheritance. Therefore, spending the night with her in the very bed she had shared with her dead husband was out of the question, no matter how much they both wanted it.

"Next time," he lied. He got out of bed and began to get dressed as she watched him.

The infamous Guy London was one of the best entertainment lawyers in the game. Guy was one of her late husband's closest friends, a friend who had steered him toward numerous ventures through which Doug Nobles had funneled tons of illegal money over the years. He was handsome and self-assured, and was married to a former supermodel who wasn't ready to let go of the limelight just yet. His trysts with Mayra had started a year ago during a dinner party at which Doug Nobles had been present, parked in his wheelchair downstairs while Guy had his wife pinned to the wall in the master bathroom.

Mayra had been eager for her slice of the Nobles fortune, but hadn't expected it to end so violently and tragically. Doug Nobles had been a sick man, diagnosed with multiple sclerosis after a twelve-year stint in prison. The disease had nearly crippled him, and Mayra had struggled to come to terms with the fact that her husband, who had once been fun and spontaneous, was now anything but. She had expected that MS would continue to debilitate him, but it had been a bloody shootout that brought his life to an end instead. As the date neared for the reading of her husband's will, she pondered what she would do with the rest of her life as a wealthy widow. For now, she walked Guy to the door and kissed him good-bye. He winked at her and she giggled like a schoolgirl.

As Guy climbed into his car and blew Mayra a kiss, Gillian watched from her car cloaked in the midnight shadows across the street.

Toya lay back in her bathtub surrounded by bubbles and candles and stared at the ceiling. She couldn't believe what was happening. Dominique had picked up Octavia and the two of them had gone home hours ago. Shortly afterward, Russell had stopped by unannounced. Usually, Toya would have told him off for coming by uninvited. But, this time Toya had

yanked him into her home by his collar, kissed him passionately, and allowed him to ravage her. More than an hour of
wild, kinky sex had followed, culminating in both of them falling asleep in her big bed. Toya had awakened, hoping it had
all been a bad dream. But it wasn't. She turned over in bed
only to find Russell's ugly face, mouth wide open as he snored.

Even then she hadn't taken her usual next step. Ordinarily
she would have awakened him and sent him home. After all,
she almost never allowed a man to spend the night in her
home, in her bed. It was a privilege that very few men had
ever enjoyed. Still she found herself reluctant to awaken him
considering the fact that he had rocked her to sleep so ex-
pertly. What he lacked in good looks, Russell more than
made up for in sexual prowess. He was, hands down, the best
fuck she'd had in a long, long time. In fact, she hoped that
when he woke up he'd be ready to go for round two.

Toya had run herself a steaming hot bath and lit all the
candles she had in order to clear her mind. As she lay now in
the expansive Jacuzzi she closed her eyes and tried to tell herself that she didn't like him that much. Sure, Russell was
smart, a good conversationalist, charming, and single. He had
no children, a great career, and made her shake like she was
seizing. But that face!

Her doorbell rang and interrupted her thoughts. Toya lay
there for a few moments, trying to figure out who might be at
her door at this late hour. She sighed, wondering if one of her
friends was in yet another crisis. As she prepared to climb out
of the bathtub, she noticed Russell watching her from the
doorway. Her body half in and half out of the steaming bath,
he stared at her and smiled.

"You stay right there," he said. "I'll answer the door and
then I'm coming back for you."

Toya smiled and got excited at the thought of what awaited her when he returned. She heard him descend the stairs and unlock her front door. And the sound she heard next caused her hair to stand on end.

"Who are you?" boomed a raspy and demanding female voice.

Toya scrambled out of the bathtub and dried off as quickly as possible.

"My name is Russell. Russell Sharp."

"Sharp?" the voice came again, then laughter.

"Yes, ma'am."

Toya frantically reached for her bathrobe and put it on, tying it tightly around her waist.

"Where are your clothes?"

Russell cleared his throat. "Well, I just woke up and—"

"Just woke up? Where is my daughter? TOYA!"

Toya ran down the stairs with an award-worthy fake smile on her face.

"Sweets!" Toya greeted her mother using the nickname she and her brothers had called her by since they were kids. "What a surprise!" Despite her steely demeanor, Toya turned to mush whenever her mother came around. She was mortified that Sweets had arrived unannounced all the way from Atlanta to find ugly-ass Russell in her home, fresh out of her bed.

Jeanie "Sweets" Blake looked from Toya to Russell and back again. "I bet it is a surprise!"

Toya smiled at Russell. "This is my mother."

Russell could see Toya's discomfort even as she smiled. He looked at her mother and apologized. "I shouldn't have answered the door dressed this way."

"Dressed?" Jeanie said sarcastically, looking at his long johns and T-shirt.

Russell could see where Toya got her straightforwardness from. "I'm just gonna go and get my stuff and head home."

Toya nodded vigorously. She looked around and saw that her mother had brought enough luggage for weeks.

As Russell scampered up the stairs to retrieve his clothes, Jeanie watched him and shook her head.

"What the—"

"Sweets, at least wait until he's gone!" Toya hissed. She stomped off toward her kitchen and poured herself a glass of wine. She could tell it was going to be a long night.

Toya watched from the kitchen as her mother strolled around her house and picked everything apart. "When's the last time you took a sponge to these floors? All the dust gets trapped in the corners and you can't get that with a broom. Sometimes you gotta get on your knees to get all that up."

"I know. I'll get to it eventually."

"Eventually?" Toya came back into the living room and saw the look of disgust on her mother's face.

Russell came back downstairs with all his clothes on and his leather jacket in hand. He wondered for a moment whether he should kiss Toya good-bye in front of her mother, but judging from the looks on both of their faces he figured it best to just leave.

"It was nice to meet you," he said to Jeanie. She only waved dismissively in response. He looked at Toya and smiled. "Talk to you soon."

Toya nodded and watched him go. The second the door shut behind him, Jeanie leered at her daughter. "You can't be that desperate. That is the ugliest man I've ever seen. He looks deformed!"

Toya took a deep breath and blew it out. She sipped her wine and looked at her mother. "You could have called to tell me that you were coming to New York. I would have been ready for your visit."

"I'm your mother. I shouldn't have to call. Your door should always be open to me." Jeanie set her purse down on the coffee table and sat on Toya's sofa. "How long have you been letting that man in your house? You know once you let them in it's hard to get rid of 'em. They see you got all this going on and they latch on like bloodsuckers."

"This was his first time over here."

"Don't even think about having kids with him, either!"

Toya rolled her eyes. "What are you talking about kids for? I'm not having any kids! I don't know how many times I can say it before you finally get it." Toya sat across from her mother, careful to shield her nakedness beneath her bathrobe. "And he may not be cute, but he's very nice. He's a fireman."

"All he has to do is *look* at the fire and—"

"Cut it out!" Toya was not in the mood to defend her love life to her mother, especially because she hadn't made complete sense of it herself. She understood then how much her parents had affected her outlook on men and relationships. It seemed she had inherited her mother's shallow and judgmental ways as well as her father's biting and vicious verbal tenacity. The way she was being torn to shreds by her mother sounded eerily similar to her rants at her friends. "I don't fly down to Atlanta unannounced and pick apart your sex life."

"You're not supposed to meddle in my business. *I'm* the mother."

"Yes, you are. But I don't want to talk about Russell anymore." Toya sipped some more of her merlot and let the warm liquid coat her insides. She smiled at Jeanie. "How are you? What brings you to town?"

Jeanie scowled playfully at her daughter, still disapproving of her choice in bedfellow. "I spoke to Nate."

Toya rolled her eyes again. She hadn't heard from her father since their lunch date weeks ago, and she liked it that way.

"He told me that you had lunch with him, that you heard him out. He said that he promised to leave you alone after that, and he has kept his word. But he was hoping that you would call him and—"

"So you flew all the way up here to tell me that?" Toya was angry now. "You could have saved yourself the airfare."

"He's your father," Jeanie said, leaning forward in her seat.

"You know what?" Toya sat forward as well. "You got a lot of nerve, Sweets. Coming to town with your criticism about who I spend my time with when all the while you spent your whole life with a loser like Nathaniel Blake."

"All right, now," Jeanie warned.

"Even after all these years, he's still got you like a puppet on a string."

Jeanie stood up. "Now, look here, Miss Thang," she said, pointing at Toya. "I'm nobody's goddamned puppet!"

Toya stopped talking, aware that she had touched a nerve.

"Nate didn't do any more to me than I let him do. I was the one who stayed, and kept letting him back in." Jeanie slowly sat back down under the gravity of that statement. "And it was a long time ago. It's time to let go of old pain, that's what I came here to tell you."

"Well, I don't have nothing else to say to him." Toya set her glass on the table. There were things her mother just couldn't understand. "He said his piece, I listened. He said he'd leave me alone, and that's cool with me. I don't see what else we need to talk about."

Jeanie sat back down and looked at Toya coyly. "Forgiveness, Toya."

Toya felt like a little kid again, scolded by her mother, a lesson forced on her when she wasn't in the learning mood.

"Your brothers invited him over for dinner at Derrick's house on Sunday night."

Toya felt her temper flaring. *Fucking traitors—especially Derrick!*

"You should be there," Jeanie said.

Toya sneered at her mother. "So is that why you flew into New York, to reunite with him after all these years? You can't be that desperate." Toya watched her mother react to her own words tossed back at her.

Jeanie didn't respond.

"What is it?" Toya asked, really searching her mother's face for an answer. "What's so great about this guy all of a sudden that everybody can forget all the shit he used to do? He claims to be sick and gets some new clothes and a shower and just like that he's a changed man! Gimme a break! We *all* know better than that."

Jeanie felt her eyes well up with tears. She looked down as a couple fell into her lap and Toya felt bad. She hadn't meant to make her mother cry.

"I'm sorry."

"Don't be sorry. You're right. Nate was a horrible person when he was getting high." She shook her head at the memory. "But before that, before all the drugs and the liquor, he was a good man. He was a good father and a good friend. He loved you so much. His only girl." Jeanie's face softened at the memory of Nate cradling Toya in his arms when she was a baby, comforting her whenever she cried. "Then he started drinking and that made him mean. Then the drugs got a hold of him and he was never the same. I didn't know him anymore. For years I hung around hoping and praying that the man I married would walk back in that door one day or wake up from out of one of those twenty-four-hour naps he used to take when he was coming down from being high for days at a time." She shook her head. "All that time I was waiting and hoping and praying, you and your brothers were watching and living with a whole lot of bullshit. And y'all didn't deserve that. I should have left him a long, long time before I actually did."

Toya felt better hearing her mother admit that. At least she wasn't completely delusional.

"But rejecting him now ain't the right kind of payback for what he did. He's dying, Toya. It's time to let it go." Jeanie took a deep breath and looked at Toya with a serious expression on her face. "I don't claim to be a saint. But I believe in God and I know that He wants us to let go and move on. You and I will go to dinner at Derrick's house on Sunday and then I'll see how long I need to stay in town before I head back." She clapped her hands together as if the matter was settled and stood up.

Toya watched her mother get up off the couch, retrieve her carry-on bag and purse and head upstairs to get settled in. She guzzled the rest of the wine in her glass and closed her eyes in exasperation.

Parental Discretion Advised

Gillian watched her mother flirting with the new Brazilian maître d' and bit her lip angrily. She drummed her fingers on the table impatiently and rolled her eyes. Her cell phone rang and interrupted her silent temper tantrum.

"Yeah?" she answered after seeing Baron's number flash across the screen.

"Hello to you, too," he said sarcastically. "Sounds like I caught you at a bad time. Should I make an appointment with you and Frankie? Call your secretary or sum'n?"

Gillian took a deep breath and glanced at her watch. She had no time for her mother's or Baron's game-playing today. "Baron, what do you need? I'm in the middle of something right now so I need you to cut to the chase."

He snickered, amused. Baby sis was sounding irritated. Sounded like she was playing the role of boss bitch to the hilt. "I owe you some money," he said. "How's that for cutting to the chase?"

Gillian recalled the fifty-five-thousand-dollar loan he'd begged her for in order to pay off a gambling debt. She'd taken the money out of her mother's restaurant and had waited months for Baron to pay it back. Frankie had eventually put the money back before anyone noticed the deficit, saving Gillian from having to admit to her father that she had given Baron the loan in the first place. Since then, she had practically forgotten about that money, it being the least of her troubles after losing her father and watching Frankie battle his wife and her family.

"Yes, you do," she said. "But consider it a gift. No need to repay it." She watched her mother bend over to wipe up a spill off the restaurant floor, giving the new guy a bird's-eye view of her plump assets.

Baron frowned. His sister was turning down a lot of money. "Why?" he asked.

She considered telling Baron that business was booming for them ever since Angelle had come through with an increase in prescription drugs, which was the new "crack epidemic" as far as Gillian could tell. OxyContin, Percocet, diazepam, and dozens of others—everybody from college kids to soccer moms, corporate workers, and hoodrats alike had an affinity for some prescription medication these days and it was a cash cow for them. That was one reason why she had managed to push her brother's debt to the back of her mind. But it certainly wasn't the main reason. Gillian was sick of beating around the bush—with everybody.

"Because I don't want it, Baron" she said honestly. "Daddy's gone, and it's your fault. You might as well have pulled the trigger yourself as far as I'm concerned, because *you* killed him!" Gillian hissed into the phone with such venom that Baron could hear her anger. "I'm glad you're out of the hospital," she said, trying to calm down. "I'm happy to know that you're gonna make it and go on to fuck up some more before you die. But my father is dead because of you. And I can't forgive that. You're on your own now. Keep the fucking money and go away." She turned her cell phone off, tossed it in her bag, and stormed over toward her mother.

Mayra was seductively sipping on a drink through a skinny straw while eyeing Phillipe. Glancing over his shoulder, she saw Gillian heading in her direction and got a glimpse of the steam coming out of her daughter's ears.

"Excuse me for a moment while I see what's wrong with my Gigi," she said, dismissing the sexy help. He nodded and walked away just as Gillian approached. "Sorry to keep you waiting," Mayra said, smiling at her child in order to cut the immediate tension. "You look like you've got somewhere else to be."

Gillian glared at her mother. "Just take him in the back and let him hit it, Ma," she said. "You might as well."

Mayra stood speechlessly and stared at her daughter.

"I came here to talk to you over half an hour ago. I waited patiently, sitting over there and watching you flirt with this guy and bend over in front of him and—"

"I was picking up a piece of—"

"Fucking spinach, yes, I saw you, Ma!" Gillian yelled. "And I saw your black thong and your tramp stamp."

"Gigi, don't make me slap you in front of all these people."

Gillian laughed.

Mayra didn't. "I'm your mother and you *will* show me respect. I don't care how old you are. You watch your tone when you speak to me." Mayra looked around at her staff busying themselves nearby and eavesdropping. "Especially here," she said.

Gillian shook her head, smirking. "You don't even own this place anymore. That's what I came to tell you."

She watched the blood drain from her mother's face.

Mayra tried to smile and laugh it off as an insane notion. "What are you talking about?"

Gillian took her phone out of her bag and turned it back on. She then pressed send and waited. She looked at her mother and had to hand it to her. Mayra was still a beautiful woman at the age of fifty-six. She could easily pass for a woman years younger—smooth skin, lovely Cuban features, and a great body that women half her age often envied. Gillian had inherited her mother's eyes—bottomless wells of seduction that lured any man in deeper. She watched her mother's expression as she reached for her BlackBerry and read the message Gillian had just forwarded to her.

Did you ever love Daddy?

Mayra scrolled down to see a picture of her and Guy London locked in an embrace on her doorstep at two o'clock in the morning. She looked at her daughter, but found no words to say to her as the next message came through—this one a picture of Guy palming her ass near the window, as they had been careless enough to leave the curtain ajar. Mayra's and Guy's lips were inches apart as he gazed into her eyes—those same eyes that Gillian now realized had the power to turn any man, even the father she thought was smarter than any other, to mush.

"I don't want you to think that I hate you," Gillian said. "'Cuz I don't. But you know Guy was Daddy's friend—at least Daddy thought so." Gillian shook her head. "I've tried to put myself in your shoes, Ma. Maybe you married him when you were younger and he was *Doug Nobles*. That must have impressed you back then."

"Gigi—"

"No, no, I get it. And then he went to prison, came home

and got multiple sclerosis, lost his stamina. Maybe you got bored or you felt like you didn't bargain for this."

"Gillian—"

"But of all the men you could creep with . . . Guy? He's my godfather, Ma! Damn!"

"I didn't mean for this to . . . I did love your father." Mayra was choking up. Gillian couldn't stick around to watch that.

"I just thank God that Daddy was on to you before he died. At least I think he was. Frankie told me a few weeks ago that Daddy took this restaurant out of your name, that he signed it over to Frankie. He told me that Daddy was suspicious that someone close to him was out to get him. I narrowed down the short list of people who were close to Daddy. Me, Baron, Frankie, you, Guy, Celia . . . that's a pretty easy list. There wasn't much digging needed. I thought about the fact that Daddy chose to share his suspicions with Frankie and not with me. I figured he must have thought I was too close to a particular person to be impartial. So I started watching *you*. I imagined that Daddy might have suspected that you were fucking around and maybe he told Frankie about it. Turns out that I was right." Gillian shook her head at her mother. "He took the restaurant out of your name and put together a new will with a new attorney and even fired his old accountant. He knew something wasn't right, that it had to be someone close to him who you were creeping with. He may have even wondered if I knew about it." Gillian's jaw clenched as she pondered that thought. If she knew for sure that her father had questioned her loyalty to him because of her mother's treachery and deceit and died not knowing the truth, she would never have been able to forgive Mayra. It seemed, based on Nobles's actions in the days and weeks before he died, that he had no one he felt he could trust one hundred percent besides Frankie.

"Anyway, the new lawyer filed Daddy's will in probate court this morning." She handed her mother some paperwork. "Two hundred thousand is what you're getting, plus you can stay in the house. You pay Greta and any other staff you decide to keep out of your own pocket." Gillian dusted her hands off demonstratively. "That's it."

Mayra erupted in sobs and the staff kept on preparing to open up the restaurant for the night. Gillian turned on her heels and walked away from her mother, unable to stomach the drama Mayra was unleashing—crying, clutching her chest as if she were having an immediate heart attack.

"Tell Guy not to try to fight it or we'll show the pictures to his wife, and to all the magazines, too," Gillian called out over her shoulder.

She walked out of her mother's restaurant—out of her mother's life, she hoped, and Baron's, too—and into her destiny. She was right where she always knew she'd be—at the helm of her father's empire. He may not be around to see her do it, but she was going to make him proud of his baby girl.

Mary watched Frankie eat his sandwich and she smiled. He still chewed the same way he did when he was a kid.

He smiled back, feeling a little awkward with her watching him this way. His mother was different this visit than he had ever seen her before. She seemed more attentive, more focused on him than she ever had been previously.

He swallowed and sat back. "How come I never see you eat when I come over here?"

Mary seemed to blush a little as she fanned her hand at the question. "I eat," she said. "Mostly soups, black-eyed peas, ham hocks. You don't eat all that."

Frankie nodded. "You're right. I never liked stuff like that." He smiled, comforted by the thought of his mother knowing his habits and preferences. She had been such a silent character in his upbringing that he wondered at times if she had been paying attention.

"I made some chicken soup the other day," she said softly. "Put it in a thermos and took it on down there with me to sit with Steven."

Frankie stared at her. "You went to the cemetery?"

Mary nodded.

Frankie frowned a little. "When?"

Mary seemed to whisper to herself. "I go all the time."

Frankie thought about that. His mother didn't drive, had never ventured out much past their neighborhood without his father. Yet, she must have taken two trains and walked a couple of blocks each time she went to the cemetery to visit Steven's grave.

"Why go see him now?" he couldn't help asking.

She looked at him, her eyes sad and despondent, and then looked at her hands. She wrung them together before placing them in her lap in an attempt to calm her nerves. She had been a mess ever since her youngest son's death, haunted by it in a way that no one understood but her.

"I think about him," she said, "every single day."

Frankie sat rapt and was grateful that the volume on the television was low. His mother's voice was so soft as she spoke.

"I dream about him. He calls my name, and I wake up and go looking for him around the house." Mary chuckled as if she knew it sounded crazy. "And when the morning comes, I go there. I sit with him."

She closed her eyes and smiled a faraway smile that Frankie had never had the pleasure of witnessing before. He thought his mother looked so pretty that way, so youthful with her face happy for once.

"Sometimes I even see his face in my dreams. I see him as a child, just a little boy running around laughing. He was a happy baby."

Frankie watched as she opened her eyes and blinked a few times, her usual demure expression returning to her face, smile fading ever so slightly.

"He loved you, Frankie. He would clap his hands whenever you stepped in the room and smile so bright. You were his hero from the second he could see straight."

Frankie smiled, remembering. He had almost forgotten fun times like that.

"He loved your pancakes," Frankie recalled. "And you would always sneak him extra ones behind Dad's back." The minute he said it, he knew he shouldn't have. Mary folded her arms across her chest, lowered her chin, and hunched her shoulders. Her body language conveyed exactly what was happening inside. Every time she thought about her husband—her sons' father—and the horror he had subjected them to, she cringed. She had allowed it. She had allowed all of it.

Mary didn't say another word until Frankie coaxed her back from the place she had gone in her mind.

"I wish you wouldn't slouch like that," he said. "You should sit up straight, 'cuz neither one of us blamed you for what he did." It wasn't true. Frankie actually did blame his mother, at least to some degree. But seeing her so wounded now, he wanted to hug her but didn't know how. "You can look me in the eye and know that I'm not mad at you."

"I'm mad at myself," she said softly.

Frankie sat in silence for a few moments, surprised to hear his mother talking about this. Like Steven, she had never wanted to before.

Mary found the courage to look at her son. "You stayed away all these years . . . you and your brother." She tilted her head thoughtfully. "Feels a little like I don't know who you are . . . as a man. To me, you and Steven are both still my boys."

Frankie felt bad for that. It had been so hard for him to see his mother this broken down and sad. In fact, the conversation they were having now was the most he'd heard her speak in years. She had become a recluse, a willful prisoner in her own home.

"Well, I'm here now," he offered. "It's not too late." He took another bite of his sandwich.

She smiled again, though her smile didn't reach her eyes. "It's too late for Steven."

Frankie lost his appetite midchew. It seemed like his mother was being tormented by what had happened to Steven. Concerned that she was already emotionally fragile, he needed her to talk about it before she did something crazy. Frankie clasped his hands together and looked at Mary directly.

"What's on your mind, Ma?"

She looked at him, her eyes full of sorrow and longing. "He's gone, Frankie. I can't ever see him or talk to him again. I can't tell him I'm sorry."

Frankie watched her staring absentmindedly at her hands, her voice clear but low.

"You know what I pray for?" she asked.

Frankie shook his head.

"That my soul won't burn in hell for all these years I kept my mouth shut." She laughed cryptically, her head thrown back and her hands splayed across her lap. When she was done, Mary looked at her only remaining son and told the truth. "Steven can never defend himself. He can never stand up in court and tell his side of the story because he's dead. That girl killed him, but he didn't deserve it, Frankie." She shook her head and looked like she wanted to cry but had run out of tears after spending countless nights crying. "I'm the one who deserves to be laying in that grave, not Steven."

"Why do you keep saying that?" Frankie asked. "You said the same thing at his funeral."

She shrunk back into her seat. "Because I didn't speak up about it. I didn't stop the things your father did to him, the things your father did to you. I didn't talk about it even after your father was dead, I just . . . stayed quiet. That makes me just as guilty."

Frankie frowned. "What happened when we were kids don't have nothing to do with what happened to Steven." He thought his mother was losing her mind. "Misa thought—"

"She thought he was abusing her son. That's what you told me."

Frankie nodded. "But we know that he wouldn't really do something like that."

His mother shot him a look that sent chills up his spine. "Do we know, Frankie? After all the years of what your father did, all the things Steven watched him do to me and—"

Frankie stood up off the couch and walked toward his mother. In that moment, he was so angry that he surprised himself. He didn't know why he wanted to slap the taste out of her mouth for even suggesting what Steven had been accused of could have been true. He just knew that he wanted her to stop talking.

Mary shrunk away, but she kept her eyes fixed on Frankie's.

"He didn't do nothing to that little boy!" Frankie's voice was louder than he meant for it to be.

Mary choked back a sob and Frankie felt instantly sorry for being so mad. Standing over her, watching her shrink away from him the way he had seen her do when his father was in one of his rages, Frankie softened. He knelt before Mary and pulled her into a hug, stroking her back and comforting her as she cried. It felt almost as if she were the child and he were the parent, comforting her, assuring her that her nightmares were nothing more than just that.

"He didn't do it, Ma," Frankie whispered to her. With his whole heart, he believed that it was the truth.

"My God!" Jeanie shrieked, gripping the phone tightly.

Toya heard her mother yelling and rushed from her bedroom to the spare room where Jeanie was supposed to be asleep. It was early—just past nine o'clock on Saturday night—but Jeanie had turned in already, exhausted after a long day of shopping in New York City.

As Toya entered the room, she saw her mother sitting on the edge of the bed, one hand covering her mouth in apparent shock, the other gripping the telephone tightly.

"Yes," Jeanie was saying. "Yes, okay. Okay. Yes."

Toya grew impatient and stepped closer to her mother. "What's wrong?" she whispered.

Jeanie held one hand up as if to silence Toya and listened

to whoever was on the other end of the phone. "Oh my God," Jeanie said, sighing. "Was he alone?"

Instinctively, Toya knew that her father was dead. She wasn't sure how she knew, but there was no doubt in her mind that Nate was gone and her mother was shaken by the news.

Toya watched her mother scribble an address down on the back of a Macy's receipt and listened as she thanked the mystery caller. The second she hung up the phone, Toya asked if her suspicions were correct.

"He's dead?"

Jeanie's eyes flooded with tears and she nodded, sending them pouring down her face.

Toya hugged her mother, rocked her as she cried. "I'm a widow," Jeanie wailed and Toya had to fight the urge to laugh at her melodramatics. Her parents hadn't been together for years, yet her mother was carrying on like she had lost her soul mate.

"Sweets, it's okay," Toya told her. "He made his peace with everyone before he died. He's in a better place now."

She waited a few minutes for her mother to calm down before she probed further. "What happened?"

Jeanie took a deep breath and looked her daughter in the eye. "He was renting a studio apartment and the landlord lives upstairs and hadn't seen Nate for a few days. Then he didn't show up for work at his job as a porter. Finally, the landlord rang the bell, knocked on the door, and called his phone. When he got no answer, he called the cops and they went in there—found him lying dead on the floor."

Toya gasped.

"They think he had a stroke, but they won't know until they perform an autopsy."

Toya's emotions got the best of her as she wondered how

long her father had lain there before anyone found him. Even an animal like Nate didn't deserve to die alone on the floor like that.

Together, she and her mother prepared to go down to the medical examiner's office and formally identify the body. As Toya got dressed and thought back on her recent conversations with her father, she felt chills run down her spine. Her father had come back into her life to seek her forgiveness and had died without receiving that. She couldn't help feeling somewhat relieved that they hadn't been forced to begin the tough work of reestablishing a relationship as father and daughter. She knew that it would have required her to confront some painful parts of her past, and she hoped now she would be able to bury that painful history along with him.

She paused as she pulled her shoes out of her closet. She recalled something Nate had said to her during their last conversation at Junior's.

"I don't know if this means anything to you, but I'm real proud of you."

Toya sat down on her bed and closed her eyes, realizing how much it had meant for her to hear those words come out of her father's mouth. In so many ways, she had waited a lifetime to hear them. And now he was gone forever.

Opening Arguments

March 2008

The excitement in the courtroom was at a fever pitch. Packed with lawyers, family members, spectators, police, and plenty of press, the place felt like an arena right before a concert.

Weeks of jury selection had culminated in twelve men and women plus six alternate jurors who would decide Misa's fate. Those jurors hadn't filed into the courtroom yet, and neither had the defendant.

Camille sat as close as possible to the defense table, hoping that Misa would be able to glance at and hopefully gain strength from her sister during the tough moments that lay ahead. Today, Camille was feeling empowered. She wore a Calvin Klein suit and a glow that could only emanate from a woman with child. Lily and Celia flanked her, and Camille drew strength from them. She tried not to be fazed by the reporters and sketch artists analyzing her every detail.

Toya and Dominique sat behind Camille, both of them lovely in basic black. Toya was explaining to Dominique how sick she was of having her mother as a houseguest.

"Sweets won't leave," Toya said. "She came to town over a month ago. My father died, she handled her wifely duties, and now she needs to go back to Atlanta!"

"You'll miss her when she's gone," Dominique said.

Toya gave her a look that cast sufficient doubt on that theory.

Frankie stepped into the room and the buzz in the room swelled even more. He walked in with his mother, Mary, at his side, followed by Gillian and Tremaine. Mary wore all black as if she were still in mourning, a pair of wire-rimmed glasses perched on her nose, her innocent eyes peering from behind them. She held a rosary and appeared to have a firm grip on Frankie's hand as he led her to a seat close to the front. Gillian looked like a different person. She wore a simple ponytail and a demure gray dress with a high collar and black pumps. Her look was so understated that Toya had to admit that if she were a juror, she would think the woman was legit.

"If she's trying to look the part of a sweet family friend lending support, she's doing it," Toya said. "I wish we could tell the jury the whole truth."

"Yeah," Dominique agreed. "Look, there's Gillian's mother. She's a hot tamale, ain't she?"

Mayra sauntered in wearing a skintight Dolce & Gabbana suit with a neckline down to there.

Turning around in her seat, Celia chimed in. "She's gonna catch a cold."

They all giggled and Lily shook her head at Gillian's mother, noticing that she sat rows behind her daughter and Frankie. "She's feeling young again now that her husband is dead."

Camille didn't look. She didn't want to sneak a glance at

Frankie and Gillian and see them looking happy, see them looking like a couple. She wanted to focus on Misa and on keeping her out of jail.

Toya and Dominique checked Frankie out, though. He wore a custom-fitted Armani suit and a pair of cuff links he had incidentally gotten as a gift from his wife. He looked very handsome and seemed eager for the trial to get under way.

Celia and Lily each grabbed hold of one of Camille's hands and held it. Camille smiled, faced forward and tried not to think about Frankie. Misa was in for the fight of her life.

Louis arrived with his frowning girlfriend, Nahla, and the social worker, Ms. Thomas. Lily couldn't help wondering if it was mere coincidence that he arrived at the same time as the woman who would ultimately have the biggest say in where Shane was placed on a long-term basis. Ms. Thomas sat two rows behind Louis and Nahla and began taking notes about God knows what.

Finally, Teresa Rourke led Misa into the courtroom, surrounded by court officers. Misa noticed her family seated up front and smiled at them weakly, hoping to reassure them that she was being strong. But inside, Misa was scared to death.

After getting seated and going over some quick notes, Teresa turned to her client. "Today will be over before you know it. Just keep your game face on, no sudden outbursts. But don't be a zombie, either. Show some emotion, just make sure it's not too much."

Misa nodded. "I'm ready."

Teresa hoped so. The Staten Island district attorney, Dean Davidson, stood with two of his assistants going over notes for the day's opening arguments. This case had garnered a ton of publicity, making it the most sensational trial the borough had seen in years. Dean was staking his career on a win, and Teresa was determined to prevent that from happening.

The jury was led in, followed by Judge Travis Felder. Misa sized him up, surmised that he was about fifty years old, and noticed that he was sizing her up, too, as he looked at her over the rim of his glasses. Once all those present were seated and the court officers placed themselves around the perimeter of the room, the judge gave the jury its instructions and then the prosecution set forth its case.

"Ladies and gentlemen of the jury, Misa Atkinson murdered Steven Bingham in cold blood. She gunned down an unarmed man in the middle of the night as he went to the refrigerator for a beer in his brother's home. This was no accident! Misa Atkinson didn't mistake her brother-in-law for an intruder. In fact, *she* was the one who was in the house unexpectedly that night. She entered the home using a key she had procured months prior and she waited in the dark for Steven Bingham. She waited until Mr. Bingham—a man with no criminal past, no known enemies or even angry creditors— came into the kitchen for a late-night drink. And she ambushed him. She pumped him full of bullets until the illegal handgun she brought was empty."

Misa noticed some members of the jury looking at her to see if she seemed capable of such atrocities. She did her best to keep her poker face on as the prosecution painted Steven as an angel.

"On the night of January 5, 2008, Misa Atkinson acted as judge, jury, and executioner. As the victim lay bleeding to death on the kitchen floor, she pulled up a chair in the dining room. Blood was splattered on the dining room wall, indicating that she wiped the victim's blood off of her, and then sat down and waited for Steven Bingham to die!" Misa sat stone-faced as the DA instructed the jury to pay close attention to the evidence and to find her guilty of murder in the first de-gree. She watched in silence as Teresa Rourke stood up, walked to stand in front of the center of the jury box, and faced the twelve as if speaking only to them. Though her voice was au-dible throughout the room, she made eye contact with each juror as if she were addressing them specifically.

"A young, uneducated, single mother is left to raise her child virtually on her own. We've all heard the story over and over. Some of us have even lived it. But Misa Atkinson had the added misery of discovering that her child had been victim-ized, sodomized by someone entrusted with his care. While she worked hard as a dental assistant, struggling to make ends meet, Misa Atkinson entrusted her son to her family members— her sister, Camille, her brother-in-law, Steven Bingham." Teresa paced the floor slowly, her eyes scanning the jurors.

"When Camille became troubled by problems in her marriage, Steven volunteered to keep an eye on Misa Atkin-son's son so that she could keep food on the table. Imagine the horror she felt when she discovered that while in Steven Bingham's care, her son had been molested. Her three-year-old baby boy sodomized repeatedly by someone he was sup-posed to trust. The evidence will show that my client went over to her sister's home to confront her brother-in-law, Ste-ven Bingham. She did use her key and entered the home where she eventually encountered Steven. And when she presented him with her questions, he lunged at her, forcing her to draw the weapon she had brought with her for protection. Only when Mr. Bingham charged at her did Ms. Bingham fire her weapon. In a sense, she just snapped." Teresa snapped her fingers for good measure, the sound echoing off the walls of the old courtroom. "And as she pulled the trigger, she was in a trance—a mother who only sought to protect her child from a predator."

Misa wanted to applaud but held her composure. She listened as Teresa coaxed the jury to ask themselves what they would have done, to wait until they heard all the facts of the case before they made up their minds about a woman's life, a child's life, as well. "When the evidence shows that this was a case of self-defense, I ask that you find Misa Atkinson not guilty and give a young single mother and her son a second chance."

She sat back down and the judge gave the jury a long list of instructions on what was expected of them for the duration of the trial. Glancing around the room, Misa saw just about everyone she knew and she was embarrassed to be on display in this way. Her mother gave her a reassuring wink and it made Misa feel better. She caught Camille's eye and the sisters smiled at each other. Despite the differences between them, the events of the past few weeks had brought them closer than they had ever been. Misa knew that Camille was still—probably would always be—the one who cared about public perception as much as personal happiness. But at least she had finally let Frankie go. As hard as it had been for her, Camille was still standing firmly by Misa's side, and she was grateful to her sister for that.

Misa glanced at Dominique and Toya and felt the love coming from them. "Face forward. You don't want to appear disinterested," Teresa urged her.

Misa snapped forward and listened as the judge scheduled testimony in her trial to begin the following day. She was anxious to get out of that courtroom and back to the safety, comfort, and isolation of her mother's home—away from the news cameras, the jury's stares, and the cold, menacing expression she saw on Frankie's face as she peeked at him now.

He stared at Misa with such intensity that Gillian whispered in his ear: "Frankie, look at me." He did and she squeezed his hand. "She's gonna pay for what she did. Don't worry."

He nodded, tried not to look at Misa anymore. But he couldn't help it. She seemed so convinced that she had done the right thing. He wanted to kill her just as she had killed Steven.

Gillian glanced over at Camille sitting on the opposite side of the courtroom and noticed that she was seated beside Celia. Apparently, Baron's mother had chosen sides, and that was fine with her. Camille, Baron, her mother, and anyone else who stood in the way of her happiness would be cut off soon enough.

The judge adjourned the court for the day, reminding everyone to arrive on time tomorrow morning for the start of the prosecution's case. Misa let out a sigh, grateful that she had survived the first part. Teresa urged her to stay behind until the courtroom emptied out and the court officers were able to clear out the lobby. The two busied themselves with paperwork and small talk as the courtroom slowly emptied.

Camille stood in the aisle and watched as Gillian walked past her. She wanted to snatch the bitch, but instead she waited until Frankie walked behind her. "I need to talk to you," she said. "It can't wait, and this is the last time I'm going to ask nicely. Let's go back to the house and have a discussion. Just me and you."

Frankie stopped in his tracks and looked at Camille like she had lost her mind. "Right now?" He didn't even know why he was entertaining the thought.

Camille nodded. "Meet me at our house, Frankie." Camille walked off and left him standing there with a confused expression on his face. He watched her leave, followed by Lily, Dominique, and Toya.

Celia stood at Frankie's side and touched him gently on the arm. "I need to serve you with these," she said softly. Celia handed Frankie the divorce papers Camille had asked Teresa to draw up. She watched him look over the paperwork and then at her, perplexed. "Camille has been a good wife, Frankie," Celia said honestly. "You know I love you. Doug loved you, too. And if he were here, he wouldn't like the way you've been handling this." Celia noticed Frankie looking convicted. "You may say that it's none of my business."

Frankie shook his head. "I respect you, Miss Celia," he said.

"So, go and talk to Camille," Celia urged. "I think you two have a lot to discuss."

She walked off and didn't bother to speak to Gillian. Gillian pretended not to notice and looked on as Frankie read through the papers he'd just been given.

"What's that?" she asked.

He looked at her. "Camille filed for divorce," he said.

Gillian beamed with joy. Finally, Camille was giving up. "That's a good thing, right?"

He nodded. "She wants me to come over to the house to talk to her about it." His eyes scanned her face, saw the flash of hesitation. "I'm gonna go and put an end to everything. Finish it once and for all."

Gillian didn't have time to protest before Mayra appeared at their side. "Frankie, we need to talk," she said. Looking at her daughter, she forced a smile. "Gillian."

Gillian smirked. It was clear that her mother was mad at her and she didn't care. "Mother."

Mayra turned her attention back to Frankie. "When did my husband sign Conga over to you and when were you going to tell me?"

Frankie looked like this was the last thing he needed. "Mayra, let's talk about this some other time," he said. "I have to go and take care of something." He kissed Gillian good-bye and then turned to his mother. "Ma, Tremaine is gonna drive you and Gillian home, all right? I have to go and handle some business."

Mary nodded and smiled weakly when Frankie kissed her on the cheek. As he left the courtroom, Mary, Gillian, and Mayra watched him leave, all three of them oblivious to Misa as she and her attorney slipped past them and out into the lobby.

Mayra looked at her daughter. "Why don't you call me after you drop off Frankie's mom?" she suggested. "Then you and I can grab some lunch. We have some things we need to talk about."

Gillian didn't blink before answering, "No. I don't have time today. I'll call you." She walked out ahead of the rest of them, leaving Mayra standing alone in the empty courtroom.

Camille watched from the front window as Frankie's car pulled up in the driveway. She thought back on the countless times over the years when she had watched her husband arrive home this way; recalled the anticipation she felt whenever she knew he was about to grace their home with his presence. She laughed at herself now, realizing that she had lost herself in their marriage. She had become Mrs. Frankie Bingham and had lost Camille in the process.

She watched as her husband climbed out of his truck and

up the stairs. She saw him do a double take when he saw the FOR SALE sign posted on the lawn. Finally, he let himself in with his key and stood in the foyer for several moments.

Frankie looked around. It felt strange stepping into his home. He hadn't been back here since the night his brother was killed. He remembered the way his knees had all but buckled as Sergeant Denton told him the bad news.

"Your wife . . . arrived home to find that your brother had been shot in the kitchen."

He walked toward the kitchen now, entered it, and looked around. It had been cleaned up since the night of the murder, but it didn't matter. Frankie could still see the pool of blood in his mind, could still hear the crunch of broken glass from the beer bottle underneath his feet.

He glanced at the walls, which had been smeared with his brother's blood. It was gone now, but the hairs on the back of his neck still stood up. He looked over at the refrigerator, pictured his brother opening it, taking out a beer and then being gunned down right where he stood.

Camille came into the kitchen and saw her husband standing there frozen in the spot where Steven had been shot. She knew he was reliving that night, as she had done countless times over the past few months. Frankie turned and faced her and she stared back at him, unsure how else to greet him.

"Thanks for coming to meet me," she said. "I won't keep you too long. I just want to go over some things real quick before the trial starts and everything gets crazier than it already is."

Frankie nodded, but gawked at her in silence. She looked so beautiful standing there, her face and body showing signs of her pregnancy. Earlier in court, he hadn't noticed how full her face had gotten, how her skin glowed and her hair had grown since the last time they'd seen each other. Her belly was swollen with his child inside and it dawned on him fully in that moment.

He followed his wife as she led the way to the living room. They sat down and Camille couldn't help wondering when they'd last sat down in this room together. It had been months, she was certain, and she felt a wave of sadness wash over her as they began to discuss the situation at hand.

Frankie watched her lay out some paperwork on the table. He was relieved that Camille was seeking a divorce, but increasingly torn about the baby she was carrying. He had so many questions, so many things to talk to her about, but he didn't know where to begin. He was so glad that she wasn't crying this time. "What's up with the 'For Sale' sign outside?" he asked.

Camille sat back and looked at him. "I had Toya list it since I can't live here anymore. Aside from everything that happened here, I can't afford this place by myself and I can't keep going hungry waiting for you to talk to me."

Frankie stared at her. "How can she list the house for sale without my permission? I'm the owner."

Camille nodded, stared back at him. "Yes, you are," she said. "In fact, you own everything. Or at least your mother does," she said sarcastically. "I thought you bought this house for me, Frankie. Remember that? I thought we were a team, that everything was ours, regardless of whose name it was in. But I guess you don't see it that way." She shook her head. "You put all the businesses in Mary's name so that I couldn't lay claim to anything."

Frankie didn't respond. It was clear that Camille and her attorney had done their homework.

"But what's yours is mine," Camille said. "I'm your wife. And as your wife, I've been very loyal to you. I've been there through sickness and in health, for better or worse, for rich or for poor . . . kept your secrets." She let the meaning sink in.

Frankie shifted a little in his seat.

Camille turned to a particular page in the stack of papers before her. She read aloud her requests—the proceeds from the sale of the house plus monthly spousal support of five thousand dollars and child support totaling ten thousand dollars a month.

"All I want is for you to give me my fair share. That way me and my child can go on living the life we've become accustomed to and you can run off with Gillian and live happily ever after."

Frankie stared at his wife. Her demeanor was stoic. Gone was the frail and fragile Camille and in her place was a no-nonsense woman with an agenda. *My child*," she had said. Frankie didn't blame her. She had every reason to exclude him. She was nearly six months pregnant and he hadn't even talked to her about it.

"What happened to us, Frankie?" she asked, as if reading his mind. "How the hell did we get to this?"

Frankie met her gaze, saw the pain in her eyes. He tilted his head slightly and spoke sincerely to his wife for the first time in years.

"I should have left a long time ago," he said. "I should have been man enough to tell you that I was getting bored, or that I don't want the same things you want. I really don't want kids, and there's a lot of reasons for that." Frankie looked away, thoughts of those reasons never far from his mind these days. "And I don't want to be with somebody whose only hobby is *me*. Truth be told, I fell out of love with you a long time ago. I just didn't know how to leave you when you were so good to me."

Camille sat back, shaken by the truth finally spilling forth from Frankie's lips.

"You're a good wife, a good woman, period. And you were by my side when nobody else was there. I appreciated that so much I let myself stay even when I wanted out." He looked at her again glaringly. "I let your sister take advantage of your generosity—paying her rent, buying her a car, baby-sitting her son."

"We're not here to talk about her," Camille reminded him, aware that whenever Misa crept into his mind, Frankie shut Camille out.

"How can we not talk about her?" he asked, his handsome face appearing pained.

"Tell me why you stopped loving me."

He felt the familiar tug of guilt then, but pressed past it. He was eager to come clean. He sat back and crossed his leg across his lap. "You changed," he said truthfully. "You used to be fun and sexy. You had a goal to become the next top model." He smiled at the memory of her posing at her photo shoots. "You were focused. Then we got married and you wanted the picture-perfect family and I never promised you that. You wanted a baby and it seemed like sometimes that was all you talked about. I got tired of that. And then you started gaining weight, you stopped doing anything but putting on a show for your friends."

"To me, it wasn't a show. I thought we had the real thing," she said.

"We did," he answered, nodding. "At one time we did."

"But you let Gillian come between that," Camille said. "You let her break us up."

He shook his head. "She's not the reason I was unhappy."

"Oh no?" Camille asked rhetorically. "All those late-night phone calls, all those trips, the dinners, the parties. I should have been smart enough to see it for myself, but I didn't. I trusted you, Frankie. When you told me that she was just your friend, I believed you. And look where we are now." Camille stared at him, such a beautiful man who had been so ugly toward her. "You treated me like shit in front of her, more than once. You were supposed to be my husband." Her face furrowed in disbelief. She still couldn't believe the way things had changed. "Frankie, I can admit that I wasn't perfect. Maybe I didn't fix myself up like I could have. I stopped working out and started drinking and eating all the time. But I did everything I could to keep you happy. I never disrespected you. In fact, I disrespected myself before I ever dreamed of doing it to you." She laughed at herself, sadly. "You owed me more than this."

"You were smothering me and I was fucked up. Nobles was dead—"

"I understand that, Frankie."

"Do you understand, Camille?" Frankie's voice rose.

"Absolutely. He was like a father to you, so instead of letting me help you mourn his loss, you ran to Gillian and fucked her for comfort."

Frankie shook his head. Camille didn't understand that his connection to Gillian was more than sexual. She was, to him, everything Camille had ceased to be.

He looked at his wife and noticed again how pregnant she was. She looked so angelic sitting there, and so hurt. Frankie knew she was crushed by his decision to leave her. But too much had happened between them to reconsider. One look around reminded him of the fate his brother had suffered here at the hands of her sister, and he cringed.

"I don't expect you to believe me," he said. "But, Gillian really was just my friend until the night her father died." Frankie looked sincerely into Camille's eyes.

"Gillian has never been *just* your friend," Camille scoffed. "I can see that now. You might not have slept with her until after you walked out on me, but you were cheating on me with her for years. Whispers, private jokes, late-night phone calls, all of that was part of it. So don't give me that."

Camille felt her baby move within her womb and instinctively stroked her belly. Frankie noticed, watching her closely. He was still in disbelief that he would soon be a father.

"Do you know if it's a boy or a girl?" he asked, curious. Camille shook her head no. He wished she would elaborate, but she didn't volunteer any more information. He had been wondering about this child—what it would look like, if she would be better off aborting it. He hadn't spoken about it to anyone, but it had certainly been on his mind. Seeing his pregnant wife now made him anxious to find out more. "I don't even know when you're gonna have it."

"Well, whose fault is that?" Camille snapped. She caught herself and steadied the tone of her voice. The last thing she wanted was for Frankie to see how deeply this was hurting her. "July. The baby is due in July."

"July what?"

"Fourteenth."

He thought about that and smiled slightly. "That's your birthday," he said.

"How nice of you to remember," she said sarcastically.

Frankie stared at her, tried to get excited about the thought of being a father, but he couldn't. All he felt was anxiety at the idea of it. He felt as if everything was being forced on him. The baby, the terms of the divorce, even the death of his brother. Everything was happening around him and he was powerless to stop any of it.

"I won't fight you on this," he said, gesturing toward the paperwork. He knew that if he did there was no telling what Camille could and would reveal about his business and his finances. "I'll sign the papers once my lawyer looks them over." He didn't want this house anymore, didn't blame Camille for not wanting it, either. He didn't care about the money. Having lost his brother and watching his mother unravel before his eyes, money seemed so insignificant these days. Camille wasn't the one to blame for what had gone wrong in his life. He felt bad for punishing her for what her sister had done. Still, the child growing in Camille's belly was causing him to lose sleep.

"But I don't know how to be a father, Camille."

She looked at him, staggered by his honesty.

"It's natural to be nervous about becoming a parent for the first time," she said. "How do you think I feel?"

Frankie was willing to bet that she didn't feel the way he did. A sense of dread had taken up residence within him and it felt like the walls were closing in on him. "I'm just trying to get you to understand that I'm not ready to be a father. I don't have the patience it takes or the understanding." He felt sweat forming on his forehead then and tried to will himself to calm down. It felt sort of like he was having a panic attack at the very thought of fatherhood.

Camille saw him going through changes and frowned.

"I'm not asking you to be involved," she said. "I'm willing to raise the baby by myself. All I want from you is the financial support to give him or her the best opportunities."

Frankie felt his blood pressure rising. "And then I walk away and act like I don't have a kid?" he asked, his face incredulous. "I would never do that."

"You're doing it now," she said. "Right now, while I'm pregnant. You cut me off from everything, Frankie. I don't have a damn dime to my name." Baron had sent over a couple thousand dollars the other day, but Frankie didn't need to know about that.

His gaze turned icy. "I'm supposed to hand you a stack of money when your freeloading sister killed my brother?"

Camille sucked her teeth. "I'M NOT THE ONE WHO DID IT, FRANKIE!" she yelled. "Misa did it. *Misa* shot Steven. She's the one who you're supposed to be mad at. Not me! I'm your fucking wife. I didn't cheat on you, you cheated on me! And you took away all that we worked hard for overnight because you want to punish *me* for what *she* did!" Camille was nearly out of breath by the time she finished. "I need you to stop making excuses for the bullshit you've put me through over the past few months. I know you're hurt about Nobles and about your brother. I get it. But you're not the only one suffering. My nephew is an innocent little boy, Frankie. And I'm sure that even in your cold heart you can find some sympathy for a child. Surely you must remember what it feels like to be a scared little kid. So you're not the only victim here. My family is in ruins just like yours is."

Frankie felt a headache creeping up on him. Part of him knew that Camille was right. But another part of him wasn't ready to make nice.

Camille was done trying to end things amicably. "Anyway, I just wanted you to know that I'm not asking you to participate if you don't want to. This is *my* child, and I'm fine with doing it by myself."

"I don't want you to do it by yourself," Frankie said softly.

Camille stared at him, wondering what was going on inside of Frankie's head. She had never seen him so reflective, so sincere.

He was thinking about his own childhood, and all the horrible images it conjured up. His family life had been so utterly dysfunctional that he wouldn't know the first thing about being a good father. "I mean . . ." Frankie searched for the words to say what was in his heart. "Camille, I didn't want any kids in the first place."

"I know. You already said that a thousand times," she reminded him.

"Now that it's happening, I have a lot of shit to process . . . mentally." He looked at her seriously. "I've been thinking about it ever since you told me that you're pregnant. And I can't come up with one positive memory of my father."

Camille watched him trying even now to think of one.

"I keep coming up empty. So, I don't have any idea what I'm supposed to do or how I'm supposed to act . . ."

Camille felt her baby move again. She cleared her throat. "I can tell you this much. You're not supposed to ignore my phone calls, take everything we own, and allow your girlfriend to disrespect me."

Frankie looked at her coldly. He should have known that Camille wouldn't understand.

She pointed at Frankie. "You may have had a fucked-up childhood, but so have thousands of other people. It's no excuse for the way you've treated me."

"You're right," he acknowledged.

His admission did little to comfort Camille, who was on the verge of tears yet again. She wouldn't allow him to see her cry anymore, so she looked away. She gathered her papers together and folded them, placing them in her purse. She stood up, her bulging belly clearly visible as she grabbed her coat and looked at her husband. "See you in court."

Frankie watched Camille leave, and listened as her car pulled away. He sat there in the home he bought for her when they first fell in love and he knew their marriage was officially over. Still, the relief he had been longing for—the sense of calm and liberation—eluded him once more.

Repentance

Baron had had enough. He was sick of being confined to a
chair, sick of being nursed and tended to twenty-four hours a
day. All he wanted was to walk, to take a step or two and
know that he was on the road to recovery.

He put his wheelchair in park and steadied himself on its
arms. Gripping tightly, his big hands wrapped firmly around
the armrests, he pulled himself up on his feet. Still clutching
the chair, he smiled, encouraged. He felt the muscles in his
forearms protruding as he willed himself to put some weight
on his legs. Baron planted his feet on the floor and his arms
trembled under his heaviness. His legs felt like Jell-O no
matter how hard he tried to steady himself. His knees buckled, and he lunged forward. The wheelchair came crashing
down behind him and he fell to the floor, face-first. Baron
cursed through clenched teeth and writhed in pain, praying
that his nurse didn't come in and find him so vulnerable and
pathetic. Fuming, he sat up on the floor and set the chair upright. Several agonizing minutes passed as he slowly dragged
himself up from the floor, using his wheelchair for leverage.
His legs had no strength to aid him, and his jaw throbbed

where he had fallen on it with the wheelchair on top of him. Finally, he managed to pull himself up. Frustrated, he slumped back down in the chair, his chest heaving breathlessly.

Anger pulsed through his veins as Baron struggled to catch his breath. Hot tears spilled down his cheeks, and quietly Baron cried. There were so many reasons why—his father was dead and it was all his fault, the empire they'd spent years building was no longer his to control, his legs were useless, and the police were searching for Danno, zeroing in on Baron. He felt like the world was closing in on him and for the first time in his life he was powerless.

If he had been able to walk, to run or even drive, Baron knew in his heart he would have killed Danno. He would have murdered his friend just to prevent him from testifying against Baron in connection with Trina Samuels's murder. Considering how he'd been feeling lately and all the wicked thoughts running through his head, he may have even killed Frankie and Gillian, too. As Baron thought about that his conscience overwhelmed him. He had been so ruthless, so brutal in his business that he took lives mercilessly. Trina had certainly not been the first. Her gang rape and murder was only one of the many devilish schemes that Baron's psychopathic mind had devised. Dusty and countless others had fallen victim to his murderous rage.

He thought about his father, about what Gillian had said to him on the phone. He may as well have pulled the trigger himself. His father had given him everything, and had died because of it.

For weeks, Baron had sat in his bed or in his wheelchair or endured hours of physical therapy, all the while plotting his revenge. He wanted to make Frankie and Gillian pay for turning their backs on him, wanted Danno to disappear before he could do the same. But now, as he sat there with snot in his nose and tears staining his face, he knew no amount of vengeance could help him atone for what he'd done. Baron wanted nothing more at that moment than to end his own life and to stop feeling the shame of having failed everyone.

Surely, God was punishing him. He was being forced to pay for all the wrong he'd done by being crippled, abandoned, and demeaned. But it was more than he could bear. Gone was his arrogance, his bravado, his dominance. In its place sat a man with legs that didn't work and pride that had been wounded beyond repair.

He was so distraught that it scared him. It felt as if the angel of death were looming over him, eager to snatch his soul and cart it off to hell. He knew that's where he was going, had dreamed of it almost nightly since waking up from his coma. Baron was afraid, terrified really, of what he was feeling and of the evil he knew lurked within him.

He squeezed his eyes shut and prayed for the first time in his life. With tears steadily streaming, in a hushed and humbled voice he talked to God.

"I'm sorry. I'm so sorry," he said. He didn't know how to pray, had never been much for church or anything religious. His mother had always been a God-fearing woman, but he had been his father's child. The streets had been his church and Doug had been its pastor. Now, as he sat alone and tried to talk to God, he didn't know where to begin.

Baron opened his eyes and looked up toward the ceiling. "I'm not gonna sit here and pretend like I've done anything good in my life," he said. "I never have. I've been a fuckup my whole life. You know that. I've lied, cheated, stole. I've killed." Baron's body trembled. "And I was a bad son. I didn't honor my father. I never honored nobody but myself." He wiped his eyes with his hands and gripped the wheelchair again. "I know I'm being punished for everything I did. I deserve it. Even now, I still have evil in my heart. I still want to kill." He shook his head. "But I want to change. Take this urge away from me, God. Take these demons off me and help me change. Let me walk again, and I swear I'll do right. I swear to you, God. I just want to walk again."

He took a deep breath and let it out. A sense of peace washed over him, and he couldn't tell if it was the crying or the praying that caused it.

Dominique lay in Archie's bed watching him put together a customer's package. Half an ounce of weed sat atop a scale he had put on the island in his kitchen.

She had spent the night in his arms again. Dominique had called Archie up after a late night at work and asked if she could come over. He had happily allowed that but she was getting sick of this arrangement. It seemed that the only time she saw him was when she called and asked for an audience with him. He never turned her away, but she was longing for the day when he would make the first move and show her he was just as open as she was.

She felt like a plaything for the king's amusement; a jester in his court. While he sat on the throne wielding that powerful sword of a dick like King Henry VIII himself, she was playing right into his hands. Dominique got up, stuck her weed in her purse, and reminded herself it was time to quit smoking so much. It was a costly habit and it was really a weakly disguised excuse to see this sexy warrior.

"I have to go."

"Your daughter needs you?" Archie asked, noticing her glancing at her cell phone.

She smirked. She knew this would be her last time seeing him, so she took in all of his features. His cocoa-brown skin, smooth as a candy bar, yet so weathered from his lifestyle as a hustler; his hair, coarse, long, and neat smelling like Moroccan spices; his eyes as bright as flames. She shook her head. Damn!

"I have to go."

He frowned, a little bit confused. But he nodded and stood up, offered a smile. She looked at his luscious lips, his pearl-white teeth, and couldn't resist the urge to kiss him. Then she turned and walked to the door. Archie followed, opened it for her just as she reached for the knob, and he pulled her close for one more kiss.

"See you soon," Archie said.

She waved over her shoulder and scampered off toward her car, eager to put some space between the two of them. She realized she was looking for something more than he was willing to offer her, and for once in her life she wasn't willing to settle for less than she deserved. Archie was a beautiful man, handsome, exotic, and his sex rendered her speechless. But he was too vague, too unavailable, too much of a puzzle for her to piece together at a time in her life when she was longing for stability. Maybe what she needed was some time to be alone without the distraction of a man.

She drove away, and didn't look back. As she reached the corner and turned right, she let out a deep breath and turned the radio up loud. She didn't wallow in it this time the way she had when she walked away from Jamel. That time she had felt like she'd made a terrible mistake, and that he owed her an explanation, some kind of apology. She had loved Jamel. With Archie, it was different, and she recognized the difference between love and lust. Archie—well, she had mostly loved his sex.

She smiled as she thought of it that way and wondered how long it would be before she found the man who could balance out her odd blend of street and class.

"How 'bout a round of applause . . ." She sang along to Rihanna as she kept searching.

Toya signed for the package and thanked the UPS guy. As he retreated toward his truck, she glanced across the street and saw Russell standing on the porch of his house across the street. He waved at her and she waved back, shutting the door before he felt encouraged to come over. Her mother was still visiting and she was in no mood to hear her criticism.

The package was from someone named Pat Rushen from Cobble Hill. Stepping into her living room, Toya tore at the packaging and pulled out a box with her name scrawled across it in her father's chicken-scratch handwriting.

Jeanie stepped into the room and noticed her daughter looking like she'd seen a ghost. Toya glanced at her mother and frowned. "It's from him. This is his handwriting," she said, knowing that her mother would figure out who she was speaking of. "There's a note here, let me read it."

Toya sat down and her mother sat beside her, both of them anxious to read what was written in fancy lettering on a piece of tan stationery. Toya read the note aloud.

"My name is Pat and I was a friend of your father's. We never met, but I feel like I know you. Nate spoke of you often and he was overjoyed when you had lunch with him. He told me about his past struggles with drugs and all of that. He had gotten clean long before we met. The Nate I knew was very different from the person he described to me from his past and I'm sure you have a lot of bad memories because of that. But if it means anything to you, your father was a changed man before he died. He had made his peace with God and I pray that you made peace with your father, as well.

"Before he died, he gave me this box and asked me to send it to you if anything ever happened to him. I stuck it up in the top of the closet and forgot about it. I was holding out hope that he would find a bone marrow donor and be given a second chance. But God had other plans. Here is the box your father wanted you to have. I understand how it feels to lose a parent. If you ever need to talk or want to meet me, my number is below. My deepest condolences to you and your family." The note was signed simply "Pat," with her telephone number listed beneath it.

Jeanie looked at Toya and saw her struggling with her emotions. "I wonder what's inside," she said. She didn't tell her daughter that she also wondered who the mystery woman had been in Nate's life. Their marriage had been over for years, but Nate had been Jeanie's first love. Her heart still held a special place for him despite all the madness.

Toya didn't waste any time tearing into the box, pulling back tissue paper to reveal a bunch of old records. "These are his old forty-fives that he used to play." James Brown, Jackie Wilson, Sam Cooke, Al Green, and old Motown records were scattered throughout the box. Toya smiled and handed them to her mother, certain that Sweets must have a dozen memories attached to each song.

Jeanie beamed as she flipped through the records. Toya reached back into the box and pulled out a manila envelope full of old pictures—photos of her father with his hair conked, his shoulders broad and his face full of pride. He was smiling in every one, so handsome that Toya could see instantly why her mother had fallen so hard. Jeanie set the records aside and began looking at the pictures Toya handed to her. She laughed out loud when she came across one of Nate carrying her across the finish line during a sack race at one of his friends' barbecues. She remembered it like it was yesterday. Those had been the early days when things were happy in their marriage. Jeanie wiped a tear that fell from her eye and didn't care that Toya had noticed.

Toya didn't say anything. She understood what her mother must be feeling. Talking about Michael with her friends had opened up a cache of emotions. She had secretly been wondering what might have been and she saw no need to judge her mother for having similar thoughts of her own husband.

Toya peeked inside the box and retrieved the last of its contents—a heavy white envelope that looked worn and used. She opened it up and frowned.

Inside the envelope was a bunch of paperwork regarding the purchase of a house in their old Brooklyn neighborhood and it appeared that Nate was the buyer. Looking closer at the papers, she recognized the address and held her hand over her mouth in shock.

"He was in the process of buying the house we grew up in." Toya felt tears threatening to plunge forth and she fought them back.

"Oh my God," Jeanie sighed. "I can't believe it."

Toya couldn't believe it either. After all the years of abuse and torment, Nate had not only turned his life around and sought his family's forgiveness, but it appeared that he was trying to buy back their family home as some sort of apology. She shook her head in disbelief and looked at her mother.

"You think this is why he wanted to have dinner with the whole family on Sunday? To tell us about this?"

Jeanie shook her head. "I guess now we'll never know."

Toya stared at the papers in her hands and felt a surge of so many emotions. She closed her eyes and said a silent prayer for her father's soul. She hadn't forgiven him while he was alive. But seeing the human side of the monster she had grown up in fear of had softened her somewhat. Despite his flaws, she felt he deserved to rest in peace. Maybe people could change after all.

"We need to talk."

Frankie looked at Gillian and wondered what could possibly be going on inside that pretty little head of hers to make her utter those dreaded words no man ever wanted to hear. He chewed his breakfast and took her all in. Her hair was braided into a single plait down her back and she wore a simple navy blue dress and diamond stud earrings. Even as modest as she looked, she could still make heads turn.

"Okay," he said. "Let's talk."

The two of them were seated at Against Da Grill, a popular restaurant on Staten Island, where they were enjoying a rare meal together. These days, Frankie had become so consumed by the upcoming trial, the end of his marriage, and the task of cleaning up Baron's messes that he rarely had time to sit still for long.

The first day of testimony in Misa's murder trial was scheduled to begin that afternoon and the couple had arrived in Staten Island early, as much for ADG's delicious pancakes as for the opportunity to slip into the courtroom undetected.

Gillian sipped her tea and set the mug back down on the saucer. "What's going on with you?" she asked.

Frankie frowned. "What do you mean?"

"Lately, you're working harder than ever. I've watched you for the past few weeks rushing off from one thing to the next—things you know you could give to me or to Tremaine to do. And I think you're running from something. I'm not sure what it is, but there's definitely something on your mind that has you so antsy."

Frankie chewed his turkey bacon and looked at Gillian. He cracked a smile. "You think you know me or something?" he joked.

She smiled back. "I do know you. I know there's something you're not telling me, and we talked about this. So spill it."

Frankie shrugged, scanned the room, and nodded in greeting in the direction of one of his cronies walking in. Turning his attention back to Gillian, he sighed.

"You want the truth?"

Gillian nodded.

He leaned forward with his elbows on the table and looked her in the eye.

"I'm thinking about this baby," he said.

Gillian tried to keep her game face on, but the mere mention of the child Camille was carrying made her green with envy.

"Wondering how it's gonna feel to be a father." He shook his head as if still in disbelief. "And how it's gonna affect me and you."

She was surprised to hear him say that. "It won't affect us," she said.

He nodded. "Yes, it will. Camille is having my baby. No matter what, she's going to be a part of my life forever now.

I'll always have to interact with her, and you'll be forced to deal with that."

Gillian knew he was right. "I trust you," she said. "I think you'll handle the situation just fine. I'm sure it won't be easy, but that's nothing to stress about." She stroked Frankie's hand across the table. "I'm in this for the long haul," she said. "Camille's not gonna come between us. And neither will the baby."

Frankie hoped that was true. "I still don't know how to feel about the whole thing. I just feel . . . scared."

"Scared of what?"

He shrugged his shoulders. "I don't know. I never wanted kids."

"Why not?"

He stared at her, wishing he could express what he was feeling in words. "Too much responsibility," he said at last. "What if I don't do enough of something or if I do too much of something else? What if I fuck the kid up for life?"

Gillian wanted to laugh, but she could see that Frankie wasn't playing. "You're not gonna do that."

"How do you know? There's no way to know that for sure." Frankie wondered if his parents had been aware of the irreversible damage that was done to their children. "I think about my father and how he was . . ." Frankie stared at the table absentmindedly. "I wonder sometimes if I'll be too hard on my kid like that. Or will I be too demanding? I feel like maybe I'm not built for this. But I can't back out now, because it's not my decision to make. Just like everything else in my life, this is being forced on me."

Gillian understood where he was coming from. She knew that he was just beginning to peel back the layers of abuse he'd suffered as a child at the hands of his father. Steven's death had forced him to take a long hard look at what had happened to them as kids. Having a baby of his own on the way made it more imperative that he come to terms with it.

"So that's what's been on your mind?" she asked.

Frankie nodded. "That," he said, "plus the trial, the divorce, and business. That's enough to keep anybody stressed out."

Gillian sipped her tea again and looked at Frankie. "Okay," she said. "But just talk to me when something's on your mind. I don't want us to get in the habit of keeping problems to ourselves."

"You're right," he said. "Won't happen again." They continued their meal, talking about the trial and what to expect. Then a familiar voice interrupted their conversation.

"I thought they had a strict no animal policy in here!"

Frankie turned around to see who it was and a big smile spread across his face when he saw Born.

"Wow!" Frankie stood up and greeted his friend whom he hadn't seen in months. Born had once been in the drug game and had done business with Frankie extensively over the years. These days, he had gone legit, managing an up-and-coming rapper's career. Born greeted Gillian and she smiled. Frankie was clearly happy to see him. "Born, what's good?"

"Ain't shit. Just came up in here to get my breakfast before I take DJ to Sony. They want to talk shop with him, see if they can offer him something worthwhile."

DJ was the son of Born's deceased best friend, Dorian. When Dorian was killed by DJ's mother in a jealous rage, Born had taken the young man under his wing and become a father figure to him. These days, he was trying to steer the promising young MC toward a great career.

Frankie smiled. "That's a good look."

Born nodded. "Speaking of a good look," he said, smiling

broadly, "I was in Pathmark the other day and I saw Camille. I didn't know you two were having a baby. Congratulations!" Born had heard all about Steven's murder and had been following the case in the newspapers just like everyone else on Staten Island. But apparently, he hadn't heard that Frankie and Camille had called it quits.

Frankie smiled, glanced uneasily at Gillian, and saw that she was occupying herself with her tea bag, pretending not to hear. "Thanks," he said.

"Yo, this is your first kid, right?" Born asked.

Frankie nodded.

"That's big! Camille looks so beautiful, too. Pregnancy definitely agrees with her. She's glowing, her face is all full. She was telling me about her cravings for peanut butter and bananas." Born laughed, assuming that Frankie was well aware of the foods his wife was craving during her pregnancy. "I bet she got you running to the store at all hours of the night for that shit."

Frankie stood there feeling terrible. Not only was he struggling to find the words to explain that he had left his pregnant wife, but he was having a hard time digesting the fact that Born knew more about what Camille was experiencing than he did.

Gillian stirred her tea and wished she could disappear.

Frankie looked at his friend. "Me and Camille split up," he said, his voice low. "We're getting a divorce."

Born looked shocked. He looked at Frankie, confused, then looked at Gillian, and it all made sense. "Ohhhhhh," he said. "Damn, son. I'm sorry to hear that."

Frankie nodded, thanked Born for his condolences on the demise of his marriage.

Born glanced at Gillian and saw how uneasy she looked.

He thought about it then. He and his girlfriend Jada had attended the surprise birthday party Frankie had thrown for Camille the previous summer. At the party, Jada and her friend Sunny noticed how intimately Frankie and Gillian were behaving, and Jada had mentioned it to Born afterward. Looking at Gillian now, he surmised that she had succeeded in breaking up Frankie's marriage. Camille had always been so sweet and Born felt sorry for her now, pregnant and abandoned.

Frankie stood there awkwardly and summoned the waitress over for his bill. Born, too, felt uncomfortable about the situation, and he stuck his hands in his pockets and cleared his throat. "Well, I'm gonna go on over here and order my food," he said, gesturing toward the counter. He looked down at Gillian. "Nice seeing you again," he said. Gillian smiled and nodded at him. He shook Frankie's hand and gave him a man hug. "Keep in touch, son," Born said.

If Frankie had been white he would have been red in the face. "No doubt," he said. He watched Born go over to the counter to place his order. Frankie paid the bill, left a ten-dollar bill on the table as a tip, and exited the restaurant with Gillian hot on his heels.

Testimony

Misa sat nervously at the defense table tapping her pencil against the legal pad her attorney had given her to scribble notes on. The prosecution had just finished calling a forensics expert who refuted Misa's claim that Steven had lunged at her before she started firing. The expert had testified that the first bullet had hit Steven at an angle that suggested he had been standing still. The trajectory of that bullet would have been curved if he had been in motion at the time of the shooting, according to forensic science. Misa couldn't argue with that and was wondering how her attorney was planning to do so.

Teresa stood up and approached the witness stand. She greeted the forensics expert and smiled. "Mr. Kaufman, your testimony indicates that it would have been impossible for the deceased to have been in motion at the moment that the first bullet entered his body. Is that correct?"

"Yes, ma'am," the witness answered. "That's correct."

"What position would he have been in?"

The witness seemed befuddled by the question. "You're

asking what position he was standing in at the moment of impact?"

"Yes," Teresa confirmed.

The witness began to sweat a little. "We can't determine the exact position that he was standing in at the moment of impact."

Teresa frowned. "You just testified with absolute certainty that the bullet couldn't have hit Mr. Bingham while he was in motion. Yet, you can't describe for us what position he was standing in at the moment of impact?"

The witness stammered for several moments before regaining his composure. "Science tells us that the bullet would have entered the body on a curved path had the victim been in motion. The first bullet took a straight path to suggest that both the victim and his assailant were standing still at the time."

Teresa faced forward and extended her arm toward the witness. "Was he standing like this?" She turned to the side, her arms hanging limply. "Like this?" She turned forward again and raised both hands in the air. "Like this?"

The witness was unable to answer her definitively. "We can't determine—"

"You can't determine if he was standing with his arms in the air, if he was standing with his arms outstretched, or if he was standing with his arms at his side. But you know that he was standing still?" Her tone was skeptical and it was convincing.

"He was definitely standing still," the witness confirmed.

Teresa frowned a little. "Is it possible that he was standing still but reaching forward for the gun when Misa shot him?"

The witness looked at the prosecutor and at the judge for some assistance but neither spoke up. Teresa looked at the judge. "Please instruct the witness to answer the question."

The judge ordered Mr. Kaufman to answer the question and, reluctantly, he did so. "We can't exclude that possibility."

Teresa smiled. "So it *is* possible that Steven Bingham was reaching for the gun Misa Atkinson was holding for protection and that she fired in an attempt to prevent him from taking the weapon?"

The witness nodded. Teresa wasn't satisfied with that.

"Mr. Kaufman?"

"Yes," he said aloud. "That scenario is possible."

"Thank you," Teresa said. "No further questions." She returned to her seat and watched as the witness climbed down from the stand.

Misa turned to her and whispered, "That was good!" She knew that Steven hadn't actually lunged at her. In fact, he hadn't really expected her to use the gun. None of that mattered now that Teresa had cast sufficient doubt on the prosecution's contention that Steven was standing still when he was shot.

The DA stood to call his next witness. "The state calls Mr. Frank Bingham to the stand."

Misa turned around for the first time all day and watched Frankie stand up. He looked so clean-cut and so polished as he made his way to the front of the courtroom. All eyes were on him, particularly Camille's as she watched him being sworn in. She still loved him, regardless of the state of their marriage, and seeing him today looking so good was enough to make her swoon.

Frankie was sworn in and took his seat in the witness box. He looked directly at Misa, watching her every move. She wore a black business suit and her hair was in a sophisticated updo. He had to resist the urge to laugh since he was more accustomed to seeing her in club clothes ready to paint the town red. Misa looked right back at him, their stare down broken only when the prosecutor began his questioning.

"Mr. Bingham, you're a successful entrepreneur in the community, is that correct?"

Frankie smirked. "Yes, I guess it's fair to say that." He leaned forward slightly and spoke into the microphone.

"You own and operate numerous local businesses such as Top Cuts Barbershop, Eight Ball Billiards, Frankie B's Bar and Grill, and Conga, a popular Manhattan restaurant. Is that right?"

"Yes, it is."

"Would you list for us the people who resided on your property at the time of your brother Steven's murder?"

Frankie nodded. "Myself, my wife Camille, and my brother lived in the guesthouse."

"What was the age difference between you and Steven?"

"Four years."

"Describe for the court what type of person your brother was."

Frankie thought about Steven and fell silent for a moment. "He was a good brother. Quiet, laid-back. He didn't bother nobody. He kept to himself, loved sports."

"What did your brother do for a living?"

Frankie fidgeted with his hands a little. "His last job was as a security guard. But he fell asleep at a job site. They fired him and he got evicted from his apartment. I let him stay with me. He was living in the guesthouse and I looked out for him, made sure he had everything he needed."

"Would it be fair to say that the two of you were close?"

"Yeah," Frankie answered. "We were very close."

The prosecutor nodded. "Describe for the court your relationship with the defendant."

Frankie looked at Misa and she wished she could crawl underneath the desk. His eyes spilled over with hatred.

"She was always around," he said. "She spent a lot of time at our house, usually dropping off her son."

The prosecutor frowned. "Was she working long hours?"

Frankie snickered a little. "No," he answered. "Usually, she was on her way out to some party and she wanted my wife to babysit her son."

"Did you ever babysit your nephew?"

"Me, personally?" Frankie shook his head. "No," he said. "I'm not really good with kids."

Camille shifted in her seat under the weight of her pregnancy.

"So the defendant would drop off her three-year-old son for your wife to babysit on weekends so that she could go out and party with her friends."

"Something like that," Frankie said. "It wasn't just weekends, though."

Misa watched several women on the jury shake their heads disapprovingly and knew that they were judging her.

"How often would you say that your nephew spent the night at your house?"

Frankie thought about it and answered, "About four nights out of the week."

Misa watched her attorney take notes and wondered when she was planning to object or something. Frankie was painting a terrible portrait of her.

"And your wife babysat your nephew while the defendant went out with friends?"

Frankie nodded. "That's right."

"Would you consider the defendant to be a good mother?"

"Objection!" Teresa said at last. "This witness is not qualified to speak to my client's competency as a mother."

"Sustained," the judge grunted.

"No," Frankie answered anyway. "She was not a good mother."

The judge banged his gavel, Teresa stood up and yelled about the previous objection, and the courtroom buzzed with chatter. "Mr. Bingham," Judge Felder bellowed. "When an objection is sustained, you are not permitted to answer that question. Do you understand? The next time you do that, I will hold you in contempt."

Frankie apologized, although he wasn't really sorry. He was glad that the jury had heard him say it, even as the judge directed them to disregard his response and had it stricken from the record.

The prosecutor continued.

"Had your wife ever expressed her displeasure with the defendant's parenting skills?"

Frankie nodded. "Absolutely. She complained all the time about Misa never taking care of her own kid."

"She complained to you?"

Frankie nodded. "To me, to her friends, to my mother-in-law, and to Misa directly. Last Thanksgiving they had an argument because Misa wanted to go out and leave her son with us again. My wife said no and told Misa that she was neglecting her kid."

"And how was that situation resolved on Thanksgiving?"

Frankie smirked. "My mother-in-law volunteered to watch Shane and Misa went out anyway."

Again, she noticed several jurors shaking their heads. Misa knew that this wasn't going well for her.

"Were you aware of any conflict between your brother and the defendant?"

Frankie shook his head. "None whatsoever. To my knowledge, the two of them didn't even speak to each other at all unless it was in passing."

"Were you aware that your brother had been babysitting the defendant's young son while she worked?"

Frankie laughed. "She wasn't working," he said. "She was at the hospital waiting for her boyfriend to wake up out of a coma."

The courtroom buzzed with chatter and a court officer shushed the crowed, reminding them that they had to keep order in the court.

"Her boyfriend?" the prosecutor asked, frowning.

"Yeah," Frankie said. He was tempted to clarify that Baron hadn't actually been Misa's boyfriend, that in fact she had been little more than his plaything. But he didn't want to tell the court too much. "She wanted to be at the hospital, so from what I understand, she had dropped Shane off with my wife."

"I see," the DA said. "At some point during this period of time, your brother began to babysit the defendant's young son. Do you know how that came about?"

Frankie shook his head. "No," he said. "I wasn't there and I have no idea how that went down."

"Very well. Mr. Bingham, had you ever seen or heard anything about your brother harming a child?"

Frankie shook his head again. "Never."

"Ever notice any questionable behavior when he was in the presence of children?"

"No."

"Do you have any thoughts on the allegations the defendant has made against your brother?"

The courtroom fell dead silent. Frankie leaned forward and spoke clearly into the mic, wanting everyone to hear his answer. "Steven didn't touch that little boy."

"No further questions," the prosecutor said before sauntering back to his seat.

Teresa referred to her notes as she stood up and addressed the witness.

"Mr. Bingham, by your own admission, you and your brother were very close. It must have been kind of nice to have him living so close by."

Frankie nodded. "It was."

"Was your wife happy to have your brother as a houseguest?"

Frankie glanced at Camille and thought back on all the times she'd asked when Steven was getting out. "No," he answered honestly. "She felt like he was taking advantage and that he was lazy. She didn't understand why I looked out for him."

"Why did you look out for him, Mr. Bingham? Your brother was an able-bodied adult with nothing holding him back from getting a job or an education. Why did you feel the need to take care of a grown man?"

Frankie's jaw clenched. "For the same reason that my wife found it necessary to take care of her sister. We bought her a car, paid her bills, babysat her son, and she was an able-bodied adult."

Teresa could tell that Frankie was getting irritated so she kept prodding. "Back to your brother," she said. "Had Steven ever gone out seeking employment during the time that he lived at your house?"

Frankie stared at Misa's defense attorney. She was cute, but her questioning was detracting from her sex appeal in Frankie's eyes. "No, not that I know of."

Teresa smirked. "So your brother was content to stay in your guesthouse and mooch off of you and your wife. Did that cause any problems in your marriage?"

Frankie shook his head. "No."

"No?" Teresa raised her eyebrows. "Really?" she asked.

"Well, I'm sure she wasn't thrilled about it," Frankie clarified. "But she wasn't raising hell or nothing like that. She understood that he was family and we always looked out for family. Mine *and* hers."

Teresa nodded. "Makes sense." She paced the floor in front of Frankie and then stopped and looked directly at him. "You testified earlier that my client dropped her son off for babysitting an average of four nights a week."

He nodded.

"How many of those nights were you actually at home?"

Frankie didn't answer right away. "I'm not sure," he said at last.

"Isn't it true, Mr. Bingham, that you were rarely home on the occasions when Misa brought her son over?"

He shrugged. "That's probably true."

"In fact, each of the times when your brother babysat your nephew, you were not in the home. Is that correct?"

Frankie nodded. "Yes."

"Where were you, Mr. Bingham? A man like you who owns so many businesses must be tired after a long day at work. Surely, you would want to come home at night to that beautiful house you own, and relax in the comfort of your own bed. So where were you on average four nights out of the week while your wife and brother were babysitting young Shane?"

Frankie glared at Teresa. "I was out taking care of business."

"In the middle of the night?" Teresa asked, garnering giggles from some of the spectators. "Isn't it true that you were having an affair?"

A few salacious gasps could be heard in the courtroom and the judge banged his gavel again. Frankie sighed. He had known that it would come to this. "Yes," he admitted. "That's true."

"So you testified earlier that you thought my client was a bad mother. Guess this makes you a bad husband?"

"Objection!" the prosecutor bellowed.

"Withdrawn," Teresa countered.

"Ms. Rourke, you're walking on thin ice," Judge Felder warned.

Teresa apologized and continued. "Have you ever had an argument with my client, Mr. Bingham?"

Frankie thought about it and shook his head. "No. Never."

"Is it reasonable to suggest that she's an easy person to get along with?"

Frankie thought this might be a trick question. It seemed as if Teresa was trying to get him to say something positive about Misa. Frankie refused.

"I wasn't around her enough to have anything to argue with her about."

Teresa nodded, impressed by how he'd sidestepped the question. "You've been married for close to eight years and you've never had so much as a spat with your sister-in-law." She paced some more. "Three years of babysitting and never any allegations of Shane being abused. But when your brother started babysitting the child—"

"Objection!" the prosecution interrupted.

"Overruled."

Teresa continued. "Once your brother started babysitting Shane, allegations of molestation surfaced. The child was sodomized repeatedly by someone in his care." Teresa looked at the jury, took in each of their faces, before turning back to Frankie. "Misa—who by all accounts has been relatively easy to get along with—thought your brother did it. And you think it was unreasonable for her to think that way?"

Frankie bit the inside of his cheek and looked at Misa's attorney. He glanced at his mother and noticed that she was wringing her hands.

"Yeah," he said. "I think it was ridiculous."

Misa's heart sank. This wasn't going very well, in her opinion.

Frankie sipped from the glass of water in front of him. Teresa referred to her notes, looked at him over the rim of her glasses and took a deep breath. She was about to go in for the kill.

"Mr. Bingham," she said. "I want to remind you that you're under oath."

Frankie nodded.

"How many girlfriends had Steven had in his lifetime?"

Frankie sat stone-faced and glanced at his mother again. Mary pushed her glasses up higher on her nose and smiled weakly at her son for encouragement.

He shook his head. "I never met any of his girlfriends."

Whispers could be heard throughout the room and Teresa frowned again.

"Your brother was thirty years old and had never had a steady girlfriend? Did you find that odd?"

"No."

Teresa turned to the jury box, still frowning.

"No job. No home to call his own. No girlfriend." Teresa scratched her head. "Did Steven have any friends?"

Frankie wiped his mouth with his hand. "No."

"No job, no home, no lady in his life, no friends," Teresa repeated for good measure. "Would you describe Steven as a loner?"

Frankie shrugged. "I don't know."

Teresa nodded. She hadn't expected him to answer honestly and he didn't disappoint her. "What was Steven like as a kid growing up?"

"He was quiet, shy."

"How about you? Were you shy?"

Frankie smiled a little. He had never been accused of possessing that trait. "No," he said. "I was the more outspoken one."

Teresa nodded. "How would you describe your childhood overall?" she asked. "Yours and Steven's?"

Frankie looked at his mother again. He thought about their conversations and knew that she was already feeling guilty for what she'd witnessed in silence. Here he was now, having to rehash the horrors in open court.

"It was tough," he answered, shifting slightly in his seat.

"Please elaborate, Mr. Bingham," Teresa urged. "Tough how?"

Frankie saw Mary cover her mouth with one hand, watched Gillian glance at her to see how she was holding up. He cleared his throat.

"We were broke, didn't have much, you know what I'm saying?" Frankie hoped that would be enough.

Teresa pressed on. "Aside from the financial hardships, would you describe your childhood as a happy one?"

Frankie shrugged. "I'm not sure."

Teresa frowned. "You're not *sure* if you had a happy child-hood?"

Frankie wanted to spit in her face. "I wouldn't describe it as happy," he said. "Like I said, it was tough."

Teresa tilted her head to one side. "Well," she said. "What aspects of your childhood were unhappy?"

"My, um . . . my father used to . . . he had a problem with his hands."

Teresa stopped pacing and stood directly in front of Frankie. She noticed some of the jurors leaning forward in their seats to hear better. Frankie's voice had gotten substantially lower.

"Your father beat you?"

"Yes."

There was some chatter throughout the courtroom. Camille was mesmerized by what she was hearing. She had never known of the abuse her husband had endured as a child. Frankie hadn't shared that with her. She wondered how Teresa had known and what else would be revealed about the man she'd spent most of her adult life with.

Teresa folded her arms across her chest. "Did he beat your brother?"

"Yes."

"Was your mother abused by your father as well?"

"She was," he acknowledged. "But he didn't hit her, really. He just intimidated her, yelled at her, cornered her and punched the wall behind her, screamed at her. He saved his fists for me."

"And this abuse took place all throughout your childhood?"

He nodded. "Yes, it did."

Camille couldn't believe what she was hearing. Frankie's reluctance to be a father was beginning to make perfect sense.

Teresa started pacing slowly again.

"So from as far back as you can remember, your father terrorized your family. Is that fair to say?"

Frankie sighed. "Yes."

"So when you turned eighteen, you must have been in a hurry to move out," Teresa said, already knowing that Frankie hadn't lasted in his father's household past his freshman year of high school.

Frankie shook his head. "I left my parents' house when I was still in school," he said.

"Which month and year was that, Mr. Bingham?"

Frankie thought about it, trying to recall when he'd fled his parents' home for the last time. He recalled he had spent his first Christmas at the Nobles family home that year, that he had arrived two weeks before the holiday and had been amazed at how jolly everyone was in Baron's house. His own home had been such a hotbed of conflict that it had come as quite a shock to find that some households were actually merry at Christmastime.

"December 1987," he answered.

"So you were only fourteen at the time. And you were still attending school?"

Frankie shook his head. "I was at first. But eventually, I dropped out and started working odd jobs." He had actually started selling hard drugs.

"Where were you living?"

"At my friend Mikey's house at first. Then his mother got arrested, he got put into foster care, and I started staying with my friend Baron and his family." Frankie left out the fact that Baron's father had been the notorious Doug Nobles.

"Did your parents know where you were?" Teresa asked.

Frankie shrugged. "I don't think my father really gave a

shit. I came around to see my mother from time to time when I knew my father wasn't there. So she knew that I was okay."

"And Steven remained in the custody of your parents?"

"Yes," Frankie said, his eyes downcast. He was still tormented by the fact that he'd been forced to leave Steven behind.

Teresa pulled out a file folder stuffed with papers. "The defense presents exhibit A, documentation outlining seventeen emergency room visits by Steven Dennis Bingham escorted by his mother Mary to Kings County Hospital with dates ranging from December 1987 through April 1988."

Frankie frowned, glanced at his mother and saw that she was crying. He was confused. Teresa didn't leave him puzzled for long.

She looked at Frankie. "Your mother escorted your brother, Steven, who was only nine years old at the time, to the emergency room seventeen times with injuries ranging from black eyes to broken arms in the months following your departure from your family home. So it seems that once you left the family home, Steven became the object of your father's rage."

Frankie felt his blood boiling. His mother seemed distraught as she cried silently in her seat. Gillian had wrapped her arm around Mary but it seemed to do little to comfort her as tears continued to fall.

"Your mother, Mary, brought Steven to the ER so often that she was warned that the next visit would result in a call to child protective services," Teresa continued. "After that, Steven was never seen in that hospital's emergency room again. Were you aware of that?"

Frankie sipped his water again. "No, I wasn't." He bit his lower lip to keep it from shaking.

Teresa pulled out a second file. "Defense exhibit B, your

honor." She plopped the folder down in front of Frankie, and opened it up to page one. "This is Steven's school attendance record." She pointed to a highlighted section. "Can you read this part aloud to the court, Mr. Bingham?"

Frankie stared at the paper before him and felt his palms sweating, his pulse quickening. He cleared his throat and spoke into the microphone in front of him.

"It says that he had twenty-eight absences that marking period," Frankie said.

"Please read the note attached to the page, Mr. Bingham."

Frankie took a deep breath and read it.

" 'Steven Bingham has been excessively absent, and appears listless and unfocused on the few occasions he does make it to school. A number of his fellow students taunt him, making fun of his shyness and teasing him about his clothes. Bruises have also been observed on his legs and forearms on occasion when he changes clothes for gym class. A recommendation is being made to follow up with his parents to determine if there is an issue at home.' " Frankie finished reading. "It's signed Christine Mahon."

"Let the record show that Ms. Mahon was Steven's fifth-grade teacher, and that she made this recommendation to the principal of PS 236 on April 15, 1988." Teresa looked at Frankie. "A visit was made to your family's home and the principal spoke with your father, who assured him that everything was fine and that Steven was just a clumsy kid who played too hard and injured himself from time to time. But that wasn't really the case, was it, Mr. Bingham?"

Frankie looked at the file in front of him and felt like shit. "Probably not."

"Isn't it true that you allowed Steven to stay with you as an adult, to live off of you and to take advantage of you and your wife's generosity because you felt guilty about leaving him behind to be abused as a child?"

Frankie's hands fisted involuntarily. "No."

"Isn't it true that you suspected all along that your father had substituted one punching bag for another once you moved out?"

"No!" Frankie yelled. "I spoke to Steven all the time and I asked him if my father was still hitting him and my mother. He told me that he wasn't."

"And you believed him?"

Frankie couldn't stop the tears from plunging forth then. He looked at his mother and knew that he couldn't run from the truth anymore. "No," he said honestly, his voice full of emotion. "I thought he was lying. But I couldn't prove it. And even if I could, I couldn't stop it. I was just a kid my-self."

The jurors were transfixed and the courtroom erupted in chatter. Judge Felder called for order in the court.

Teresa compassionately set a box of tissues in front of Frankie and waited as he took two tissues and wiped his eyes and nose. When he had composed himself somewhat, she got back to her line of questioning.

"You felt guilty for leaving Steven behind, didn't you, Mr. Bingham?"

Frankie nodded. "Yeah," he said with a sigh, wiping his eyes.

"Isn't it probable, Mr. Bingham, that Steven lied to you and to the teachers at school and to the doctors in the emergency room out of fear of your father?" Teresa didn't wait for Frankie to answer that. "And isn't it true that you knew all along that the abuse had continued? That you gave your brother whatever he wanted as an adult in order to make up

for the fact that you left him behind as a child? That you allowed him to take advantage of you out of guilt that you were
the only one in your family who escaped your father's wrath?"

"I don't know," Frankie said with tears still falling even
though he wanted desperately for them to stop.

"You knew that something wasn't right about Steven,
didn't you? You suspected that he had been damaged by the
abuse he suffered in a way that was very different from you?"

Frankie pounded his fist on the witness stand, startling
Teresa, who jumped back. Two court officers rushed forth
and told Frankie to calm down. Teresa looked at Judge Felder
and softly asked, "Can you instruct Mr. Bingham to answer
the question?"

The prosecutor rose to his feet and requested a recess. "I
think the witness could use a break."

The judge agreed. "Court will take a fifteen-minute recess," he ordered, banging his gavel again.

Frankie stepped down from the witness stand feeling like
he'd just gone through an emotional trauma. Gillian rushed
to his side and could tell by the look on his face that he needed
to get out of there as quickly as possible. Mary stood nearby,
her face tearstained, as well.

"Come with me," Gillian urged, leading him and Mary
out of the courtroom and down a corridor to an empty case
room she'd noticed earlier on her way to the bathroom. She
shut the door behind them and Frankie sat down on a chair
nearby. Gillian walked over to where he sat and held his face
in her hands, kissing his lips gently. She loved him so much
and hated seeing him this hurt and vulnerable. "Talk to your
mother. She's very upset," Gillian said. She smiled at him,
kissed him on the bridge of his nose, and walked out, leaving
Frankie alone with his mom.

Mary stood against the wall, her face ashen and distraught.

Frankie looked at her. "Why didn't you tell me?" he asked. "I used to come around all the time to bring you money when he wasn't home." Frankie had always avoided his father, waiting hours for him to leave the house at times before he climbed the stairs to visit his mother and brother. "You could have told me what was really going on."

Mary's voice was surprisingly steady as she spoke, though barely above a whisper. "There's a lot you don't know, Frankie."

His brow furrowed and he licked his lips, dry after such an emotional outpouring. "What don't I know?"

Mary all but collapsed into a nearby chair under the weight of what she'd held inside for so long. She took a deep breath and looked her only surviving child in his eyes. It was time to stop keeping quiet.

"When you left," she began, "your father was so mad. He drove around the neighborhood looking for you, but he couldn't find you. He came home that night and he beat Steven bloody because he thought Steven knew where you were."

Frankie closed his eyes as if to block out the enormity of what he was hearing. He opened them again and Mary was staring at the floor as if entranced.

"Steven didn't know where you were, though. So John got even madder and he . . . raped me. He beat me and raped me for so long that I passed out. When I woke up, he was gone and Steven was there with a cold rag on my head, begging me to get up and leave. He wanted us to run away like you had." Mary squeezed her eyes shut and tears spilled forth. "But I wouldn't go." She shook her head. "I wouldn't leave John."

"Why not?" Frankie asked. He had always wondered why.

"I loved him." She seemed to laugh at how ridiculous that

was now. "He was your father, and I wanted us to be a family. I thought it was better to be with him than to be without him."

Frankie stared at his mother and felt such contempt for her. She could have left, could have spared her children the horror of growing up with a monster. But she had chosen to stay, and no matter how noble her reasons were, no matter how hard he tried not to, he resented her for it.

"After you left, he got worse. That lawyer lady was right. The school did contact us about how Steven was coming to school. So John stopped hurting him in ways that left visible marks. If Steven did anything wrong, if he moved too slowly or spoke too loudly, John would take a broomstick and beat him across his back."

Frankie grimaced, picturing little Steven enduring such abuse. Steven had been a frail and lanky kid, skinny and weak. Their father's blows must have all but broken him.

Mary was crying harder now. "I remember that Steven got to the point that he stopped crying when John would beat him. John didn't like that. He took it as a challenge. So one day I came home from food shopping and found him . . . he had Steven tied down . . . and the broomstick . . ."

Frankie stared at his mother with his mouth agape. "Ma . . ." he stammered. "Please don't tell me—"

She nodded, confirming his worst fears. "Steven was screaming and I yelled for John to stop. He did, and Steven was laying on the floor, crying and screaming. John said it was the only way he could get Steven to cry as hard as he wanted him to. He penetrated him with that broomstick and I don't know how many times he had done that before I found out about it." She was sobbing now. "Steven wasn't strong enough to fight back. And I just stayed. I just stayed and kept my mouth shut!" She looked at Frankie, her face so pained. "I deserve to be the one in that grave, Frankie. I'm the one who should be dead, not Steven. He didn't have a chance! And all I did was sit back and let it happen."

Frankie stared at his mother in disbelief. He had a sick feeling in the pit of his stomach and he worried that he might be nauseous. Mary was trying to stop crying, but talking about what she had witnessed in silence for the first time was hard to handle.

Gillian came back in the room and saw Frankie sitting with his head in his hands and Mary sobbing quietly in the corner. She frowned. This wasn't what she'd expected to happen when she'd left the two of them alone together.

"Court is about to reconvene," she said. "The prosecutor says they need you back on the stand."

Frankie couldn't move. He stared at his weeping mother and shook with contempt and pure rage. His father had done them all a favor when he shot himself. He looked at Mary and wondered why she hadn't done the same.

Slowly, Frankie got to his feet and walked back to the courtroom, his mother and Gillian trailing behind him in silence.

He walked up to the witness stand more upset than he had been when he left it. The judge reminded Frankie that he was still under oath and Frankie took his seat and a long guzzle of water before Teresa got started.

She picked up right where she'd left off before the recess.

"Had you ever suspected that Steven was affected by the abuse in a very different way from you?"

Frankie told the truth. "Yeah," he said. "I could tell that it was different." He shook his head. "He was human. Anybody would have been damaged after going through what he did."

Teresa nodded. "Were you sexually abused as a child?"

Frankie frowned, hating that she would even suggest that. "No!"

"To your knowledge, was your brother ever sexually abused?"

Frankie looked at his hands, replaying what his mother had just told him in his head. He didn't know how to answer the question so he said simply, "I don't know."

Teresa stared at him. "Your father is deceased, correct?"

"Yes."

"How did he die?"

Frankie looked out across the courtroom, hating that his family business was being laid bare for all the world to see. He watched reporters staring at him in anticipation of his answer and knew they would cream themselves when they heard his response.

"He committed suicide. He put a forty-five in his mouth and blew his brains out."

"How did you feel when you found out?"

Frankie shrugged. "Relieved."

The courtroom was abuzz again and Judge Felder was banging his gavel once more.

"Just one final question," Teresa said. She saw the look of relief on Frankie's face. "Mr. Bingham, do you believe that Steven sodomized your nephew when he was left in his care?"

Frankie looked at his mother, thought about what she'd just revealed to him. It was entirely possible that what their father had done to Steven had warped him in unimaginable ways. He shook his head and then looked at Camille, her belly bulging with his unborn child. He thought about how cruel he'd been to her, how hearing Born describe her preg-

nancy cravings had made him feel like shit. He looked then at
Misa and his eyes filled with tears.

Misa had never done anything to Frankie. In fact, he had
practically watched her grow up in the years he'd been with
Camille. He thought about Shane. Although he wasn't much
for children, Shane was a good kid. He had been so happy, so
carefree, and now this. Frankie couldn't help wondering if
what his brother had been accused of was true.

"Mr. Bingham, please answer the question."

Frankie shook his head. "I don't know what to believe
anymore."

Teresa was satisfied with that. She had gotten him to go
from absolute denial to the possibility of Misa's suspicions
being correct.

"No further questions," she said, returning to her seat.

"Your honor, may I redirect?" the DA asked.

The judge nodded and the DA stood up, addressed Frankie.

"Mr. Bingham, do you believe that Steven deserved to die?"

Frankie got choked up. Fighting back tears, he looked at his
mother again and then looked at the jury. "No," he said, shaking his head. "No, he didn't." He squeezed his eyes shut and
shook his head. His father had done a number on them all.

One Step at a Time

"Did you know about all that stuff that Frankie went through growing up?" Lily asked. Celia, Misa, Dominique, Toya, and Lily all waited anxiously for the answer. They had gone out to eat dinner after court recessed for the day. Now, as they sat at a table in R.H. Tugs surrounded by tons of food, they were all eager to chew the fat of what they'd witnessed.

"No," Camille answered, shaking her head. "Frankie never told me that he was abused as a kid. I had no idea."

"It makes sense," Celia said, looking at Misa, "that Steven had been abused by their father and then he would turn around and become an abuser. I watch Oprah faithfully, and she always says that abusers abuse others. It's a cycle."

Camille thought about that. She thought about Frankie and his reluctance to be a father. It all made sense to her now, and she wondered whether or not his past would affect their baby.

"I felt kind of sorry for Frankie," Misa said, her voice low and sad. "I know that might sound crazy . . ."

"It doesn't sound crazy to me," Camille said. "Not crazy at all."

Misa glanced at Camille and smiled at her weakly.

Lily shook her head. "Well, it sounds like he had a terrible childhood. Frankie's mother was over there falling apart today. She seemed like hearing all of the details of her son's life like that was too much for her."

"She sat there and watched her husband abuse her kids and she stayed," Toya said, thinking back on how her own mother had done the same thing. "She should feel like shit." Hearing Frankie breaking down in court that day as he recounted his tough childhood had touched her. She understood the torment Frankie and Steven had endured at their father's hands and her heart went out to Frankie. She agreed with Celia. Abuse victims tended to continue the cycle. Toya wondered how her own past had shaped the woman she was today.

Dominique chewed her food and shook her head. "All I know is that Teresa Rourke is worth every penny she's being paid. If I was sitting on that jury, I would be thinking that Steven was guilty of what Misa says he did. I think there is sufficient evidence to suggest that Steven was abused, and that he would have had the potential to abuse Shane. So far, I think you've got a good chance for acquittal."

Misa crossed her fingers tightly. "From your mouth, to God's ears," she said. "I pray that you're right."

"I loved him," Mayra was saying. "I know you may not believe that, but I did."

Gillian sat across from her mother in the living room of her parents' house. Mayra had summoned her there so that she could plead her case regarding her affair with Guy London. Gillian's face was set in a permanent grimace, her hands crossed in her lap as she listened to her mother's excuses.

"I married him knowing that I wanted to spend the rest of my life with him. But then he got sick and he stopped being the same Doug I fell in love with."

"And you blame him for that? You think he wanted to get sick?" Gillian's face was twisted into a look of pure loathing.

"No, no," Mayra hurriedly clarified. "I'm the one who was at fault. I guess I thought that he was bionic or something. It never seemed possible to me that anything—not any disease or any human being or any bullet—could ever overpower your father. When he got sick and the disease weakened him . . ."

"You started sleeping with his friend," Gillian said flatly.

Mayra looked at her daughter and shook her head. "Why are you being so cold, Gigi?"

Gillian laughed then. "*I'm* being cold? You're the one who carried on an affair with Daddy's friend while he was confined to a wheelchair. Sounds pretty cold to me."

"No, Gigi. It's not as simple as that. I'm trying to get you to understand, but it's pointless. You're not hearing anything I'm saying." Mayra shook her head in frustration.

"I'm serious. Something is very different about you and it's not in a good way."

Gillian rolled her eyes.

"Ever since Doug died, you've been so distant. I know you're mad at me. You have every right to be. But we're family, Gigi. You can't keep acting this way towards me when all we have left is each other."

Gillian leaned forward, looking her mother squarely in the eyes. "Guy probably doesn't want you anymore now that you're not the wealthy heiress that he thought you'd be," she said. "And Daddy's gone, so maybe you think I'm all you've got." Gillian picked up her purse and held it in her hand as she continued. "But you are not all that I have left. I have Frankie. And to be honest with you, he's all that I need to keep me sane these days. I don't hate you, Ma. I just want to be left alone for a little while. Just give me time to forgive the fact that you lied to me and to Daddy for God knows how long." Gillian rose to leave. "And please don't keep showing up at court with your breasts hanging out. You're still supposed to be playing the role of grieving widow."

Gillian got up, and walked out, leaving her mother sitting speechlessly in her wake.

She sat in her car with the key in the ignition and stared blankly at her reflection in the rearview mirror. Gillian knew that her mother was right about one thing. She *had* become colder since her father's murder. She was angry that she had been robbed of him so unexpectedly and she was furious with Baron and Mayra for their transgressions against him. She realized, though, as she looked in the mirror, that Nobles probably wouldn't fully approve of how she was handling things.

It was almost as if she could hear his voice clearly in her ears, telling her to forgive her mother and brother. Baron was confined to a wheelchair and had been stripped of his role in the family business. Gillian had cut Mayra off financially and emotionally. But it still wasn't enough for her. Gillian wanted them both to suffer more for what they'd done to her father.

But Nobles hadn't raised her that way. He had drilled the notion of family loyalty into her head so effectively over the years that she could hear him reminding her now, telling her that Baron needed her help, that Mayra was too weak to survive on her own. Gillian had little sympathy for either of them. They alone were to blame for the way things had turned out. But she knew that she couldn't turn her back on them completely, knowing that both of them needed her desperately.

Tremaine had made Gillian aware of a situation concerning Baron. Apparently, Danno's DNA had turned up during an investigation into Trina Samuels's murder. Gillian didn't need a PhD to figure out that Baron had been involved in the killing, since Trina had set him up to be shot by Jojo. Danno was on the run now, and Gillian knew that if he were caught, he could very well implicate Baron in Trina's murder. She shook her head now as she thought about what a fuckup her brother was.

And now Mayra was begging for her forgiveness. Gillian turned the key in the ignition and fastened her seat belt. She put her sunglasses on and looked at her reflection in the mirror one last time.

"Being in charge ain't all it's cracked up to be," she said aloud to herself and peeled out, her tires squealing as she made her exit.

Celia couldn't believe her eyes. She peeked through the partially open door and watched as Baron slowly, and ever so gingerly, put one foot in front of the other and took his first step since the shooting. Out of breath and clearly exhausted, he took another step, holding on to his walker for dear life. His physical therapist had been trying for weeks to get Baron back on his feet, to no avail. The entire process had frustrated him, causing Celia to feel sorry for her only child as he struggled to feel like a man again. Baron had grown increasingly annoyed and discouraged and had expressed his displeasure with the whole process. What she hadn't known was that each night, after his physical therapist and his nurse had gone

home, Baron had been working hard to walk on his own, doing the exercises they'd taught him and struggling through
them in a sweat-soaked determination to walk again.

And now he had done it—two small steps that felt more
like a marathon. As he collapsed onto his bed, winded and
drained, he smiled. He had walked!

Celia stepped into the room, applauding. Baron was clearly
surprised to see his mother. He had no clue that she had been
watching from the wings, willing him forward as she watched
him take his first steps in months.

"I'm so proud of you," she said, rushing to his side and
kissing him on his cheek.

His smile spread. He was proud of himself.

"I knew you would get your strength back. You're going
to be up and at 'em in no time."

Baron nodded. He caught his breath and sat up on the bed.

"I'm sick of sitting in that chair," he said. "I'm too young
to settle for being a cripple for the rest of my life."

Celia smiled. "Yes, you are," she said. She sat down on the
chair near her son's bed and crossed her legs. Baron was doing
much better these days. Emotionally, he still seemed distant
and perhaps depressed. But he wasn't as downtrodden as he had
been. He had a sense of calm about him that hadn't been there
in the days and weeks after he'd first regained consciousness.

Celia looked at him now and thought it was time she got
to the bottom of what was really troubling her son. "Gillian
called."

Baron's smile faded, morphing slowly into a frown. "She
wanted to talk to me?" It had been weeks since their last conversation.

"No," Celia said. "She just asked me to give you a message. She said that Danno was killed last night."

Celia noticed all the blood drain from Baron's face and saw his green eyes narrow. "What happened?" he asked. He couldn't believe this. It seemed that his prayers had been answered after all.

"Gillian said that Danno was on the run from the cops. He had been hiding out in Queens, but he was struck by a black Lexus SUV while he was crossing Queens Boulevard late last night. The vehicle fled the scene, but witnesses gave a description of it."

Baron's heart was racing. Gillian herself drove a black Lexus. Baron was wondering if his sister had handled Danno for him.

Celia confirmed it. "She also said to tell you 'no more favors.' Whatever that means."

Baron felt a flood of emotion wash over him. He knew exactly what it meant and he was relieved. Danno was dead and he prayed that Trina Samuels's murder investigation had died with him. He also felt so grateful to Gillian, whom he knew had run Danno down on the boulevard of death. Although he knew the two of them would never be close again due to Baron's stupidity, he was grateful that Gillian hadn't turned her back on him altogether. Celia was looking at him questioningly, so Baron fought to keep his emotions under control lest she notice.

"Baron," she said. "I want to talk to you about your father."

He stared back at her. "Okay."

"Are you in any way responsible for what happened to him?"

Baron looked at his mother and felt so ashamed. He had been doing his best to run from the truth, but there was no escaping it. For months, he'd sat in that wheelchair and beat himself up for what he'd done, for causing his own problems and for setting the events in motion that led to his father's death. Now, as his mother sat beside him looking so angelic and understanding, he stopped running from the truth.

"Yeah," he admitted, his voice low and monotone. "And you deserve to know the whole story."

As difficult as it was, Baron finally came clean, using his mother as his temporary priest in his makeshift confessional. For the rest of the afternoon he told his mother the truth about the costly decisions he'd made in the months before his father was killed. Baron admitted his role in it and placed all the blame squarely on his own shoulders, no longer willing to point the finger at everybody else. He felt that God had given him a new start. He still had a tremendous amount of shame and guilt inside. But with Celia's help, that day was the first step on a long road to forgiving himself and changing like he had promised God he would.

Toya kissed her mother good-bye and watched as Sweets climbed into the taxi and shut the door. She waved as the cab pulled away from the curb, en route to take her mother back to Atlanta at last. Toya had to resist the urge to kick up her heels and dance for joy as her unexpected houseguest finally vacated her home. Her mom had been there for weeks and Toya was thrilled to see her go.

She waited until the cab was out of sight and then she crossed the street, approaching Russell's house for the first time. She wondered why she felt a little nervous. This wasn't like her. As she neared Russell's front door, she took a deep breath and blew it out. Finally, she rang the bell and waited.

Russell came to the door wearing an FDNY T-shirt and a pair of jeans, his beef-and-broccoli Timberlands untied and a beer in his hand. He smiled slightly when he saw Toya, but she noticed right away that his face hadn't lit up the way it usually did at the sight of her.

"Good morning," she said. "I just wanted to come by and say hello."

Russell's brow furrowed. "Hello," he said. "This is a pleasant surprise."

Toya shifted her weight from one foot to the other and waited to be invited in. When that didn't happen, she sucked her teeth and said, "Well, can I come in or not?"

"Not." Russell just stood there.

Toya felt herself getting angry and she frowned. "I can't come in?"

"Nope," he said, sipping his Corona. "After the way you've been treating me, why would I invite you into my house?"

Toya mentally counted to ten, told herself not to go off on this ugly bastard, and reminded herself that she had been avoiding him ever since her mother came to town.

"I had a houseguest," she explained, surprised that she was actually giving this fool an explanation. "My mother was here and I didn't want to have you coming over while she was staying with me."

He nodded. "So I guess that's why you couldn't bother to call or to come over here and ring my bell after she went to bed. Maybe that's why you didn't keep our appointment to go house hunting like we discussed. And I bet your mother being here is the reason why you practically shut your door in my face every time I so much as looked across the street."

Toya knew she had been hard on Russell. Still, she didn't appreciate being forced to stand out on his porch instead of being invited inside. "I apologize," she said halfheartedly.

"You don't mean that."

"Listen here, bitch. I'm not about to stand here and beg you—"

"See?" he said. "That's what I'm talking about."

"What?" she asked, perplexed. "I came over here to say hello and I apologized for not returning your calls. If that's not enough, then I don't know what to tell you."

He smirked, thinking she was too hard for her own good. "I don't know why you feel like you have to be so tough all the time. It's really not attractive." Russell shook his head. "At first I used to think it was cute. But now I think I'm kinda turned off by it." He thought back on all their interactions and realized that she was always pushing him away no matter how close he tried to get. He was tired of being rejected. "Look," he said, "I know I'm not the handsomest guy in the world. I don't own my house or drive a fancy car like you do. But that doesn't give you the right to treat me like you do, hiding me from your mother and then coming by the second she leaves town. I thought we had a good time when you finally let me take you out. I found out that underneath all that crusty exterior is a really intelligent, funny, and sexy woman." He shook his head again. "But then you went right back to acting like a bitch."

"I'm a bitch now?" she asked, her hands on her hips. She was about to go off on Russell something terrible.

"No," he said. "But you play the part really well." He sighed. "I like you. I think you know that. But I don't want to be your toy. That's not the role I'm meant to play."

Toya didn't know why she was turned on by Russell at that moment. Maybe it was because he had the nerve to tell her no, or that he had found the balls to stand up to her. Most men ran for cover when she unleashed her mean streak. But Russell was different. She had realized, after weeks of reliving

TRACY BROWN

the past with her parents, how her upbringing had hardened her to the extreme. She had inherited her father's brutal and cutting vernacular and her mother's holier-than-thou demeanor and it had resulted in this. She pushed men away to avoid them doing it to her instead.

She wanted to change that. "Listen," she said, opting not to curse him out. She was going to turn a new page and start again. "I've been very nasty to you. And you have been very nice to me. So I apologize. I mean it." She wasn't used to this. Sorry never came easy for her. "I understand if you don't want to let me in your house. But my father just died and I had to confront some terrible things from my past. And with my mother being here . . . I just needed some time to sort all of that out before I let myself get involved with you." She shrugged. "But if you don't want to accept my apology, I'll leave." She turned to go, praying that he would stop her and allow her to save face.

Russell felt sorry for her, unaware that she was mourning her father's loss. "No, wait." He watched as she stopped her retreat and turned back to face him. He held the door open and smiled softly. "Come in," he said. "Apology accepted."

Toya smiled back and stepped inside Russell's home. She decided that she was going to stop being so negative and truly let go of all the pain from her past. The first step in doing that would be to look past Russell's lack of good looks and enjoy the good qualities he had to offer—great conversation and fantastic sex. He shut the door behind them and pulled her in close for a kiss. And she didn't even fight back.

Witness for the Prosecution

"The people call Camille Bingham to the stand."

Misa looked around in desperation and saw the same expression on her sister's face. The whole courtroom began to buzz with chatter as Camille slowly rose and made her way to the front. She locked eyes with her sister on her way up to the witness stand and Misa's heart galloped in her chest.

Camille was sworn in and sat down, her pregnant belly lifting her breasts up better than any pushup bra could. Frankie marveled at how each time he saw her she looked more maternal than the day before.

"Mrs. Bingham, what is your relationship to the defendant?"

"She's my sister." Camille glanced at Misa and smiled at her.

"Please tell us what happened when you arrived home on the night of January 5, 2008."

Camille licked her lips and thought back to that fateful evening.

"I came home and saw that my sister's car was parked outside in my driveway. I found that odd since my nephew Shane wasn't there."

"What time was it when you arrived home?"

Camille tried to recall. "About two o'clock in the morning."

The district attorney seemed surprised by that. "Where had you been?"

Camille looked at Frankie, Gillian seated beside him and holding his hand. "I had been at my husband's mistress's house on the Upper East Side, telling him that I was pregnant."

The chattering commenced, causing the judge to call for order—a daily occurrence in this trial. All of Staten Island seemed to be packed into the courtroom each day, eager for a morsel of gossip to take back to their block.

The DA nodded. "You gave your husband the good news and then returned home to find your sister's car in the driveway?"

"Yes, that's right," Camille said. "I walked into the house and noticed that it was dark and quiet."

"Was that unusual?"

Camille nodded. "Most nights my brother-in-law, Steven, came in from the guesthouse to watch my husband's flat-screen plasma TV. Apparently, the TV in the guesthouse wasn't good enough." A few jurors snickered, mostly the men who understood exactly how he'd felt.

"So typically late at night, your brother-in-law would be in your living room until the wee hours of the morning watching TV."

"That's correct."

"But on this night?"

Camille took a deep breath. "I walked into my kitchen and saw Steven lying in the middle of the floor."

"What else did you see?"

"Blood was on the walls and on the floor in a pool around

his body. I also saw a gun on the floor and a broken beer bottle."

The DA's brow was furrowed compassionately. "You must have been terrified."

She nodded. "I was."

"What did you do next?"

"I noticed a light coming from the dining room, so I picked up a knife from the block on the counter and went to see what was going on."

"Weren't you afraid that the assailant might still be in the house?"

Camille shook her head. "At that point, I wasn't thinking straight. I probably should have ran out of the house, but I guess seeing my sister's car in the driveway made me think that she might be in the house and that she might be in danger. So I went into the dining room with the knife."

"And what did you discover there?"

Camille sighed. "I saw my sister sitting at the table, a candle lit in the center of it."

"What was she doing?"

Camille shook her head. "She was just sitting there staring at the wall like she was in a daze."

"What did you say to her, if anything?"

Camille looked at Misa and then back at the prosecutor. "I asked her what she had done."

"You assumed immediately that she had killed your brother-in-law? Why?"

"Because she had blood on her clothes and on her hands. I could see blood on the wall near her also. Plus, she was sitting there so calmly that I assumed she was aware that Steven was dead in the kitchen."

The prosecutor looked at the jury panel. "She was sitting there *calmly*," he repeated.

Camille knew she had fucked up. "Well . . . she was quiet I mean. She was just sitting there in a daze. Her hands were shaking," she offered.

"To your knowledge, had she called 911 to summon an ambulance for Mr. Bingham?"

Camille looked at Misa again. Misa was staring at her legal pad, though the page was blank. She could tell that Camille's testimony today would be damaging to her case, but she also understood that her sister had to tell the truth under oath.

"No."

"So," the DA said. "You arrived home, found Steven Bingham lying in a pool of his own blood on the kitchen floor. Then you walked into the dining room where you found your sister sitting calmly with blood on her clothes and hands. And she had not even bothered to summon help for the victim. So, in essence, you arrived to find your sister waiting for Steven Bingham to die."

"OBJECTION!" Teresa bellowed.

"Sustained. Watch it, Mr. Davidson," Judge Felder snarled.

"I'll rephrase it, your honor." The DA smirked ever so slightly at Camille. "Did your sister exhibit a sense of urgency concerning Mr. Bingham's condition?"

Camille shook her head. "No. But at that point, I believe he was already dead."

The DA ignored her and kept going. "What explanation did your sister give you for what had happened?"

"She told me that Steven had molested Shane. That she had come over to confront him and brought the gun she had gotten years ago for protection."

Louis looked like he wanted to disappear when the subject of the illegal gun came up. He had given the .38 to Misa years earlier, and he certainly didn't want the DA to know that.

"She said that she caught Steven by surprise while he was in the kitchen getting a beer. She told him what she suspected and they had words. She told me that he lunged at her and she pulled out the gun, but he kept coming toward her. She said she fired in self-defense."

"Yet, she didn't call the police?"

"Objection!" Teresa interjected. "This witness can't speak to what was going on in my client's mind at that time."

"Sustained."

The DA moved on. "You finally called 911, Mrs. Bingham, is that correct?"

"Yes," Camille answered.

"Did you call your husband to tell him what had taken place?"

Camille looked at Frankie, recalled speaking to him on the phone that night and hanging up without telling him that his brother was dead on their kitchen floor.

"No, I didn't."

"Why not?"

"I was afraid."

"Of your husband?"

She nodded. "Yes."

"Why?"

She thought it was a dumb question. "His brother had just been shot by my sister. I thought he might flip out. He and Steven were very close."

"How about you, Mrs. Bingham? Were you and the deceased close?"

She thought about that and answered honestly. "Not at

first," she admitted. "I thought he was a freeloader who lounged around all day and took advantage of our kindness. I don't think he liked me, either."

"Any idea why not?"

She shrugged again. "Maybe he sensed that I didn't want him around. Maybe he thought I was stuck up. I don't really know. But there was definitely tension between us at first."

"That changed?"

Camille nodded.

"When?"

She looked at Misa again, held her gaze for a moment before the DA snapped her back to the question at hand.

"I developed a drinking problem," she admitted. "My marriage was unraveling and drinking was how I coped. There were times when I would wake up with a hangover and my nephew was there and . . ." Her voice trailed off as she wondered for the hundredth time whether Steven had used those opportunities to prey on Shane. "Steven would come over from the guesthouse and make Shane some cereal or put on his favorite cartoons. He would let me sleep off my hangover." She looked at her hands. "I was grateful to him for that. I thought we were starting to get along better."

"During those times that you were sleeping off your drunkenness," the prosecutor began. Camille glared at him, pissed that he was making her sound like a lush. "Did you ever awake to find Shane traumatized in any way?"

She tried to recall if she ever had. "No," she said honestly.

"Did Shane ever cry or exhibit fear of Steven Bingham in your presence?"

Camille knew this wasn't the answer that would help her sister's case, but she was under oath. "No," she said softly.

The prosecutor sneered at her. "So it sounds as if Steven

Bingham was blamed for such an atrocity based solely on
your sister's imagination."

"OBJECTION, your honor!"

"Rephrase that, counselor," Judge Felder ordered.

"Gladly," the DA answered. He looked at Camille pointedly. "Did you think your brother-in-law was a child molester when you left your nephew in his care?"

"Objection!" Teresa was on her feet now.

"Overruled, Ms. Rourke."

The DA looked at Camille. "Please answer the question."

Camille wanted to cry. "No," she said. "I didn't think he
was. But—"

"You spent a lot of time with your nephew, did you not?"

"Yes, I did."

"In fact, it's fair to say that you spent more time with him
than his own mother. Am I right?"

Camille looked at Misa and shook her head.

"That's not the case?" the prosecutor asked, pulling out
the sign-in sheet from Shane's day care showing that Camille
had dropped him off and picked him up far more than his
mother had.

"Yes," she admitted. "That may be true."

"And had you ever noticed Steven exhibit more than a
passing interest in the child?"

Camille had to admit that she hadn't. "No."

The DA seemed satisfied so far. "Would you say that
Shane was afraid of his uncle Steven?"

Camille wiped her nose with a tissue from a nearby box
and wished she could answer differently. "No."

"No further questions, your honor." The DA went back
to his seat and got a pat on the back from his colleague on a
job well done.

Camille felt sick to her stomach. But before she could ask the judge for a time-out, Teresa was on her feet and walking her way for cross-examination.

"Mrs. Bingham, is it true that you were distracted by your failing marriage in the days leading up to January fifth?"

Camille brightened a little. This much was true! "Yes," she answered. "My husband was ignoring my phone calls and had run off with someone else. I was very distracted by that."

"Is it possible that Shane had exhibited some change in behavior but that you were too preoccupied to notice?"

Ashamed, Camille answered, "Yes."

"No further questions."

Camille stepped down from the witness stand, relieved, but praying that she hadn't done too much damage to Misa's case with her testimony. She felt terrible. But as she passed the defense table, Misa winked and smiled weakly at her, letting Camille know that the truth hadn't cost her the only sister she had.

Reasonable Doubt

Today it was the defense's turn. Misa rubbed her hands together in anticipation, eager to change the jury's minds about what they had heard so far.

"The defense calls Louis Crowley to the stand."

Misa watched her ex-husband stand up, watched his girlfriend, Nahla, give him an encouraging smile, and she couldn't wait for Teresa to tear his ass apart. He got up on the stand, took the oath, and sat down. His brown suit fit him well, but Misa thought he looked like a broke-ass church deacon sitting up there with his tan tie and pocket square. She shot daggers at him and listened as Teresa got started.

"Mr. Crowley, you were married to the defendant for three years, is that correct?"

"Yes, that's correct."

"How would you describe your marriage?"

He chuckled a little. "Looking back on it, we got married for the wrong reasons," he said. "We dated for two years and things were good. Then, Misa got pregnant with our son and we thought the right thing to do was to get married and make a real family."

"I see," Teresa said. "At what point did the marriage begin to collapse?"

"Well, it became clear pretty fast that we wanted different things," Louis said.

"You wanted another woman, isn't that right?" Teresa asked, cutting to the chase.

Louis looked like he'd swallowed the canary. He recovered quickly and responded. "Well, I did meet someone else. But that wasn't the only problem."

"Really?" Teresa asked. "What were the other problems?"

"Well," Louis said, "Misa didn't want to get a job. And I was fine with that. But the money was slow coming in and I think she expected us to be doing as well as her sister and Frankie were."

Teresa tilted her head, contemplatively. "You discouraged your wife from working outside the home, didn't you? Didn't you tell her that you didn't want her working in some office with a bunch of men leering at her every day?"

Louis recalled saying that, but it seemed so long ago now. "I guess I might have said that."

"But in fact, it was you who met someone at work, isn't that right?"

Louis looked at Nahla and then at Misa, who was scowling at him. "Yes, I did."

"You abandoned your wife and son for a woman who made double your salary, am I correct?"

"I wouldn't say abandoned . . ."

"Did you leave your wife and son?"

He seemed tormented by that question. "I left my wife. I never left my son."

"Oh no?" Teresa asked. "Defense exhibit C, your honor." She held up a child support order and had it entered as evidence. "This is an order of child support that my client had drawn up after you refused to provide for your son. In this filing it's painfully clear that your son's day-to-day expenses, including tuition, food, clothing, shelter, entertainment, medical, and dental costs were all paid for by your wife. You, in fact, had not a single receipt or bill to prove that you had contributed in any way to your son's financial well-being prior to this filing."

Louis had no response for that.

"In fact," Teresa continued, "this order stipulates that you owed your wife arrears totaling seven thousand dollars plus a monthly support order of one thousand dollars a month." She raised an eyebrow at Louis. "So you didn't only leave your wife, Mr. Crowley. You abandoned your son as well—physically and financially. In fact, you didn't even bother to visit with your son until after the courts ordered you to pay child support."

While Louis fidgeted in his seat he noticed that many of the women in the courtroom were looking at him like he was the gum on the bottom of their shoes. He felt vilified. Misa, meanwhile, felt such contempt for Louis as her attorney rehashed the lengths she'd been forced to go in order to get him to be a father to his child. She still remembered his reaction when the judge ordered him to pay child support and asked if he wanted to set up visitation with his son. "Yeah, I guess so," he had said. "If I'm gonna be paying child support, I might as well see him." Misa hated his guts, and would have given anything to have chosen a different father for her son.

Teresa moved on, her tone suggesting that she was interrogating a hostile witness. "Mr. Crowley, prior to Christmas Day, 2007, when had you last seen your son?"

Louis tried to recall the exact date, but couldn't pinpoint it. "I'm not sure," he admitted.

"Had you seen him at all in the month of December 2007?"

Louis answered hesitantly, "I don't think . . . no. No, I didn't."

"How about November 2007? Had you seen your son at Thanksgiving?"

Louis had not. "No."

"Isn't it true that you saw Shane on average once every two months prior to Christmas 2007?"

Louis glanced at Misa and saw the expression of pure hatred on her face. "That sounds about right."

"Why hadn't you been a consistent part of Shane's life?"

"I work very long hours."

"Twenty-four hours a day, seven days a week?"

"Objection," the prosecution interrupted.

"Withdrawn," Teresa countered. "How does your new girlfriend feel about children, Mr. Crowley?"

Louis frowned. "I'm not sure."

"Does she have any?" Teresa asked.

"No."

"Have you discussed having any?"

Louis shook his head. "No."

"Isn't it true that you told your mother that your girlfriend doesn't like children?"

Louis remembered telling his mother that, but wondered how the hell Misa's attorney had gotten that information.

"I might have said that."

"So you lied when you said that you weren't sure how she felt about children."

"No . . . what I meant . . . I'm saying that she might not feel that way anymore."

Teresa tilted her head to the side and looked at Louis like the liar that he was. "But she felt that way at some point, did she not?"

Louis sighed. "When we first got together she mentioned that she wasn't particularly fond of children."

"What does your girlfriend do for a living, Mr. Crowley?"

"She's a dentist."

"And when the two of you met, you were working two odd jobs in order to provide for your family, correct?"

"Yes."

"When you left your wife and moved in with your girl-friend, did you continue to work?"

"No."

"You quit your jobs?"

"Yes, I did."

"How did you support yourself?"

He glanced at Nahla and then replied. "Nahla supported me while I went back to school and got my degree."

Teresa looked at the women on the jury and was happy to see them looking at Louis with some contempt.

"Is it true that you went on vacation with your mistress to Saint Vincent and the Grenadines and to Acapulco, Mexico, while Misa was left to try her best to provide for your son?"

"Yes," he said. "But I didn't pay for those vacations, so it's not as if I was taking food out of my son's mouth."

Teresa frowned. "While you were cavorting on exotic beaches, your wife was getting financial assistance from her sister and brother-in-law. They purchased a car for Misa so that she could transport your son to and from school. They helped her to pay her rent and to buy food and clothing for your child. And you were off enjoying a child-free environment with your mistress."

He looked at Nahla and noticed she seemed just as embarrassed as he was. "I did feel bad about not seeing my son that often," he said, his voice cracking a little as the guilt he'd suppressed for years spilled forth.

"Did you?" Teresa challenged him.

"Yes, I did. And that's why when Misa called me on Christmas Day and told me to come and get him, I didn't hesitate. I went and got my son."

"You went and got him and brought him back to the home that you shared with your girlfriend who hates kids?"

"Objection, your honor!"

"Sustained."

"Mr. Crowley, what happened when you brought Shane home with you on Christmas?" Teresa asked, standing in front of him with her arms folded across her chest, her Louboutins making her tower over the witness.

"Well, the first night, everything was good. He was happy to see me but he was being really clingy and I didn't know why."

"Did you attribute that to the fact that he hadn't seen you in over a month?"

Louis knew that was a dig at him and he deserved it. "I just thought he was used to being babied or something. He slept in bed with me and Nahla that night, and in the morning he seemed fine."

"When did you notice a change?"

"About two days later, he started saying curse words that I had never heard him say before."

Teresa frowned. "What kinds of words?"

Louis thought back to that day and sighed. "Shit, fuck, bitch. Words like that."

"Was he just saying those words or was he directing them at anyone in particular?"

"He was just saying them, sitting on the floor playing with his toys and saying them."

"And how did you respond to that?"

Louis looked at Nahla again. The truth was she had insisted that he spank Shane for using such foul language. Louis had been hesitant to do so, since he rarely even saw his son. He hadn't wanted to spank him and make him upset. "At first, I warned him that if he kept saying those bad words that I was gonna spank him."

"Did that work?"

He shook his head. "He kept doing it, almost as if he was challenging me. So I went over to where he was sitting on the floor and I pulled him to his feet and started to spank him on his butt." Louis felt himself getting choked up at the memory of that horrible night. "But then he started to cry—hard! He was sobbing and he was screaming, begging me not to hurt him back there."

Teresa allowed Louis a moment to compose himself as he dabbed at his eyes with a tissue. She knew it had to be difficult for him to remember that night.

"What was your reaction to that?"

Louis took a deep breath. "I tried to pick him up and get him to stop crying, but he just fell into a ball at my feet and kept crying, begging me not to hurt him. So I scooped him up off the floor and sat on the couch with him, rocking him. I asked him what was wrong, what he meant by 'don't hurt me back there' . . . he told me that a bad man hurt him back there."

Misa was crying now and Camille leaned forward and

handed her sister a tissue. The judge glanced at her and asked if she needed to take a recess, but she shook her head. She wanted to get this part over with as quickly as possible. It was horrible hearing the details of what had been done to her son.

"Did you ask Shane who the bad man was?" Teresa asked.

Louis nodded. "I kept asking him that. But he wouldn't tell me. He said that the bad man would hurt him and hurt his mommy if he told anybody. I told him that I would never let anybody hurt him again, but he was petrified. He just kept promising that he was gonna be good, begging me not to send him back home, telling me that he didn't want to play those games anymore."

"Games?" Teresa asked.

Louis shrugged. "I had no idea what he was talking about. So I calmed him down, got him dressed, and I took him to the doctor."

Teresa looked at her notes and nodded. "What did the doctor tell you?"

"He confirmed that my son had been sodomized. He told me he was obligated to report it to the authorities. So we sat there in the doctor's office and called the police. We tried to call my ex-wife to find out what she knew, tried calling my sister-in-law and got no answer. So I filed the report and gave them my statement. I took my son home with me and kept trying to get in touch with his mother."

"When were you able to contact her?"

"She called to speak to Shane later that night. It was the first time she had called to check on him since I picked him up three days earlier." Louis wanted the jury to know what a terrible mother Misa had been. "And I told her what happened to my son on her watch."

Teresa looked at Louis like he had a lot of nerve. "On her watch, Mr. Crowley?"

He nodded. "Exactly!" Now he was angry. "On her watch," he repeated.

"Is it true that my client asked to speak with Shane and you refused?"

"Yes, I did."

"Did she sound upset?"

"She was crying, but I didn't give a damn. It was her fault."

"You felt that your ex-wife had sodomized him?" Teresa asked for clarification.

"No," he said. "But she was supposed to be taking care of him and she allowed it to happen."

"How about you, Mr. Crowley?" Teresa asked. "Didn't you have a responsibility to Shane, as well?"

"Yeah, but I wasn't the one who was leaving him for days at a time with whoever would babysit him!"

"Did you ever think that if you had been there for your son more often that Misa may not have been forced to leave him in the custody of others?"

Louis fought back tears. He wasn't about to let this bitch turn the blame on him. "She wasn't forced! She could have stayed home and took care of Shane instead of running off—"

"The way you did?"

"OBJECTION!"

"Sustained."

"Isn't it possible that Misa was out searching for happiness the way that you ran off in search of the same thing years ago? Is it possible that perhaps she was out looking for a way to complete the family structure that you tore apart when you upgraded to a new child-free life?"

Louis was tearing up now.

Teresa took the opportunity to go in for the kill. "Is it true that when you delivered the blow to my client that her son had been molested, that you further traumatized her by telling her that she and her family would never see your son again as long as you were alive?"

"I did say that," he admitted.

"And did you threaten to kill my client?"

"I was upset."

"Did you threaten to kill my client?"

"Yes," Louis said reluctantly.

The courtroom hummed with chatter and Misa stared at Louis, watched him reliving the worst day of their lives.

"So after hearing about her son's molestation, being told that she would never see him again, and having her life threatened, how did my client respond?"

Louis shrugged. "I was mad so I hung up on her. She kept calling back so I turned the ringer off."

"Why did you do that?"

"I had said everything I needed to say to her. I wanted her to get to the bottom of who tortured my son and then we could talk."

"So what happened then?"

"Then she came over to my house demanding to see Shane."

"And did you let her see her son?"

Louis stared at his hands. "No."

Teresa stared down at Louis. "Didn't you curse at my client, calling her a slut, a whore, and a myriad of other names before spitting on her?"

"I didn't spit on her. I missed."

Some people in the courtroom snickered then and Judge Felder ordered silence.

"And she left at that point?"

Louis nodded. "Yes."

"When was the next time you heard from your ex-wife after that?"

He looked at Camille. "I got a phone call from my sister-in-law Camille. She told me that Misa had killed Steven, that she suspected he was the one who had hurt my son."

"And what was your reaction?"

He shrugged. "It didn't change what happened to Shane," he said. "The damage has been done."

Teresa moved closer to Louis and spoke sympathetically to him. "How is Shane's mental state today?"

Louis sniffled a little, wiped his nose. "He has nightmares. He wakes up crying and it's hard to get him to go back to sleep sometimes." He took a deep breath. "But he's coming along. My mother helps me take care of him. I hate being away from him."

Teresa smiled encouragingly. "And he visits with his mother twice a week, correct?"

"Yes."

"And how is his demeanor after those visits? Is he sad, withdrawn, angry?"

Louis hated to admit the fact that Shane never came home that way. "Actually, he usually comes back happier than he was before he left. I think he enjoys seeing his mother."

Teresa was happy to hear him acknowledge that. So was Misa.

"Mr. Crowley, I commend you for stepping up to care for your son at a time like this. It can't be easy for you to help him recover from such a traumatic experience."

Louis thanked her, told her that it was very difficult to know that his son had suffered. He dabbed at his eyes, clearly hurting for Shane.

"Do you feel guilty, Mr. Crowley?"

Louis looked at Teresa and frowned, prepared to deny it.

"Do you feel guilty, knowing that you had all but abandoned your son in the process of leaving your wife; knowing that you hadn't been there for him in the months and years prior to the abuse? Do you ever think about what you may have done to prevent this from happening to Shane?"

Louis nodded. "Yes."

"Do you think your ex-wife was justified in killing Steven Bingham?"

"Objection!" The prosecutor was on his feet.

"Your honor, I'm seeking to establish that Mr. Crowley has had an epiphany today. That perhaps he no longer sees his ex-wife as solely responsible for what happened to their son."

Judge Felder seemed to think about it for a moment. Then he grunted, "Overruled."

Teresa was thrilled. "Mr. Crowley, do you think your ex-wife was justified in killing Steven Bingham?"

Louis pictured Shane's sweet, innocent face and thought of the terror he had suffered at some grown man's hands. He looked then at Misa and realized she had killed Steven in order to get some kind of justice for what had been done to Shane. And he had to admit that if he had been in her shoes—if he had had any idea who may have hurt his child—he would have done the same thing she had.

He choked back a sob and finally felt some of the anger he had toward Misa abate.

"I think she did the right thing," he said honestly. "And if I had been in her shoes I would have done the same thing."

The courtroom erupted in bedlam and Misa couldn't believe what she'd just heard. As Teresa stated that she had no

more questions and returned to her seat, Misa locked eyes
with Louis and knew that his mind had been changed. Finally, he felt her pain. She was grateful and squeezed Teresa's
hand when she sat down beside her. For the first time since
her trial began, Misa felt hopeful that she might walk away a
free woman.

Order in the Court

Ms. Thomas raised her right hand and swore to tell the truth, the whole truth, and nothing but the truth. As Shane's social worker, she was here today to describe how he had been affected by the trauma he'd suffered.

Teresa had already questioned the doctor who'd examined Shane, making the determination that the child had been abused. Dr. Ahmed had delivered graphic testimony, saying that Shane had suffered excruciating tears he couldn't have caused himself. Dr. Ahmed had testified that the injuries described in Shane's medical report were consistent with being sodomized by an adult male, resulting in anal lacerations. He also noted that Shane later developed an abscess slightly smaller than a golf ball—consistent with being assaulted.

Today was Ms. Thomas's turn to deliver equally difficult testimony. She adjusted her glasses on her nose and watched as Teresa walked in her direction, smiling.

"Ms. Thomas, you have been monitoring the progress of little Shane Crowley throughout this entire ordeal, is that right?"

"Yes, I have."

"And can you describe for the court how you found the child on the first day you visited with him?"

Referring to her notes, Ms. Thomas went back to the day in early January when she'd met Shane for the first time. "The child was in the custody of his father when I saw him for the first time. He was clean, well fed, and his surroundings were suitable, but he was clearly traumatized."

"How so?"

"He was withdrawn. He clung to his toys more than what is typical for a child his age. He was sucking his thumb, which I learned later was not something he had been doing prior to that. And he was crying, more like whining, for his aunt."

"Even while he was being cared for by his father, he was still asking for his aunt Camille?" Teresa toyed with the pencil in her hand as she asked the question.

"Yes," Ms. Thomas confirmed.

"Is that normal behavior, or does it suggest perhaps that Shane wasn't very familiar or even very comfortable with his father?"

"It was my understanding that Shane didn't have a consistent relationship with his father prior to being placed in his custody. In fact, I came to understand that the child didn't have a consistent relationship with either parent." Ms. Thomas felt sorry for the little boy handed around like a burden nobody wanted. "So, while he felt comforted to some extent by his father, he was still longing for the familiarity of the aunt he loves so much. Coupled with the abuse he suffered, the separation from his aunt was causing the child more distress."

"I see," Teresa said. "Did you express that to Shane's father?"

Ms. Thomas nodded. "I did. However, Mr. Crowley was

unwilling to contact Mrs. Bingham to tell her that her nephew had been asking for her extensively."

"And why did he refuse to call his sister-in-law?"

"Objection," the DA interjected. "The witness can't be asked to explain someone else's decision."

"She can if Mr. Crowley expressed his reasons to her, your honor." Teresa prayed that the judge sided with her.

"Overruled."

Teresa smiled. "Ms. Thomas, can you tell us why Louis Crowley refused to contact his sister-in-law to tell her that Shane was asking for her?"

Ms. Thomas shot a glance at Louis and saw him sneering at her. But she was under oath so he could give her dirty looks all day as far as she was concerned. "He said that he blamed Mrs. Bingham just as much as he blamed his ex-wife. He faulted that entire side of the family for what happened to Shane, and he said that he didn't trust any of them around his son."

"And what was your reaction to that?"

"Well," Ms. Thomas began, talking with her hands for emphasis, "I asked him if he felt that one of them had personally abused the child. He said that he didn't believe so, but that since it happened under their watch, they were all responsible. I told Mr. Crowley that the child's best interests were the important factor, and that all visitation with him would be strictly supervised. I told him that it would be beneficial to Shane if he were able to see his aunt at least once in order to establish some sense of normalcy in his new surroundings. But he refused, at least at first."

"And when did that change?"

"When the court ruled that the child's mother could have supervised visitation with him, we agreed that it would be best to conduct those visits at the maternal grandmother's house as opposed to Mr. Crowley's residence."

Teresa frowned. "Any particular reason for that?"

"Well, for one thing, the maternal grandmother's home was familiar and safe. It was a place where he could visit with his mother, grandmother, and his aunt at the same time. And that proved to be very beneficial for the child." She glanced at Louis again. "But another factor in our eventually arranging to conduct the visits at the maternal grandmother's home was Mr. Crowley's contention that he needed some 'alone time' with his girlfriend." Ms. Thomas used air quotes as she said "alone time," indicating that those were Louis's exact words.

The courtroom buzzed with conversation as she said it. Teresa pounced on the opportunity to turn the tide in their favor.

"So, Mr. Crowley admitted to you that wanting alone time with his girlfriend was a factor in allowing the visits with Shane's mom to take place elsewhere?"

"Yes."

The judge had to bang his gavel to get the courtroom back under control. Louis looked like he wished he could dig a hole and crawl inside. All eyes were on him.

"So is it fair to suggest that he was more concerned with his girlfriend's happiness than his son's safety at that point?"

"Objection!"

"Sustained."

Teresa moved on. She'd made her point. "And what did you observe during Shane's visits with his mother and her family?"

"At first, he was unwilling to interact with his mother at all. He ran from her. I observed that Misa seemed equally reluctant to initiate conversation with the child. When I arrived at the grandmother's house with Shane, Misa was a little standoffish, perhaps waiting for her son to come to her. But he wasn't willing to do that."

"Did that initial visit end without the two of them interacting?"

Ms. Thomas smiled a little as she recalled that day. She shook her head. "No," she said. "I urged Misa to coax Shane out of his seclusion. Eventually she found a very effective way to get Shane to come around. She pulled out toys of his and told a story about each one. In the end, Shane was hanging on to her for dear life and I almost hated to end the visit."

Teresa was pleased to hear that. "And in subsequent visits, how has Shane responded to his maternal family?"

"He has bonded with his mother, often crying when it's time for us to leave. He also exhibits pure excitement whenever he sees his aunt Camille." Ms. Thomas looked at her notes. "Although, lately, with his aunt's pregnancy becoming more and more obvious, he is exhibiting some jealous behavior toward her, which is typical of a child whose mother is expecting."

Teresa seemed confused. "But Camille is not Shane's mother."

Ms. Thomas nodded. "Yes, I know. However, our investigation has concluded that Mrs. Bingham cared for the child perhaps just as often as his mother did. And in a situation like that, it is natural for the child to feel some apprehension at the prospect of a new baby taking their place or pushing them out of the picture."

"And aside from that, Shane has been excited and happy to see his mother and her family?"

"Yes, he has."

Teresa nodded. "With regard to the sexual abuse, what has Shane told you?"

Ms. Thomas clasped her hands together. "Well, with a child Shane's age it is often difficult to get them to explain in words what was done to them. So we use dolls to have the child demonstrate what happened and that is what we did with Shane."

Teresa held up two dolls in front of the witness stand. "These are the dolls you used with Shane, is that correct?"

"Yes."

"Can you please demonstrate what Shane showed you?"

Ms. Thomas took the dolls from Teresa and positioned them so that one was facedown with its pants down around its knees and the other was straddling it. She spoke into the microphone, narrating for the court what Shane had described.

"At first, the child was unwilling to do more than position the dolls in a manner such as this. He wouldn't talk about what happened, but would only show us what had taken place. We asked him to point to which of the dolls was 'Shane' and he pointed to the doll on the bottom. We asked him to point to where Shane had been hurt and he pointed to the doll's buttocks area. We also showed him a dollhouse and asked him to point to where in the house he was victimized. He pointed to the couch and to the living room floor."

Many of the jurors were moved to tears by what Ms. Thomas described and the judge interrupted and asked if they needed to take a break. The jurors declined taking a recess and Judge Felder told Teresa to continue with her questioning.

"And so far Shane has not talked about what happened to him, is that right?"

"Well," Ms. Thomas said, "that was the case until our last session with Shane yesterday."

Some jurors leaned forward in their seats, while many in the courtroom began to talk among themselves, all of them eager to hear what Shane had finally said about his abuser. Misa almost jumped out of her seat and Louis's mouth hung open in shock.

Teresa seemed caught off guard, as well. "Shane spoke about it for the first time yesterday?"

"Yes," Ms. Thomas said. "He was very quiet as he spoke about it, his voice was barely audible. But he did tell us that he still sees the bad man in his dreams at night. We assured him that the bad man was not going to hurt him anymore, but it was clear that the very thought of his molester tormented him. He told us that he did not want to play hide-and-seek anymore."

Misa's heart stopped for a moment as she recalled Steven telling her how he liked to play the game with Shane. She sat transfixed as Ms. Thomas continued.

"We asked Shane if the bad man had hurt him while they were playing hide-and-seek and he nodded. He whispered, 'When I hide, I be quiet. But he still find me.' I asked Shane who finds him. And he told me that it was 'Unca Steben.' And we understood that to mean Uncle Steven."

The courtroom was filled with gasps and so much of an uproar that the judge was banging his gavel and yelling for the court to come to order. Misa turned and locked eyes with her sister and mother, tears streaming down her face, and saw that they were crying, too. Emotions surged through them—anger about what had been done to poor Shane and relief that Misa hadn't killed the wrong man after all.

Mary Bingham ran from the courtroom, having heard the evidence that her son was guilty of molesting Shane. There was no doubt in her mind as she fled the room that Steven had victimized the little boy in the same manner in which his father had preyed upon him. Frankie ran out after his mother, his own emotions running wild. Behind him, he heard Teresa announce that she had no further questions, heard the judge calling for a five-minute recess with the commotion continuing in the courtroom.

Frankie followed his mother out into the vestibule and down a flight of stairs leading to the restrooms. He called out after her and finally caught up to her, grabbing her by the arm and pulling her to his chest in a firm embrace. Clinging to her son, Mary cried so hard that her body quaked in agony. Frankie felt his heart breaking, and he was powerless to stop it.

"Ma . . ." His voice trailed off as the words escaped him. He didn't know what to say to her.

He noticed cameras flashing as reporters perched nearby, snapping pictures of the two of them as if they were part of a freak show. Frankie pulled his mother into the nearby men's room and locked the door behind them.

"Stop crying," he said, thinking instantly that he was asking his mother to do the impossible. He hated to see her cry. It brought him right back to the old days whenever he saw her in tears. "We gotta get you out of here."

He thought about weighing the enormity of the situation—that Shane had named his brother, that his mother was racked with guilt. But right now, if he took the time to digest what was happening, it might swallow him whole.

"I'm gonna have Tremaine take you home," he said. He was determined to stay in court and hear the outcome of the day's events. "Wait right here. Keep the door locked until I come back."

Frankie reached for the doorknob, but his mother stopped him, placing her hand over his. "I won't be quiet this time. You have to accept that he did it, Frankie. And she's that child's mother. Should she go to jail for the rest of her life for protecting her son?" Mary's voice shook. "I wish I would have protected you that way. And Steven."

Frankie stared at her. He was at a loss for words. Finally, Mary let go of his hand and he quickly exited, heading back into the courtroom to get Tremaine. His feet felt heavy as he walked amid the stares and chatter in the courthouse. Frankie's mind was reeling. Steven couldn't have been that twisted without him knowing it. Shane wouldn't lie about it, would he? Had Misa been justified? Could Mary handle the truth? Could he?

These things and more raced through his mind as he stepped back inside the courtroom. Aware that all eyes were on him, he walked over to Tremaine and whispered to him. Tremaine nodded and hurriedly left the courtroom in search of Frankie's mom, with instructions to bring her home and stay with her.

Gillian looked different when Frankie sat beside her again. He could tell that she was having doubts about his brother's innocence. He couldn't help wondering if she was second-guessing him as well. Her back was stiff, her hands folded in her lap, legs crossed. Her eyes searched his for something Frankie hoped she found. And then she looked away, no reassuring words, no touch of comfort. Frankie noticed this as the court officer called them all back to order.

Everyone listened as Ms. Thomas was cross-examined by the prosecution.

"You say that young Shane points to the deceased as his predator only now, after months of saying nothing?" The DA sounded skeptical.

"It's normal for a child to withhold the identity of their attacker out of fear. Particularly a child as young as Shane."

"What explanation has he been given for being removed

from his mother's custody? How has that been explained to Shane?"

Ms. Thomas reviewed her notes once more. "He's been told that his mother is away for a little while, but that she's coming back for him soon."

"And what about the 'bad man' as Shane refers to his predator? What has he been told has happened to the bad man?" DA Dean Davidson was staking his career on a win in this case. No amount of theatrics was going to allow Teresa Rourke to score an acquittal.

Ms. Thomas checked her notes again. "That the bad man was destroyed, and will never hurt Shane again."

Dean was practically salivating now.

"Shane has been tormented by nightmares of his attacker, which he shared with us and with his father. In order to get Shane to fall back asleep at night, Mr. Crowley told his son that the bad man was gone forever."

"Has Shane mentioned his uncle Steven by name since your investigation began?"

"No."

"So how did he just spit out 'Uncle Steven did it!' all of a sudden?"

Ms. Thomas didn't appreciate the prosecutor's sudden shift in tone. He was being downright accusatory. "Well, we asked him specifically about each of his closest family members, teachers—"

"So you *asked* him about his uncle Steven?"

"Yes, we—"

"What specifically did you ask him?"

"We just said the names of different people who've been close with Shane over the years and watched to see what his reaction would be."

"Please give us the order of the names you recited to Shane."

Ms. Thomas listed them: Misa (Mommy), Aunt Camille, Uncle Frankie, Grandma Lily, Uncle Steven. "His response to each name was noted. Each solicited a positive reaction. It was when we got to Uncle Steven that Shane stopped playing, laughing, and reacting positively. He grew quiet, withdrawn, went back to sucking his thumb. We repeated 'Uncle Steven' to Shane and he said, 'No!' His voice was loud and defiant and then his facial expression changed. He began to cry. We assured Shane that there was no need to cry and he eventually stopped. When we asked Shane if Uncle Steven was the bad man—"

"You *asked* the child point-blank if his uncle was the bad man?"

Ms. Thomas frowned slightly, nodding. "Yes, we did."

"So is that what you're trained to do, Ms. Thomas? To tell a child what you want them to say? To imply that Uncle Steven was the bad man that haunts this toddler in his dreams?"

"OBJECTION!" Teresa was on her feet and her voice boomed loudly over the prosecutor. But Dean wasn't having it. He kept right on peppering Ms. Thomas with accusations.

"It's very likely that Shane, crying and afraid after being barraged with a list of names and questioned about his nightmares, just told you what you wanted to hear. Three years old, separated from his mother, and told that the bad man won't bother him anymore as long as he says that the bad man is Steven Bingham!"

"OBJECTION!" Teresa looked like she was ready to fight Dean Davidson as she stormed toward the bench.

Judge Felder banged his gavel and Misa looked on as the jury took it all in. She wondered what they were thinking, prayed that their minds hadn't been changed by the DA's twisted logic. The judge was fuming and the courtroom had erupted in anarchy. Demanding to see the lawyers in his chambers, court was recessed for the second time.

Camille rushed to Misa's side and hugged her sister tightly. "Are you all right?" she asked, pulling back but holding tight to Misa's hand.

Misa shook her head. "I knew it, Camille. I knew all along that it was him. I don't care what the DA says. My baby told the truth, Camille."

Toya, Dominique, Lily, and Celia had formed a circle around the sisters as the nosy spectators looked on, hanging on their every word and movement. Leaning in, Toya whispered to Misa.

"Stay strong, girl. I'm watching the jury. They're paying attention and Teresa is doing a great job."

"That's right," Celia cosigned. "The truth always prevails."

Frankie stared across the room at the circle of women surrounding Misa and Camille. He was oblivious to the *Staten Island Advance* reporter snapping a picture of him in profile, looking so perplexed as he stared at his brother's killer. The photo was a poignant one, showing the inner battle being waged within a man torn between a painful truth and his quest for justice.

Gillian didn't know how to feel. To her, it seemed that there was no victory for any them. Shane had been molested, Steven killed, Misa jailed. Camille had lost Frankie, but she was having his child. Gillian had lost her father, her mother, too, in some ways. Baron had fallen from grace, and Frankie had lost it all.

She wondered now if she and Frankie could survive this. Once, she had been so sure. Now, she couldn't imagine what the future held.

The attorneys and the judge finally emerged from chambers, Dean red-faced and Teresa looking as if she'd just been scolded by her high school principal. Judge Felder had warned them both to tone down their melodramatic camera-posturing or else.

Ms. Thomas took the stand for the third time that day, easily the most controversial witness called by either side so far.

The prosecution got back down to business. "I asked you if you've been trained to suggest possible suspects to children who've been victimized."

Ms. Thomas didn't like the DA at all. "We did not *suggest* anything to the child. We are trained to make a child feel safe in speaking about what has been done to them and that was what we did."

"You said that Shane had a negative reaction to hearing his uncle's name. And then you repeated 'Uncle Steven' to which Shane yelled 'No!' according to your testimony. Had you repeated any of the other names more than once?"

"No, because none of the other names elicited the reaction that Steven's did."

"Please answer simply yes or no to the following questions," Dean instructed. "Shane was told that the bad man was gone forever, correct?"

"Yes."

"He was asked about the nightmares he has and he told you that he sees the bad man in his dreams, correct?"

"Yes."

"You asked him to tell you who the bad man was and he refused?"

"Yes."

"Then you listed names for him, repeating his uncle Steven's name twice, and everyone else's name only once. Is that correct?"

Ms. Thomas wanted to elaborate but knew she could only answer yes or no. This bastard was crafty. "Yes."

"The second time you mentioned Uncle Steven, the child yelled 'No!' Is that correct?"

"Yes."

"And you asked Shane if Uncle Steven was the bad man who hurt him, right?"

"Yes."

"How long had you been questioning the child at that point?"

Ms. Thomas reviewed her notes. "For less than an hour."

Dean Davidson smirked at her. "You questioned a three-year-old child for close to an hour," he remarked, "and when he told you that his uncle Steven was the bad man, did the questioning end?"

Ms. Thomas shrugged. "Not immediately."

"So you continued to question him beyond that?"

"No," she stammered. "What I'm saying is that we assured him that he was not in danger, that his mother would not be harmed. And he was upset. So we ended our session for the day and returned him to his family's care."

"So you rewarded him by ending the session when he told you what you wanted to hear?"

"Objection!"

"I'll withdraw the question," Dean said. "Ms. Thomas, why didn't you tell Mr. Crowley what his son had revealed to you during your session yesterday?"

"Mr. Crowley did not pick Shane up yesterday. His paternal grandmother did, and we decided to wait until we were able to meet with both parents before revealing our findings. Unfortunately, I was called to testify before I was able to meet with them."

Misa felt so guilty then. Louis was pawning Shane off on his mother just as she had pawned him off on Camille. She wanted nothing more than to get her son back so that she could get a do-over.

"Ms. Thomas, one final question," Dean said, much to her relief. "Do children often make mistakes when identifying their attackers?"

Ms. Thomas sighed. "From time to time, they do. But I wouldn't say that it happens often. And in this case, I believe Shane. I don't think he was making it up. I've seen hundreds of cases over the years. I've seen children lie and I've witnessed them fall apart when they face the adults who preyed upon them. And in my professional opinion, Shane is telling the truth. His uncle Steven sodomized him."

"No further questions," the prosecutor said, scowling as he sat back down.

After giving the jury some instructions on which testimony to consider and which things to disregard, the judge adjourned for the day, sending everyone home until first thing tomorrow morning.

Misa noticed that her lawyer and the DA were huddled together instead of retreating to their corners like boxers in the ring the way they usually did at the end of each day. She waited and watched as Frankie and Gillian sulked out of the courtroom. Camille watched, too, amazed at how little she had known about the man she called her husband for so many years. She wondered if she'd ever know the whole truth, even as she carried his child in her womb.

Self-Defense

Camille stood and stared out of the living room window, watching the flowers blooming on her sprawling lawn as spring arrived in New York City. This view had been one of her favorite parts of living in this house over the years. She looked around now at all the boxes labeled for the movers to take them to a storage unit until she could decide on where she wanted to go next. Her beloved house was being sold, her divorce papers had been signed, and her baby was due in only eight more weeks.

She marveled at how drastically things had changed in a year. The doorbell rang and she wobbled over to it and ushered her friends inside. Teresa had suggested that everyone meet at Camille's house that morning before heading to court. She had something she wanted to discuss and felt that everyone should gather together in private to weigh in.

Toya, Dominique, Misa, Lily, and Celia were all assembled in Camille's living room by the time Teresa arrived at eight-thirty in the morning. Misa sat there in the same room where she and Frankie had faced off on the night of the murder and she shuddered a little. So much time had passed, yet not nearly enough for the healing to begin. Teresa breezed in, thanked everyone for coming and got right down to business.

"The DA realizes that he may not win this case," she said. "So he's offering you a plea deal."

Misa's heart raced, wondering whether or not this was good news. "What kind of deal?"

"You plead guilty to second-degree manslaughter in exchange for five to fifteen years in prison."

"Wow!" Lily muttered.

"What kind of a deal is that?" Toya asked.

Teresa unbuttoned her suit jacket and sat down among the forum of women. "The murder one charge carries a maximum sentence of—"

"Twenty-five to life," Misa finished, fully aware of what she was facing.

The room fell silent, everyone weighing the odds.

"We've put on a good case," Teresa said at last. "Obviously, the fact that Shane points to Steven as his attacker is in our favor. It shows the jury that you were correct in your assumption. Shane corroborates your theory. We've shown that Louis was no saint, either, and explained why you may have been flawed, as well." Teresa shook her head, looking seriously at her client. "But you confessed. You claimed self-defense. So now, all we have is your testimony. If you roll the dice and proceed with the trial, you have to know that everything is riding on your performance on that stand."

Misa didn't know what to do. She looked around at her mother, her sister, her friends. All of them loved her, but she alone was facing serious hard time in prison for murder. She wondered if she should take the deal, if she should accept responsibility for what she had done.

But when she thought about Shane, she shook her head. There was no way she could be away from her son for that long, no way that she could endure the horrors of prison knowing that her already wounded son was growing up without her. To her, going to prison would be the equivalent of a death sentence. If the jury decided that was what she deserved, so be it. She was prepared to accept it. But there was no way she was going down without a fight.

"For me, it's not a performance," she said, correcting Teresa. "My life is riding on this. My son was all that I thought about that night and he's all I'll think about every day for the rest of my life if I get another chance. But I just want to tell my story, and explain why I did it. So then if they want to send me away for life, fine. But I have to have my say and I really need to know if I'm crazy for doing what I did."

"You're not crazy," Celia said, squeezing Misa's hand. She thought that Misa was incredibly brave. Aware that she and Baron were financing Misa's defense, she reassured her. "And you have my son's support regardless of what you decide. You will not be left alone, Misa."

"Thank you, Miss Celia," she said. Looking at Teresa, she said, "I don't want the deal. I'm ready to testify."

Teresa nodded. "All right, well, today's the day."

"Let's pray," Lily suggested.

Misa and Camille looked at each other and struggled to suppress their laughter as they recalled the countless times their mother launched into evangelical sermons whenever she was called on to pray. They snickered at their private joke as Lily prayed that they all would gain the strength it took to endure the day ahead.

Misa stood up in front of the packed courtroom, her long hair hanging loosely at her shoulders, her pretty face uncertain as she took the oath and sat down in the witness seat. She wore very little makeup and a simple black suit. Her trembling hands were barely noticeable as Teresa began.

"Misa, we've heard weeks of testimony regarding the type of parent that you were to your son Shane—some of it good, some of it not so good. How would you honestly describe your relationship with your son?"

Misa took a deep breath, glanced warily around the courtroom. She was so nervous, but so anxious to put this day behind her. She finally spoke, her voice strong and slightly melodic.

"I love my son. I wanted the best for him, for him to have the best of everything." She paused for a moment. "I wasn't always there like I should have been. But I just wanted to have the perfect family. He deserved two parents, a big house, lots of toys, nice clothes, and the best schools. And I was doing what I thought I had to do to make all of that possible for him."

"Who cared for Shane besides you?"

"My sister Camille mostly. My mother sometimes, his teachers at preschool."

"Did you ever suspect that Shane had been abused in any way?"

Misa shook her head. "Never. I paid attention to Shane and he was a happy kid, just being his usual sweet self."

"When did Steven Bingham begin babysitting your son?"

Misa clasped her hands together, squeezing. "When I left Shane with my sister. I had been at the hospital, visiting a friend. Camille was babysitting for me and nothing was wrong with Shane when I left."

"How long were you gone?"

Misa shrugged, trying to remember. "A day or so."

"Had you called to check in on Shane?"

Teresa had warned her that she would have to ask her questions with tough answers. It was a risky tactic, which would deprive the prosecution of pointing out Misa's flaws. If Misa's attorney revealed her best and worst traits, the prosecution would be robbed of the opportunity to do it themselves.

"No, I didn't call. I trusted my sister with Shane and I knew that he was in good hands with her. My friend was recovering from a coma and I wanted to be there for him."

Some members of the jury—mostly the women—were studying Misa like she was an art exhibit. They were observing her body language, following her eyes when she looked around, and hanging on her every word. Teresa moved on, knowing that what they saw and heard today was crucial.

"So when did you discover that Steven Bingham had been caring for your son?"

"When I came to pick Shane up, he opened the door—"

"Who opened the door? Shane?"

"No."

"Who opened the door?"

Misa squeezed her eyes shut, clearly struggling to even utter the name of the bastard who had sodomized her son. "Steven," she managed through clenched teeth, her hands still clasped tightly together and her eyes staring intently at Teresa.

Teresa was glad that the jury could see how devastated Misa was by what had happened to her son. Any mother would understand Misa's rage.

"Did you observe Shane behave strangely in the presence of Steven Bingham?"

Misa looked at her hands, nodded slowly. "When I got there, he . . . Steven . . . opened the door and I asked where my sister was. He told me that Camille had been upset that her and Frankie broke up. I was surprised to hear that because my sister and I hadn't talked. I didn't know that she was having . . . I didn't know that Frankie had left her."

Teresa nodded. "And what happened then?"

"He told me that he had been babysitting Shane while Camille was gone. I asked where Shane was and he told me that he didn't know. He said that Shane liked to play hide-and-seek a lot." Misa's voice caught in her throat.

"Hide-and-seek? The same game that Shane has told his social worker that he doesn't want to play anymore?" Teresa asked.

"Yes," Misa said.

"Where did you eventually find Shane?"

"He was curled up in the bathtub hiding and he wouldn't come out. Not until . . . Steven . . . he told Shane to get up and go with me and Shane jumped up. He wasn't talking, though. Shane wasn't acting the same after that."

"What did you think after that incident?"

Misa shook her head. "I thought Shane was upset that I wasn't spending enough time with him. I thought he was acting up because he was mad at me. So I just took him home. It was Christmas Day and I had a whole bunch of presents for him at home. But he wasn't really happy like he usually was. He didn't want to talk to me. He just played in his room by himself. I tried to play with him and tried to talk to him, but he was ignoring me for some reason. I didn't know why he was mad at me. So I asked him if he wanted to go back to

Aunt Camille's house. He didn't answer me. I thought that was a 'yes' so I said, 'Fine. I'll take you back to Aunt Camille's house and Uncle Steven can watch you.' And . . . Shane got so mad! He threw a toy car at me and he started crying for his daddy."

Misa started to get emotional, recalling how angry Shane had been at her, as she unknowingly threatened to bring him back to the very monster who haunted him.

"Did you call your ex-husband then?" Teresa nudged.

"Yes. He came and got Shane about an hour later."

Teresa nodded, placed a box of tissues on the witness stand for Misa's use, and continued.

"When were you told that Shane had been molested?"

"It was January 4, 2008. I came home from the hospital and I called Louis to check up on Shane. He cursed at me, told me that I was never going to see my son again. He called me an irresponsible bitch and told me that some-body . . ." Misa began to cry. Teresa plucked out a few tissues and handed them to her client while she struggled to compose herself. "He told me that somebody had been molesting my son."

Teresa waited a few minutes for Misa to compose herself.

"He hung up on me, and when I called back, nobody answered. So I went over there."

"Did your ex-husband allow you to see your son?"

Misa shook her head, sniffling. "No. He tried to spit on me, he lunged at me, cursed at me. His girlfriend held him back, otherwise he might have hit me."

"What did you do then?"

"I drove back home. I thought about killing myself. I was so distraught, and so . . . my son had been raped. I don't know how to describe what I was feeling. I was scared of the way that I was feeling and I just had to sit and figure out who had done that . . . who had hurt my son."

"And who did you think of?"

"Everyone," Misa said, honestly. "Everybody was a suspect in my mind. But I started eliminating people who I knew would never hurt my son. I thought of all his teachers at school—male and female. But Shane hadn't been in school for weeks because of the holiday break. It had to have been someone he had been around recently. Frankie was never around. When Steven came to mind, I just . . . I felt it in my gut that it was him."

"Why?" Teresa pressed her. "Why did you dismiss Frankie as a suspect easily but know intuitively that Steven had been the one?"

"I thought about that day when Shane was hiding in the bathtub. I thought about all the times I had noticed how weird Steven was, how he used to stare at people. I had never had a problem with Shane misbehaving until the day that I mentioned returning Shane to Camille's house and letting Steven watch him. It just made sense to me."

"So what did you do then?"

"I decided to go and confront Steven."

"Why didn't you call the police?" Teresa asked.

Misa took a deep breath. Oath or no oath, she couldn't answer that question truthfully. The truth was that no amount of legal justice would have been enough for her. No arrest could have made it all right. She wanted Steven dead for what he had done to her son and she set out to kill him when she went to Camille's house that night.

"He was a part of my family," she lied. "I didn't want to call the police until I had proof that he had done it. I wanted to see what he would say when I confronted him."

"Why did you bring the gun?"

"I was afraid for my safety," she answered. Misa gestured with her hands emphatically, trying to express her frame of mind that night. "So many things were going through my mind," she said. "I was so upset about what happened to my son, scared that I would never see him again. I thought I knew who had done it, and I wanted to know for sure. But I was scared, too. I was afraid that if I was right that Steven might try to keep me quiet, that he might hurt me. So I brought the gun with me for protection."

"Where did you get the gun?"

Misa stared at Louis. She stared at him and a smirk lingered on her lips as she watched him squirm. He knew that he had given her that gun years earlier, that she could easily throw him under the bus now. But she was no snitch. Lily had raised her better than that, although the thought of revenge was tempting. "I found it," she said. "Years ago when I used to live in the Stapleton projects."

"And you kept the gun for protection as a single mother concerned for the safety of you and your child?"

"That's right," Misa said, liking how Teresa made it sound so noble.

"Walk us through the early morning hours of January 5, 2008."

Misa took a long sip of water and glanced at the jury box. Each of the twelve people sitting there looked mesmerized as she began to tell her story.

"I remember looking at the dashboard clock in my car and it was 12:03 A.M. when I pulled up at my sister's house. I don't remember driving there. It's like I was in a dream or something. But I recall seeing that time on the digital clock. I got out of the car and I let myself into the house with my key."

"Why did you have a key to your sister's home?" Teresa asked.

"Shane was there a lot and Camille had given me the key months ago."

"What did you find upon entering the home that night?"

"It was dark. Nobody was home. I sat in the dining room and tried to get my thoughts together. I was upset and I couldn't think straight. I kept trying to think if I had missed a clue . . . if Steven could really be the one who did that to my son. There was a candle in the center of the table and I lit it. I sat there and I was just . . . lost in thought." Misa stared at her hands, recalling the murderous thoughts she'd had that night. "I imagined what had been done to my son." Misa looked at the jury, made eye contact with a few of the women. "It would kill any mother to know that someone has molested your child. To think of somebody touching your little boy, thinking of him crying in pain . . ." Misa cried. "To think of some sick, disgusting man getting pleasure from hurting my child . . . I just felt so powerless and so hurt, so angry!" She blew her nose, wiped her eyes and saw a few of the jurors crying, too. "Steven came in from the guesthouse and I heard him walk into the kitchen."

Frankie's eyes watered as he imagined his brother walking into an ambush unknowingly.

"I got up and walked into the kitchen, too. I was standing behind him and he didn't know it. He turned around and saw me and he jumped. I think I scared him."

Teresa nodded. "Did he say anything?"

"He kinda chuckled. He said, 'Damn, girl. You scared me.'" Misa felt her anger growing as she thought about the smug expression on Steven's face that night. It felt like he was laughing at her, laughing at Shane. "I asked him what he had done to my son."

Teresa saw that the jurors were literally on the edge of their seats.

"He asked me what I was talking about. And I told him that I knew he had touched Shane. I started yelling. I called him a fucking freak and I was yelling that he had molested my son." Misa's voice rose now as she thought back on that night. "He laughed at me. He laughed in my face! He told me that Shane was lying."

Misa had snapped right at that moment. She had pulled out the .38 special that Louis had given her, pointed it at Steven and watched the smile slowly drain from his face.

"Put that away," Steven had said, his face suddenly serious. "The little muthafucka is lying."

Misa had pulled the trigger then, kept pulling the trigger until it clicked empty, and Steven lay dead in a bundle at her feet.

Teresa's voice lured her back to the present and to her carefully crafted story for this moment. "What happened then?"

"I told him that I knew what he had done to Shane and all of a sudden, he lunged at me. I jumped back and I pulled out the gun. I held it up, but my hands were shaking. I was scared to death."

"Did he stop advancing toward you?"

Misa thought about the forensics expert who had testified that Steven couldn't have been in motion at the moment the first bullet struck him. "He reached for the gun real quick," she lied. "And I fired just to stop him. But he didn't stop. I thought I had missed the first time, because he kept coming toward me. So I fired again and again. I was just trying to keep him away from me. Then he fell on the floor and I had no more bullets. So I dropped the gun and I ran back into the dining room. I was distraught, crying, I was scared. I sat down and tried to stop my heart from racing, my hands were shaking. And that's how my sister came in and found me."

Teresa was proud of her client. "Did you go over to your sister's home that night with the intention of killing Steven Bingham?"

"No," Misa said convincingly. "I did not." She looked at the jury. "I only shot Steven in self-defense because I was in fear for my life."

"No further questions," Teresa announced, and took her seat.

The district attorney stood up and applauded. "Very nice performance, Ms. Atkinson. Did you and your attorney work on that long?"

"OBJECTION!" Teresa yelled, back on her feet.

"Sustained." Judge Felder glowered at Dean Davidson. "I've warned you about the theatrics, Mr. Davidson. Cross-examine the witness!"

"Sorry, Your Honor," the prosecutor lied. He looked at Misa, his facial expression conveying his lack of faith in her testimony.

"Ms. Atkinson, you've painted quite a vivid picture for the court today," he said. "You described yourself as a mother who wasn't always perfect, but who wanted the best for her son. Is that an accurate depiction?"

Misa nodded. "Yes."

"Yet, you left Shane in your sister's care for more than a week while you sat at your boyfriend's bedside?"

Misa didn't answer. She stared at the prosecutor contemptuously.

"Speaking of your boyfriend, Baron Nobles, can you please tell us the nature of his injuries?"

Misa looked confused.

"Why was he in a coma?"

"He got shot."

The jury squirmed and so did Misa.

"He got shot," the prosecutor repeated. "For those present in the courtroom today who are unaware of the circumstances of that shooting, Baron Nobles was injured when he and his father—the notorious drug kingpin Doug Nobles—were ambushed in a recent gunfight." He held up a copy of the *Daily News* with the headline reading NOTORIOUS NOBLES DEAD IN AMBUSH!

"And this hoodlum is the man you dropped everything for?"

"Objection."

"Overruled."

Teresa sat back down, dejected.

"I was very close with Baron," Misa explained, "It was the holiday break and I thought Shane was safe with my sister."

"The date of this newspaper article was December 15, 2007. You admittedly spent the days leading up to Christmas Day at the hospital with Baron Nobles. So let's see . . ." Dean began to count off the days on his fingers demonstratively. "Ten days passed before you returned to pick up your son, not the day or so you testified to earlier, Ms. Atkinson. Isn't that correct?"

The courtroom hissed with condemnation. Misa thought about that. She hadn't realized that ten days had passed. It hadn't seemed that long at the time. But she had to admit the facts were correct. "Yes."

The jury seemed to have turned on her as evidenced by their body language. A few were shaking their heads in contempt. Misa hung her own head in shame.

"What else have you lied about?" the DA asked.

"Objection!"

"Careful, Mr. Davidson," the judge snarled.

"You testified that you became suspicious when you arrived at your sister's house to find Steven babysitting Shane and Shane curled up and hiding in the bathtub?"

"Yes."

"You found that odd?"

Misa frowned. "Hell, yeah, I found it odd. My son was hiding and he looked scared."

"You found that strange, and yet you still suggested bringing your son back to Steven Bingham later on that night. Isn't that how you testified, Ms. Atkinson? That you asked your son if he wanted to go back to Aunt Camille's house? Back to Steven's care?"

"I didn't know that he was—"

"You didn't think that he was a pedophile then, did you?"

"No. Not right then. But when I thought about it later on . . . after Louis told me that Shane had been hurt, I thought about it . . ."

"You crafted this scenario in your mind that Steven Bingham was the one who molested Shane because you really had no clue who could have victimized your son."

"That's not true."

"You were never around. You didn't even know that Shane had been left in Steven's care. You had no clue that your sister's marriage had fallen apart. You didn't even know what the top story was on the news at that time because all you were concerned about was catering to your gangster boyfriend!"

"OBJECTION!" Teresa yelled. "Mr. Davidson is badgering the witness. He hasn't asked a single question in the past ten minutes!"

"I'll get right to it, Your Honor," the prosecutor hurriedly assured him. "You testified that your ex-husband came and got Shane on the night of Christmas 2007. You went back to the hospital and continued to attend to Baron Nobles until the night of January fourth. So yet another ten days passed before you checked in on your son again. Is this right?"

"Yes," Misa allowed, her voice low and sad.

"This time when you disappeared, Shane was with his father and the news wasn't good. Shane had been molested. Understandably angry, Shane's father tells you that it's all your fault; that you're irresponsible; that you should never see your son again." The DA looked at Misa like she was a worthless piece of shit. "Don't you think Mr. Crowley was right?"

"Objection!"

"Overruled."

Misa looked out at the courtroom and heard the question echoing in her ears. She looked at people she'd lived close to, girls she had gone to school with, her family, reporters, court personnel, at Frankie, and finally at the prosecutor. She felt her eyes well up with tears. "He might have been right," she admitted. Misa was crying now, guilty tears that rolled down her face the way a ball rolls down a hill, picking up speed on the way down, slowing at the bottom, hanging from her chin.

She looked at the jury. "I was a bad mother. Louis was a bad father. But that didn't give Steven the right to hurt my son. It didn't give him the right to touch him!"

"What right did you have to take a man's life without getting all the facts?"

Misa was crying now, not bothering to answer.

"You didn't even know for sure that it was Steven. You couldn't have known for sure that night."

"I knew in my gut," Misa said defiantly.

"You took the law into your own hands! You brought the gun with you because you wanted to kill Steven for what you believed he did to your son. Isn't that right?"

"I brought the gun for protection."

"You went into that house and you waited for him. You waited in the dark like a hunter stalking its prey."

"I was thinking about what I should say . . ."

"You were thinking about how you were going to blow his brains out when he came in from the guesthouse."

"Your Honor—" Teresa interrupted.

"Weren't you mad as hell that night?"

"I was mad!" Misa yelled. "Anybody in my shoes would be mad."

"And you wanted somebody to pay for what had been done to your son. So you ambushed Steven Bingham when he came into that kitchen. You had the gun drawn and you confronted him about what had been done to Shane. And when he denied it, you shot Steven Bingham in cold blood while he stood motionless, posing no threat to you."

"He was coming at me!"

"You shot him in the chest. Then twice in the head. Surely he must have fallen then."

"I blacked out."

"You blacked out, firing until the gun was empty, is that what you want us to think?"

"That's what happened!"

"Then, when the gun was empty and Steven Bingham lay dying on the floor, you didn't bother to call for help, did you?"

"No . . . I was in shock."

"You wanted Steven Bingham dead and you sat there and made damn sure he wouldn't survive."

"Your Honor!" Teresa was having a fit.

The prosecution pushed on, not waiting for the judge's response. "You accused him, convicted him, put him on trial, and executed him all within a matter of hours and you didn't need the police to help you do any of that."

Teresa's objections were barely heard beneath the DA's booming voice.

"If you could go back to that night and do it all again, would you spare Steven Bingham's life?"

"No!" Misa yelled over all the commotion. "No, I wouldn't spare that bastard's life after what he did to my son!" she seethed.

"No further questions, Your Honor," Dean Davidson spat.

Misa kept right on talking. "Any mother out there should thank me for killing him! He deserved to die for what he did to my son. Anybody sick enough to hurt an innocent child deserves to die!"

Teresa walked quickly over to her client, eager to silence her. "Misa, come down off the stand," she instructed, her voice stern yet soothing.

Slowly, Misa climbed down from the witness stand, completely aware that she may have just ruined her one shot at freedom.

In Summation . . .

As the warm spring morning unfolded before him, Frankie lay awake in bed watching Gillian sleep. Things had changed between them somehow without either one realizing it. Gone was the twinkle in her eye that used to greet him whenever he looked at her. And he assumed that she had noticed his distance, how he had withdrawn from her ever since the truth about his family had been laid bare. He hadn't meant to pull away from her. But it was the only way he knew how to handle things when they overwhelmed him. He pulled away and secluded himself as a defense mechanism rather than facing whatever was making him feel vulnerable.

He looked at Gillian now, sleeping peacefully, and wished he'd never fallen for her. If he hadn't complicated their friendship with love, it would be easier for them to continue doing business together. Now, even as he knew their future together was impossible, he was forced to find a way to end it without hurting her too badly. He touched a strand of her hair, swept it out of her face, and touched her lips lightly. She was so beautiful and he loved her. But uncovering the ugliness of his past had changed him in a way that made it clear that he wasn't ready to start a new relationship. He needed time to sort everything out by himself—without the added burden of having to love her right.

He climbed out of bed, got dressed in silence, and crept out of her house before the sun had fully peeked its head above the clouds.

Camille was in her Staten Island home packing up the last of her belongings while talking with Officer Eli King on her cell phone. An early bird, Camille was up before the sun rose trying to finish boxing what remained of her life with Frankie before court that day. It was the day of closing arguments in Misa's trial and Camille was feeling antsy. When Eli called, fresh off the night shift, she was wide awake and eager for the distraction of hearing about his night. She was laughing at a joke he had just told her about a rabbi, a priest, and a Buddhist when she noticed headlights pulling into her driveway.

"Now, who could this be?" she wondered aloud, happy that she was on the phone with a cop just in case she needed backup.

Eli was concerned. "It's only five-thirty in the morning. Who would be pulling up at your house this early?"

She gasped a little when she saw Frankie get out of his car. Camille felt her pulse quicken. "It's my husband," she said. "Can I call you back?"

Eli agreed, not bothering to point out that he was no longer her husband since signing the divorce papers a week ago. They hung up and Camille greeted Frankie at the front door, a look of confusion etched on her face.

He held up a bag. "I brought breakfast from Perkins," he said. "Figured you're pregnant . . . you might be hungry." He knew he sounded just as awkward as he felt. He had been so mean to Camille that it was hard to know where to start now.

Camille stared at Frankie. She had been pregnant for seven months, and hungry every minute. And *now* he decided to come by with breakfast? She wondered what was up as he stepped inside the house. Seeing everything packed up, Frankie froze. It was all so real now—the marriage, the house, everything was coming undone.

"Thanks," Camille said, taking the bag out of his hand. "But I must say this is a big surprise."

Frankie nodded, led the way to the couch where they both sat side by side. He watched as Camille unpacked the food. She sat back and looked at him questioningly.

"What do I do now?" he asked her, his eyes searching hers desperately.

Camille stared back at him, not sure what he meant. She could tell that he was tormented by the way he looked at her—his confusion causing his face to collapse under the weight of it.

"I don't understand," she said softly.

"My brother . . ." Frankie's voice broke off.

Camille sat speechlessly, not knowing how to respond to him.

"I didn't know that he was . . ."

"I know, Frankie." Camille could tell that he was still struggling with what Steven had done. She didn't believe for a minute that Frankie had known about the demons that haunted his brother.

"My mother blames herself," he said at last. "I blame myself, too. I left them behind. He must have suffered when I left." Frankie shook his head, the thought of that too much for him.

Camille knew that there was clearly plenty she didn't know about Frankie's childhood. Watching him battle his emotions now, she wondered how much he didn't even know.

He kept stammering. "Nobody told me anything. And Steven . . . he's dead. Shane . . ." Frankie knew he wasn't making sense as all his thoughts spilled out of his mouth in the same random order in which they were conceived. "Shane is just a little boy," he said. Frankie sighed, held his face in his hands and shook his head. Looking at Camille again, he shrugged. "And Misa . . . what about . . . the baby . . ." He seemed like he was slowly coming apart.

Camille knew that the enormity of the situation had just begun to settle in for Frankie and she shook her head. "It's all one great big mess," she said.

Frankie nodded. That it was. He looked at Camille and spoke, his voice full of sincerity. "I'm so sorry."

Camille looked at Frankie for a long time, his words resounding in her head. He was sorry. Well, so was she.

"I went about this all wrong," he said. "You didn't deserve what I did to you, Camille. I needed a way out and I went too far. I abandoned you. When I found out that my brother was dead . . . that Misa killed him . . . to me you both became the villains and I hated both of you. It never even occurred to me that Steven could do something so sick to Shane." Frankie shut his eyes for a moment as if to block out the thought. "I can't apologize for what he did to that little boy. But I can tell you that I'm sorry that Shane was hurt. I'm sorry for what happened to Misa's son." His voice cracked, then. He was still trying to come to grips with the fact that Misa had killed his brother. As much as he wanted to forgive her, he wasn't there yet.

Camille touched Frankie's hand. She wanted to hate him,

but she couldn't. He had been cruel to her since deciding he wanted out of their marriage. But she still loved him and hated to see him hurting so badly.

"We all have regrets," she said. "And all of us can find reasons to blame ourselves. But the truth is that none of us are at fault for what Steven did. None of us could have known . . . Frankie, all we can do is try to pick up the pieces and move on. Soon, we're going to be parents and we've gotta figure out how to get along and get past what happened."

He smiled slightly. "That's why I came over here," he said, chuckling uneasily. "Figured breakfast would be my olive branch."

Camille smiled weakly at him. "It's a good start."

Frankie reached out his hand, inching it slowly toward her swollen belly. Camille watched him as he touched her stomach softly, feeling the tightness and drawing his hand back in shock. "Oh my God!" he said, surprised by the way it felt.

Camille took his hand and placed it back on her belly, holding it there this time as Frankie's face contorted in amazement. His eyes widened in wonder as the baby moved within her womb, kicking his hand.

Frankie wanted to laugh and cry at the same time. "That feels crazy!"

Camille smiled at him, happy that he was sharing in the excitement of her pregnancy at last. Better late than never.

Frankie questioned her for more than an hour about her pregnancy—what she was feeling, what foods she craved, how often the baby moved, what vitamins she was taking, how often she went to the doctor, and even how she handled swollen ankles. Finally, as the hour drew near for court to begin, Frankie rose to leave. He looked at Camille awkwardly. He wanted to give her a hug, but worried that she might think that he wanted to reconcile. He didn't. Frankie wanted nothing more than to sort out what happened in his childhood so that he could be a better parent to the child he was about to have. He prayed that both Gillian and Camille would give him the space he needed to do that.

But as he stared down at his wife, glowing with his child in her womb, he felt so much love for her. Despite all that he had done to her, she was still willing to listen to him, still willing to forgive him. He thought she looked more beautiful standing there then she had in years. Taking her face in his hands, Frankie kissed Camille softly on her lips. Looking at her for a moment, he paused before kissing her again. Then he turned and left. Camille lingered in the doorway long after his car pulled away. She hated how much she loved that man.

The prosecutor was presenting his grand finale and the jury was spellbound.

"Misa Atkinson showed a depraved indifference for human life when she shot Steven Bingham in cold blood on January 5, 2008. It was a premeditated act of murder, nothing less. She went to her sister's house in the middle of the night, stalking her brother-in-law because she decided that he was guilty of a crime he may or may not have committed."

Frankie cringed a little then. He looked at his mother who sat with her eyes straight ahead, her hands clutching a rosary as usual.

"We'll never know beyond a reasonable doubt whether or not Steven Bingham molested Shane because he's no longer alive for us to determine that. Misa Atkinson took matters into her own hands that night. She went there armed with a gun and she waited in the dark. By her own admission, she sat there and waited for Steven for close to an hour—time enough for her to reconsider, to come to her senses and call the police. She didn't share her suspicions about Steven with anybody—not a single soul. Instead, she ambushed him.

"She shot him six times, ladies and gentlemen. The first shot hit him in the chest. Forensics has determined that he was not moving, therefore posing no threat to Misa Atkinson when she plugged a bullet in his chest. According to her testimony, he continued advancing toward her—perhaps in a desperate attempt to stop her before she pulled the trigger again. But she did just that. She shot him twice more—both shots to the head."

Mary couldn't stop the tears that fell now, slowly down her face, as she imagined her son riddled that way.

"He had surely fallen by then," the prosecutor surmised. "And yet Misa Atkinson continued firing, hitting Steven Bingham three more times in the legs and torso." He paused for dramatic effect, letting the jury imagine that. "When all her ammunition was gone, she sat there, showing no regard for the law or for human life, and waited for her sister to come home." He looked at Misa with such contempt that she wondered if he'd been friends with Steven or something. He was taking this far too personally.

The jury was watching everything.

"Misa Atkinson was a terrible mother. She abandoned her son for weeks at a time with his aunt, hiding behind single motherhood as an excuse for poor parenting. Rather than admit her own flaws, she's more content to remind us that Shane's father has a new girlfriend he's more interested in than anything. There are thousands of single women across the country who manage to spend more than a few days a month with their children. When her shortcomings as a mother were brought to the forefront, she went looking for someone else to blame for it. And she set her sights on a target, and executed that target, showing no remorse. She hasn't apologized once for what she did. In fact, she said—under oath—that Steven Bingham deserved it. *She* decided that he deserved it."

He looked at the jury, standing close to them and making eye contact with each one. "That's vigilante justice. Imagine if it was your son, or your brother. As a favor to a friend, he babysits a toddler. And God forbid, that toddler has been victimized. Your brother, your son is the first person the parents suspect. And rather than giving your loved one the chance to defend themselves, the parents take matters into their own hands. They kill *your* loved one and then claim self-defense. That's not justice. That's murder. And that's how we ask you to find Misa Atkinson—*guilty* of murder in the first degree."

Misa was shaken by the prosecutor's closing argument. He had made her sound so completely guilty that she wondered if the plea deal was still on the table.

Teresa rose from her seat and walked slowly toward the center of the jury pool.

"Sometimes the justice system insults our intelligence," she said. "Sometimes, when lawyers get caught up in filing motions and objections, the process of finding out the truth gets clouded by a whole bunch of rhetoric. You can almost miss the bottom line.

"The facts of this case are simple. Shane Crowley, three years old, was molested. We heard grueling testimony about the anal lacerations he suffered, the sure signs that he had been violated by an adult entrusted with his care. Misa Atkinson, perhaps not the most attentive mother, but without question a mother who loves her son, was tormented by the suspicion that Steven Bingham was the predator who assaulted her son. She was almost certain that it was him, but she wasn't sure. Put yourself in her shoes for a moment. My client testified that she was suicidal that night. She was so overwrought with grief over what had been done to Shane that she wasn't thinking straight. She was angry, confused, desperate for answers, and afraid when she went over to her sister's house that night.

"Misa Atkinson wasn't a woman hell-bent on revenge. She was a mother frantically searching for answers about what had been done to her only child. She told Steven Bingham what she suspected and he laughed at her. Put yourself in her shoes. Upon hearing that three-year-old Shane Crowley had been sodomized, Steven Bingham didn't show concern. He didn't act in any way compassionate. We heard testimony that he was abused himself as a child, and yet he showed no sympathy towards Shane. When Misa Atkinson told Steven Bingham what had been done to her son, he laughed at her. 'The little muthafucka is lying!' he said. And he laughed at her, laughed at her son, and at the pain that he had caused them.

"Faced with the reality of the situation—that Misa was certain to share her suspicions with her sister, with his brother, Frankie, Steven charged at Misa. She was grateful in that moment that she had brought the gun with her for protection. Her hands trembling in fear, she testified that she hoped the sight of the gun would be enough to stop him in his tracks. She was praying the entire time that he wouldn't make her pull the trigger."

Teresa paused and looked at the jury seriously. She deserved an Oscar for best summation. "But Steven Bingham didn't stop. He didn't possess the self-control necessary to

stop that night. He certainly wouldn't have stopped with
Shane. He would have gone on to abuse other children and to
try and intimidate other mothers, but Misa Atkinson didn't
let him win that night. As he charged at her, prepared to take
the gun out of her very hands, she reacted in self-defense, firing. This single mother born and raised in the Stapleton projects is not a card-carrying member of the NRA. She was
never trained to shoot a gun, had never been to target practice. When that gun went off, she wasn't even sure she had hit
her mark. She testified that even after being struck by the first
bullet, Steven kept advancing on her. Misa Atkinson—seeing
the man who she believed had assaulted her son barreling
down on her with a sinister smile on his face—she snapped! In
that moment, she lost all ability to reason. The gun in her
hands kept firing, her finger kept squeezing the trigger. But
she was a mother blinded by thoughts of what had been done
to her son. Her ears were filled with a pedophile's laughter,
taunting her and daring her to defend herself.

"Throughout this trial, some of the testimony may have
made it hard for you to remember the bottom line. The bottom line is Shane Crowley was molested. His mother knew
who did it and she went to confront him. Steven Bingham—
the man who Shane himself has pointed to as his molester—
charged at Misa Atkinson, causing her to fire her weapon in
self-defense. When that first shot didn't stop him, she kept
firing until he stopped moving. That's a case of self-defense,
ladies and gentlemen of the jury. And self-defense is not first-
degree murder. That's the bottom line."

Teresa went back to her seat and prayed she had said
enough to get her client the acquittal she deserved.

Judge Felder gave the jury instructions on their delibera-
tions, reminding them that to find Misa guilty, they must

agree beyond a reasonable doubt that she had intentionally
set out to kill Steven that night. When the jury had been dismissed to deliberate, court was adjourned and everyone began to leave in order to await their decision.

Gillian was right by Frankie's side as usual, and she watched
him staring at Camille across the courtroom. Camille was
standing in a semicircle of women, all of whom were admiring
her pregnant belly. Frankie's face spread into an involuntary
smile as he watched them all admiring the child he had helped
create—the child he hadn't even wanted until now. He wasn't
sure when his mind had changed, but suddenly he had been
filled with a deep desire for fatherhood. He couldn't help
wondering if it was some subconscious attempt to right so
many of the wrongs in his life.

Camille looked up and caught him staring at her, his facial
expression so proud. She smiled back at him and noticed Gillian standing close by, looking furious.

Dominique noticed, too, and she discreetly whispered to
her friend. "Looks like the tables are turned. Gillian wants to
scratch your eyes out."

Camille nodded and strolled right on over toward Frankie
and Gillian. Shocked, Toya and Dominique followed at a safe
distance.

Gillian noticed Camille heading in their direction and
frowned. "Frankie," she said, to snap him out of whatever
trance he was in. "What's all this about?" She was referring to
the way he was smiling at his supposed ex-wife.

He looked at Gillian and shrugged. "I don't know," he
said honestly. He really didn't know what had changed in
him. But suddenly, all he wanted was the baby Camille had
been begging him for years to give her.

Camille arrived at Frankie's side and she pretended not to

see Gillian leering at her nearby. "Hey," she said to Frankie. "Just wanted to come and tell you that my sonogram is next week. Thursday. If you want to come—"

"I definitely want to come," he said, cutting her off.

Gillian looked at Frankie like he was an alien.

"All right," Camille said, nodding. "I'll text you the information." She smiled at Frankie, happy that he was coming back around. "I enjoyed breakfast this morning," she said, aware that Gillian was listening to every word. "Let's do it again soon."

Camille walked off with Dominique and Toya exchanging confused looks. They trotted out after her, anxious to hear about this morning's breakfast.

Gillian was, too. She watched as Frankie looked at her, his expression showing that he knew he was busted.

"Let's go somewhere and talk," he said.

And just like that, Gillian knew that her love affair with Frankie Bingham was over.

The Verdict

Everyone had poured into Celia's New Jersey home. She had insisted that everyone come back to her New Jersey estate to await word of the jury's decision. It was only two o'clock in the afternoon and it was possible that they could render a decision that day. Gathering at this house would ensure that they were all close enough to Staten Island to get back there immediately in case there was breaking news.

Toya and Dominique were floored by the splendor of the opulent home. Baron had lived here after Celia had moved to North Carolina, so Misa was very familiar with this house. She had spent many nights being ravaged by him within the confines of these four walls and she marveled now at the different circumstances under which she was there today.

Camille's house was being sold and Misa had relinquished her Staten Island apartment. Both of them had been living with their mother out on Long Island. Misa and Baron had bonded under their recent circumstances, talking on the phone often, and Misa believed he had become a different man. Since the trial started, though, she hadn't had the time to visit with him.

Aware of that, Celia had arranged to have Baron brought to the New Jersey home. Misa was ecstatic when she entered the huge living room and found Baron seated in his wheelchair smiling at her.

She ran to him and threw her arms around his neck, hugging him tightly. He smiled and returned the embrace, flattered that she was so clearly happy to see him.

"You act like you missed me or something," Baron joked.

Misa climbed into his lap as he sat in his wheelchair. "Thank you, Baron," she said. "Thank you so much for everything you did."

He looked away, shyly, as she heaped him with praise.

"You didn't have to help me out the way you did—paying my bail, paying my lawyer, giving Camille money . . . I don't know how I can ever thank you enough."

Baron loved the way her eyes danced when she spoke. "I wasn't always good to you," he said. "Helping you out this time was the least I could do."

The smile on her face as she looked at him now made up for all the times he had made her cry and Baron realized she made him feel like such a man, even as he sat there crippled. He hugged her, grateful he had been given a second chance at life. He planned to make the most of it this time.

Celia smiled from the doorway and left the two of them alone together. She saw that Camille and her crew had gathered out on the patio, enjoying the warm sunny day. So, Celia joined Lily in the kitchen for a cup of coffee. She poured a steaming cup and then sat across from Lily as she watched Camille, Toya, and Dominique chatting outside.

"Looks like Baron and Misa are getting close," Lily said, smiling at Celia.

"I noticed that," Celia agreed. "I like Misa. I think she's a smart young lady with a lot of courage and just the right amount of diva."

Lily laughed. She did think her youngest child was the stronger of the two.

"Baron has done a lot of soul-searching lately," Celia shared. She thought back to the conversation she'd had with him about the things he'd done in his past. "He has a lot of blood on his hands," Celia said, locking eyes with Lily. "And it's going to be a long road to redemption for him. But, he has acknowledged his mistakes, and that's half the battle. The other half is forgiving himself." She smiled at Lily. "And he's getting there," she said.

The two of them gazed out the window for a few moments, watching Camille enjoying some down time with her friends.

"Camille is absolutely glowing," Celia observed.

Lily smiled and nodded. "Yes, she is." She glanced knowingly at Celia. "And I think Frankie sees it, too."

Celia raised an eyebrow. "What do you mean?"

"I noticed Frankie watching Camille over the past few days, when he thinks that nobody's looking at him." She peeked toward the window to make sure that Camille wasn't listening. Confident that her daughter was occupied with her friends, Lily spoke freely. "He's looking like he's having second thoughts about leaving his wife. But it's too late now. The paperwork is already filed, the ink is dry, and Camille should keep on moving if you ask me."

Celia sipped from her mug. "You know it's never that simple when you love a man, Lily."

Lily rolled her eyes and stirred her coffee briskly. "Love, my ass! Frankie left her with nothing—"

"I know what he did," Celia said, crossing her legs and

looking at Camille's mother. "Frankie made a lot of mistakes and I will not sit here and defend him."

Lily slanted her eyes at Celia. "I know you love that boy like he's your son."

Celia nodded. "I do. Frankie's not a bad person. He just handled this situation very badly. And hearing about his childhood makes me understand him just a little bit more." Celia fanned her hand dismissively. "Anyway, like I said, I'm not here to make excuses for him. And I happen to agree with you. Camille should leave him. She should raise her baby and be as happy as she can without him. But . . ." Celia leaned forward toward Lily as if she were a teenager telling a secret to her girlfriend. Lily had to chuckle despite herself. *"She loves him!"* Celia whispered. She smiled and thought back to how that felt. "You remember what it was like when you were a young girl and you just *loved* a young man."

Lily had to admit that she did know that feeling. Young love had resulted in her bearing two children and struggling to raise them alone in the projects. She didn't want that or anything close to that for her daughters.

"Camille is probably very emotional right now, pregnant and going through a divorce. I'm sure that her hormones are wreaking havoc on her. Let her do what feels right to her right now. When the baby comes and Frankie has to figure out how to juggle fatherhood and Gillian's spoiled ass, things will change. Camille will be in a better position to decide what's best for her."

Lily looked like she wanted to agree but was still not convinced. "Frankie thinks he can bounce in and out of her life and Camille deserves more than that."

"She sure does," Celia agreed. She glanced out the window and watched Camille looking lovely as ever in a pastel green maternity dress swaying back and forth on the swing. "She deserves a whole lot more than that."

"I'm in love."

Toya said those three words and stunned both Camille and Dominique speechless.

She looked at her friends and at their shocked expressions and shook her head. "Don't act like that. It's not that surprising."

"Wait," Camille said, clutching her belly in mock labor pain. "You're in love with whom?"

Dominique was on the edge of her seat. "Please don't tell me . . ."

Toya smiled at her friends, shook her hair in the breeze, and said proudly, "I'm in love with Russell."

Camille burst out laughing, her eyes filling with tears of hysteria. Dominique threw her hands up in the air as if surrendering.

"The gremlin?" she demanded.

Toya shook her head in shame. She had called him so many horrible names before she stopped fighting what she was feeling.

"Wait," Dominique said again. "You're sitting here telling us that you're in *love* with Russell?"

"Yes," Toya answered.

"The same Russell that you said was a beast?"

"She called him Shrek so many times I thought it was his real name," Camille chimed in.

"She said he had teeth like Chiclets!"

"All right!" Toya exclaimed, laughing along with her friends at some of the things she had said as she described

Russell. "Yes! That's him." She fluttered her eyelashes and shrugged. "I love him."

"Whew!" Dominique exclaimed, trying to catch her breath after laughing for so long. She took a deep breath and blew it out as Camille fanned herself in the warm spring sunshine.

"When did you realize that you love him?" Camille asked, happy to hear her usually crusty friend being soft and pink.

Toya smiled again. "The entire time my mother was here, I couldn't stop thinking about him. Jameson was calling me. Alvin, too. I had plenty of opportunities to go out and I chose not to. I sat home night after night with Sweets and I watched his car come and go out my living room window."

Dominique was amazed. "You watched him?"

Toya nodded. "I watched him leave for work in the morning, watched him come home with groceries. All I could think about was how he made me laugh and how intelligent he was. He didn't judge me when I had a little too much to drink. He fed me. I had such a good time with him."

"Mmm-hmm," Camille said, teasingly. "And he grabbed you by the throat and fucked you when you got home. That has a lot to do with how you feel about him!"

Dominique and Toya cracked up.

"True," Toya admitted. Her eyes drifted skyward whimsically. "The way he fucks me!"

"Shhh!" Camille hissed. "My mother and Miss Celia are in there!"

The ladies giggled and chastised Toya for her loud mouth.

"I'm happy for you," Dominique said. "Finally, you found somebody who can handle you!"

"Amen!" Camille said.

"So what if he's not too cute? I know a whole bunch of cute guys with ugly ways." Dominique winked knowingly.

"Thanks," Toya said. She wasn't sure whether Russell would stand the test of time. But, for now, she was willing to try to turn a new page and stop judging a book by its cover.

"How about you, miss?" Dominique asked, nudging Camille playfully. "What was all that at court today about?" Dominique put on a sultry face and lowered her voice seductively as she imitated Camille. " 'I enjoyed our breakfast together . . .' "

Toya laughed but Camille blushed slightly, punching Dominique playfully in her arm.

"Frankie surprised me and came by the house this morning with breakfast. It was early. The sun hadn't even come up yet."

"How did he know you'd be up?" Dominique asked.

"They were married forever. I'm sure he knows her habits," Toya reminded her.

"He just showed up," Camille said. "He seemed like he needed to talk about the baby, about what his brother did." Camille briefly filled her friends in on what Frankie had said. She braced herself for their remarks and said, "He kissed me before he left."

Toya stared at Camille in silence and Dominique's mouth hung open in disbelief.

"Camille . . ." Toya started.

"I know," Camille said, holding her hands up defensively. "I know." She sighed. "But I would be lying if I said that I didn't love him."

Toya rolled her eyes and Dominique shook her head. "Just because you love him doesn't mean you have to be with him," Dominique said. "Frankie really hurt you."

"He did," Camille admitted. "And I'm still angry. But

when he kissed me, I just . . ." Searching for the words, she shrugged her shoulders helplessly.

"Let me ask you this," Toya said. "If he came crawling back tonight, bags in hand, and tore up the divorce papers . . . would you take him back?"

Camille thought about it. She felt the baby move within her belly as if urging her to answer honestly. "Yeah," she said, her voice low and somewhat ashamed. "I'm not proud of it. But I would take him back."

Toya shook her head. "I don't understand that kind of love."

Dominique didn't either—at least not anymore. "It doesn't pay," she said. "Loving a man like that, forgiving him, ignoring his faults and trusting him with your heart . . ." She shook her head. "Dangerous business."

"You're so wise," Toya said, only half joking. "You sound so different from the wide-eyed dumb bitch you were last year."

Dominique laughed at the backhanded compliment. "Thanks. A lot has changed in the past few months."

Camille and Toya both nodded. Everything had changed.

Misa had just finished describing Teresa's closing arguments in court that day.

"It sounds like your lawyer did her thing. The jury can't find you guilty."

"From your mouth to God's ears," Misa said again. It had become one of her favorite phrases.

Baron smirked a little. "Did they really call me a hoodlum in court the other day?"

Misa nodded. "They called me worse," she offered as a

consolation. She chuckled and looked at Baron, smiling. "What a couple of fuckups we are, huh?"

Baron laughed. The two of them had indeed managed to change their families' lives forever without truly meaning to.

Misa's cell phone rang and she fished it out of her bag. Seeing Louis's number flash across the screen, she lost her breath momentarily, worrying that something might be wrong with Shane. Anxiously, she answered it.

"Mommy?"

Misa's hands began to shake and Baron sat forward in his chair, concerned.

"Sh-Shane?"

"Hi, Mommy," Shane spoke into the phone, his voice conveying his excitement upon hearing his mother's voice. "Daddy said I could call you."

Misa didn't even realize that she was crying tears of joy as she gripped the phone. Maybe Louis wasn't such a rat bastard after all.

"Shane, I miss you," she said. "Mommy misses you so much."

"I miss you, too, Mommy. Where are you?"

Misa laughed, still shocked that she was having a phone conversation with her son. "I'm in New Jersey, baby."

"Ohhh," Shane said, as if he knew exactly where New Jersey was. "Is Aunt Tamille with you?"

Misa smiled. "Yes, she is. She's outside with her friends."

"Tell Aunt Tamille I said hi." Shane burped loudly then and said, " 'Scuse me."

Misa laughed and Shane did, too. She had never felt happier than she did at that moment, giggling on the phone with her son.

"I'm coming to get you soon," she said. "Mommy's gonna come and get you and give you a big kiss."

"I love you, Mommy," he said.

Misa closed her eyes and pictured his sweet face. "I love you, too, Shane." She held the phone to her ear even after Shane hung up, the sound of his precious voice echoing in her mind.

Frankie stared at Gillian's lips as she spoke. The two of them were sitting in Silver Lake Park, a warm breeze blowing softly around them as they sat on a bench. Frankie thought Gillian was such a beautiful woman. He was spellbound, listening to what she was saying. In fact he was hanging on her every word.

"I feel like you're not giving us a real chance to be a couple, Frankie. You're already shutting me out and we're still supposed to be in the honeymoon phase." Gillian was disappointed. She and Frankie had been so drawn together in the beginning. It had been hard for them to keep their hands off each other, and when he finally walked away from his marriage their hunger had finally been satisfied. They had been passionate, affectionate, honest, and uninhibited with one another. These days, she was finding Frankie so aloof, finding their relationship so typical of what most couples were about. She and Frankie had always been different, never typical.

"What's this about you having breakfast with Camille this morning?" she asked. Frankie had wondered how long it would take before she brought that up. "I woke up this morning and your side of the bed was empty. Is it because you left my bed to go climb into Camille's?"

Frankie shook his head. "No," he answered truthfully. He licked his lips, his mouth suddenly arid. "I couldn't sleep. So I got up and went to see her. I wanted to talk to her about her pregnancy and about how we go about being a family with this baby when Misa killed my brother." He shrugged his shoulders. "I brought breakfast. It was as simple as that."

Gillian stared at him, believing him. "That's not so simple, Frankie. That's a whole lot to deal with."

He nodded. It was. "That's why I want to ask you if we can put 'us' on hold for a little while."

Gillian continued to stare at him. She didn't respond. Instead, she searched his face for a clue as to what went wrong.

"I love you," Frankie said. "I know that you're the woman I want to spend my life with. But I need some time to think about everything that's going on in my family. I need to think about my father and try to come to grips with what he did to me and to my brother. And then I have to figure out how to *be* a father to a child I never expected to have." He sighed, exasperated. "I just need some time to myself so I can deal with all of that."

Gillian wanted to flip out. She wasn't about to be put on some back burner like Camille, pathetically waiting her turn while Frankie took his time thinking things through. Too proud to allow Frankie to see how crushed she really was, she cleared her throat and blinked back angry tears.

"Fine," she said. "If that's what you want to do—"

"It's not what I want to do. It's what I need to do."

"You're full of shit, Frankie," she said. He seemed surprised and she sucked her teeth. "You know you don't have to be by yourself while you sort all that out." She felt herself growing angrier and she fought to keep her voice under control. "You didn't need to slip out of bed with me to go and talk to Camille in secret. You could have told me what you were feeling about the baby, about your family. *I'm here,* Frankie! You're pushing me away."

Frankie was caught off guard. "I am not. I love you," he said again.

Gillian laughed at that. "Love ain't supposed to feel like this," she said. She felt so silly for having thought that Frankie was different. She had never expected him to break her heart this way.

"I'm not pulling away from you," he said. Staring out at the lake, he thought about that. "Maybe I am," he admitted.

Gillian looked at him. Finally, he was being honest with himself.

"Maybe I am," he said again. "But not because I don't love you or because I don't want you." He looked at her. "I just want some time to myself to get my shit straight. Otherwise, I'm not gonna make you happy. I'm not gonna make anybody happy until I sort this shit out."

Gillian took a deep breath. She was sad, angry, and very dissatisfied. But she was also grateful. At least Frankie hadn't strung her along for years the way he had done to Camille. At least he hadn't wasted her valuable time chasing an elusive dream.

The two of them sat in silence, watching the ducks swimming on the lake. Frankie's cell phone rang a few minutes later. He looked at it and saw the DA's office number appear on the screen. He answered it, looking at Gillian apprehensively.

"The jury just came back," Dean Davidson said. "They have a verdict."

Reporters milled about the courtroom like sharks sensing blood in the water. Outside the courthouse, news crews from each of the major networks were staked out in anticipation of the jury's decision. A caravan of black SUVs pulled up in front of the Supreme Court building in St. George. Out of the first few vehicles spilled Toya and Dominique, Camille and Celia. The last vehicle with its heavily tinted windows was immediately swarmed by cameras and reporters with microphones in hand, eager for Misa's sound bite.

Teresa Rourke stepped from the vehicle's passenger side and immediately opened the rear passenger door, ushering Misa into the crush of the crowd. Shielding her client as best she could, Teresa led her up the steps and into the courthouse, yelling repeatedly that Misa would have no comment to any of their questions.

Finally inside the courthouse, the ladies hurriedly entered the courtroom where the buzz was at a fever pitch. Misa saw that Frankie, his mother, Mary, Tremaine, and Gillian were already seated. She saw all the familiar faces that had been present for the entire duration of Misa's fight for her freedom.

When her gaze fell on Louis, she couldn't help but notice that Nahla wasn't with him for once. She walked over to him, only slightly apprehensive about how he would respond to her.

Louis watched as Misa approached him, his hands in his pockets, palms sweaty.

"Hi," she said.

"Hi." Louis bit the inside of his cheek.

"I want to thank you for letting Shane call me," she said, her face beaming at the thought of it. "That really meant a lot to me."

Louis nodded, happy that it had meant so much to her. "He asks for you all the time," he said. "I should have been letting him call you all along."

Misa was happy to hear him admit that. Silence fell between them and Louis glanced around awkwardly. He didn't know what to say to her.

"I'm gonna go now," Misa said, gesturing toward the defense table.

Louis nodded. As Misa turned to go, he called her name and watched as she turned around. "Good luck," he said.

She nodded. "Thanks."

Misa joined her lawyer and stood breathlessly as the judge entered the courtroom. The judge ordered everyone to be seated and Misa clung to her lawyer's hand tightly. The jury was brought in and Misa looked at each of their faces one by one. As they took their seats, she watched them, eager to see any clue as to what they'd decided. None of them held her gaze for very long and Misa choked back a sob.

"They're not looking at me," she whispered to Teresa. "None of them will look at me. I'm going to jail," she cried. "I should have took the deal!"

"Calm down," Teresa urged. "You don't know anything yet. Let's wait and see what happens."

Misa shook her head. Teresa was going home tonight regardless of what the jury said. But Misa's life hung in the balance and the last thing she could do was to calm down. "You said yourself that if they come back with a verdict right away, it means they found me guilty."

Teresa shook her head. "I said *usually* it means that they had little to deliberate over. That could mean that the prosecution did his case well or it could mean that we presented our case well. We're going to have to wait and see." She squeezed Misa's hand. "Don't fall apart on me now," she said. "You have a good chance, Misa. Even if they find you guilty today, we will file an appeal. Don't worry."

"Will the defendant please rise?" the judge's voice boomed.

Misa stood up, Teresa by her side, and faced the judge.

Judge Felder motioned for the jury to bring forth its decision. First the verdict was handed to the judge. He read it, nodded his head and handed it back, gesturing toward the microphone.

Misa took a deep breath as the jury foreman came to the mic.

"In the case of the *State of New York vs. Misa Atkinson,* how do you find?" Judge Felder asked.

The foreman still did not look at Misa as he spoke. "On the charge of murder in the first degree, we the jury find the defendant . . ."

Misa held her breath, squeezed her lawyer's hand and waited. Camille, Lily, Celia, Dominique, and Toya all prayed silently. Louis sat with his head in his hands as he waited. Frankie felt his heart roaring in his chest. Mary clung to her rosary beads breathlessly. Gillian and Tremaine stared at the jury foreman expectantly.

"Not guilty."

Bedlam erupted in the courtroom as Misa's legs went weak and she collapsed into her attorney's arms. Shouts and applause, tears of joy and laughter could be heard as Misa and her supporters celebrated her acquittal.

"Thank you, Jesus!" Misa was yelling, her voice rising above the crowd and happy tears pouring forth from her eyes.

In the midst of all the chaos, Frankie took his mother by the hand and together they slipped out of the courtroom, beset by reporters and photographers. He guided Mary through the rowdy crowd, steering her toward his waiting car and ushering her inside of it. Frankie climbed behind the wheel amid the flashbulbs and news cameras, started his car, and pulled away slowly, eager to get his mother home to Brooklyn.

On the way, he looked over at her and took her small frail hand in his. Mary glanced at him with tears in her eyes, still mourning the loss of her youngest son and the acquittal of his killer. She sighed and managed to smile weakly at Frankie. "Nobody really wins," she said sadly.

Frankie stared back at her, and couldn't help thinking that she was absolutely right.

Starting Over

June 21, 2008

"SURPRISE!" the crowd yelled, and Camille felt like she was experiencing déjà vu. The last time she had been given a surprise party it was thrown by her husband to celebrate her thirtieth birthday. But that seemed so long ago. Frankie was no longer her husband and everything had changed since then. Today, as she looked around Dominique's spacious apartment, she smiled at the sight of all the baby shower decorations. All of Camille's family and friends were assembled in Dominique's Manhattan high-rise apartment to help her celebrate the upcoming arrival of her first child.

"Oh, my goodness!" Camille exclaimed. "I can't believe you guys did all of this!" The whole place was covered in baby decorations. Balloons, streamers, cutouts of storks, rubber duckies, rattles, and teddy bears filled the space and Camille was overwhelmed. She saw a throne against the far wall surrounded by dozens of balloons. Toya gestured toward it.

"Come take your seat. You are queen for a day!" Toya

said. She led Camille to her seat and placed a tiara on her head and a "Mommy to Be" sash around her torso.

Camille couldn't stop smiling. Misa rushed over and started snapping pictures of her seated on her throne while Dominique played hostess to the many guests milling about her home. Camille wore a lavender sundress that clung to her pregnant belly. Her skin seemed to glow, draped in the soft hue, and Misa stood back and took her all in.

"You look beautiful, Camille," she told her.

Lily came over and sat down beside her older daughter. After posing for a few pictures with her, Lily shooed Misa away. "Okay, enough, Miss Paparazzi!"

Laughing, Misa scampered off to help Dominique serve the finger sandwiches. Lily turned to her pregnant daughter and beamed with joy. "I'm so proud of you," Lily said.

Camille smiled back at her mother. "Proud of me for what?" she asked.

"For holding your head up high all these months. A lot has changed in the past year and you've been dealing with your breakup with Frankie plus your pregnancy. You've been in Misa's corner one hundred percent. Now, you're about to be a mother and I'm just . . . so proud of you." The usually stoic Lily got choked up.

Camille smiled, stroked her mother's hand, and felt her baby shift within her womb. Her tears were happy ones for once as she held Lily's gaze. Misa appeared out of nowhere and snapped a picture of the special moment. Laughing, Camille chastised her sister. "Stop snapping pictures and come take my shoes off for me!" Lily and Camille wiped their tears of joy and chuckled.

Misa laughed, too, and did as she was told. "I can't wait until you have this baby so you can stop bossing me around."

"Shut up," Camille said jokingly. "I'm always going to boss you around."

Lily smiled at her daughters just as Toya turned the music up.

"This is a celebration!" Toya yelled over the sound of R. Kelly singing about happy people. "Everybody get up!" She danced and snapped her fingers and Lily quickly joined in along with Celia, Misa, Dominique, and at least a dozen other guests.

Camille laughed as she watched her loved ones celebrating for her. But as she watched Misa smiling brightly again, watched her dancing again the way that she used to, Camille knew that they were celebrating so much more than just the baby. Their prayers had been answered, although perhaps not in the way they had hoped. Though their lives would forever be fractured by the choices they'd made in love, the sisters had landed on their feet with a second chance to get things right in the lives of their children. Misa had been awarded joint custody of Shane. She and Louis had been working together to be better parents and were getting along for once. Shane seemed to be recovering from the trauma he suffered with the help of therapy and Misa was grateful for her new lease on life.

Camille's baby kicked again, harder this time. She rubbed her belly and thought about Frankie. She hadn't spoken to him much since the trial had ended. He had accompanied her to her sonogram and afterward they'd shared lunch. But since then, the two had retreated to their separate corners as they awaited the birth of their child. Camille wondered how things would be between them once the baby came. She had finally given up hope that she and Frankie could make things right. Too much had happened between them to turn back now. She realized now that an invisible line had been drawn down the center of their family, with Frankie and his mother on one side and Camille and her loved ones on the other. As much as she still hated the thought that her marriage was over, Camille had finally accepted its demise. Toya had sold the house on Staten Island and gotten top market value to boot. Camille was set financially and had decided to continue living with Lily for the time being. She figured she'd need all the help she could get once the baby was born. Plus it was nice living under the same roof as her mother and sister again after all these years.

Camille had also found comfort in a most unlikely source. Officer Eli King had been picking her up on Mondays and Wednesdays (his days off) and taking her for walks around her neighborhood park. Camille's doctor had suggested that walking was good for her in preparation for childbirth. So Eli would walk with her and then together they would share a cup of ice cream from Coldstone. It gave Camille something to look forward to for a couple of days a week and it gave Eli the chance to get to know this woman he was becoming enamored with. She thought about him now as she stroked her belly. She had made up her mind that once her baby was born, she was going to take Eli up on his offer for a date. She smiled at the thought of that.

For the next hour and a half the ladies shared advice on motherhood, ate delicious food, and played baby shower games that Octavia had come up with. The time came for Camille to open the tons of gifts that were piled high on the table and on the floor surrounding it. As Misa sat beside her sister and handed her the presents, Camille began to open each gift, taking time to read each card and thank each benefactor. *Oohs* and *aahs* could be heard repeatedly as one adorable item after another was unwrapped.

The doorbell rang and Dominique left the party in full swing to go and answer it. She was shocked when Archie stood there, his beautiful face smiling at her, with a bottle of Hennessy in his strong yet gentle hands. For a moment, she was speechless, caught off guard by his unexpected visit.

Archie said, "Hello. How are you?"

She watched his lips as he spoke and then caught herself. "Fine," she said, clearing her throat and forcing herself to look into his eyes. Staring into them did little to quiet her speeding heartbeat. "I'm hosting a baby shower for my friend, Camille," she said, wishing deep down inside that she had been home alone so that he could have ravaged her again. Even though she had decided weeks ago that he wasn't the man for her, at night she still thought of him, and even sometimes during her busy workday. Seeing him standing before her now dressed in crisp white Nikes, blue jeans, and a button-up, she licked her lips.

"I know," he said, to her surprise. "Well . . . kind of. My aunt told me that you came in to get your hair done the other day. You told her that you were busy running around for this party at your house." He smiled, disarming her. "I didn't know it was a baby shower. I thought you were just having a party and I just—"

"You just decided to come and crash my party?" Dominique asked, her hands on her hips and a fake frown on her face. Archie's aunt Karen had been her hairdresser for years and she often confided in her—perhaps a little too much.

Archie seemed to ponder that assessment. Then he nodded. "Yes," he said honestly. "You don't call me anymore. And when I call you, I always get your voice mail. I leave a message. No reply. So I asked my aunt to give you a message for me. She said she would, but then when you came to get your hair done, she told me that she forgot to tell you what I said. You were so busy talking about this party you were having that my message slipped her mind." He shrugged his shoulders. "So I came to tell you myself."

Dominique stood there wanting to be mad, but feeling somewhat turned on by the fact that he had gone to such lengths to see her again. "Okay, so what's the message?" she asked.

Archie looked at her. She was beautiful. Her salmon-colored Donna Karan pantsuit hugged her sexy hips perfectly. She wore her hair off her face for once, and she looked so natural to him standing there, so effortlessly pretty as she pretended to be pissed. "I miss you."

She melted instantly, her frown turning slowly into a bashful smile. Toya came up behind her then and craned her neck to see who Dominique was talking to. She saw Archie and clutched her chest dramatically.

"Who is *this*, Dominique?" she asked.

Dominique looked at Toya out of the corner of her eyes and shook her head.

"I'm Archie," he said, extending his hand to Toya in introduction. Toya took it and smiled at him seductively. "I'm Dominique's friend," he said, looking at Dominique. "At least I think I am." She smiled at him and he turned his attention back to Toya. "I didn't know that she was having a baby shower for someone tonight and she was just explaining that I can't stay."

Toya looked appalled. "Of *course* you can stay! You have Hennessy and everything!" She nudged Dominique aside and cleared the way for Archie to enter the apartment.

He laughed and looked at Dominique for the okay.

Dominique laughed, too. "Come on in, Archie," she said. "This is my friend Toya. She's the loud one as you can see."

Archie smiled and stepped inside. "I like you, Toya," he said.

Toya looked him up and down and stroked the back of her neck absentmindedly. "Likewise."

Dominique shoved her friend. "Archie, you can set the bottle on the bar over there and make yourself comfortable."

He nodded and walked across the large living room packed with women. He felt like a spotlight was on him as he strode toward the bar with every woman's adoring eyes on him.

Toya nudged Dominique. "Who the fuck is *that*?"

"I already told you—"

"Is *that* the one you were telling us about? The one who you screwed while the convict was—"

"*Yes,* Toya, damn!" Dominique felt like she couldn't talk fast enough for her friend.

"Wow!" Toya said, watching Archie as he was being visually undressed by every woman present.

"I'm gonna tell Russell," Dominique warned, teasingly.

"Tell him!" Toya said, shrugging. "I love Russell, but ain't nothing wrong with looking." Toya laughed.

Dominique chuckled, shook her head again and looked at Archie. "I like him a lot," she admitted. "I just don't want to make another mistake."

Toya looked at her friend. "Then take it slow. Don't rush in and get your heart all into it. Let him take the lead and you go along for the ride. Enjoy yourself."

Dominique smiled and thought about that.

"He's all long and strong!" Toya fiddled with her necklace.

Dominique laughed and walked off to keep the vultures at bay. Archie stood by the bar looking as if he felt out of place. "Can I see you in the kitchen for a minute?" she asked.

He agreed, eager to get away from all the eyes on him. They entered the kitchen and Dominique walked over to the refrigerator and retrieved two bottles of wine. Turning to the island in the center of the room, she retrieved the corkscrew and began to open them. Peeking at him, she smirked. "So, you miss me, huh?"

He walked closer to her and stood on the opposite side of the island, gently taking the wine bottle and corkscrew out of her hands. As he began to open the bottles for her, she folded her hands on the counter and watched, waiting for an answer.

"Yes," he said. "Why did you disappear?"

She hadn't seen it that way. "It wasn't disappearing. I just figured that we'd be better off as friends."

He nodded. "Okay," he said. "I can understand if that's how you feel. But is there a reason why you feel that way?"

She thought about saying something that sounded good, something phony. But she was sick of doing that. She had learned from her relationship with Jamel, and from watching her daughter struggle with getting over her broken heart, that it was best to tell it like it is.

"My last relationship ended badly. He took me for granted, and he was wrong for that. But I was wrong, too, for trying to make something out of nothing with him. I don't want to make the same mistake with you."

Archie finished uncorking one bottle and moved on to the next one. "So you're saying what me and you had going on was nothing?"

Dominique shook her head quickly. "No, that's not what I'm saying at all."

"So why do you compare me to him?" he asked calmly, staring into her eyes. "I don't think I take you for granted."

"I'm just saying that . . . I know you're two different people. But there are some similarities."

"Like?"

"Well . . . for one thing you both hustle."

Archie laughed and shook his head. "I'm no saint. I never pretended that I was. But I'm sure that I'm nothing like any other man you've been with. And I don't *just* 'hustle,' as you put it. I have a landscaping company, you know?"

Dominique didn't know that. "You never mentioned that," she said.

"You never asked me," he pointed out. "Mostly, we would talk about your work, your daughter, but never much about me. I figured maybe I was a . . . release for you. But now I see that you just thought you had me figured out already. You had already decided that I was just like your ex."

Dominique looked convicted as he uncorked the second bottle and set the corkscrew down on the top of the island.

"I also noticed that you never called *me* to hang out. It was always the other way around," she said.

"That's because I was being respectful of your schedule. You're a single mother of a teenaged daughter. You told me that she was dealing with a lot of problems and I wanted to give you the room to handle that. Plus you have this big job at Def Jam and you're always working hard. So I just gave you space to do your thing. I figured you would get at me when you weren't busy."

Dominique nodded, understanding his logic.

"I think maybe you're scared of me," Archie said, folding his arms across his chest.

Dominique frowned. "*Scared* of you?"

"Yes. I think you are not used to a man like me. I don't take you for granted, and maybe you're not used to that. I respect you and your busy life. You have a hectic job, you have friends, a daughter. So, I try not to crowd you. Instead, I sit back and wait for you to contact me when you are not busy. But it seems like the only time you would call me was late at night. And then in the morning you always tried to rush off. It's like you're afraid."

"No, I'm not," Dominique mumbled.

"Then, out of the blue you stop calling me altogether. You don't answer my messages. We're both adults. I just want you to tell me to my face that you're scared."

"I'm not scared!" Dominique snapped.

Misa walked into the kitchen at that moment. She could sense the tension between the two of them and had overheard her friend's outburst, so she scanned the room quickly. Rushing over, she snatched the two bottles of wine off the island, and scurried back out.

Dominique sighed. "I like you, Archie," she said. She looked at him and wondered if a man this good could really be hers. He seemed to be the perfect combination of rugged and refined. "I really do."

"Good. 'Cause I like you, too. And if you stop running, I can take you out sometime and I can tell you who I am and what I'm all about." He smiled. "Maybe you'll like me even more."

Dominique smiled at him. "That sounds very nice."

Toya peeked into the kitchen and cleared her throat. "Um, sorry to interrupt," she said. She looked at Dominique anxiously. "But Camille's cop friend just showed up. And he's cute!"

Dominique's eyes widened and so did Archie's. "Cop?" he repeated for confirmation.

Dominique nodded. "He's harmless. Camille met him

recently and he's been really nice to her. I can't wait to meet him!" She followed Toya out into the living room, with Archie trailing behind. They all saw Eli standing near the doorway as if he was having second thoughts about being there.

Octavia had welcomed him inside and he stood awkwardly near the door holding a shower gift in his hand. From where he stood, he could see Camille opening her gifts with Misa seated beside her, assisting. Camille looked radiant as she held up a tiny baby outfit. Seeing her smile caused Eli to do the same. Dominique walked over and introduced herself.

"Camille has told me a lot about you," she said.

"Same here," Eli replied, still smiling. He had heard all about Camille's friends and their sisterly bond.

"Come on in and have a seat," she urged. "You're not the only guy here, either." She nodded toward Archie who was helping himself to a plate of food. "That's my friend Archie. I'm feeling him out."

Eli laughed. "Okay. I can tell that me and Archie have a lot in common already." He winked at Dominique and she led him to a seat nearby.

Camille smiled even brighter when she saw Eli. She paused while opening Toya's gift and said, "Elijah, I'm glad you came. You really *are* a good guy."

They laughed at their private joke and everyone else noticed the chemistry between them. For once, Camille didn't care what rumors might get started or what people might think. Misa smiled, seeing her sister throw caution to the wind, and Dominique's eyes widened in surprise.

Toya cleared her throat. "Um . . . can you please finish opening my present? I put a whole lot of thought into—"

"Okay, okay," Camille interrupted, laughing. She tore at

the packaging and revealed a beautiful handwoven baby blanket. It was dotted with pastel colors and lined with ruffled edges. Camille's mouth hung open in awe. "This is so beautiful!"

Everyone agreed.

"Did you make it?" Eli asked innocently.

Dominique and Misa both burst out laughing so hard that everyone else joined in. Toya stood stone-faced as they all got their digs in.

"Toya's not the type to sew," Camille explained. "She has people for that."

"You don't know *what* I do in my down time," Toya sniffed, her arms folded across her chest defensively.

"Who made the blanket, Toya?" Celia asked, admiring the beautiful handiwork.

Toya reluctantly came clean. "My mother stitched it while she was visiting me." As everyone commented, she spoke over them. "But, it was *my* vision. I told her how I wanted it and she simply produced it."

"Yeah, yeah," Dominique dismissed her.

"It's beautiful, Toya. Thank you," Camille said. She moved on to the next gift as Toya discreetly gave Dominique the finger.

Octavia sidled up beside her mother while everyone's eyes were on the mom-to-be. She nudged Dominique playfully as Camille opened the next present.

"So," she said. "Who's your friend?" Octavia nodded in Archie's direction as he sat beside Eli tearing into some chicken.

Dominique felt like she was on the hot seat. Her relationship with Octavia was so much better than it had ever been and she didn't want to jeopardize it in any way. Since ending her relationship with Jamel, she was wary of bringing a new man into her child's life so soon. The last thing she wanted was to jump out of the frying pan and into the fire.

"That's Archie," she said. "I'm dating him, but we're not serious. Not yet anyway. We're just getting to know each other for now and we'll see if it goes anywhere."

Octavia gave her a sly look. "Well, he gets my vote. 'Cause he's mad cute!"

Dominique laughed. "He is cute, ain't he?" Mother and daughter shared a laugh and rejoined the festivities.

Once all of the gifts had been opened and the cake had been sliced, the guests began to wane. One by one they offered their congratulations to Camille and her family and left. Misa and Lily sorted through all the baby clothes like two kids in a candy store while Octavia and Toya looked on.

Archie decided to make his exit and Dominique walked him to the door.

He towered over her at six one and she felt so small standing beside him. He smiled down at her and pulled her into an embrace. Dominique wrapped her arms around his waist and rested her head against his chiseled chest. She closed her eyes and wondered again if this could be the start of something big.

"So," Archie said, still holding her close. "I will call you tomorrow and hopefully we can get together."

She nodded, forced herself to step out of his arms. "Sounds like a plan," she said, smiling.

He smiled back, leaned down and kissed her softly on the lips. His eyes lingered on hers for a moment. And then he turned and left.

Dominique watched him walk away and fought the urge

to call after him. She wasn't even sure what she wanted to say to him, only that she hated to see him go. She watched until he got to the end of the hallway and turned the corner. Reluctantly, she shut the door to her apartment and returned to the few guests that remained.

Camille was drained. As the last handful of guests filtered out, Eli sat beside her and put his arm around her.

"You look tired, gorgeous," he said. "You need to get all the sleep you can get now. Because once the kid gets here, it's a wrap!"

Camille laughed, and couldn't help thinking that it was nice having Eli's arm wrapped around her this way. "Gorgeous, huh?" she repeated. "That was sweet, but we both know you're lying."

Eli looked shocked. "I am not! I've seen some hideous pregnant women in my lifetime."

Camille cracked up laughing.

Eli laughed, too. "Word! Noses spread all out across their faces like King Kong. Their necks get all dark and their ankles all swollen." He shuddered for emphasis. "You're nothing like that." He watched Camille smile bashfully. "Your skin is glowing, your hair is long and thick, your nails are done, pedicure is official." He smiled back at her. "You're gorgeous."

Camille wanted to kiss him. Instead, she took his hand in hers and squeezed it. "Thank you," she said. Eli had no way of knowing how crucial he had been to Camille's sanity over the past several months. Since Frankie had abandoned her, Camille had been left feeling undesirable, less attractive, and she had almost forgotten what it was like to smile. But Eli had come into her life and made her feel wanted, appreciated, and respected. She had no idea how she could repay him for making her life livable.

"You don't have to thank me," he said. "Just keep being you." He kissed her on her forehead and stood to leave. "I'll see you on Monday for our walk," he said.

Camille stood awkwardly and hugged Eli. "Monday, it is," she said.

She walked him to the door and he bid farewell to her family and friends and left. Camille joined her loved ones in Dominique's living room and made herself comfortable on the chaise lounge. Celia, Lily, Misa, Toya, Dominique, and Octavia were all that remained and Camille felt surrounded by love.

"I like him, Camille," Lily said, smiling. "He's a real gentleman!"

Camille beamed. "I like him, too," she said. "If he's being this sweet while I'm pregnant, just imagine what it'll be like when I'm not."

Toya laughed. "You'll be pregnant again in no time," she predicted.

Everyone laughed. Camille blushed.

Misa sighed. "I can't wait for this baby to get here. Shane is so excited to have a cousin to play with."

Lily nodded. "It's all he talks about. 'Is Aunt Tamille gonna have the baby *today*, Grandma?' I keep telling him that his cousin will be here very soon."

Camille smiled as she imagined Shane playing with her baby, the two of them growing up side by side. "I'm so happy that Shane is doing well," she said. "I love him so much."

Misa nodded. "He loves you, too." She looked around at all the people in the room and reflected on how supportive they had all been of her and Camille.

"Thank you, everybody," she said, seemingly out of nowhere. She noticed the puzzled expressions on all of their faces—all except Camille, who understood completely where her sister was coming from.

Misa continued. "We never got the chance to say thank you to all of you for everything you did over the past few months. I'm not just talking about the trial and the fact that you all were there every single day. But, you've all done so much. You've opened your homes to us, opened your wallets." She looked knowingly at Celia, who smiled. "We're so grateful."

"We sure are," Camille chimed in. "We couldn't have survived all of this without you ladies."

Toya waved her hand dismissively. "That's what friends are supposed to do. We stick together, and we will continue to do so."

Everyone agreed and Misa turned her attention to Celia. "How is Baron?" she asked. "I haven't spoken to him much since we started planning the baby shower. I've been obsessed with baby stuff lately."

Celia smiled. She was proud of her son for the strides he was making. "He's still undergoing physical therapy a few days a week. He's hoping to be able to walk without having to use a cane or a walker eventually. But he's taking it one day at a time." She looked at Misa, hoping she understood the underlying message in what she was about to say. "Lately, Baron has been doing some soul-searching and coming to terms with the monster that he used to be. He admitted to me that he's made a lot of mistakes, hurt a lot of people."

Misa understood exactly what Celia was saying as she stared directly at her.

"It's not always easy admitting when you've been wrong. So that's been hard for Baron . . . he's being hard on himself.

But the first step in correcting a problem is admitting that you have one. He's finally admitted that to himself and with God's help, he'll be okay. I believe that Baron will emerge from all of this stronger than he was before." She looked around the room at all the women present and realized that was true for all of them. "We all will," she added.

"I know that's right!" Lily agreed. "Stronger than ever!"

Epilogue: A New Beginning

"Push!" the doctor was urging Camille as she panted and sweated, her legs spread-eagle on the delivery bed.

It was ten minutes to four on the morning of July 11, 2008, and the baby had decided to arrive on a lucky day—7/11. Camille didn't feel lucky at all as the pain seared through her. She groaned and grunted as she bore down hard, squeezing Frankie's hand for dear life. He was amazed by her strength as she crushed his fingers together painfully. "That's it," he urged her. "You can do it!"

Camille had called Frankie just after midnight to tell him that her water broke and she was en route to the hospital. He had climbed out of bed frantically and rushed to meet her at the hospital. He had arrived to find that all of her family and friends were gathered in the waiting room, and he had been humbled to find out that Camille wanted him to be by her side. For hours now, he had been coaching her to push, to breathe, and telling her that she was the strongest woman he had ever met.

Camille felt the contraction ceasing and fell back against

the bed, breathless and exhausted. "I can't do it," she said. "Just take it out." She looked at the doctor pleadingly.

"You're almost there, Camille," the doctor reassured her. "One or two more pushes and the baby will be here."

"You can do it," Frankie said, convincingly. "Just one or two more pushes," he repeated.

Camille stared at him in silence. Had she been in her right state of mind, she imagined that he may have looked quite handsome standing there smiling at her, urging her on. Instead, at the moment he looked and sounded like a complete fucking idiot. He made one or two more pushes sound like an easy task when, in fact, Camille feared that the pain might kill her.

She felt another contraction coming and she squeezed his hand again. "I'm gonna try and push it out one more time. If it doesn't come out, I'm not pushing anymore." She said it so matter-of-factly that the doctor just agreed with her.

"One, two, three, *push*!"

Camille pushed with all her might and Frankie felt his hand go numb. She was straining so hard that he thought she might self-destruct if this push wasn't successful. She squeezed his hand with such force that *he* wanted to cry out in pain. Then in one swift motion the squirming baby sprang from her womb and into the doctor's arms. They cleared out its airways and the baby's first cries filled the room.

"It's a girl!" the doctor proclaimed.

Frankie held on to Camille's hand as they watched their baby being cleaned and bundled. He couldn't believe the miracle he was witnessing.

"A girl," he breathed, gripping Camille's hand tighter.

Camille watched her ex-husband's face as he laid eyes on his daughter for the first time. She watched his apprehension at the thought of being a father give way to pure love. His eyes filled with tears and he laughed as several streamed down his face. "I have a daughter."

Camille smiled brightly as she watched him. He felt light-headed, but her hand steadied him as he stood staring at their squirming eight-pound-seven-ounce baby girl. The nurse finally brought the baby to them.

"Let me have her," Frankie said eagerly. Smiling at the happy dad, the nurse handed the child to Frankie and he took her carefully into his strong arms. He cradled her so gently and so carefully that Camille chuckled a little. "She's beautiful," he said.

The baby lay serenely in Frankie's arms and he couldn't take his eyes off her. Camille beamed with joy as she wrapped her mind around the fact that they now had a little girl to love forever. The doctor tended to her and the nurses swarmed around her. But all Camille could focus on was the vision of Frankie holding his baby girl.

Finally, Frankie handed the baby to Camille. It seemed like he hated to give her up, but he did. He watched Camille cry as she held her daughter for the first time. The sight of mother and child lying together there that way filled Frankie with such joy. He smiled at them and shook his head in amazement. "She looks like you," he said.

Camille thought she looked like an angel. "She has your nose."

Frankie laughed. It was unthinkable to him that he had helped to create this perfect little girl who lay before him, that he and Camille together had formed something so magnificent.

"I want to name her Bria," Camille said. "What do you think?"

Frankie smiled and nodded. "If you like it, I love it." He scooped the baby back into his arms again and cradled her close to him, inhaling her scent. "Bria," he repeated, staring at her chocolate-brown skin, the same color as his own.

"It means 'beautiful one,'" Camille explained.

"She is beautiful," he said again.

Camille smiled. She had a feeling that Bria would be the apple of his eye from that day forward.

The nursing staff came to take the baby to be inoculated and they explained that Camille would be taken into recovery where she would get rest and have a chance to recuperate. Frankie reluctantly watched as the two of them were taken away.

He wasn't sure how to feel as he stripped out of his scrubs and left the delivery room. He took a seat just outside of the delivery room and waded through a flood of emotions. He was a father.

He looked around at the staff at North Shore University Hospital hustling to and fro and he took a deep breath. Hospitals had always been a place of sadness, distress, and so much pain in his life until that point. But this time was different. He smiled as he thought of his baby.

Frankie got up and entered the waiting room where Camille's loved ones sat anxiously. He looked around at everyone and a broad smile crept across his face. "It's a girl," he announced proudly. "Her name is Bria."

Everyone smiled, laughed, and congratulated Frankie. They also flooded him with questions.

"How much did she weigh?"

"How long is she?"

"What time was she born?"

"Who does she look like?"

"How is Camille?"

He fielded their questions happily, still slightly dazed by all the excitement. Celia pulled him into an embrace and he had to resist the urge to cry on her shoulder. He felt so many different things in that moment—gratitude, humbleness, joy, and a little bit of fear.

"Congratulations, Daddy," she said, rubbing his back as she hugged him. "You're gonna do just fine."

He nodded, blinked back the tears that threatened to plunge forth at any moment and took a deep breath. Frankie licked his lips before speaking.

"Misa, do you think I can talk to you in private for a minute?" His voice was low and even, his eyes fixed on Misa's face.

Lily squirmed slightly, feeling uncomfortable at the thought of Frankie being alone with her child after all that had happened. "Frankie, you can say what you need to say in front of all of us," she said.

Misa held her hand up to stop her mother from speaking. "No," she said. "It's okay." She looked at Frankie and nodded. She led the way to an empty waiting room at the end of the hall and shut the door behind them. Standing uncomfortably before Frankie, she waited to hear what he had to say.

He stared at her for a long time, thinking about what she had done, thinking about what had been done to her son. Try as he might, he couldn't hate Misa for killing Steven. Not now that he had heard the truth about his brother's past.

"I want to tell you that . . ." Frankie's voice trailed off and he wiped a few errant tears that fell from his eyes. He hadn't anticipated that becoming a father would make him so emotional. "Misa, I practically watched you grow up. I remember you when you were younger, when you got married, when you had your son, and I've watched Shane growing up, too." He looked at the floor. "All of the shit that's happened lately . . . I can't front like I'm not hurt by what you did." He got choked up but caught himself. "But I know you and Shane got hurt in all of this, too. We . . . we gotta put it behind us. Since Camille and I have this baby, we're gonna have to be a family. She's gonna be a part of all our lives and we're gonna have to be around each other and everything." Frankie was stumbling over his words and he realized it. But he was powerless to control his stammering. "I just don't want us to . . . hate each other . . ." He bit the inside of his cheek nervously, wishing he could find the words to say what he really wanted to say to Misa.

She watched him struggling and then she spoke up at last. "Frankie," she said. "I could never hate you, even after all that's happened." Misa looked into his eyes as she said it. "I never meant to cause you any pain, and I know that sounds crazy because he was your brother. But from the very start, I was never mad at *you*. My anger that night was toward him alone," she said, still too bitter to utter Steven's name. "I wasn't thinking about you or about Camille, or even about myself. All I could think about was Shane and what had been done to him." She shook her head. "But I never intended to hurt you, Frankie. You were always good to me. All those years when Louis was nowhere to be found, it was you and Camille's generosity that made it possible for Shane and I to have what we needed. I will never forget everything you did for me over the years." She shifted her weight from one leg to the next as she stood. "You hurt my sister, though. You made it really hard for her for the past few months, and she's done you no harm. It's me you were mad at, and I feel like it's my fault she had to suffer all this time."

Frankie sighed. "I know I hurt Camille. I can't take back

what I did to her. But, I'm gonna do my best to make it up to
her. I just want to be a good father to this baby and I want
peace in my family . . . what's left of it."

Misa didn't reply.

"And it's *not* your fault," he corrected her. "I'm a man and
I take responsibility for my own actions. I shouldn't have
treated Camille the way that I did." He stared back at her.
"I'm sorry, too," he said. "For a lot of things. What happened
to Shane was horrible." He looked down at the floor. "Nothing I can say will fix what was done to him. But I am sorry
for what happened."

Misa looked away. No one was sorrier than she was.

"How is he?" Frankie asked.

Her face spread into a smile instantly. "He's doing great.
He can't wait to play with his new cousin." She watched
Frankie smile at the thought of Shane playing happily again.
"You know," she said. "I think you're going to be a great
father, Frankie."

He smiled at that. "I hope so," he said, rubbing his head
as if he wasn't so sure. "I don't know the first thing about
fatherhood, but I'm gonna do my best."

Misa nodded. "Well, you've got a lot of help coming your
way. Regardless of what has happened before today, we're
still a family. Maybe we're a dysfunctional family, but we're
still a family nonetheless."

Frankie laughed a little. She was right. He thought about
reaching to hug her, but decided against it. Sensing his hesitation, Misa hugged him instead. Frankie squeezed her tightly
and was glad that the first steps toward reconciliation had
been taken. They pulled away and walked back out into the
waiting room where everyone waited eagerly for some sense
of what had transpired.

Frankie quickly made his exit. "Good-bye, everybody," he called out. They all said good-bye and he walked to the elevators. On the ride down, he realized that he hadn't slept in close to twenty-four hours. He yawned and felt his eyes growing heavy. But before he went home to sleep, he had to make one detour.

Gillian answered her door wearing one of her old T-shirts and a pair of boy shorts and her hair hung loosely around her shoulders. Frankie bent down, kissed her on the cheek, and entered her Upper East Side town house. It had taken him an hour to get there driving from Syosset and he was drained. Still, he noticed again what a beauty Gillian was.

He had driven there in a fog mentally, still sorting through all the new revelations that had been made about his family, his past, still reeling from the fact that he was now a father. But he suddenly yearned to be in Gillian's presence. He needed to hold her, to kiss her, and to talk to her, to hear her voice in his ears. He had been avoiding her—in fact, he'd been avoiding everyone lately. It was his way of coping with all that he'd recently discovered. But now, as the emotions plunged forth with the birth of his child, he found himself longing for Gillian's presence in his life again. He realized now how much he loved her, how desperately he needed her.

"It's six o'clock in the morning. What are you doing here?" she asked, her voice raspy, sexy to him.

They sat down in her living room and Gillian folded her legs beneath her and pulled a throw blanket across her body. She stared at him closely and could tell that he hadn't slept. She knew him well enough to tell that he was anxious about something, and she wondered what was wrong. Since the trial had ended, Frankie had distanced himself from her, from everyone. He had moved out of her house and into a luxury apartment of his own in Downtown Brooklyn. His role in the family business had been scaled back considerably and Gillian had been hoping that it wouldn't be long before he decided to talk to her about what was happening.

"Camille had the baby," he said. "A girl."

Gillian's expression shifted ever so slightly and Frankie could see that she was getting better at maintaining her poker face. But he knew her too well. He could tell that she was hurt.

She smiled weakly, her eyes sad. "Congratulations. What's her name?"

"Bria." Frankie pictured his daughter's perfect little face and smiled.

"That's a beautiful name," Gillian said. She was jealous of Camille for the first time. It was an emotion she was very unfamiliar with. "So what are you doing here?" she asked bluntly.

Frankie looked at her, somewhat caught off guard by her rawness. He longed to tell her what he had come there to say, that he wished she had been the one giving birth to his daughter that morning instead of Camille. He just didn't know if it would comfort Gillian to know that.

"I love you," he said.

Gillian stared at Frankie. It had begun to rain outside and she heard the raindrops drumming against her windowpane. It reminded her of the tears she'd shed in secret late at night as she did her best to get over him. He had broken her heart and she wanted to hate him for it.

"Yeah?" she asked.

He smiled at her, knowing she was trying to be tough. He

had watched her take the helm of the family business with ease. Being in control of such an empire required her to be stern and direct, unafraid. Gillian was all of those things, and she was respected by their whole crew. Frankie knew that she could handle it on her own. If ever there was a time for him to leave the Nobles family business behind and focus on the task of being a father, this was it. But he loved Gillian, and he didn't want to let her go so easily.

"Yeah," he responded. "I love you very much."

She nodded. "That's nice to know," she said. "But I don't like the way you love people. And I still don't understand why you're here."

He frowned. "What do you mean you don't like the way I—"

"I'm not Camille!" Gillian was pissed, but she chuckled a little at the irony that she was now walking a painful mile in Camille's shoes. "What me and you had was supposed to be different."

"It is different."

She shook her head. "No, it's not. Otherwise, we'd still be together."

"I just needed some space, Gigi. I never stopped loving you. I just had to get my thoughts together—about the baby, about my brother and everything. I've been rebuilding my relationship with my mother and trying to forgive her, trying to forgive myself." He looked at her sadly. "You know me better than anybody. So you should understand that I just needed some time to figure things out."

Gillian looked into his melancholy eyes. "You used to talk to me and tell me things. But when it mattered—when your brother died and your family secrets came out, you shut down on me, just like you did to Camille. You need to figure out why you do that to the women you claim to love. But I'm not gonna be the one to help you figure it out."

Frankie sat in silence and let her words sink in.

"Congratulations on the baby, Frankie."

He felt like he was being dismissed. "Gigi, I know I hurt you."

She shrugged and looked away.

"I'm sorry."

"That's not enough for me. I'm not Camille."

"Stop saying that. I don't want you to be her." He frowned, confused.

"You can't run in and out of my life like that—"

Frankie closed in on her so quickly that she was amazed. Quickly, he slid into position beside her on the sofa and cupped her chin firmly in his hand. He looked intensely into her eyes. Gillian stared back at him, speechless.

"Come on, Gigi," he said, pleadingly. "Don't do this."

Gillian stared at Frankie. Even with his hand gripping her face so tightly she felt no fear. She knew that Frankie would never hurt her. But the desperation in his eyes was unmistakable.

Prying his hands from her face, she spoke firmly. "*You* did this. Not me."

Their faces merely inches apart, they stared at each other in a face-off of wills. Seconds elapsed with neither of them budging. Finally, without warning, Frankie covered Gillian's mouth with his own. He kissed her deeply and pulled her eagerly toward him. Gillian resisted at first, pushing him away, but soon she gave in under the force of his kiss. Her intensity matched his as they went at each other. He pulled her onto his lap and gripped her hungrily.

Frankie slid his hands underneath her shirt, stroking her

breasts as she straddled him. His hands seemed to know her the way a pianist knows the ebony and ivory keys. It was the perfect combination of squeezing and caressing. He bit at her, nibbled on her mouth and she at his. Their kisses told a story—a tale of pleasure and pain, danger, discovery, and the ultimate safety they still found in each other's arms. Frankie's lips explored her body, tasting and sucking on her in the most erotic fashion, reducing her to moans that escaped her involuntarily. Clutching his head, Gillian pulled him closer, her body so desperate for him even though her mind was screaming no. Frankie tore at his belt, eager to free his rock-hard dick as it pressed against his jeans. Gillian reached for it, stroking it and feeling how rigid it was as she grinded in Frankie's lap. He pulled her panties to the side and entered her raw, plunging into her silky wetness.

Gillian felt an incomparable rush. All her senses responded to him and she was flooded with pleasure. His strong hands squeezed her ass as she grinded on top of him, swirling her hips in a way that caused his face to fall into ecstasy, his lips to part and his voice to sound.

She called his name.

"Yes?" he whispered softly, searching her eyes for the answer.

". . . feels so good . . ." she managed.

"Yes," he whispered again, so confident. "Yes, mami."

His voice in her ears made her creamy. She rocked her hips around in circles, then back and forth. She wrapped her arms around his muscular torso, his back and shoulder muscles so well defined and his arms encircling her tightly. They were meshed together—their mouths, their hands, arms, legs, their whole selves. He sucked her breasts, alternating between sucking them and sucking her lips, her tongue, her neck. Gillian felt herself building up to a fever pitch within. Frankie felt it, too, and he watched her—the way that her face contorted into a look of pure surrender. Gillian looked him dead in the eye as she came, riding him. He watched her face, her eyes narrowed, lips parted. He loved to see that expression on her face and he kissed her again, their tongues so good together, their breathing hungry.

Gillian came some more, kissing his neck, his collarbone, his face, sucking on his beautiful brown skin. Her pace quickened as he glided in and out of her. She gripped him with her sugar walls and he couldn't fight it anymore. She took him to his climax with the sway of her hips and the warmth of her pussy.

Gillian moved to dismount him but he pulled her back, held her closer to him. Her head rested on his shoulder, and she inhaled his beautiful scent. They held each other, her arms still tightly linked around his body, his arms encasing her in a wonderful embrace. His chest rose and fell as his breathing steadied. The rhythm of her breath fell into step with his, and soon she could hear him softly snoring, his eyes closed serenely, his arms still tightly wrapped around her. She lay there with him still inside of her, not wanting to disrupt the absolute bliss she felt in his embrace.

While he slept, she tried to come to terms with what had just happened. She hadn't meant to lose control that way and she felt angry with herself for allowing it to take place.

Gillian felt conflicted. She loved being in control of the Nobles family empire. But it meant nothing without Frankie by her side to share it with. Still, she felt as though she was letting him off the hook too easily and she wondered how long it would be before he went running from her again. She wasn't sure what to do.

Gillian climbed slowly off his lap and sat beside him on the couch, her mind reeling. She looked at Frankie, still asleep, his mouth open and his head laid back against her sofa.

Gillian stared at him. Try as she might, she couldn't stop loving him. She had gained control over every other aspect of her life—Baron had been removed from power, and his troubles with Danno were history; Mayra had been stripped of her father's fortune and was groveling at Gillian's feet in search of forgiveness; the Nobles crew was answering to her and her alone. She had achieved every goal she'd set for herself in recent months. But when it came to Frankie and her love for him, Gillian was powerless.

She kissed Frankie's sleeping face and went to take a shower. As the steamy water dripped all over her body, she closed her eyes and inhaled. Stepping into the stream of the shower, she let the water glide down her face as she flashed back to how Frankie had made her feel only moments ago.

Then she thought back on the pain he had caused her, how he had made her cry. She remembered how it had felt to learn that he had climbed out of the bed he shared with her and gone home to Camille in the middle of the trial. And now he had left Camille in the hospital recovering from childbirth to make a plea for Gillian's forgiveness. He always managed to get his way. She grew angrier the more she thought about it.

Who does he think he is? she thought to herself.

She opened her eyes and lathered up, washed the scent of Frankie off her. This was a test, she decided. Him coming here this way—making love to her the way he had, taking control—it was a power move. He had come there today to reclaim her, to make her submit to him. She was not about to lie down, roll over, or jump through hoops the way Camille did for him. In the weeks since he had walked out of her life,

Gillian had risen to a position of influence unlike anything she could have possibly dreamed up. Running an empire, having control over so much money, being able to decide who lived or died, it all gave her an incredible high. Her love for power—for control over the men who answered to her and over her own heart—was being put to the test.

She rinsed off and thought about how taking Frankie back into her life would change everything. The line would be blurred between which one of them was actually in charge of the Nobles family. Gillian wanted there to be no question as to who was running this show.

Her father had asked her once what she was looking for, what she wanted out of life. She knew now. She wanted the power, the influence, and the life of luxury she had now become accustomed to. She wanted the respect of her friends and enemies alike. They didn't have to like her. But she insisted that they respect her, if only because she was Doug Nobles's heir to the throne.

Gillian stepped out of the shower, toweled off, and walked naked into her bedroom. She dressed, draped herself in her family jewels—diamonds her father had given to her upon her graduation from high school years ago—and scrawled a note for Frankie. She left it on her coffee table as he lay on the sofa, softly snoring as he dreamed of his new baby girl.

Gillian lingered for a moment as she headed for the door. She watched him sleeping, handsome even in his slumber. She would miss loving him. But loving him was too costly. And Gillian was determined that she would not lose.

Frankie shifted in his sleep, but didn't waken. Gillian's note fluttered to the floor and landed near his sneaker. Her cursive letters written in black Sharpie stood out boldly against the hot-pink Post-it.